John Sandford is the pseudonym of Pulitzer-prize winning journalist John Camp. He is the author of sixteen PREY novels and four KIDD novels. He lives in Minnesota.

Published by Pocket Books

Mind Prey

JOHN SANDFORD

POCKET
BOOKS

LONDON • SYDNEY • NEW YORK • TORONTO

First published in Great Britain by HarperCollins, 1996
This edition published by Pocket Books, 2005
An imprint of Simon & Schuster UK Ltd
A CBS COMPANY

3 5 7 9 10 8 6 4 2

Simon & Schuster UK Ltd
Africa House
64-78 Kingsway
London WC2B 6AH

www.simonsays.co.uk

Simon & Schuster Australia
Sydney

A CIP catalogue record for this book is available from the British Library

ISBN 1-4165 -0232-7
EAN 9781416502326

Printed and bound in Great Britain by
Bookmarque Ltd, Croydon, Surrey

Mind Prey

1

The storm blew up late in the afternoon, tight, gray clouds hustling over the lake like dirty, balled-up sweat socks spilling from a basket. A chilly wind knocked leaves from the elms, oaks, and maples at the water's edge. The white phlox and black-eyed Susans bowed their heads before it.

The end of summer; too soon.

John Mail walked down the floating dock at Irv's Boat Works, through the scents of premix gasoline, dead, drying minnows and moss, the old man trailing behind with his hands in the pockets of his worn gabardines. John Mail didn't know about old-style machinery—chokes, priming bulbs, carburetors, all that. He knew diodes and resistors, the strengths of one chip and the weaknesses of another. But in Minnesota, boat lore is considered part of the genetic pattern: he had no trouble renting a fourteen-foot Lund with a 9.9 Johnson outboard. A driver's license and a twenty-dollar deposit were all he needed at Irv's.

Mail stepped down into the boat, and with an open hand wiped a film of water from the bench seat and sat down. Irv squatted beside the boat and showed him how to start the motor and kill it, how to steer it and accelerate. The lesson took thirty seconds. Then John Mail, with his cheap Zebco rod and reel and empty, red-plastic tackle box, put out on Lake Minnetonka.

"Back before dark," Irv hollered after him. The white-haired man stood on the dock and watched John Mail putter away.

When Mail left Irv's dock, the sky was clear, the air limpid and summery, if a little nervous in the west. Something was coming, he thought. Something was hiding below the treeline. But no matter. This was just a look, just a taste.

He followed the shoreline east and north for three miles. Big houses were elbow to elbow, millions of dollars' worth of stone and brick with manicured lawns running down to the water. Professionally tended flower beds were stuck on the lawns like postage stamps, with faux-cobblestone walks snaking between them. Stone swans and plaster ducks paddled across the grass.

Everything looked different from the water side. Mail thought he'd gone too far, but he still hadn't picked out the house. He stopped and went back, then circled. Finally, much further north than he thought it would be, he spotted the weird-looking tower house, a local landmark. And down the shore, one-two-three, yes, there it was, stone, glass and cedar, red shingles, and, barely visible on the far side of the roof, the tips of the huge blue spruces that lined the street. A bed of petunias, large swirls of red, white, and blue, glowed patriotically from the top of a flagstone wall set into the slope of the lawn. An open cruiser crouched on a boat lift next to the floating dock.

Mail killed the outboard, and let the boat drift to a stop. The storm was still below the trees, the wind was dying down. He picked up the fishing rod, pulled line off the reel and threaded it through the guides and out the tip. Then he took a handful of line and threw it overboard, hookless and weightless. The rat's-nest of monofilament drifted on the surface, but that was good enough. He looked like he was fishing.

Settling on the hard bench seat, Mail hunched his

shoulders and watched the house. Nothing moved. After a few minutes, he began to manufacture fantasies.

He was good at this: a specialist, in a way. There were times when he'd been locked up as punishment, was allowed no books, no games, no TV. A claustrophobic—and they knew he was claustrophobic, that was part of the punishment—he'd escaped into fantasy to preserve his mind, sat on his bunk and turned to the blank facing wall and played his own mind-films, dancing dreams of sex and fire.

Andi Manette starred in the early mind-films; fewer later on, almost none in the past two years. He'd almost forgotten her. Then the calls came, and she was back.

Andi Manette. Her perfume could arouse the dead. She had a long, slender body, with a small waist and large, pale breasts, a graceful neckline, when seen from the back with her dark hair up over her small ears.

Mail stared at the water, eyes open, fishing rod drooping over the gunwales, and watched, in his mind, as she walked across a dark chamber toward him, peeling off a silken robe. He smiled. When he touched her, her flesh was warm, and smooth, unblemished. He could feel her on his fingertips. "Do this," he'd say, out loud; and then he'd giggle. "Down here," he'd say . . .

He sat for an hour, for two, talking occasionally, then he sighed and shivered, and woke from the daydream. The world had changed.

The sky was gray, angry, the low clouds rolling in. A wind whipped around the boat, blowing the rat's-nest of monofilament across the water like a tumbleweed. Across the fattest part of the lake, he could see the breaking curl of a whitecap.

Time to go.

He reached back to crank the outboard and saw her. She stood in the bay window, wearing a white dress—though she was three hundred yards away, he knew the figure, and the unique, attentive stillness. He could feel the eye contact. Andi Manette was psychic. She could look right into your brain and say the words you were trying to hide.

John Mail looked away, to protect himself.

So she wouldn't know he was coming.

Andi Manette stood in the bay window and watched the rain sweep across the water toward the house, and the darkness coming behind. At the concave drop of the lawn, at the water's edge, the tall heads of the white phlox bobbed in the wind. They'd be gone by the weekend. Beyond them, a lone fisherman sat in one of the orange-tipped rental boats from Irv's. He'd been out there since five o'clock and, as far as she could tell, hadn't caught a thing. She could've told him that the bottom was mostly sterile muck, that she'd never caught a fish from the dock.

As she watched, he turned to start the outboard. Andi had been around boats all of her life, and something about the way the man moved suggested that he didn't know about outboards—how to sit down and crank at the same time.

When he turned toward her, she felt his eyes—and thought, ridiculously, that she might know him. He was so far away that she couldn't even make out the shape of his face. But still, the total package—head, eyes, shoulders, movement—seemed familiar . . .

Then he yanked the starter cord again, and a few seconds later he was on his way down the shoreline, one hand holding his hat on his head, the other hand on the outboard tiller. He'd never seen her, she thought. The rain swept in behind him.

And she thought: the clouds come in, the leaves falling down.

The end of summer.

Too soon.

Andi stepped away from the window and moved through the living room, turning on the lamps. The room was furnished with warmth and a sure touch: heavy country couches and chairs, craftsman tables, lamps and rugs. A hint of Shaker there in the corner, lots of natural wood and fabric, subdued, but with a subtle, occasionally bold, touch of color—a flash of red in the rug that went with the antique maple table, a streak of blue that hinted of the sky outside the bay windows.

The house, always warm in the past, felt cold with George gone.

With what George had done.

George was movement and intensity and argument, and even a sense of protection, with his burliness and aggression, his tough face, intelligent eyes. Now . . . this.

Andi was a slender woman, tall, dark-haired, unconsciously dignified. She often seemed posed, although she was unaware of it. Her limbs simply fell into arrangements, her head cocked for a portrait. Her hair-do and pearl earrings said horses and sailboats and vacations in Greece.

She couldn't help it. She wouldn't change it if she could.

With the living room lights cutting the growing gloom, Andi climbed the stairs, to get the girls organized: first day of school, clothes to choose, early to bed.

At the top of the stairs, she started right, toward the girls' room—then heard the tinny music of a bad movie coming from the opposite direction.

They were watching television in the master bedroom suite. As she walked down the hall, she heard the sudden disconnect of a channel change. By the time she got to the bedroom, the girls were engrossed in a CNN newscast, with a couple of talking heads rambling on about the Consumer Price Index.

"Hi, Mom," Genevieve said cheerfully. And Grace looked up and smiled, a bit too pleased to see her.

"Hi," Andi said. She looked around. "Where's the remote?"

Grace said, unconcernedly, "Over on the bed."

The remote was a long way from either of the girls, halfway across the room in the middle of the bedspread. Hastily thrown, Andi thought. She picked it up, said, "Excuse me," and backtracked through the channels. On one of the premiums, she found a clinch scene, fully nude, still in progress.

"You guys," she said, reproachfully.

"It's good for us," the younger one protested, not bothering with denials. "We gotta find things out."

"This is not the way to do it," Andi said, punching out the channel. "Come talk to me." She looked at Grace, but her older daughter was looking away—a little angry, maybe, and embarrassed. "Come on," Andi said. "Let's everybody organize our school stuff and take our baths."

"We're talking like a doctor again, Mom," Grace said.

"Sorry."

On the way down to the girls' bedrooms, Genevieve blurted, "God, that guy was really hung."

After a second of shocked silence, Grace started to giggle, and two seconds later Andi started, and five seconds after that all three of them sprawled on the carpet in the hallway, laughing until the tears ran down their faces.

The rain fell steadily through the night, stopped for a few hours in the morning, then started again.

Andi got the girls on the bus, arrived at work ten minutes early, and worked efficiently through her patient list, listening carefully, smiling encouragement, occasionally talking with some intensity. To a woman who could not escape thoughts of suicide; to another who felt she was male, trapped in a female body; to a man who was obsessed by a need to control the smallest details of his family's life—he knew he was wrong but couldn't stop.

At noon, she walked two blocks out to a deli and brought a bag lunch back for herself and her partner. They spent the lunch hour talking about Social Security and worker compensation taxes with the bookkeeper.

In the afternoon, a bright spot: a police officer, deeply bound by the million threads of chronic depression, seemed to be responding to new medication. He was a dour, pasty-faced man who reeked of nicotine, but today he smiled shyly at her and said, "My God, this was my best week in five years: I was looking at women."

Andi left the office early, and drove through an annoying, mud-producing drizzle to the west side of the loop, to the rambling, white New England cottages and green playing fields of the Birches School. Hard maples boxed the school parking lot; flames of red autumn color were stitched through their lush crowns. Toward the school entrance, a grove of namesake birch had gone a sunny gold, a brilliant greeting on a dismal day.

Andi left the car in the parking lot and hurried inside, the warm smell of a soaking rain hanging like a fog over the wet asphalt.

The teacher-parent conferences were routine—Andi went to them every year, the first day of school: meet the teachers, smile at everyone, agree to work on the Thanksgiving pageant, write a check to the strings program. *So looking forward to working with Grace, she's a very bright child, active, school leader, blah blah blah.*

She was happy to go to them. Always happy when they were over.

When they were done, she and the girls walked back outside and found the rain had intensified, hissing down from the crazy sky. "I'll tell you what, Mom," Grace said, as they stood in the school's covered entry, watching a woman with a broken umbrella scurry down the sidewalk. Grace was often very serious when talking with adults. "I'm in a very good dress, and it's barely wrinkled, so I could wear it again. Why don't you get the car and pick me up here?"

"All right." No point in all of them getting wet.

"I'm not afraid of the rain," Genevieve said, pugnaciously. "Let's go."

"Why don't you wait with Grace?" Andi asked.

"Nah. Grace is just afraid to get wet 'cause she'll melt, the old witch," Genevieve said.

Grace caught her sister's eye and made a pinching sign with her thumb and forefinger.

"Mom," Genevieve wailed.

"Grace," Andi said, reprovingly.

"Tonight, when you're almost asleep," Grace muttered. She knew how to deal with her sister.

At twelve, Grace was the older and by far the taller of the

two, gawky, but beginning to show the curves of adolescence. She was a serious girl, almost solemn, as though expecting imminent unhappiness. Someday a doctor.

Genevieve, on the other hand, was competitive, frivolous, loud. Almost too pretty. Even at nine, everyone said, it was obvious that she'd be a trial to the boys. To whole flocks of boys. But that was years away. Now she was sitting on the concrete, messing with the sole of her tennis shoe, peeling the bottom layer off.

"Gen," Andi said.

"It's gonna come off anyway," Genevieve said, not looking up. "I told you I needed new shoes."

A man in a raincoat hurried up the walk, hatless, head bowed in the rain. David Girdler, who called himself a psychotherapist and who was active in the Parent-Teacher Cooperative. He was a boring man, given to pronunciations about *proper roles in life*, and *hard-wired behavior*. There were rumors that he used tarot cards in his work. He fawned on Andi. "Dr. Manette," he said, nodding, slowing. "Nasty day."

"Yes," Andi said. But her breeding wouldn't let her stop so curtly, even with a man she disliked. "It's supposed to rain all night again."

"That's what I hear," Girdler said. "Say, did you see this month's *Therapodist*? There's an article on the structure of recovered memory . . ."

He rambled on for a moment, Andi smiling automatically, then Genevieve interrupted, loudly, "Mom, we're superlate," and Andi said, "We've really got to go, David," and then, because of the breeding, "But I'll be sure to look it up."

"Sure, nice talking to you," Girdler said.

When he'd gone inside, Genevieve said, looking after him, from the corner of her mouth like Bogart, "What do we say, Mom?"

"Thank you, Gen," Andi said, smiling.

"You're welcome, Mom."

• • •

"Okay," Andi said. "I'll run for it." She looked down the parking lot. A red van had parked on the driver's side of her car and she'd have to run around the back of it.

"I'm coming, too," Genevieve said.

"I get the front," Grace said.

"I get the front . . ."

"You got the front on the way over, beetle," Grace said.

"Mom, she called me . . ."

Grace made the pinching sign again, and Andi said, "You get in the back, Gen. You had the front on the way over."

"Or I'll pinch you," Grace added.

They half-ran through the rain, Andi in her low heels, Genevieve with her still-short legs, holding hands. Andi released Gen's hand as they crossed behind the Econoline van. She pointed her key at the car and pushed the electronic lock button, heard the locks pop up over the hissing of the rain.

Head bent, she hurried down between the van and the car, Gen a step behind her, and reached for the door handles.

Andi heard the doors slide on the van behind her; felt the presence of the man, the motion. Automatically began to smile, turning.

Heard Genevieve grunt, turned and saw the strange round head coming for her, the mop of dirty blond hair.

Saw the road-map lines buried in a face much too young for them.

Saw the teeth, and the spit, and the hands like clubs.

Andi screamed, "Run."

And the man hit her in the face.

She saw the blow coming but was unable to turn away. The impact smashed her against her car door, and she slid down it, her knees going out.

She didn't feel the blow as pain, only as impact, the fist on her face, the car on her back. She felt the man turning, felt blood on her skin, smelled the worms of the pavement as she hit it, the rough, wet blacktop on the palms of her hand, thought crazily—for just the torn half of an instant—about ruining her suit, felt the man step away.

She tried to scream "Run" again, but the word came out as a groan, and she felt—maybe saw, maybe not—the man moving on Genevieve, and she tried to scream again, to say something, anything, and blood bubbled out of her nose and the pain hit her, a blinding, wrenching pain like fire on her face.

And in the distance, she heard Genevieve scream, and she tried to push up. A hand pulled at her coat, lifting her, and she flew through the air, to crash against a sheet of metal. She rolled again, facedown, tried to get her knees beneath her, and heard a car door slam.

Half-sensible, Andi rolled, eyes wild, saw Genevieve in a heap, and bloody from head to toe. She reached out to her daughter, who sat up, eyes bright. Andi tried to stop her, then realized that it wasn't blood that stained her red, it was something else: and Genevieve, inches away, screamed, "Momma, you're bleeding . . ."

Van, she thought.

They were in the van. She figured that out, pulled herself to her knees, and was thrown back down as the van screeched out of the parking place.

Grace will see us, she thought.

She struggled up again, and again was knocked down, this time as the van swung left and braked. The driver's door opened and light flooded in, and she heard a shout, and the doors opened on the side of the truck, and Grace came headlong through the opening, landing on Genevieve, her white dress stained the same rusty red as the truck.

The doors slammed again; and the van roared out of the parking lot.

Andi got to her knees, arms flailing, trying to make sense of it: Grace screaming, Genevieve wailing, the red stuff all over them.

And she knew from the smell and taste of it that she *was* bleeding. She turned and saw the bulk of the man in the driver's seat behind a chain-link mesh. She shouted at him,

"Stop, stop it. Stop it," but the driver paid no attention, took a corner, took another.

"Momma, I'm hurt," Genevieve said. Andi turned back to her daughters, who were on their hands and knees. Grace had a sad, hound-dog look on her face; she'd known this man would come for her someday.

Andi looked at the van doors, for a way out, but metal plates had been screwed over the spot where the handles must've been. She rolled back and kicked at the door with all her strength, but the door wouldn't budge. She kicked again, and again, her long legs lashing out. Then Grace kicked and Genevieve kicked and nothing moved, and Genevieve began screeching, screeching. Andi kicked until she felt faint from the effort, and she said to Grace, panting, three or four times, "We've got to get out, we've got to get out, get out, get out . . ."

And the man in the front seat began to laugh, a loud, carnival-ride laughter that rolled over Genevieve's screams; the laughter eventually silenced them and they saw his eyes in the rearview mirror and he said, "You won't get out. I made sure of that. I know all about doors without handles."

That was the first time they'd heard his voice, and the girls shrank back from it. Andi swayed to her feet, crouched under the low roof, realized that she'd lost her shoes—and her purse. Her purse was there on the passenger seat, in front. How had it gotten there? She tried to steady herself by clinging to the mesh screen, and kicked at the side window. Her heel connected and the glass cracked.

The van swerved to the side, braking, and the man in front turned, violent anger in his voice, and held up a black .45 and said, "You break my fuckin' window and I'll kill the fuckin' kids."

She could only see the side of his face, but suddenly thought: I know him. But he looks different. From where? Where? Andi sank back to the floor of the van and the man in front turned back to the wheel and then pulled away from the curb, muttering, "Break my fuckin' window? Break my fuckin' window?"

"Who are you?" Andi asked.

That seemed to make him even angrier. *Who was he?* "John," he said harshly.

"John *who?* What do you want?"

John Who? John the Fuck Who? "You know John the Fuck Who."

Grace was bleeding from her nose, her eyes wild; Genevieve was huddled in the corner, and Andi said again, helplessly, "John who?"

He looked over his shoulder, a spark of hate in his eyes, reached up and pulled a blond wig off his head.

Andi, a half-second later, said, "Oh, no. No. Not John Mail."

2

The rain was cold, but more of an irritant than a hazard.
If it had come two months later, it would've been a killer
blizzard, and they'd be wading shin-deep in snow and ice.
Marcy Sherrill had done that often enough and didn't like it:
you got weird, ugly phenomena like blood-bergs, or worse.
Rain, no matter how cold, tended to clean things up. Sherrill
looked up at the night sky and thought, *small blessings*.

Sherrill stood in the headlights of the crime-scene truck,
her hands in her raincoat pockets, looking at the feet of the
man on the ground. The feet were sticking out from under
the rear door of a creme-colored Lexus with real leather
seats. Every few seconds, the feet gave a convulsive jerk.

"What're you doing, Hendrix?" she asked.

The man under the car said something unintelligible.

Sherrill's partner bent over so the man under the car could
hear him. "I think he said, 'Chokin' the chicken.' " The rain
dribbled off his hat, just past the tip of a perfectly dry
cigarette. He waited for a reaction from the guy on the
ground—a born-again Christian—but got none. "Fuckin'
dweeb," he muttered, straightening up.

"I wish this shit'd stop," Sherrill said. She looked up at
the sky again. The *National Enquirer* would like it, she
thought. This was a sky that might produce an image of

Satan. The ragged storm clouds churned through the lights from the loop, picking up the ugly scarlet flicker from the cop cars.

Down the street, past the line of cop cars, TV trucks squatted patiently in the rain, and reporters stood in the street around them, looking down at Sherrill and the cops by the Lexus. Those would be the cameramen and the pencil press. The talent would be sitting in the trucks, keeping their makeup straight.

Sherrill shivered and turned her head down and wiped the water from her eyebrows. She'd had a rain cap, once, but she'd lost it at some other crime scene with drizzle or sleet or snow or hail or . . . Everything dripped on her sooner or later.

"Shoulda brought a hat," her partner said. His name was Tom Black, and he was not quite openly gay. "Or an umbrella."

They'd once had an umbrella, too, but they'd lost it. Or, more likely, it had been stolen by another cop who knew a nice umbrella when he saw it. So now Sherrill had the icy rain dripping down her neck, and she was pissed because it was six-thirty and she was still working while her goddamn husband was down at Applebee's entertaining the barmaid with his rapierlike wit.

And more pissed because Black was dry and snug, and she was wet, and he hadn't offered her the hat, even though she was a woman.

And even more pissed knowing that if he had offered, she'd have had to turn it down, because she was one of only two women in the Homicide Unit and she still felt like she had to prove that she could handle herself, even though she'd been handling herself for a dozen years now, in uniform and plainclothes, doing decoy work, undercover drugs, sex, and now Homicide.

"Hendrix," she said, "I wanna get out of this fuckin' rain, man . . ."

From the street, a car decelerated with a deepening groan, and Sherrill looked over Black's shoulder and said, "Uh-oh." A black Porsche 911 paused at the curb, where the uniforms had set up their line. Two of the TV cameras lit up to film the car, and one of the cops pointed at the crime van. The Porsche snapped down the drive toward the parking lot, quick, like a weasel or a rubber band.

"Davenport," Black said, turning to look. Black was short, slightly round, and carried a bulbous nose over a brush mustache. He was exceedingly calm at all times, except when he was talking about the President of the United States, whom he referred to as *that socialist shithead*, or, occasionally, *that fascist motherfucker*, depending on his mood.

"Bad news," Sherrill said. A little stream of water ran off her hair and unerringly down her spine. She straightened and shivered. She was a tall, slender woman with a long nose, kinky black hair, soft breasts, and a secret, satisfying knowledge of her high desirability rating around the department.

"Mmmm," Black said. Then, "You ever get in his shorts? Davenport's?"

"Of course not," Sherrill said. Black had an exaggerated idea of her sexual history. "I never tried."

"If you're gonna try, you better do it," Black said laconically. "He's getting married."

"Yeah?"

The Porsche parked sideways on some clearly painted parking-space lines and the door popped open as its lights died.

"That's what I heard," Black said. He flicked the butt of his cigarette into the grass bank just off the parking lot.

"He'd be nine miles of bad road," Sherrill said.

"Mike's a fuckin' freeway, huh?" Mike was Sherrill's husband.

"I can handle Mike," Sherrill said. "I wonder what Davenport . . ."

There was a sudden brilliant flash of light, and the feet sticking out from under the car convulsed. Hendrix said, "Goldarnit."

Sherrill looked down. "What? Hendrix?"

"I almost electrocuted myself," said the man under the car. "This rain is a . . . pain in the behind."

"Yeah, well, watch your language," Black said. "There's a lady present."

"I'm sorry." The voice was sincere, in a muffled way.

"Get out of there, and give us the fuckin' shoe," Sherrill said. She kicked a foot.

"Darn it. Don't do that. I'm trying to get a picture."

Sherrill looked back across the parking lot. Davenport was walking down toward them, long smooth strides, like a professional jock, his hands in his coat pockets, the coat flapping around his legs. He looked like a big broad-shouldered mobster, a Mafia guy with an expensive mohair suit and bullet scars, she thought, like in a New York movie.

Or maybe he was an Indian or a Spaniard. Then you saw those pale blue eyes and the mean smile. She shivered again. "He does give off a certain"—Sherrill groped for a word—"pulse."

"You got that," Black said calmly.

Sherrill had a sudden image of Black and Davenport in bed together, lots of shoulder hair and rude parts. She smiled, just a crinkle. Black, who could read her mind, said, "Fuck you, honey."

Deputy Chief Lucas Davenport's trench coat had a roll-out hood like a parka, and he'd rolled it out, and as he crossed the lot, he pulled it over his head like a monk; he was as dry and snug as Black. Sherrill was about to say something when he handed her a khaki tennis hat. "Put this on," he said gruffly. "What're we doing?"

"There's a shoe under the car," Sherrill said as she pulled the cap on. With the rain out of her face, she instantly felt better. "There was another one in the lot. She must've got hit pretty hard to get knocked out of her shoes."

"Real hard," Black agreed.

Lucas was a tall man with heavy shoulders and a boxer's hands, large, square, and battered. His face reflected his hands: a fighter's face, with those startling blue eyes. A white scar, thin like a razor rip, slashed down his forehead and across his right eye socket, showing up against his dark complexion. Another scar, round, puckered, hung on his throat like a flattened wad of bubble gum—a bullet hole and jack-knife tracheotomy scar, just now going white. He crouched next to the feet under the car and said, "Get out of there, Hendrix."

"Yes, yes, another minute. You can't have the shoe, though. There's blood on it."

"Well, hurry it up," Lucas said. He stood up.

"You talk to Girdler?" Sherrill asked.

"Who's that?"

"A witness," she said. She was wearing the good perfume, the Obsession, and suddenly thought of it with a tinkle of pleasure.

Lucas shook his head. "I was out in Stillwater. At dinner. People called me every five minutes on the way in, to tell me about the politics. That's all I know—I don't know anything about what you guys got."

Black said, "The woman . . ."

". . . Manette," said Lucas.

"Yeah, Manette and her daughters, Grace and Genevieve, were leaving the school after a parent-teacher conference. The mother and one kid were picked up in a red van. We don't know exactly how—if they were tear-gassed, or strong-armed, or shot. We just don't know. However it was done, it must have been a few seconds before the second daughter was taken off the porch over there." Black pointed back toward the school. "We think what happened was, the mother and Genevieve ran out to the car in the rain, were grabbed. The older daughter was waiting to get picked up, and then she was snatched."

"Why didn't she run?" Lucas asked.

"We don't know," Sherrill said. "Maybe it was somebody she knew."

"Where were the witnesses?"

"Inside the school. One of them is an adult, a shrink of some kind, one was a kid. A student. They only saw the last part of it, when Grace Manette was grabbed. But they say the mother was still alive, on her hands and knees in the van, but she had blood on her face. The younger daughter was facedown on the floor of the van, and there was apparently a lot of blood on her, too. Nobody heard any gun shots. Nobody saw a gun. Only one guy was seen, but there might have been another one in the van. We don't see how one guy could have roped all three of them in, by himself. Unless he really messed them up."

"Huh. What else?"

"White guy," Sherrill said. "Van had a nose on it—it was an engine front, not a cab-over. We think it was probably an Econoline or a Chevy G10 or Dodge B150, like that. Nobody saw a tag."

"How long before we heard?" Lucas asked.

"There was a 911 call," Sherrill said. "There was some confusion, and it was probably three or four minutes after the snatch, before the call was made. Then the car took three or four more minutes to get here. The call was sort of unsure, like maybe nothing happened. Then it was maybe five more minutes before we put the truck on the air."

"So the guy was ten miles away before anybody started looking," Lucas said.

"That's about it. Broad daylight and he's gone," Black said. They all stood around, thinking about that for a moment, listening to the hiss of rain on their hats, then Sherrill said, "What're you doing here, anyway?"

Lucas's right hand came out of his pocket, and he made an odd gesture with it. Sherrill realized he was twisting something between his fingers. "This could be . . . difficult," Lucas said. He looked at the school. "Where're the witnesses?"

"The shrink is over there, in the cafeteria," Sherrill said. "I don't know where the kid is. Greave is talking to them. Why is it difficult?"

"Because everybody's rich," Lucas said, looking at her. "The Manette woman is Tower Manette's daughter."

"I'd heard that," Sherrill said. She looked up at Lucas, her forehead wrinkled. "Black and I are gonna lead on this one, and we really don't need the attention. We've still got that assisted-suicide bullshit going on . . ."

"You might as well give up on that," Lucas said. "You're never gonna get him."

"Pisses me off," Sherrill said. "He never thought his old lady needed to kill herself until he ran into his little tootsie. I know he fuckin' talked her into it . . ."

"Tootsie?" Lucas asked. He grinned and looked at Black.

"She's a wordsmith," Black said.

"Pisses me off," Sherrill said. Then: "So what's Tower Manette doing? Pulling all the political switches?"

"Exactly," Lucas said. "And Manette's husband and the kids' father, it turns out, is George Dunn. I didn't know that. North Light Development. The Republican Party. Lotsa bucks."

"And Manette's the Democrats," Black said gloomily. "Jesus Christ, they got us surrounded."

"I bet the chief is peeing her political underwear," Sherrill said.

Lucas nodded. "Yeah, exactly," he said. "Can this shrink give us a picture of the guy?"

Sherrill shook her head doubtfully. "Greave told me the guy didn't see much. Just the end of it. I didn't talk to him much, but he seems a little . . . hinky."

"Great. And Greave's doing the interview?"

"Yeah." There was a moment of silence. Nobody said it, but Greave's interrogations weren't the best. They weren't even very good. Lucas took a step toward the school, and Sherrill said to his back, "Dunn did it."

Ninety percent of the time, she'd be right. But Lucas stopped, turned, shook his head at her. "Don't say that, Marcy—'cause maybe he did." His fingers were still playing with whatever-it-was, turning it, twisting it. "I don't want people thinking we went after him without some evidence."

"Do we have any?" Black asked.

Lucas said, "Nobody's said anything about it, but Dunn and Andi Manette just separated. There's another woman, I guess. Still . . ."

Sherrill said, "Be polite."

"Yeah. With everybody. Stay on their asses, but be nice

about it," Lucas said. "And . . . I don't know. If it's Dunn, he'd have to have somebody working with him."

Sherrill nodded. "Somebody to take care of them, while he was talking to the cops."

"Unless he just took them out and wasted them," Black suggested.

Nobody wanted to think about that. They all looked up at the same moment and got their faces rained on. Then Hendrix slid out from under the Lexus, with a ratcheting of metal wheels, and they all looked down at him. Hendrix was riding a lowboy, wore a white mechanic's jumpsuit and spectacles with lenses the size of nickels: he looked like an albino mole.

"There's a bloodstain on the shoe—I *think* it's blood. Don't disturb it," he said to Sherrill, passing her a transparent plastic bag.

Sherrill looked at the black high-heeled shoe, said, "She's got good taste."

Lucas flipped whatever-it-was between his middle and ring fingers, fumbled it, and then unconsciously slipped it over the end of his index finger. "Maybe the blood's from the asshole."

"Fat chance," Black said.

He pulled the mole to his feet and Lucas frowned and said, "What's that shit?"

He pointed at the leg of the mole's jumpsuit. In the headlights of the crime-scene truck, one of his pant legs was stained pink, as though he were bleeding from a calf wound.

"Jesus," Black said. He pulled on the seams of his own legs, lifting the cuffs above the shoes. "It's blood."

The mole dropped to his knees, pulled a paper napkin from a pocket, and laid it flat on the wet blacktop. When it was wet, he picked it up and held it in the truck lights. The handkerchief showed a pinkish tinge.

"They must've emptied her out," Sherrill said.

The mole shook his head. "Not blood," he said. He held the towel between himself and the truck lights and looked through it.

"Then what is it?"

The tech shrugged. "Paint. Maybe lawn chemicals. It's not blood, though."

"That's something," Sherrill said, her face pale in the headlights. She looked down at her shoes. "I hate wading around in it. If you don't clean it up right away, it stinks."

"But it's blood on the shoe," Lucas said.

"I believe it is," said the mole.

Sherrill had been watching Lucas fumble with the what-ever-it-was and finally figured it out. A ring. "Is that a ring?" she asked.

Lucas quickly pushed his hand in his coat pocket; he might have blushed. "Yeah. I guess."

"You guess? Don't you know?" She handed the shoe bag to Black. "Engagement?"

"Yeah."

"Can I see it?" She stepped closer and consciously batted her eyes.

"What for?" He stepped back; there was no place to hide.

"So I can fuckin' steal the stone," Sherrill said impatiently. Then, wheedling again: " 'Cause I want to look at it, why do you think?"

"Better show it to her," Black said. "If you don't, she'll be whining about it the rest of the night . . ."

"Shut up," Sherrill snapped at Black. Black shut up and the mole stepped back. To Lucas, "Come on, let me see it. Please?"

Lucas reluctantly took his hand out of his pocket and dropped the ring into Sherrill's open palm. She half-turned, so she could see the stone in the headlights. "Holy cow," she said reverently. She looked at Black. "The diamond is bigger'n your dick."

"But not nearly as hard," Black said.

The mole sadly shook his head. This kind of talk between unmarried men and women was another sign that the world was going to heck in a handbasket; that the final days were here.

They all started through the drizzle toward the school, the mole looking into the sky, for signs of God or Lucifer; Black, carrying the bloody shoe; Lucas with his head down;

and Sherrill marvelling at the three-carat, tear-shaped diamond sparkling in all the brilliant flashing cop lights.

The school cafeteria was decorated with hand-painted Looney Tunes characters, and was gloomy despite it: the place had the feel of a bunker, all concrete block and small windows too high to see out of.

Bob Greave sat at a too-short cafeteria table in a too-short chair, drinking a Diet Coke, taking notes on a secretarial pad. He wore a rust-colored Italian-cut suit and a lightweight, beige micro-fiber raincoat. A thin man in a trench coat sat next to him, in another too-short chair, his bony knees sticking up like Ichabod Crane's. He looked as though he might twitch.

Lucas walked through the double doors with Black, Sherrill, and the mole trailing like wet ducklings. "Hey, Bob," Lucas said.

"Is that the shoe?" Greave asked, looking at the bag Black was carrying.

"No, it's Tom's," Lucas said, a half-second before he remembered about Black and had to smother a nervous laugh. Black apparently didn't notice. The man with the incipient twitch said, "Are you Chief Davenport?"

Lucas nodded. "Yeah."

"Mr. Greave"—the man nodded at the detective—"said I had to stay until you got here. But I don't have anything else to say. So can I go?"

"I want to hear the story," Lucas said.

Girdler ran through it quickly. He had come to the school to talk to the chairperson about the year's PTA agenda, and had encountered Mrs. Manette and her daughters just outside the door, in the shelter of the overhang. Mrs. Manette had asked his advice about a particular problem—he was a therapist, as was she—and they chatted for a few moments, and he went inside.

Halfway down the hall and around a corner, he recalled a magazine citation she'd asked for, and that he couldn't remember when she'd first asked. He started back, and when he turned the corner, fifty or sixty feet from the door, he saw a man struggling with Manette's daughter.

"He pushed her into the van and went around it and drove away," Girdler said.

"And you saw the kids in the van?"

"Mmmm, yes . . ." he said, his eyes sliding away, and Lucas thought, *He's lying.* "They were both on the floor. Mrs. Manette was sitting up, but she had blood on her face."

"What were you doing?" Lucas asked.

"I was running down the hall toward the doors. I thought maybe I could stop them," Girdler said, and again his eyes slid away. "I got there too late. He was already going out the drive. I'm sure he had a Minnesota license plate, though. Red truck, sliding doors. A younger man, big. Not fat, but muscular. He was wearing a t-shirt and jeans."

"You didn't see his face."

"Not at all. But he was blond and had long hair, like a rock 'n' roll person. Hair down to his shoulders."

"Huh. And that's it?"

Girdler was offended: "I thought it was quite a bit. I mean, I chased after him, but he was gone. Then I ran back and got the women in the office to dial 911. If you didn't catch him, it's not my fault."

Lucas smiled and said, "I understand there was a kid here. A girl, who saw some of it."

Girdler shrugged. "I doubt she saw much. She seemed confused. Maybe not too bright."

Lucas turned to Greave, who said, "I got what I could from her. It's about the same as Mr. Girdler. The kid's mother was pretty upset."

"Great," Lucas said.

He hung around for another ten minutes, finishing with Girdler, talking to Greave and the other cops. "Not much, is there?"

"Just the blood," Sherrill said. "I guess we already knew there was blood, from Girdler and the kid."

"And the red stuff in the parking lot," said the mole, looking at the napkin he'd used to soak it up. "I bet it's some kind of semi-water-soluble paint, and he painted the van to disguise it."

"Think so?"

"Everybody says it was red, and this is red. I think it's a possibility. But I just don't see . . ."

"What?"

The mole scratched his head. "Why did he do it this way? Why right in the middle of the day, and three-to-one? I wonder if it could be a mistake or some spur-of-the-moment thing by a guy on drugs? But if it was spur-of-the-moment, how would he know to take Mrs. Manette? He must've known who she was . . . unless he just came here because it's a rich kid's school and he'd take anybody, and he saw the Lexus."

"Then why not just snatch a kid? You don't want the folks if you're looking for ransom. You want the parents getting the money for you," Black said.

"Sounds goofier'n shit," Sherrill said, and they all nodded.

"That could be an answer—she's a shrink, and maybe the guy used to be a patient. A nut," Black said.

"Whatever, I hope it was planned and done for the money," Lucas said.

"Yeah?" The mole looked at him with interest. "Why?"

" 'Cause if it was some doper or a goddamn gang-banger doing a spur-of-the-moment thing, and they haven't dropped them off by now . . ."

"Then they're dead," Sherrill finished.

"Yeah." Lucas looked around the little circle of cops. "If it wasn't planned, Andi Manette and her kids are outa here."

3

The chief lived in a 1920's brown-brick bungalow in a wooded neighborhood east of Lake Harriet in Minneapolis, cheek-by-jowl with half the other smart politicians in the city; a house you had to be the right age to buy in 1978.

The gabble of a televised football game was audible through the front door, and a moment after Lucas pushed the doorbell, the chief's husband opened it and peered out nearsightedly; his glasses were up on his forehead. "Come on in," he said, pushing open the door. "Rose Marie's in the study."

"How is she?" Lucas asked.

"Unhappy." He was a tall, balding lawyer, who wore a button vest and smelled vaguely of pipe tobacco. He reminded Lucas of Adlai Stevenson. Lucas followed him down through the house, a comfortable accumulation of overstuffed couches and chairs, mixed with turn-of-the-century oak, furnishings they might have inherited from prosperous farmer-parents.

Rose Marie Roux, the Minneapolis Chief of Police, was sitting in the den, in a La-Z-Boy, with her feet up. She was wearing a sober blue business suit with white sweat socks. She was smoking.

"Tell me you found them," she said, curling her toes at Lucas.

"Yeah, they were shopping at the Mall of America," Lucas said. He dropped into the La-Z-Boy facing the chief. "They're all okay, and Tower Manette's talking about running you for the U.S. Senate."

"Yeah, yeah," Roux said sourly. Her husband shook his head. "Tell me," she said.

"She was hit so hard she was knocked out of her shoes and there's blood on one of them," Lucas said. "We've got some eyewitness who says that Andi Manette and the younger of the daughters were covered with blood, although there's a possibility it was something else, like paint. And we've got a description of the guy who did it . . ."

"The perp," said Roux's husband.

They both looked at him. He hadn't seen the inside of a courtroom since he was twenty-five. He got his cop talk from the television. "Yeah, the perp," Lucas said. And to Rose Marie, "The description is pretty general: big, tough, dirty-blond."

"Damnit." Roux took a drag on her cigarette, blew it at the ceiling, then said, "The FBI will be in tomorrow . . ."

"I know. The Minneapolis AIC is talking to Lester," Lucas said. "He wanted to know if we were going to declare it as a kidnapping. Lester said we probably would. We're covering the phone lines at Tower Manette's office and house. The same for Dunn and Andi Manette, offices and houses."

"Gotta be a kidnapping," Roux's husband said, getting comfortable with the conversation. "What else could it be?"

Lucas looked at him and said, "Could be a nut— Manette's a shrink. Could be murder. Marital murder or something in the family. There's lots of money around. Lots of motive."

"I don't want to think about that," Roux said. Then, "What about Dunn?"

"Shaffer talked to him. He's got no alibi, not really. But we do know it wasn't him in the van. He says he was in his car—he's got a phone in his car, but he didn't use it within a half-hour of the kidnapping."

"Huh."

"You don't know him? Dunn?" Rose Marie Roux asked.

"No. I'll get to him tonight."

"He's a tough guy," she said. "But he's not crazy. Not unless something happened since the last time I saw him."

"Marital problems," Lucas suggested again.

"He's the type who'd have some," Roux said. "He'd manage them. He wouldn't flip out." She grunted as she pushed herself out of the La-Z-Boy. "Come on, we've got an appointment."

Lucas looked at his watch. Eight o'clock. "Where? I was gonna see Dunn."

"We've got to talk to Tower Manette first. At his place, Lake of the Isles."

"You need me?"

"Yeah. He called and asked if I'd put you on the case. I said I already had. He wants to meet you."

The chief traded her sweat socks for panty hose and short heels and they took the Porsche five minutes north to Lake of the Isles.

"Your husband said *perp*," Lucas said in the car.

"I love him anyway," she said.

Manette's house was a Prairie-style landmark posed on the west rim of the lake, above a serpentine driveway. The drive was edged with a flagstone wall, and Lucas caught the color of a late-summer perennial garden in the flash of the headlights. The house, of the same brown brick used in Roux's, was built in three offset levels, and every level was brilliantly lit; peals of light sliced across the evergreens under the windows and dappled the driveway. "Everybody's up," Lucas said.

"She's his only child," Roux said.

"How old is he now?"

"Seventy, I guess," Roux said. "He's not been well."

"Heart?"

"He had an aneurysm, mmm, last spring, I think. A couple

of days after they fixed it, he had a mild stroke. He supposedly made a complete recovery, but he's not been the same. He got . . . frail, or something."

"You know him pretty well," Lucas said.

"I've known him for years. He and Humphrey ran the Party in the sixties and seventies."

Lucas parked next to a green Mazda Miata; Roux struggled out of the passenger seat, found her purse, slammed the door, and said, "I need a larger car."

"Porsches are a bad habit," Lucas agreed as they crossed the porch.

A man in a gray business suit, with the professionally concerned face of an undertaker, was standing behind the glass in the front door. He opened it when he saw Roux reach for the doorbell. "Ralph Enright, chief," he said, in a hushed voice. "We talked at the Sponsor's Ball."

"Sure, how are you?" Roux said. "I didn't know you and Tower were friends."

"Um, he asked me to take a consultive role," Enright said. He looked as though he were waxed in the morning.

"Good," said Roux, nodding dismissively. "Is Tower around?"

"In here," Enright said. He looked at Lucas. "And you're . . ."

"Lucas Davenport."

"Of course. This way."

"Lawyer," Roux muttered, as Enright started into the depths of the house. Lucas could see the light glittering from his hair. "Gofer."

The house was high-style Prairie, with deep Oriental carpets setting off the arts-and-crafts furniture. A touch of deco added glamour, and a definite deco taste was reflected in the thirties art prints. Lucas knew nothing of decoration or art, but the smell of money seeped from the walls. *That* he recognized.

Enright led them to a sprawling center room, with two interlocking groups of couches and chairs. Three men in suits were standing, talking. Two well-dressed women sat on chairs facing each other. They all had the expectant air of a group waiting for their picture to be taken.

"Rose Marie . . ." Tower Manette walked toward them. He was a tall man with fine, high cheekbones and a trademark shock of white hair falling over wooly-bear white eyebrows. Another man, tanned, solid, tight-jawed, Lucas knew as a senior agent with the Minneapolis office of the FBI. He nodded and Lucas nodded back. The third man was Danny Kupicek, an intelligence cop who had worked for Lucas on special investigations. He raised a hand and said, "Chiefs."

The two women were unfamiliar.

"Thanks for coming," Manette said. He was thinner than Lucas remembered from seeing him on television, and paler, but there was a quick aggressive flash in his eyes. His suit was French-cut but conservative, showing his narrow waist, and his tie might have been chosen by a French president: the look of a ladies' man.

But the corner of his mouth trembled when he reached out to Roux, and when he shook hands with Lucas, his hand felt cool and delicate; the skin was loose and heavily veined. "And Lucas Davenport, I've heard about you for years. Is there any more news? Why don't we step into the library; I'll be right back, folks."

The library was a small rectangular room stuffed with leather-bound books, tan, oxblood, green covers stamped with gold. They all came in sets: great works, great thoughts, great ideas, great battles, great men.

"Great library," Lucas said.

"Thank you," Tower said. "Is there anything new?"

"There have been some further . . . disturbing developments," Roux said.

Tower turned his head away, as though his face were about to be slapped. "That is . . . ?"

Roux nodded at Lucas, and Lucas said, "I just got back from the school. We found one of your daughter's shoes in the parking lot, under her car, out of the rain. There was blood on it. We've got her blood type from medical school, so we should be able to tell fairly quickly if it's her blood.

If it *is* hers, she was probably bleeding fairly heavily—but that could be from a blow to the nose or a cut lip, or even a small scalp wound. They all bleed profusely . . . But there was some blood. Witnesses also suggest that your daughter and her younger daughter, Genevieve . . ."

"Yes, Gen," Manette said weakly.

". . . apparently were bleeding after the assault, when they were seen in the back of the kidnapper's van. But we've also found that the kidnapper may have tried to disguise his van by painting it with some kind of red water-soluble paint, so that may be what was seen on your daughter. We don't know about that."

"Oh, God." Manette's voice came out as a croak: the emotion was real.

"This could turn out badly," Roux said. "We're hoping it won't, but you've got to be ready."

"There must be something I can do," Manette said. "Do you think a reward? An appeal?"

"We could talk about a reward," Roux said. "But we should wait awhile, see if anyone calls asking for ransom."

"Do you have any ideas—anything at all—about what might be going on?" Lucas asked. "Anybody who might want to get at you, or at Miz Manette?"

"No . . ." But he said it slowly, as if he had to think about it. "Why?"

"She may have been stalked. This doesn't look like a spontaneous attack," Lucas said. "But there's an element of craziness about it, too. All kinds of things could've gone wrong. I mean, he kidnapped three people in broad daylight and got away with it."

"I'll tell you what, Mr. Davenport," Manette said. He took three shaky steps to an overstuffed library chair and sat down. "I've got more enemies than most men. There must be several dozen people in this state who genuinely detest me—people who blame me for destroying their careers, their prospects, and probably their families. That's politics. It's unfortunate, but that's what happens when your side loses in a political contest. You lose. So there are people out there . . ."

"It doesn't feel political," Roux said. Lucas noticed that she'd taken a cigarette out of a pocket and was rolling it, unlit, in her left hand.

Manette nodded. "I agree. As crazy as some of those people may be, I don't think this kind of thing would ever occur to them."

Lucas said, "There's always the possibility . . ."

Roux looked at him. "Political people always leave themselves escape hatches. With this, there's no escape hatch. Even if he just dropped them off on the corner, he'd be looking at years in prison for the kidnapping. A political mind wouldn't do that."

"Unless he was nuts," Lucas said.

Roux nodded, and looked at Manette and said, "There is that possibility."

"Which brings us to your daughter's psychiatric practice," Lucas said to Manette. "We need access to her records."

"The woman on the couch"—Manette tipped his head toward the living room—"the younger one, is Andi's partner, Nancy Wolfe. I'll talk to her."

"We'd like to start as soon as we can," Lucas said. "Tomorrow morning."

"I hope it's a kidnapping," Manette said. "I hope it's for profit—I don't like to think of some nut taking them."

"How about George Dunn?" Lucas asked. "He says he was in his car during the attack. No witnesses."

"That sonofabitch," Manette said. He pushed himself out of the chair and took a quick turn around the room and made a sound like a dog's growl. "He's a goddamn psycho. I didn't think before tonight that he'd do anything to hurt Andi or the girls, but now . . . I don't know."

"You think he might?"

"He's a cold-hearted sonofabitch," Manette said. "He could do anything."

They talked about the case for a few more minutes, then the two women came to the door and looked inside. "Tower? Are you okay?"

"I'm fine," he said.

The women stepped inside. The younger of the two, Nancy Wolfe, was a slender, well-tanned woman. She wore a soft woollen dress, but no jewelry or makeup, and her auburn hair showed a few threads of gray. Speaking to Manette, she said, "You need some quiet. I'm telling you that as an M.D., not as a psychiatrist."

The other woman was paler, older, with a loose, jowly face touched expertly with rouge. She nodded, stepped closer to Manette, and took his arm. "Just come on upstairs, Tower. Even if you can't sleep, you could lie down . . ."

"I don't go to bed until two o'clock in the morning," Manette said irritably. "There's no point in going up now."

"But it's been exhausting," the woman said. She seemed to be talking about herself, and Lucas realized that she must be Manette's wife. She spoke to Roux: "Tower's under a lot of stress, and he's had health problems."

"We wanted him to know that we're doing everything we can," Roux said. She looked back at Manette. "I've assigned Lucas to oversee the investigation."

"Thank you," Manette said. And to Lucas: "Anything you need, anybody that I know, that you want to talk to, just call. And let me know about that reward, if it would be useful."

"George Dunn," Lucas said.

"Get him on the phone, will you, Helen?" Manette said to his wife. "I'll talk to him."

"And after that, Tower, I want you to kick back and close your eyes, even if it's just for half an hour," Wolfe said. She reached out and touched his hand. "Take some time to think."

Lucas dropped the chief at her house, promising to call back at midnight, or when anything broke.

"Lester's running the routine," Roux said as the car idled in her driveway. "I need you to pluck this thing out of the sky, so to speak."

"Doesn't have a plucking feel about it," Lucas said. "Something complicated is going on."

"If you don't, *we're* gonna get plucked," Roux said. Then: "You want fifteen seconds of politics?"

"Sure."

"This is one of those cases that people will talk about for a generation," Roux said. "If we find Manette and her kids, we're gold. We'll be untouchable. But if we fuck it up . . ." She let her voice trail away.

"Let me go pluck," Lucas said.

George Dunn's house was a modest white ranch, tucked away on a big tree-filled lot on a dead-end street in Edina. Lucas left the Porsche in the driveway and climbed the stone walk to the front door, pushed the doorbell. A thick-faced cop, usually in uniform, now in slacks and a golf shirt, pushed open the door.

"Chief Davenport . . ."

"Hey, Rick," Lucas said. "They've got you watching the phones?"

"Yeah." In a lower voice. "And Dunn."

"Where is he?"

"Back in his office—the light back there." The cop nodded to the left.

The house was stacked with brown cardboard moving boxes, a dozen of them in the front room, more visible in the kitchen and breakfast area. There was little furniture—a couch and chair in the living room, a round oak table in the breakfast nook. Lucas followed a hall back to the light and found Dunn sitting at a rectangular dining table in what had been meant as a family room. A large-screen TV sat against one wall, the picture on, the sound off. A stereo system was stacked on a pile of three cardboard boxes.

Dunn was huddled over a pile of paper, with a crooked-neck lamp pulled close to them, his face half-in and half-out of the light. To his left, a half-dozen two-drawer file cabinets were pushed against a wall. Half of them had open drawers. Another stack of cardboard boxes sat on the floor beside the file cabinets. On the far side of the room, three chairs faced each other across a glass coffee table.

Lucas stepped inside the room and said, "Mr. Dunn."

Dunn looked up. "Davenport," he said. He dropped his pen, pushed back from the table, and stood to shake hands.

Dunn was a fullback ten years off the playing field: broad shoulders, bullet head, beat-up face. His front teeth were so even, so white and perfect, that they had to be a bridge. He wore a gray cashmere sweater, with the sleeves pushed up, showing a gold Rolex; jeans, and loafers without socks. He shook hands, held the grip for a second, nodded, pointed at a chair, sat down, and said, "Ask."

"You want a lawyer?" Lucas asked.

"I had one. It was a waste of money," Dunn said.

Lucas sat down, leaned forward, an elbow on his thigh. "You say you were in your car when your wife was taken. But you don't have any witnesses and you made no calls that would confirm it."

"I made one call to her, while she was on her way over to the school. I told that to the other guys . . ."

"But that was an hour before she was taken. A prosecutor might say that the call tipped you off to exactly where she'd be, so you'd have time to get there. Or send somebody," Lucas said. "And after that call, you were out of your office, and out of everybody's sight."

"I know it. If I'd done . . . this thing . . . I'd have a better alibi," Dunn said. He made a sliding gesture with one hand. "I'd have been someplace besides my car. But the fact is, I spend maybe a quarter of my business day in my car. I've got a half-dozen developments going around the Cities, from west of Minnetonka to the St. Croix. I hit every one every day."

"And you use your car phone all the time," Lucas pointed out.

"Not after business hours," Dunn said, shaking his head. "I called the office from Yorkville—that's the job over in Woodbury—and after that, and after I talked to Andi, I just headed back in. When I got here, the cops were waiting for me."

"Who do you think took her?" Lucas asked.

Dunn shook his head. "It's gotta be one of the nuts she handles," he said. "She gets the worst. Sex criminals, pyromaniacs, killers. Nobody's too crazy for her."

Lucas gazed at him for a moment. The gooseneck lamp

made a pool of light around his hands, but his pug's face was half in shadow; in an old black-and-white movie, he might have been the devil. "How much do you dislike her?" Lucas asked. "Your wife?"

"I don't dislike her," Dunn said, bouncing once in the chair. "I love her."

"That's not the word around town."

"Yeah, yeah, yeah." He put his fingers to his forehead, scrubbed at it. "I screwed a woman from the office. Once." Lucas let the silence grow, and Dunn finally launched himself from his chair, walked to a box, opened it, took out a bottle of scotch. "Whiskey?"

"No, thanks." And he let the silence go.

"We're talking about a major-league cookie, this chick, in my face five days a week," Dunn said. He made a Coke-bottle tits-and-ass figure with his hands. "Andi and I had a few disagreements—not big ones, but we've got a lot going on. Careers, busy all the time, we don't see each other enough . . . like that. So this chick is there, in the office— she was my traffic manager—and finally I jump her. Right there on her desk, pencils and pens all over the place, Post-it notes stuck to her butt. The next thing I know, she gets her little handbag and her business suit and shows up at Andi's office to announce that she loves me and I love her." He ran his hands through his hair, then laughed, a short, half-humorous bark. "Christ, what a nightmare that must've been."

"Doesn't sound like one of your better days," Lucas admitted. He remembered days like that.

"Man, I wish I hadn't done it," Dunn said. He lipped the bottle of whiskey in his hand, caught it. "I lost my wife and a pretty goddamn good traffic manager on the same day."

Lucas watched him for a long beat. He wasn't acting.

"Is there any reason you might've killed your wife for her money?"

Dunn looked up, vaguely surprised: "Christ, you don't fuck around, do you?"

Lucas shook his head. "Could you have done that? Does it make sense?"

"No. Just between you and me—there isn't that much money."

"Um . . ."

"I know, Tower Manette and his millions, the Manette Trust, the Manette Foundation, all that shit," Dunn said. He flicked a hand as if batting away a cobweb, then walked across the room, stepped through a doorway and flicked on a light. He opened a refrigerator door, dropped a couple of ice cubes in his glass, and came back. "Andi gets a hundred thousand a year, more or less, from her share of the Manette Trust. When the kids turn eighteen, they'll get a piece of it. And they'll get bigger pieces when they turn twenty-five and forty. If they were . . . to die . . . I wouldn't see any of that. What I'd get is the house, and the stuff in it. Frankly, I don't need it."

"So what about Manette? You said . . ."

"Tower had maybe ten million back in the fifties, plus the income from the trust, and a board seat at the Foundation. But he was running all over the world, buying yachts, buying a house in Palm Beach, screwing everything in a skirt. And he was putting the good stuff up his nose—he was heavy into cocaine back in the seventies. Anyway, after a few years, the interest on the ten mil wasn't cutting it. He started dipping into the principal. Then he got into politics— bought his way in, really—and he dipped a little deeper. It must've seemed like taking water out of the ocean with a teacup. But it added up. Then, in the late seventies and eighties, he did everything wrong—he was stuck in bonds during the big inflation, finally unloaded them at a terrific loss. Then sometime in there, he met Helen . . ."

"Helen's his second wife, right?" Lucas said. "She's quite a bit younger than he is?"

Dunn said, "I guess she's . . . what? Fifty-three, fifty-four? She's not that young. His first wife, Bernie—that's Andi's mother—died about ten years ago. He was already seeing Helen by that time. She was a good-looking woman. She had the face and real star-quality tits. Tower always liked tits. Anyway, Helen was in real estate and she got him deep into REITs as a way to recoup his bond losses . . ."

"What's a *reet*?" Lucas asked.

"Sorry; real-estate investment trust. Anyway, that was just before real estate fell out of bed, and he got hammered again. And the crash of eighty-seven . . . Hell, the guy was the kiss of death. You didn't want to stand next to him."

"So he's broke?"

Dunn looked up at the ceiling as if he were running a calculator in his head. After a moment, he said, "Right now, if Tower hunted around, he might come up with . . . a million? Of course, the house is paid for, that's better'n a mil, but he can't really get at it. He has to live somewhere and it has to be up to his standards . . . So figure that he gets sixty thousand from the million that's his, and another hundred thousand from the trust. And he's still got that seat on the Foundation board, but that probably doesn't pay more than twenty or thirty. So what's that? Less than two hundred?"

"Jesus, he's eating dog food," Lucas said, with just a rime of sarcasm in his voice.

Dunn pointed a finger at Lucas: "But that's *exactly* what he feels like. *Exactly*. He was spending a half-million a year when a Cadillac cost six thousand bucks and a million was really something. Now he's scraping along on maybe a quarter mil and a Caddy costs forty thousand."

"Poor sonofabitch."

"Listen, a million ain't that much any more," Dunn said wryly. "A guy who owns two good Exxon stations—he's worth at least a mil, probably more. Two gas stations. We're not talking about yachts and polo."

"So if you took your wife off, you wouldn't have done it for the money," Lucas said.

"Hell, if anybody got taken off, it should've been me. I'm worth fifteen or twenty times what Tower is. Of course, it ain't as good as Tower's money," he said ruefully.

"Why's that?"

" 'Cause I earned it," Dunn said. "Just like you did, with your computer company. I read about you in *Cities' Biz*. They said you're worth probably five million, and growing. You must feel it—that your money's got a taint."

"I've never seen any of it, the money," Lucas said. "It's all paper, at this point." Then: "What about insurance? Is there insurance on Andi?"

"Well, yeah." Dunn's forehead wrinkled and he scratched his chin. "Actually, quite a bit."

"Who'd get it?"

Dunn shrugged. "The kids . . . unless . . . Ah, Christ. If the kids died, I'd get it."

"Sole beneficiary?"

"Yeah . . . except, you know, Nancy Wolfe would get a half-million. They do pretty well in that partnership, and they both have key-man—key-woman—insurance to help cover their mortgage and so on, if somebody died."

"Is a half-million a lot for Nancy Wolfe?"

Dunn thought again, and then said, "It'd be quite a bit. She pulls down something between $150,000 and $175,000 a year, and she can't protect any of it—taxes eat her alive—so another half mil would be nice."

"Will you sign a release saying that we can look at your wife's records?" Lucas asked.

"Sure. Why wouldn't I?"

"Because a lot of medical people think psychiatric records should be privileged," Lucas said. "That people need treatment, not cops."

"Fuck that. I'll sign," Dunn said. "You got a paper with you?"

"I'll have one sent over tonight," Lucas said.

Dunn was watching Lucas's hand and asked, "What're you playing with?"

Lucas looked down at his hand and saw the ring. "Ring."

"Uh-oh. Coming or going?" Dunn asked.

"Thinking about it," Lucas said.

"Marriage is wonderful," Dunn said. He spread his arms. "Look around. A box for everything and everything in its box."

"You seem . . . sort of *lighthearted* about this whole thing."

Dunn suddenly leaned forward, his face like a stone. "Davenport, I'm so fuckin' scared I can't spit. I honest-to-

God never knew what it meant, being scared spitless. I thought it was just a phrase, but it's not . . . You gotta get my guys back."

Lucas grunted and stood up. "You'll stick around." It wasn't a question.

"Yeah." Dunn stood up, facing him. "You're a tough guy, right?"

"Maybe," Lucas said.

"Football, I bet."

"Hockey."

"Yeah, you got the cuts . . . Think you could take mè?" Dunn had relaxed again, and a faintly amused look crossed his face.

Lucas nodded. "Yeah."

Dunn said, "Huh," like he didn't necessarily agree, and then, losing the smile, "What d'you think—you gonna find my wife and kids?"

"I'll find them," Lucas said.

"But you won't guarantee their condition," Dunn said.

Lucas looked away, into the dark house: he felt like something was pushing his face. "No," he said to the darkness.

4

The Homicide office resembled the city room of a slightly seedy small-town daily. Individual cubicles for the detectives were separated by shoulder-high partitions; some desks were neat, others were a swamp of paper and souvenirs. Three different kinds of gray or putty-colored metal file cabinets were stuck wherever there was space. Old fliers and notes and cartoons and bureaucratic missives were tacked or taped on walls and bulletin boards. A brown plastic radio the size of a toaster, the kind last made in the sixties with a big, round tuning dial, sat on top of a file cabinet, a bent steel clothes hanger jammed into the back as an antenna. An adenoidal voice squeaked from the primitive speaker.

". . . is one of the most historical of crimes, from the Rape of the Sabine women to the Lindbergh kidnapping of our own era . . ."

Lucas was drinking chicken noodle Soup-in-a-Cup, and paused just inside the door with the cup two inches from his lips. The voice was familiar, but he couldn't place it until the DJ interrupted:

You're listening to Blackjack Billy Walker, go ahead, Edina, with a question for Dr. David Girdler . . .

Dr. Girdler, you said a minute ago that kidnapping victims identify with their kidnappers. All I can say is, that's a perfect example of what happens when the liberal school system shoves this politically correct garbage down the kids' throats, teaching them things the kids know are wrong but they gotta believe because somebody in authority says so, like these union hacks that call themselves teachers . . .

Girdler's voice was consciously mellow, hushed, artificially and dramatically deepened. He said:

I understand your feelings—heh heh—about this, although I don't entirely agree with your sentiments: there are many good teachers. That aside, yes, that identification often takes place and begins within hours of the kidnapping; the victims may actually suggest ways that the police can be more effectively foiled in their efforts . . .

Lucas stared at the radio, not believing it. Greave was sitting at his desk, eating a Mr. Goodbar. "Sounds like a fuckin' politician, doesn't he? He couldn't wait to get on the radio. He walked out of the school and drove right down to the station."

"How long has he been on?" Lucas finished the Soup-in-a-Cup and dropped the cup in a wastebasket.

"Hour," Greave said. "Lotta newsies have been looking for you, by the way."

"Fuck 'em," Lucas said. "For now, anyway."

A dozen detectives were milling around the office—everybody from Homicide/Violent Crimes, more from Vice, Sex, and Intelligence. Some were at desks, others were parked on swivel chairs, some were leaning against file cabinets. A very tall man and a very short one were talking golf swings. A guy from Sex elbowed past with a cafeteria tray full of cups of coffee and Coke. Almost everybody was eating or drinking. The office smelled like coffee, microwave popcorn, and Tombstone pizza.

Harmon Anderson wandered over to Greave's desk, eating a chicken-salad sandwich. A glob of mayonnaise was stuck to his upper lip. "Anything for a buck," he said between chews. Anderson was a hillbilly and a computer expert. "Girdler is *not* a doctor. He has a B.A. in psychology from some redneck college in North Carolina."

Sherrill, still damp, strolled in, pulled off the tennis hat, slapped it against her coat, then took off her coat and hung it up. She nodded at Lucas, tipped her head at the radio, and said, "Have you been listening?"

Lucas said, "Just now," and to Greave, "Did you ask him not to?"

Greave nodded. "The standard line. I said we should keep it to ourselves so the perpetrators don't know exactly what we have, and so we can present a better image if we get to court."

"Did you say perpetrator?" Lucas asked.

"Yeah. So shoot me."

"I'd say he didn't give a fuck," Sherrill said, fluffing her hair. "I was listening on the way over. He's remembering stuff he didn't give to us . . ."

"Making it up," Lucas said.

"Everybody's gotta be a movie star," Greave said. And they paused for a moment to listen:

Dr. Girdler, you know, the police don't stop crime; they simply record it, and sometimes they catch the people who do it. But by then, it's too late. This kidnapping is a perfect example. If Mrs. Manette had been carrying even a simple handgun, or if you had been carrying a handgun, you could've stopped this thug in his tracks. Instead, you were left standing there in the hallway and you couldn't do anything. I'll tell you, the criminals have guns; it's time we honest citizens took advantage of our Second Amendment rights . . .

"Damnit," Sherrill said. "It's gonna turn into a circus."

"Already has." They all turned toward the door. Frank

Lester, deputy chief for investigation, stepped inside with a handful of papers. He was tired, his face drawn. Too many years. "Anything more?"

Lucas shook his head. "I talked to Dunn. He seems pretty straight."

"He's a candidate, though," Greave said.

"Yeah, he's a candidate," Lucas said. To Lester: "Have the Feds come in yet?"

"They're about to," Lester said. "They can't avoid it much longer."

Lucas twisted the engagement ring around the end of his forefinger, saw Lester looking at it, and pushed it down in his pocket. Lester continued, "Even if the Feds come in, Manette wants us working it, too. The chief agrees."

"Jesus, I wish this shit would stop," Greave said, rubbing his forehead.

"Been doing it since Cain and Abel," said Anderson.

Greave stopped rubbing: "I didn't mean crime. I meant politics. If crime stopped, I'd have to get a job."

"You could probably get on the fuckin' radio with that suit," Sherrill said.

Lester waved them silent, held up a yellow legal pad on which he'd scribbled notes. "Listen up, everybody."

The talk died as the cops arranged themselves around Lester. "Harmon Anderson will be passing out assignments, but I want to outline what we're looking at and get ideas on anything we're missing."

"What's the overtime situation?" somebody called from the back.

"We're clear for whatever it takes," Lester said. He looked at one of the papers in his hand. "Okay. Most of you guys are gonna be doing house-to-house . . ."

Lester dipped his head into a chorus of groans—it was still raining outside—and then said, "And there's a lot of small stuff we've got to get quick. We need to know about the paint in the parking lot, by morning. And we need to check the school, for that color or type of paint. Jim Hill here"—he nodded at one of the detectives—"points out that you hardly ever see poster paint outside a school, so maybe the school is somehow involved."

"Her old man did it," somebody said.

"We're checking that," Lester said. "In the meantime, we got the blood on that shoe, and we need somebody to walk the blood tests around, 'cause we need to know quick if the blood's Manette's or one of the kids'. If it's not—if it's somebody else's—we'll run it through the state's DNA offender bank. And we need to talk to the University medical school, get Manette's blood type. I'm told she occasionally volunteered for medical studies, so they may even have a DNA on her, and if the blood on the shoe belongs to one of the kids, a DNA might tell us that . . ."

"DNA takes a while," said a short, pink cop who wore a snap-brim hat with a feather in the hatband.

"Not this one," Lester said. He looked at the paper again. "We need Ford Econolines checked against all her patients, against the school staff, all relatives, and against whatever data base we can find on felony convictions, Minnesota and however much of Wisconsin we can get. We need to see if any Manette- or Dunn-related companies own Econolines. Go to Ford, see if we can get a list of Econolines from their warranty program—they said it was an older one, so go back as far as you can. We need to run the registration lists for Econolines against her patient list, which we're trying to get . . ."

Anderson broke in. "I'm setting up a data base of patient names. Any name that pops up in the investigation, we can run against the list—so get all the names you can. All the teachers at the school, her phone records, anything."

Lester nodded and continued. "We need to check Manette's and Dunn's credit ratings, see if anybody's got money problems. Check insurance policies. What else?"

"Manette's putting together an enemies list," Lucas said.

"Run that, too," Lester told Anderson. "What are we missing?"

"Public appeals," said a black cop in a pearl-gray suit. "Pictures of Manette and the kids."

"All the news outlets already have some kind of pictures,

but we're putting out some high-quality stuff in the next couple of hours," Lester said. "There's some talk of a reward for information. We'll get back to you on that. And I want to say now, all the news contacts should go through the Public Affairs Department. I don't want anybody talking to the press. Everybody clear on that?"

Everybody was. Lester turned to Sherrill. "How's the house-to-house going?"

"We've hit all the houses where the residents could see the school, except for two, where there's nobody home, and we're looking for those people in case they were there during the kidnapping," Sherrill said. "The only thing we have so far is one woman who saw the van, and she picked out Econoline taillights as the lights she saw. So we think that ID is solid. Now we're going back for a second round, to talk about what people might've seen in the past couple of days—and we're doing the same thing in Manette's neighborhood. If this was planned out, he must've been scouting her. So, that's about it."

"Okay," Lester said. He looked around the room. "You all know the general picture. Get your assignments from Anderson and let's get it on the road. I want everybody breaking their balls on this one. This one's gonna be tough, and we need to look good."

As the other detectives gathered around Anderson, Lucas leaned toward Greave and asked, "Did the kid, the witness kid, did she see anything different from what Girdler gave us?"

Greave scratched the back of his head, and his eyes defocused. "Ah, the kid, I don't know, I didn't get much from her. She was fairly freaked out. Didn't seem like much."

"You got her phone number?" Lucas asked.

"Sure. You want it?"

"Doesn't she live over in St. Paul? Highland Park?"

"Someplace around there . . ."

Lester caught Lucas outside his office as Lucas was locking the door.

"Any ideas?" he asked.

"What everybody else says—money or a nut," Lucas said. "If we don't get a ransom call, we'll find him in her files or in her family."

"There could be a problem with the files," Lester said. "Manette talked to the Wolfe woman and she hit the roof. I guess there was a hell of an argument. Medical privilege."

"Doesn't exist, Frank," Lucas said. "Subpoena the records. Don't talk about it. If you talk about it, it'll turn into a big deal and the media will be wringing their wrists. Get a judge out of bed, get the subpoena. I'll take it over myself, if you want."

"That'd be good, but not tonight," Lester said. "We've got too much going on already. I'll have it here at seven o'clock tomorrow morning."

Lucas nodded. "I'll pick it up as early as I can drag my ass out of bed," he said. He didn't get up early. "I'm gonna stop and see the kid, too. Tonight."

"Bob talked to her," Lester said, uncomfortably.

"Yeah, he did," Lucas said. And after a moment, "That's your problem."

"Bob's a nice guy," Lester said.

"He couldn't catch the clap in a whorehouse, Frank."

"Yeah, yeah . . . did you talk to the kid's folks?"

"Two minutes ago," Lucas said. "I told them I was on the way."

Clarice Bernet wore a suit and tie. Her husband, Thomas, wore a cashmere sweater and a tie. "We don't want her frightened any more than she is," Clarice Bernet said. She hissed it, like a snake. She was a bony woman with tight blonde hair and a thin nose. Her front teeth were angled like a rodent's, and she was in Lucas's face.

"I'm not here to frighten her," Lucas said.

"You better not," Bernet said. She shook a finger at him: "There's been enough trouble from this already. The first officer questioned her without allowing us time to get there."

"We were hoping to stop the kidnapper's van," Lucas said mildly, but he was getting angry.

Thomas Bernet waggled his jowls: "We appreciate that, but you have to understand that this has been a trauma."

They were standing in the quarry-tiled entry of the Bernets' house, a closet to one side, a framed poster on the opposite wall, a souvenir from a Rembrandt show at the Rijksmuseum Amsterdam in 1992. A sad, middle-aged Rembrandt peered out at Lucas. "*You* have to understand that this is a kidnapping investigation and it could become a murder investigation," Lucas snapped, his voice developing an edge. "One way or another, we'll talk to your daughter and get answers from her. We can do it pleasantly, here, or unpleasantly down at Homicide, with a court order." He paused for a half-beat. "I'd rather not get the court order."

"*We* don't need threats," Thomas Bernet said. He was a division manager at General Mills and knew a threat when he heard one.

"I'm not threatening you; I'm laying out the legal realities," Lucas said. "Three people's lives are in jeopardy and if your daughter has a bad night's sleep over it, or two bad nights, that's tough. I've got to think about the victims and what they're going through. Now, do I talk to, uh, Mercedes, or do I get the court order?"

Mercedes Bernet was a small girl with a pointed chin, a hundred-dollar haircut, and eyes that were five years too old. She wore a pink silk kimono and sat on the living room couch, next to a Yamaha grand piano, with her ankles crossed. She had recently developed breasts, Lucas thought, and sat with her back coyly arched, making the best of what was not yet too much. With her mother sitting beside her, and her father hovering behind the chair, she told Lucas what she'd seen.

"Grace was standing there, looking back and forth, like she didn't know what was going on. She even walked back toward the door for a minute, then she went back out. Then this van pulled around in front, going that way." She pointed to her left. "And this guy jumps out, and he runs up to her and she started to back up and the guy just grabbed her by her blouse and by her hair and he jerked her right off the porch-thing . . ."

"The portico," Clarice Bernet said.

"Yeah, whatever," said Mercedes, rolling her eyes. "Anyway, he pulled her toward the van and slid the door back and threw her inside. I mean, he was this *huge* dude. He just threw her. And before he closed the door, I saw two other people in there. Mrs. Dunn . . ."

"Mrs. Manette," her mother said.

"Yeah, whatever, and she had blood on her face. She was, like, *crawling*. Then there was another kid in there that I thought was Genevieve, but I couldn't see her face. She was, like, lying down on the floor, and then the guy closed the door."

"Where was Mr. Girdler during all of this?"

"I didn't see him until afterwards. He was behind me somewhere. I told him to call 911, but he was like, *Duh*." She rolled her eyes again and Lucas smiled.

Then: "Think about this," Lucas said. "Tell me exactly what the kidnapper looked like."

Mercedes leaned back, closed her eyes, and a minute later, eyes still closed, said, "Big. Yellow hair, but it looked kinda weird, like it was peroxided or something. 'Cause his skin looked dark, not like a black dude, but you know . . . dark." She opened her eyes, and studied Lucas's face. "Like you, kinda. His face didn't look like yours—he had, like, a real narrow face—but he was about your color and big like you."

"What was he wearing? Anything special?"

She closed her eyes again and lived through the scene, then opened her eyes, looking surprised, and said, "Oh, shit."

"Young lady!" Clarice Bernet was shocked.

Lucas wagged his head once and asked, "What?"

"He was wearing a GenCon shirt. I *knew* there was something . . ."

He said, "GenCon? Are you sure? Did you see what year?"

"You know what it is?" A skeptical eyebrow went up.

"Sure. I write role-playing games . . ."

"Really? My boyfriend . . ."

"Mercedes!" Her mother's voice took a warning tone and Mercedes swerved into safer territory.

"A friend at school has one. I recognized it right away—the shirt isn't the same as my friend's, but it was a GenCon. Great big GenCon right on the front, and one of those weird dice. Everything black and white, kinda cheap . . ."

"What's a GenCon?" asked Thomas Bernet, looking suspiciously from his daughter to Lucas, as though GenCon might somehow be linked to ConDom.

"It's a gamer's convention, over in Lake Geneva," Lucas said. To Mercedes: "Why didn't you tell the other officer?"

"I could barely get his attention," she said. "And that asshole Girdler . . ."

"Mercedes!" Her mother was on the word like a wolf on a lamb.

"Well, he is," she said, barely defensive. "He kept talking all over me—I don't think he saw hardly any of it. He was mostly hiding down the hall."

"Okay," Lucas said. "What about the truck? Anything unusual about it?"

She nodded. "Yeah, there was, and I told the other cop. They'd painted over the sign on the truck. I don't know what it said, but there were letters on the door and they were painted right over."

"What letters?"

She shrugged. "I don't know. It was just something I sorta noticed when I went up closer to the windows and he was driving away. It wasn't a good paint job, you know? They just slopped right over the old letters."

Lucas used the Bernets' phone to call back to the office, and dropped the t-shirt and truck information with Anderson.

"Heading home?" Anderson asked.

"Not much more to do tonight, unless we get a call. Are we still doing the door-to-door?"

"Yeah, up in Manette's neighborhood now. Asking for suspicious activities. Haven't heard anything back."

"Let me know."

"Yeah, I'll be putting together a book on it . . . Have you asked Weather yet?"

"Jesus Christ . . ." Lucas laughed.

"Hey, it's primo gossip."

"I'll let you know," Lucas said. He could feel the engagement ring in his pants pocket. Maybe ask her, he thought.

"I got a feeling about this," Anderson said.

"About Weather?"

"No. About the Manettes. There's something going on here. So they're not dead yet. They're out there waiting for us."

Weather Karkinnen made a bump on the left side of the bed, near the window. The window was open an inch or two, so she could get the fresh cold air.

"Bad?" she asked, sleepily.

"Yes." He slipped in beside her, rolled close, kissed her on the neck behind the ear.

"Tell me," she said. She rolled onto her back.

"It's late," he said. She was a surgeon. She operated almost every day, usually starting at seven o'clock.

"I'm okay; I've got a late starting time tomorrow."

"It's Tower Manette's daughter and her two children, her daughters." He outlined the kidnapping, told her about the blood on the shoe.

"I hate it when there are kids involved," she said.

"I know."

Weather was a surgeon, but she looked like a jock—a fighter, actually, somebody who'd gone a few rounds too many. She had wide shoulders and she tended to carry her hands in front of her, fists clenched, like a punch-drunk boxer. Her nose was a little too large and bent slightly to the left; her hair was cut short, a soft brown touched with white. She had the high Slavic cheekbones of a full-blooded Finn, and dark blue eyes. For all of her jockiness, she was a small woman. Lucas could pick her up like a parcel and carry her around the house. Which he had done, on occasion; but never fully clothed.

Weather was not pretty, but she reached him with a power he hadn't experienced before: His attraction had grown so strong that it scared him at times. He'd lie awake at night, watching her sleep, inventing nightmares in which she left him.

They'd met in northern Wisconsin, where Weather had been working as a surgeon in a local hospital. Lucas had run down a child-sex ring, and the killer at the heart of it. In the final moments of a chase through the woods, he'd been shot in the throat by a young girl, and Weather had saved his life, opening his throat with a jack knife.

Hell of a way to get together . . .

Lucas put his hands on her waist. "Just how late can you go in?" he whispered.

"Men are animals," she said, moving closer.

When she went to sleep, Lucas, relaxed, warm, moved against her. She snuggled deeper into her pillow, and pushed her butt out against him. The best time to ask her to marry him, he thought, would be now: he was awake, articulate, feeling romantic . . . and she was sleeping like a baby. He smiled to himself and patted her on the hip, and let his head fall on his pillow.

He kept the ring in the bottom of his sock drawer, waiting for the right moment. He could feel it there and wondered if it made black sparkles in the dark.

5

The room was a concrete-and-stone hole that smelled like rotten potatoes. Four fist-sized openings pierced the top of one wall, too high to see through. The openings reminded Andi of the holes that a child would punch in the top of a Ball jar, to give air to his insect collection.

A stained double-bed mattress lay in one corner, and the girls slept on it. John Mail had been gone for three hours, by Andi's watch. When he'd left, the steel door banging behind him, they'd all crouched on the mattress, waiting wide-eyed for his return.

He hadn't come back. The fear burning them out, the girls eventually curled up and fell asleep like kittens in a cat box, too exhausted to stay awake. Grace slept badly, groaning and whimpering, Genevieve slept heavily, her mouth open, even snoring at times.

Andi sat on the cold floor, with her back to the gritty wall, taking inventory for the fiftieth time, trying to find something, anything, that would get them out.

There was a light socket overhead, with a single sixty-watt bulb and a pull-chain. She hadn't yet had the courage to turn the light off. A Porta-Potti sat in a corner, smelling faintly of chemical rinse. The portable toilet was meant for small sailboats and campers, and was made of plastic. She could think of no way to use it as a weapon, or as anything other than a toilet. A Coleman cooler sat next to the door, half-full of melting ice and generic strawberry soda. And beside her, on a low plastic table, a game console and a monitor. The console and monitor were plugged into a four-socket power bar, which was plugged into an outlet above the light bulb.

And that was all.

A weapon? Perhaps one of the cans could be used as a club . . . somehow? Could the cord be used to strangle him?

No. That was all absurd. Mail was too big, too violent.

Could you wire the door, somehow? Strip the wire out of the cord to the computer, connect it to the door handle?

Andi knew nothing about electricity—and if all Mail got was a shock, he'd simply turn off the power, and then come down, and . . . what?

That was what she couldn't deal with: what did he want? What would he do?

He'd obviously planned for this.

Their cell had once been a root cellar in a farm house, a deep hole, well below the frost line, with walls of granite fieldstone and concrete. Mail had knocked out part of an interior wall and had rebuilt it with concrete block to accommodate a steel fire door. The wiring was all new, nothing more than a cord run in from the outside.

Although the walls were old, except for the part Mail had redone, they were solid: Andi had pushed or kicked at every stone, had probed the interstices with her fingernails. Her hands were raw from it, and she'd found no weaknesses.

Overhead, between two-by-ten joists, was a plank ceiling. They could reach it by standing on the Porta-Potti, but when they beat on it, the sound was frighteningly dead: Andi feared that if they somehow pulled out a board, they'd find themselves buried underground.

The door itself was impossible, all steel with a simple slide latch on the outside. No amount of patience with a hairpin would pick the lock—if she'd known how to pick a lock in the first place, which she didn't.

She did the inventory again, straining to think of ways out. The chemical in the toilet? If it were harsh enough, perhaps she could throw it in his eyes and slip past him up the stairs?

He would kill them . . .

Andi closed her eyes and relived the trip out of the Cities.

They'd rattled around the back of the van like dice in a cup—the cargo space had been stripped and was no more than a steel box, without handholds or comfort. Mail had apparently rigged the steel screen and removed the door handles for the kidnapping.

When they'd left the school, Mail had dodged from street to street, watching the rearview mirror, then took the van onto I-35, heading south, Andi thought. They were on I-35 for several minutes, then exited to an unfamiliar two-lane highway, out through the whiskey billboards and into the pastel suburbs south of the Cities, as the kids screamed and beat at the sides of the truck and then fell into an alternating, spasmodic weeping.

Andi was still bleeding inside her mouth, where her teeth had cut into her lip. The taste of blood and the smell of exhaust nauseated her; fighting to get to her hands and knees as Mail dodged through the side streets, she eventually crawled into a corner and vomited. The stench set Genevieve off; she began to retch, and Grace began to weep and shudder, shaking uncontrollably. Andi took all of it in but was unable to focus on it, unable to sort it out and react, until finally, dumbly, she simply took the children in her arms and held them and let them scream.

Mail paid no attention.

After a while, they all got to their knees and looked out the windows as the suburbs dwindled, and the truck entered the great green sea of corn, beans, and alfalfa outside the Cities.

Up front, Mail punched buttons on the radio, seemingly without purpose: he went from Aerosmith to Toad the Wet Sprocket to Haydn to George Strait to three, four, five talk shows.

Listen, most of these criminals are weaklings; the only thing that makes them anything is that we give them a gun. Take the gun away, and they'll crawl back to the gutters where they came from . . .

They spent five minutes on a rural highway, bumping over long, snaky tar joints in the cracked concrete; then Mail took them off the highway onto a gravel road, and they left a spiraling cloud of gray dust in their wake. Red barns and white farmhouses flicked past the windows, and a black rural mailbox in a cluster of orange day lilies, dusty from the gravel.

Grace staggered to her feet and grabbed the chain-link fence separating them from Mail, and screamed, "Let me out of here, you fuck, let me out of here let me out . . ."

Genevieve panicked when her sister began to scream and wailed, a high, sirenlike keening, and her eyes rolled up into her head. She fell back and Andi thought for a moment that she'd had a stroke and crawled toward her, but Genevieve's eyes rolled and got straight and she started again, the keening, and Andi put her hands over her ears and Grace shouted, *Let me out of here . . .*

Mail put a hand over the ear closest to Grace, and, without looking back at her, shouted, *shut up shut up shut up*, and spit sprayed down the length of the windshield.

Andi grabbed her daughter and pulled her down, shook her head, held her daughter's face close and said, "Don't make him mad," then gathered up Genevieve and held her, squeezed her until the keening died away.

Then came a moment, just a moment, when Andi thought something different could happen, a streak of possibility rolling through her bloodied mind. They'd turned off the gravel road and started up a dirt lane.

Ragweed and black-eyed Susans grew in the middle of the track, and along both sides; farther away to the right, ancient, gray-barked apple trees stood with branches crabbed like scarecrow fingers.

An old farmhouse waited at the end of the lane: a dying house, shot through with rot, the paint peeling off the clapboard siding, a front porch falling off to one side.

Behind it, down the far side of the hill, a barn's foundation crouched in a hollow. The barn itself was gone, but the lower level remained, covered by what had been the floor of the old structure, and by a blue plastic tarp tied at the corners with yellow polypropylene rope. An open doorway poked into the dark interior, like the entrance to a cave. Around the barn foundation, two or three other crumbling outbuildings subsided into the soil.

When they stopped, Andi thought in the recesses of her mind there would be three of them, only one of him. She could take him on, hold him while the girls ran. A cornfield bordered the farmhouse plot. There was no fence. Grace was fast and smart, and once in the cornfield, which was as dense as a rain forest, she could escape . . .

John Mail stopped the truck and they all rocked back and forth once, and Grace got to her knees and looked out the dirty window. Mail turned in his seat. He had an oddly high-pitched voice, almost childlike, and said to Andi: "If you try to run, I'll shoot the little kid first, then the next one, then you."

And the streak of possibility died.

Genetics had made John Mail a psychopath. His parents had made him a sociopath.

He was a crazy killer and he didn't care about labels.

Andi had met him as part of her post-doc routine at the University of Minnesota, a new psychiatrist looking at the strange cases locked in the Hennepin County jails. She'd recognized a hard, quick intelligence in the cave of Mail's mind. He was smart enough—and large enough—to dominate his peers, and to avoid the cops for a while, but he was no match for a trained psychiatrist.

Andi had peeled him like an orange.

Mail's father had never married his mother, had never lived with them; last heard of, he was with the Air Force in Panama. Mail had never seen him.

When he was a baby, his mother would leave him for hours, sometimes all day and overnight, stuck in a bassinet, alone in a barren room. She married a man when he was three—three and still unable to talk—who didn't care much about her and less about Mail, except as an annoyance. When he was annoyed, when he was drunk, he'd use his leather belt on the kid; later, he moved to switches and finally to broom sticks and dowel rods.

As a child, Mail found intense pleasure in torturing animals, skinning cats and burning dogs. He moved up to attacking other children, both boys and girls—the class bully. In fourth grade, the attacks on girls had taken a sexual turn. He liked to get their pants off, penetrate them with his fingers. He didn't know yet what he wanted, but he was getting close.

In fifth grade, big for his age, he started riding out to the malls, Rosedale, Ridgedale, catching suburban kids outside the game rooms, mugging them.

He carried a t-ball bat, then a knife. In sixth grade, a science teacher, who also coached football, pushed him against a wall when he called a girl a cunt in the teacher's hearing. The teacher's house burned down a week later.

The fire was a trip: five more houses went down, all owned by parents of children who'd crossed him.

In June, after sixth grade, he torched the home of an elderly couple, who ran the last of the mom-and-pop groceries on St. Paul's east side. The old couple were asleep when the smoke rolled under the door. They died together near the head of the stairs, of smoke inhalation.

A smart arson cop finally found the pattern, and he was caught.

He denied it all—never stopped denying it—but they knew he'd done it. They brought Andi in, to see exactly what they'd caught, and Mail had talked about his life in a flat lizard's voice, casually, his young eyes crawling around her body, over her breasts, down to her hips. He scared her, and she didn't like it. He was too young to scare her . . .

Mail, at twelve, had already shown the size he'd be. And he had tension-built muscles in his body and face, and eyes like hard-boiled eggs. He talked about his stepfather.

"When you say he beat you, you mean with his fists?" Andi asked.

Mail grunted, and smiled at her naivete. "Shit, fists. The fucker had this dowel he took out of a closet, you know, a clothes rod? He whipped me with that. He beat my old lady, too. He'd catch her in the kitchen and beat the shit out of her and she'd be screaming and yelling and he'd just beat her until he got tired. Christ, there'd be blood all over the place like catsup."

"Nobody ever called the police?"

"Oh, yeah, but they never did anything. My old lady used to say that it was none of the neighbors' business."

"When he died, it got better?"

"I don't know, I wasn't living there any more; not much."

"Where'd you live?"

He shrugged: "Oh, you know: under the interstate, in the summer. There's some caves over in St. Paul, by the tracks, lots of guys over there . . ."

"You never went back?"

"Yeah, I went back. I got really hungry and fucked up and thought she maybe had some money, but she called the cops on me. If I hadn't gone back, I'd still be out. She said, 'Eat some Cheerios, I'll go get some cake,' and she went out in the front room and called the cops. Learned me a lesson, all right. Kill the bitch when I get out. If I can find her."

"Where is she now?"

"Took off with some guy."

After two months of therapy, Andi had recommended that John Mail be sent to a state hospital. He was more than a bad kid. He was more than unbalanced. He was insane. A kid with the devil inside.

The girls had stopped weeping when Mail opened the van door. He took them out, single file, through the side door of the old farmhouse and straight into the basement. The basement smelled wet, smelled of fresh dirt and disinfectant. Mail had cleaned it not long ago, she thought. A small spark of hope: he wasn't going to kill them. Not right away. If they had a little time, just a little time, she could work on him.

Then he locked them away. They listened for him,

fearful, expecting him back at any moment, Genevieve asking, over and over, "Mom, what's he going to do? Mom, what's he going to do?"

A minute became ten minutes, and ten minutes an hour, and the girls finally slept while Andi put her back to the wall and tried to think . . .

Mail came for her at three in the morning, drunk, excited.

"Get out here," he growled at her. He had a beer can in his left hand. The girls woke at the sound of the latch, and they crawled across the mattress until they had their backs to the wall, but curled, like small animals in a den.

"What do you want?" Andi said. She kept looking at her watch, as if this were a normal conversation and she was on her way somewhere else. But the fear made her voice tremble, as much as she tried to control it. "You can't keep us here, John. It's not right."

"Fuck that," Mail said. "Now get out here, goddamnit."

He took a step toward her, his eyes dark and angry, and she could smell the beer.

"All right. Don't hurt us, just don't hurt us. Come on, girls . . ."

"Not them," Mail said. "Just you."

"Just me?" Her stomach clutched.

"That's right." He smiled at her and put his free hand on the doorsill, as though he needed help staying upright. Or maybe he was being cool. He'd teased his hair into bangs, and now she realized that in addition to the beer, she could smell aftershave or cologne.

Andi glanced at the girls, then at Mail, and at the girls again. "I'll be right back," she said. "John won't hurt me."

Neither of the girls said a word. Neither of them believed her.

Andi walked around him, as far away as she could. In the outer basement, the air was cooler and fresher, but the first thing she noticed was that he'd dragged another mattress down the stairs. She stepped toward the stairs as the steel door clanged shut behind her and Mail said, "Don't move."

She stopped, afraid to move, and he walked around her,

until he was between her and the door. He stared at her for a moment, a little out of balance, she thought. He was seriously drunk, and his eyes looked closed in, heavy-lidded, and his lips curled in an ugly, contemptuous smile.

"They don't have any idea where you're at or who took you," he said. He nearly laughed, but somewhere, under there, he was a bit unsure of himself, she thought. "They been talking about it on the radio all night. They're running around like chickens with their heads cut off."

"John, they'll come sooner or later," Andi said. "Your best option, I believe . . ." She automatically fell into her academic voice, the slightly dry observational tone that she used when dealing with patients on a sensitive point. A tone that seemed educated and aristocratic at the same time, and often sold her viewpoint on its own.

Not this time.

Mail moved very quickly, shockingly quickly, like a middleweight boxer, and slapped her face hard, nearly knocking her down. An instant before, she'd been a Ph.D. applying psychology; now she was a wounded animal, trying to find its balance before it became simply meat.

Mail stepped close to her, close enough to smell, close enough to see the texture in his jeans, and he snarled, "Don't you ever talk that way. And they're never gonna find us. Never in this world. Now stand up straight. Stand the fuck up."

She had her hand to her face, nothing coherent in her head: her thoughts were like Scrabble pieces on a dropped board. There was a crunching sound and she looked toward Mail, who was watching her, still angry. He'd crushed the beer can in his hand, and now he threw it into a corner, where it clattered off the wall and then bounced back toward them.

"Let's see 'em," he said.

"What?" She had no idea.

"Let's see 'em," he said.

"What?" Stupidly, shaking her head.

"Your tits, let's see your tits."

She tried to back away, one step, two, but there was no

place to go. Behind her, an old coal-burning furnace stood like an old, close-cropped oak, the coal door open and leaning to the left; and behind it, a dark space, a place she really didn't want to go. "John, you don't want to hurt me. John," she said. "I took care of you."

He thrust a finger at her. "You don't want to talk about that. You don't want to talk about that. You took care of me, all right, you sent me down to the fuckin' hospital. You took care of me, all right." He looked around wildly, then saw the beer can on the floor. He'd forgotten that he'd finished it. He came back at her. "Come on, let's see 'em."

She crossed her arms over her chest. "John, I can't . . ."

And as quickly as he had before, he hit her again, open-handed, not quite as hard. When she put her hands up, he hit her again, and then again. She couldn't block the blows, she couldn't stop, she couldn't even see them coming.

Then he was on her, slamming her back against the stone wall, ripping at her jacket, at her blouse. She screamed at him, "No, don't, John . . ."

And he swatted her again, knocked her down, pulling her hair, guiding her to the mattress, and landed on top of her, straddling her waist. She struck at him, flailed uselessly. He caught her hands, brought them together, took them in one of his, held them. She couldn't see him very well, realized that she was bleeding, that she had blood in one eye.

"John . . ." She began to weep, not believing that he could go on.

But he did.

When he was done, he was angrier than when he had started.

He made her dress, as best she could—her blouse was ripped nearly in half, and he took her bra away from her—and then thrust her back in the cell.

Both of the girls, even the small Genevieve, knew what had happened. When Andi dropped onto the mattress, they automatically curled around her and held her head, while the steel door clanged shut.

Andi couldn't cry.

Her eyes had dried, or something. When she thought of Mail—not his face, not his voice, but the smell of him—she wanted to gag, and sometimes did, a reflexive clutching of her throat and stomach.

But she couldn't cry.

She hurt, though. She was bruised, and felt small muscle pulls and tears, when she'd struggled and twisted against his strength. There wasn't any blood: she checked herself, and though she felt raw, he hadn't ripped anything.

She was dry-eyed, stunned, when Mail came back.

They felt something, a muffled part of the sound, vibrations from the floor above, and knew he was coming. They were all facing the door, sitting on the mattress, when the door opened. Andi tucked her skirt beneath her.

Mail was wearing jeans, a plaid shirt, and wrap-around sunglasses, and held a pistol. He stood in the open door for a moment, then said, "I can't keep all of you." He pointed at Genevieve. "Come on, I'm taking you out."

"No, no," Andi blurted. She caught Genevieve's arm, and the girl pulled into her side. "No, John, please, no, don't take her, I'll take care of her here, she won't be a problem, John . . ."

Mail looked away. "I'll take her out to the Wal-mart and drop her off. She's smart enough to call the cops and get back home."

Andi stood up, pleading. "John, I'll take care of her, honest to God, she won't be a problem."

"She is a problem. Just thinking about her in my head, she's a problem." He pointed the pistol at Grace, who flinched away. "I gotta keep her, because she's too old and she could bring the cops back. But the kid, here—I'll put a bag on her head and take her out to the van and drop her at Wal-Mart."

"John, please," Andi begged.

Mail snarled at Genevieve, "Get out of here, kid, or I'll beat the shit out of you and drag your ass out."

Andi got to her knees and then to her feet, reached toward him. "John . . ."

He stepped back and his hand came up and caught her throat, and for a half-instant she thought she was dead: he squeezed for a second, then threw her back. "Get the fuck away." And to Genevieve: "Get out of here, kid, out the door."

"Wait, wait," Andi said. "Gen, take your coat, it's cold . . ." Genevieve had rolled her coat into a pillow, and Andi got it off the mattress, unrolled it, and fitted it around the child and buttoned it, kneeling, looking into Gen's eyes.

"Just be good," she said. "John won't hurt you . . ."

Genevieve went like her feet were stuck in glue, and Andi called, "Genevieve, honey, ask for a policeman. When you get to the mall, ask for a policeman and tell them who you are. They'll take you home to Daddy."

The door slammed in her face. Faintly, faintly, she could hear footsteps outside in the basement, but nothing else behind the muffled steel door.

"She'll be okay," Grace said. But she was beginning to cry, and the words came hard through the tears: "She's been in lots of malls. She'll just find a policeman and she'll go home. Dad'll take care of her."

"Yes." Andi dropped to the mattress, her hands covering her face: "Oh my God, Grace. Oh my God."

6

"I hate rich people," Sherrill muttered. She was wearing the same coat as the night before, but she'd added her own hat, a green baseball cap with a pale blue bill. Her hair was tucked underneath. She finished the outfit with pale blue sneaks, a tom-boy-with-great-breasts look. With her rosy cheeks and easy smile, Black thought she looked good enough to eat.

They'd dumped the city car in the parking lot outside Andi Manette's office building. The building, Sherrill thought, had been designed by a seriously snotty architect: black windows, red bricks, and copper flashing, snuggled into the side of a cattail-ringed pond, with a twisted chunk of rusty Corten steel out front. Black paused by the sculpture: the plaque said, *Ray-Tracing Wrigley.*

"You know what that's supposed to be?" he asked, looking up at it.

"Looks like a big stick of rusty steel chewing gum that somebody twisted," Sherrill said.

Black said, "Jesus, you're an art critic. That's what it must be."

Sherrill led the way across a bridge over a moatlike finger from the pond. Somebody had thrown a half-bucket of corn into the water, and a cluster of mallards and two Canada geese rooted through the shallow water weeds for the kernels. A half-dozen koi circled slowly among the ducks, their golden bodies just under the surface. The rain had stopped, and a thin sunshine, broken up by the yellow branches of weeping willows, dappled the pond.

"There's Davenport," Black said, and Sherrill looked back at the parking lot. Lucas was just getting out of his Porsche. The lot around him was sprinkled with 700-series BMWs and S-Class Mercedeses, a few Lexuses and Cadillacs, and the odd Jaguar, among the usual Chevys and Fords. Lucas circled a black Acura NSX that had been carefully parked away from other cars, stopped to look in the driver's side window.

"Speaking of rich," Sherrill said.

They waited and, after a second, Lucas broke away from the NSX and came up the walk, nodded at Black, grinned at Sherrill, and she felt a little *thump*. "If I was gonna steal cars, this would be the place," he said. "Gotta have money to get your head shrunk."

"Or get the county to pay for it," Black said.

"Did you ask her?" Sherrill asked.

"Not yet," Lucas said.

They checked the building directory, an arty rectangle decorated with a blue bird. Manette's office was at the back of the building, a multiroom suite with quiet, gray carpets and Scandinavian furnishings. A matronly Scandinavian receptionist sat behind a blonde oak desk, writing into a computer. She looked up when Lucas, Black, and Sherrill walked in, turned away from the computer. "Can I . . . ?"

"We're Minneapolis police officers. I'm Deputy Chief Lucas Davenport and we have a subpoena for Dr. Manette's records and a search warrant for her office," Lucas said. "Could you show us her office?"

"I'll get Mrs. Carney and Dr. Wolfe . . ."

"No. Show us the office, then get whomever you wish," Lucas said politely. "Who is Mrs. Carney?"

"The office manager," the woman said. "I'll get . . ."

"No. Show us Dr. Manette's office."

Manette's office was large, informal, with a comfortable

couch and a loveseat at right angles to each other, and a glass coffee table in the angle. Two Kirk Lyttle ceramic sculptures stood in the middle of the table; they looked like crippled birds, straining for the sky.

"Where are her files?"

"In, um, there." The receptionist was ready to panic, but she poked a finger at a line of wood folding doors. Sherrill crossed to the doors and pulled them back. A half-dozen four-drawer file cabinets were lined up in an alcove, along with a short table that held an automatic espresso maker and a small refrigerator.

"Thank you," Lucas said, nodding at the receptionist. The woman stepped backwards through the door, then turned and ran. "Gonna be some noise," he said.

"Tough shit," said Sherrill.

Lucas took off his coat, tossed it on a chair, went to the first of the file cabinets, and pulled open a drawer.

"Get out of there," Nancy Wolfe shouted at him. She steamed through the door, her hands out to grab him, push him, or hit him. Lucas set his feet, and when she grabbed him and pushed, he didn't move. Wolfe went backward with a little hop.

"If you push me again, I'll arrest you and send you downtown in handcuffs," Lucas said quietly. "Assault on a police officer has a mandatory jail sentence."

Wolfe's black eyes were blazing with anger: "You're in my files, you've got no right . . ."

"I've got a subpoena, a search warrant, and the written approval of Dr. Manette's next of kin," Lucas said. "We're gonna look at the files."

She stepped toward him again, her hands moving, and Lucas turned just a half an inch and tucked his chin even less, but he saw the flinch in her eyes. She believed he'd hit her back, and she stopped, stepped sideways, and crossed her arms. "You're referring to George Dunn?"

"Yes."

"George Dunn is hardly close to Andi, not any more," Wolfe said. Her face had been white with anger, but now it was reddening, with heat. She was an attractive woman, in a professorial way—slender, salt-and-pepper hair, just a boarding-school touch of makeup. But her red face clashed with her cool, mint-green suit and the Hermès scarf at her neck. "I don't believe . . ."

"Mr. Dunn is her husband," Sherrill said. "Andi Manette and her children have been kidnapped, and even though nobody has said it, they may already be dead somewhere."

"If they're not, they may be, soon," Lucas added. "If you try to fuck us around on the records, you'll lose. But the delay could kill your partner and her daughters."

Lucas said *fuck* deliberately, to harden the statement, to shock, to keep her on the defensive. Wolfe talked right through it: "I want to call my attorney."

"Call him," Lucas said.

Wolfe looked at him, then spun on a heel and stormed out.

When Wolfe was gone, Black asked, "How solid are we?"

"Solid, but they might find a friendly judge and slow us down," Lucas said. Sherrill nodded and pulled open another file cabinet. "Skim everything, get all the names and addresses—read them into your tape recorders, transcribe later. We need speed. If there's a problem, we'll have that much, anyway. And if there is a problem, refer it to Tyler down at the County Attorney's office and just keep working. When you get all the names on the recorder, go back through the records and look for anything likely. References to violence, to threats. Sexual deviation. Males only, to start."

"Where're you going?" Sherrill asked.

"To see some guys about some games," Lucas said.

Nancy Wolfe met him in the hallway as he was going out. "My attorney is on the way. He said for you to leave the files alone until he gets here."

"Yeah, well, as soon as your attorney is elevated to the district court, I'll follow his instructions," Lucas said. Then he let some air into his voice: "Look, we're not gonna persecute your patients—we won't even look at most of them. But we've got to move fast. We've got to."

"You'll set us back years with some of these people.

You'll destroy the trust they've built up with us—the only people they can trust, for most of them. And the people who need treatment for sexual deviation, or other possibly criminal behavior, they won't be back at all. Not after they hear what you've done."

"Why do they have to hear?" Lucas asked. "If you don't make a big deal out of it, nobody'll know except the few people we actually talk to. And with them, we can make it seem like we got the information from someplace else—not deal with the records."

She was shaking her head. "If you go through those records, I'll feel it incumbent upon me to inform the patients."

Lucas tightened up and his voice dropped, got a little gravel. "You don't tell them before we look at them. If you do, by God, and one of them turns out to be the kidnapper, I'll charge you as an accomplice to the kidnapping."

Wolfe's hand went to the Hermès scarf at her throat: "That's ludicrous."

"Is it true that you'll get a half-million dollars if Andi Manette is dead?"

Wolfe's mouth tightened in a line that might have indicated disgust. "Get away from me," she said. She brushed at him with one hand and started down the hall toward Manette's office. "Just get away."

But as he was going out the door, she shouted down the hall, "Who told you that? George? Did George tell you that?"

Lucas hit a game store in Dinkytown, near the campus of the University of Minnesota, another on Snelling Avenue in St. Paul, then dropped down to South Minneapolis.

Erewhon was run by Marcus Paloma, a refugee from the days of LSD and peyote tea. The shop was just off Chicago, a few blocks below Lake, surrounded by small stucco houses painted in postwar pastels, all crumbling into their crab-grass lawns.

Lucas parked and ambled toward the shop. The cool,

rain-washed air felt alive around him, the streets clear of their usual dust, the leaves of the trees burning like neon.

The shop was exactly the opposite: dim, musty, a little dusty. Bins of comics in plastic sleeves pressed against boxes of used role-playing and war games. Lucite racks of metallic miniatures—trolls, wizards, thieves, fighters, clerics, and goblins—guarded the cash register counter.

Marcus Paloma was gaunt, with a goatee and heavy glasses. His thinning gray hair was worn bouffant; he was dressed in a gray sweatsuit with Nike cross-training shoes. He'd once finished eighth in the St. Paul Marathon. "I got a concept," he shouted down the store, past the bins of comics, when he saw Lucas. "I'm gonna make a million bucks."

John Mail was sitting in a folding chair, looking through a cardboard box of used D&D modules. He glanced down the store at Lucas, and then looked back into the box. Two other gamers, one of each sex, looked up when Paloma shouted at Lucas.

"A feminist role-playing game, modelled on Dungeons and Dragons," Paloma said, gradually moderating his voice as he walked toward Lucas. "Set in prehistoric times, but dealing with problems like heterosexual mating and child birth in an essentially lesbian-oriented setting. I'm calling it The Nest."

Lucas laughed. "Marcus, everything you know about feminism, you could write on the back of a fuckin' postage stamp with a laundry pen," he said.

The female gamer said, "Profanity is a sign of ignorance," and faced him, waiting to be challenged.

Marcus, coming up the store, said, "That was an obscenity, sweetheart, not a profanity. Get your shit straight. That's a vulgarity, by the way—shit is." To Lucas, he said, "How you been? Shoot anybody lately?"

"Not for several days," Lucas said. They shook, and Lucas added, "You're looking good."

"Thanks." Marcus's face was its usual dusty gray. "I'm watching my diet. I've eliminated all fats except a tablespoon of extra virgin olive oil, on salad, at noon."

"Yeah?"

"Yeah. Could you sign some stock since you're here?"

"Sure."

"Hey, are you Davenport?" the female gamer asked. She was a dark-haired high school senior, quivering with caffeine.

"Yes."

"I've got *Blades* at home, I'd love you to sign it."

"You still got the book on that?" Marcus asked the girl.

"Sure," the girl said.

"I'll get him to sign a book on a used one, and you bring yours in, and we'll trade," Marcus said.

"Dude," said the girl.

"Marcus, we gotta go in the back," Lucas said. "I need to talk for a minute."

"All right, let me get those games." He stepped over to the cash register stand, took a half-dozen boxes off a rack, walked to the used bin and picked up two more, and led Lucas down the length of the store into the back. Just before ducking through a gray curtain into his office, he called back to the girl, "Keep an eye on the desk, will you, Carol?"

The office was filled with cardboard shipping boxes. A roll-top desk was shoved into a corner, buried under ten pounds of unopened junk mail. There were three chairs, one overstuffed and comfortable, two folding, covered with green vinyl. The room smelled of old newsprint and slightly stale cat food. A fat red tabby was lying on the back ledge of the rolltop. The cat looked at Lucas, and Lucas's gray silk suit, and seemed to think about it.

"Sit down," Paloma said, waving one hand expansively. "Damn cat is sitting on my orders. Get off of there, Bennie."

They talked the games business for a minute or two—who was winning, who was losing, the sales wars. "Listen, Marcus, something's up," Lucas said. He leaned forward and tapped Paloma on the knee.

"Sure. Cop business?" Paloma had done a little snitching for Lucas.

"Yeah. You heard about that shrink getting snatched? And her kids? Big news in the *Strib* this morning?"

"Yeah, I saw that," Paloma said, amazed. "Took her right out of the parking lot."

"The guy who did it might be a gamer," Lucas said.

"A gamer?" Paloma asked doubtfully. Another cat came out of the back, a gray one, a solemn female. Marcus picked her up and scratched her ears, and she stared at Lucas with her yellow eyes.

"Yeah. Big guy, wearing a GenCon t-shirt, middle twenties. Probably strong, like a body builder. Has a violent streak. Blond, shoulder-length hair."

"Nice Dexie," Paloma said to the cat. Then he shook his head, slowly, thinking. "Not really. Big and tough, huh? That doesn't sound like too many gamers." He scratched his nose, thinking. "Except . . ."

"Who?"

"The guy out there now—he's a big guy." Paloma nodded toward the door to the front. "Pretty tough-looking. And I think I've seen him in a GenCon shirt."

"Where? Sitting down? He was kinda short." Lucas looked toward the curtain that separated the office from the sales floor.

"He was sitting in an old folding chair. He's probably six-four, maybe two-twenty. Strong as a bull," Paloma said.

Lucas stepped toward the door. "What's his name?"

"I don't know. I've seen him two or three times before. Never said much to me."

"Have you ever seen his car?"

"No. Not that I know of," Paloma said.

"Huh," Lucas said. He went back through the door in a hurry, but the dark-haired man was no longer sitting in the chair. To the girl he said, "Where did that guy go? The guy who was sitting over there . . ."

She shook her head. "He left. You gonna sign a book for me?"

"Who is he? You know him?" Lucas hurried toward the street door.

"Nope. Never saw him before," she said. "Why?"

"How about you?" he called back to the male gamer. "You know him?"

"Nope. I'm with her."

Out on the sidewalk, Lucas went to the corner and looked all four ways down the intersecting streets. No van in sight. Nothing but a green Mazda, driven by a redheaded woman in a green dress, who seemed to be lost.

How long had they been talking in the back? Four or five minutes, no more.

And the guy had gone, disappeared, in that time.

Lucas stood on the street corner, wondering.

The parking garage that had once faced the back entrance to City Hall had been razed, and Lucas left the Porsche on the street. Paloma, who'd been following in a Studebaker Golden Hawk, found another space a half-block further on. As they walked back toward City Hall, they could hear the City Hall bell ringer playing "You Are My Sunshine," the tune clanging out above police headquarters.

A thin man fell in step with them. As Lucas turned to him, Sloan said, looking up at the bell tower, "Hope there are no fuckin' acid-heads around right now."

Lucas grinned: "That would be hard to explain to yourself—'You Are My Sunshine' banging around your brain."

"Makes me want to jump off the tower. And I'm not even high," Paloma said.

Sherrill caught them in the hallway outside Lucas's office. She was carrying a manila file: "We've got a problem." She glanced at Paloma, then turned back to Lucas. "We need to talk. Now."

"What? They got a court order?" Lucas asked.

"No. But you're not gonna like it."

Lucas turned to Sloan: "Marcus is here to look at the composite on the Manette kidnapper. He might want to add some stuff. Could you get him down there?"

"Sure," Sloan said. And to Marcus: "Let's go."

Lucas opened his office, nodded Sherrill into a chair, and hung his coat and jacket on an old-fashioned oak coat rack. "Tell me," he said. And he decided that he liked the tomboy-with-great-breasts look. He'd never hit on Sherrill, and now couldn't think how he'd missed her.

"There's a guy named Darrell Aldhus, a senior vice president at Jodrell National," Sherrill said. "He's been diddling little boys in his Scout troop."

Lucas frowned. "Does this have anything . . ."

"No. Nothing to do with Andi Manette, except that she hasn't reported the guy. And that's a felony. What's happening is, is what everybody was afraid was gonna happen. Aldhus admits in here—" Sherrill slapped the file—"that he's had several sexual contacts with boys, and he's trying to get himself cured. If we go after him, a defense attorney is gonna tell him to get the hell out of therapy and don't say shit to anybody. Since all we've got is her notes, nothing on tape, we really don't have that strong a case—not without her to back them up. We could put the Sex guys on it, have them start talking to kids . . ."

"Do we have any of the kids' names?" Lucas asked.

"No, but if we went in hard, I'm sure we could find some," she said.

"Goddamnit." Lucas opened a desk drawer and put his feet on it. "I didn't want this."

"The press is gonna be on us like a hot sweat," Sherrill said. "This guy is big enough that if we bust him, it'll be front-page stuff."

"In that case, we oughta do the right thing."

"Yeah? And what's that?" Sherrill asked.

"Beats the shit out of me," Lucas said.

"You figure it out," she said. She handed him the file. "I'm gonna go back and look at the rest of it. I wouldn't be surprised if Black hasn't already found more of these things . . . this was like the fourth file I looked at."

"But nothing on Manette?"

"So far, no—but Nancy Wolfe . . ."

"Yeah?"

"She says you're a bully," Sherrill said.

Lucas unloaded the Aldhus file on the chief, who treated it like a live rattlesnake.

"Give me a couple of suggestions," Roux said.

"Sit on it."

"While this guy is diddling little boys?"

"He hasn't done any diddling lately. And I don't want to start a fuckin' pie fight right in the middle of the Manette thing."

"All right." She looked at the file, half-closed her eyes. "I'll confer with Frank Lester and he can assign it to an appropriate officer for preliminary assessments of the veracity of the material."

"Exactly," Lucas said. "Under the rug, at least for now. How are the politics shaking out?"

"I briefed the family again, me and Lester, on the overnights. Manette looked like death had kissed him on the lips."

Sloan caught Lucas in the corridor.

"Your friend the doper looked at the composite: he says it could be our guy."

"Sonofabitch," Lucas said. He put his hands over his eyes, as if shielding them from a bright light. "He was right there. I didn't even see his face."

Greave had on a fresh, bluish suit; Lester's eyes were red-rimmed from lack of sleep.

"They giving you shit?" Lucas asked, stepping into Homicide.

"Yeah," Lester said, straightening up. "Whataya got?"

Lucas gave him a one-minute run-down: "It coulda been him."

"And it coulda been Lawrence of Iowa," Greave said.

Lester handed over the composite sketch based on information from Girdler and the girl. "Had a hell of a time getting them to agree on anything," Lester said. "I have a feeling that our eyewitnesses . . . Mmmm, what's the word I'm looking for?"

"*Suck*," said Greave.

"That's it," Lester said. "Our eyewitnesses suck."

"Maybe my guy can add something," Lucas said. The

face in the composite was tough, and carried a blankness that might have reflected a lack of information, or a stone-craziness. "Did Anderson tell you about the GenCon shirt?"

"Yeah," Lester nodded. He stretched, yawned, and said, "We're trying to get a list of people who registered for the convention the past couple of years, hotel registrations . . . did you see the *Star-Tribune* this morning?"

"Yeah, but I missed the television last night," Lucas said. "I understand they got a little exercised."

Lester snorted. "They were hysterical."

Lucas shrugged. "She's a white, professional, upper-middle-class woman from a moneyed family. That's the hysteria button. If it was a black woman, there'd be one scratch-ass guy with a pencil."

A phone rang in the empty lieutenant's office, and Greave got up and wandered over, picked it up on the fourth ring, looked back toward Lucas.

"Hey, Lucas—you've got a call. The guy says it's an emergency. A Doctor Morton."

Lucas, puzzled, shook his head and said, "Never heard of him."

Greave shrugged, waved the phone. "Well?"

Lucas said, "Jesus, Weather?" He took the phone from Greave. "Davenport."

"Lucas Davenport?" A man's voice, young, but with back gravel in it, like a pot smoker's rasp.

"Yes?" There was silence, and Lucas said, "Dr. Morton?"

"No, not really. I just told them that so you'd answer the phone." The man stopped talking, waiting for a question.

Lucas felt a small tingle at the back of his throat. "Well?"

"Well, I got those people, Andi Manette and her kids, and I saw in the paper that you're investigating, and I thought I ought to call you 'cause I'm one of your fans. Like, I play your games."

"You took them? Mrs. Manette and her daughters? Who the hell is this?" Lucas dosed his voice with impatience, while frantically waving at the other two. Lester grabbed a phone; Greave looked this way and that, not sure of what to do, then hurried to his cubicle and a second later came back with a tape recorder with a suction-cup pickup. Lucas nodded, and while Mail talked, Greave licked the suction cup, stuck it on the earpiece of the phone, and started the recorder.

"I'm sorta the Dungeon Master in this little game," John Mail was saying. "I thought maybe you'd like to roll the dice and get started."

"This is bullshit," Lucas said, stretching for time. Lester was talking urgently into his telephone. "We run into you assholes every time something like this gets in the paper. So listen to this, pal: you want to get your face on TV, you're gonna have to do it on your own. I'm not gonna help."

"You don't believe me?" Mail was perplexed.

Lucas said, "I'll believe you if you can tell me one thing about the Manettes that's not in the newspaper or on television."

"Andi's got a scar like a rocket ship," Mail said.

"A rocket ship?"

"That's what I said. An old German V-2 with a flame coming out of the ass-end. You can ask her old man where it is."

Lucas closed his eyes. "Are they all right?"

"We've had a casualty," John Mail said, offhandedly. "Anyway, I gotta go before you trace this and send a cop car. But I'll call back, to see how you're doing. Do you have a cellular phone?"

"Yes."

"Give me the number."

Lucas recited the number, and Mail repeated it. "You better carry it with you," he said. Then, "This really turns my crank, Davenport. OK, so roll a D20."

"What?"

"On your Zen dice."

"Uh, okay . . . just a minute." In the office, Lester was bent over the desk, talking urgently into the phone. Lucas said, "I'm rolling . . . I get a four."

"Ah, that's a good roll: Here's the clue: Go ye to the Nethinims and check 'em out. Got that?"

"No."

"Well, then, tough shit," Mail said. "Doesn't look like you're gonna do too well."

"We're already doing well. We knew you were a gamer," Lucas said. "We've been on your ass since last night."

Mail exhaled impatiently, then said, "You got lucky, that's all . . ."

"Not luck: you're fuckin' up on the details, pal. You'd be a hell of a lot better off . . ."

"Don't tell me how I'd be better off. Not one fuckin' guy in a million would've recognized that shirt. Blind fuckin' luck."

And he was gone. Lucas turned to Lester, who was working two phones at once. After a moment, he put one down, then the other, looked up at Lucas, shook his head. "Not enough time."

"Jesus, half the people in town have Caller ID. And we're still calling up the company for traces?" Lucas said. "Why don't we get a goddamn Caller ID like half the civilians in the state?"

"Well," Lester said. He shrugged: he didn't know why. "Was it him?"

"I'd bet on it," Lucas said. He told Lester about the scar like a rocket ship.

"What—you think it's on her ass or something?"

"That's what I think," Lucas said. "We better check with Dunn. But the way he said it, that's what I think . . . And he said they'd had a casualty. I think somebody's dead."

"Aw, shit," Lester said.

They went over Greave's tape together, three or four other cops gathering around to listen. They played it through once without interruption, then went back and listened to pieces. They could hear cars in the background. "Pay phone at a busy intersection. Big fuckin' help," Lester said. "And what's a D20? And who are the Nethinims?"

"D20s are twenty-sided dice. Gamers use them," Lucas said. "I don't know about the Netha-whachamacallits."

"Sounds like some kind of street gang, but I never heard of them," Greave said. "Play it again."

As they rewound the tape, Lucas said, "He knew about the shirt. Who'd we tell?"

"Nobody. I mean, the family, maybe. And the kid knows . . ."

"And probably that fuckin' Girdler. We better see if we can get a tape of that radio show, see if what all he talked about . . ."

"And maybe that goddamn kid is talking to the press— everybody else is blabbing."

Greave punched the tape, and they listened to it again and Greave said, "Yeah, he said Nethinims. N-E-T-H-I-N-I-M-S or N-E-T-H-A-N-I-M-S."

Lucas looked in the phone book, Lester tried directory assistance. "Nothing."

Lucas, walking around, staring at the ceiling, came back to Lester. "Was I on the news? In the paper, about being on the case?"

Lester showed a thin grin: Lucas attracted a lot of publicity over the years. Sometimes it chafed. "No."

"This guy said he knew I was investigating, because he'd seen it in the paper . . ."

"Well, we got the *Pioneer Press* around here somewhere, and all kinds of *Star-Tribunes*, you could look—but I don't think so. I read the stories."

"TV or radio?"

He shrugged. "I don't know. Maybe. They know you by sight—they know your car. There were all kinds of reporters around that school. Or maybe somebody interviewed Manette or Dunn and they mentioned something. Or that guy on the radio last night . . ."

"Huh." And he thought about the kid he'd seen in the game store that morning, sitting down. The kid who'd left so quickly, who looked like the right guy.

"You want me to check out these Nethinims dudes?" Greave asked.

Lucas turned to him, nodded. Greave was okay with books. "Yeah. If you ask around, and nobody knows, check a couple of game stores and see if it's a new game character or set. Then check like, uh, Tolkien's Ring cycle—*Lord of the Rings*, all that. There're a couple of science fiction stores in town—call and talk to a clerk, see if anybody recognizes the name from a book series . . . a fantasy series probably."

"The guy sounds like a smart little wiseass," Lester said.

"Yeah." Lucas nodded. "And he can't help proving it. He'll last five days or a week—I just hope somebody's left alive when we get him."

7

The rape had done something to her, beyond the obvious. Had damaged her.

When Mail had finished with her, she was panicked, injured, in pain—but generally coherent. When Mail had taken Genevieve, she'd argued with him, pleaded.

An hour after that, she began to drift.

She curled on the mattress, stopped talking to Grace, closed her eyes, trembled, shuddered, tightened into a ball. She lost the most elemental sense of what was going on—how much time was passing, where sounds came from, who was in the cell with her.

Grace came to her several times, gave her strawberry soda, tried to get her to eat, took off her own coat and gave it to her mother. This last, the coat, Andi found useful: she huddled under it, away from the naked lightbulb, the Porta-Potti, the stark gray walls. With the coat over her head, she could almost believe she was at home, dreaming . . .

She seemed to wake a few times and she spoke with both Grace and Genevieve, and once with George. Sometimes she felt her mind drifting above herself, like a cloud: she watched her body huddled on the mattress, and wondered, *why*?

But sometimes she felt needle-sharp: she opened her eyes

and looked at her knees, pulled up tight to her chin, and felt herself clever not to come out from under the coat.

Beneath it all, she knew her mind simply wasn't functioning correctly. This, she thought during a passing moment of rationality, was insanity. She'd been outside of it for years: this was the first time she'd been inside.

Once she had a dream, or a vision: several men, friendly but hurried, wearing technicians' or scientists' coats, lowered her into a steel cylinder with an interior the size of a phone booth. When she was inside, a steel cap with interlocking flanges was lowered on top of the cylinder, to seal it off. One of the technicians, an intelligent, soft-spoken man with blond hair, glasses, and an easy German accent, said, "You'll only have to last through the heat. If you make it through the heat, you'll be all right . . ."

Some kind of protection dream, she thought, during one of the lucid moments. The blond man, she thought, she'd seen in a Mercedes-Benz commercial, or a BMW ad. But the man wasn't the thing. The cylinder was: nobody, nothing could get at her in the cylinder.

After a very long time of wandering in and out of consciousness, she closed in on herself. Found a ray of rationality, followed it to a kind of spark, and sat up. Grace was sitting on the concrete floor, facing the computer monitor. The screen was blank.

"Grace, are you all right?"

Andi was whispering. Grace reflexively looked up at the ceiling, as though the whisper might have come from the outside, from God. Then she looked over her shoulder at Andi: "Mom?"

"Yes." Andi rolled up to a sitting position.

"Mom, are you . . ."

"I'm getting better," Andi said, shaking.

Grace crawled toward her. Her slender daughter looked even thinner, like a winter-hungry fox: "Jeez, Mom, you were arguing with Daddy for a while . . ."

"John Mail beat me up; he raped me," Andi said. She

simply let the word out. Grace had to know what was happening, had to help.

"I know." Grace looked away, tears trickling down her cheek. "But you're better?"

"I think so." Andi pushed herself up to her knees, then stepped off the mattress, shakily, one hand on the wall. Her legs felt like cheese, thick, soft, unreliable, until the blood began to flow again. She pulled her skirt up, pulled her blouse together. He'd taken her bra: she remembered that. The assault was coming back.

She turned her back to her daughter, pulled up her skirt, pulled down her underpants, looked inside: just a spot of blood. She wasn't badly torn.

"Are you okay?" Grace whispered.

"I think so."

"What are we going to do?" Grace asked. "What about Genevieve?"

"Genevieve?" *My God. Genevieve.* "We've got to think," Andi said, turning around to look at her daughter again. She knelt on the mattress, pulled Grace's head close to her lips and whispered, "The first thing we've got to do is find out if he's listening to us, or if we can talk. We have to keep talking, but I want you to get on my shoulders, and I'm going to try to stand up. Then I want you to look at the ceiling, see if there is anything that might be, you know, a microphone. It probably won't be very sophisticated—he'd just stick a tape recorder microphone in one of the airholes, or something."

Grace nodded, and Andi said, out loud, "I don't think I'm too hurt, but I need some sleep."

"So just lie down for a while," Grace said. Andi squatted, and Grace stepped over her shoulders. She probably weighed eighty pounds, Andi thought. She had to push herself up with help from the wall, but she got straight, and they walked back and forth through the room, Grace's head almost at the ceiling, the girl dragging her fingers across the dark wooden boards, probing into corners, poking her fingers into the airholes in the concrete walls. Finally she whispered, "Okay," and Andi squatted again and Grace got off, shook her head. She'd found nothing.

Andi put her lips close to Grace's ear again. "I'm going to say some things about John Mail. We want to see if he refers to what I say, when he comes down next time. Ask me a question about him. Ask me why he's doing this."

Grace nodded. "Mom, why is Mr. Mail doing this? Why is he hurting you?" The question sounded phony, artificial, but maybe on a crude tape it'd be okay.

Andi counted out a long, thoughtful pause. "I believe he's compensating for sexual problems he had when he was a child. His parents made it worse—he had a stepfather who'd beat him with a club . . ."

"You mean, he's a sex pervert."

Andi shook her in a warning: *don't push it too far* . . .

"There's always the possibility that he has a straight-forward medical problem, a hormone imbalance that we simply don't understand. We did tests, and he seemed normal enough, but we didn't have the tools back then that we do now."

Grace nodded and said, "I hope he doesn't hurt us any more."

Andi said, "So do I. Now try to sleep."

They felt him coming, a sense of impact, a heavy body moving around. Then they heard him on the cellar steps, the footfalls muffled and far away. Grace huddled into her, and Andi felt her mind beginning to slip. No. She had to hold on.

Then the door opened: the scraping of the slide lock, the screak of the hinge. Grace said, "Don't let him take me alone, like Genevieve."

Mail's eye appeared at the crack of the door, took them in. Then he closed the door again, and she heard another rattle. A chain. She hadn't heard that before, hadn't seen that when she was outside: he had two locks, so they couldn't rush the door.

"Don't move," he said. He was wearing jeans and an olive-colored shirt with a collar, the first time they'd seen him in anything but a t-shirt. He had two microwave meals on plastic plates, with plastic spoons. He left them on the floor and backed away.

"Where's Genevieve?" Andi asked, pushing herself up. She gripped her blouse button-line with her left hand. She did it unthinkingly and only noticed when she saw Mail pick it up.

"Dropped her at the Hudson Mall," Mail said. "Told her to find a cop."

"I don't believe you," Andi said.

"Well, I did," Mail said, but his eyes shifted and a black dread grew in Andi's heart. Then: "They've got Davenport looking for us."

"Davenport?"

"He's a big cop in Minneapolis," Mail said. He seemed impressed. "He writes games."

"Games?" She was confused.

"Yeah, you know. War games and role-playing games, and some computer games. He's like this rich dude now. And he's a cop."

"Oh." She put her fingertips to her lips. "I *have* heard of him . . . Do you know him?"

"I called him," Mail said. "I talked to him."

"You mean . . . today?"

"About two hours ago." He was proud of himself.

"Did you tell him about Genevieve?"

Again he looked away: "Nah. I called him from this Wal-Mart right after I dropped her off. He probably didn't know about her yet."

Andi hadn't fully recovered from the attack and felt less than completely sharp, but she pushed herself to understand the man, what he was saying. And she thought she saw fear or, possibly, uncertainty.

"This Davenport . . . are you afraid of him?"

"Fuck no. I'll kick his ass," Mail said. "He's not gonna find us."

"Isn't he supposed to be mean? Wasn't he fired for brutality or something? Beating up a suspect?"

"Pimp," Mail said. "He beat up a pimp because the guy cut one of his stoolies."

"Doesn't sound like somebody you'd want to challenge," Andi suggested. "I wouldn't think you'd want to play with him—if that's what you're doing."

"That's sorta what I'm doing," Mail said. He laughed, seemed lifted by the thought. Then, "I'll see you later. Eat the food, it's good."

And he was gone.

After a moment, Grace crawled over to one of the plates, poked the food, tasted it. "It's not very warm."

Andi said, "But we need it. We'll eat it all."

"What if he poisoned it?"

"He doesn't have to poison it," Andi said, coolly.

Grace looked at her, then nodded. They carried the plates back to the mattress, and in a second, they were gobbling it down. Grace stopped long enough to get two cans of strawberry soda, passed one to her mother, glanced at the Porta-Potti. "God, I'm gonna hate . . . going."

Andi stopped eating, looked at the pot, then at her daughter. A daughter of privilege: she'd had a private bathroom since she was old enough to sleep in her own room. "Grace," she said, "we are in a desperately bad situation. We're trying to stay alive until the police find us. So we eat his food and we aren't embarrassed by each other. We just try to hang on the best we can."

"Right," Grace said. "But I wish Genevieve was here . . ."

Andi choked, forced herself to hold it down. Genevieve, she thought, might be dead. But Grace couldn't be told that. She had to protect Grace: "Listen, honey . . ."

"She could be dead," Grace said, her eyes wide, like an owl's. "God, I hope she's not . . ." She put down her spoon and began to cry and Andi started to comfort her, but then dropped her plate and she began to cry as well. A few seconds later, Grace crawled next to her and they huddled together, weeping; and Andi's mind flashed back to the night when they'd all sprawled on the upstairs rug, laughing, after Genevieve's "*God, that guy was really hung . . .*"

Much later, Grace said, "He didn't say anything about being a sex pervert . . ."

"He's not listening," Andi said. "He hadn't heard it."

"So what are we going to do?"

"We have to judge him," Andi said. "If we think he's going to kill us, we have to attack him. We have to think about the best ways to do that."

"He's too strong."

"But we have to try . . . and maybe . . . I don't know. Listen: John Mail is a very smart boy. But maybe we can manipulate him."

"How?"

"I've been thinking about that. If he's talking to this Davenport person, maybe we can send a message."

"How?"

Andi sighed. "I don't know. Not yet."

John Mail came back an hour later. Again they felt him coming before they heard him, the vibration of a body on the stairs. He opened the door as he had before, carefully. Andi and Grace were on the mattress. He looked at them both, his gaze lingering on Grace until she looked away, and then he said to Andi, "Come out."

8

Lucas spent the early afternoon reading the papers, then tripping around to the television stations. After his last stop, he called in to Homicide and asked that Sloan be sent to meet him at Nancy Wolfe's office.

When Lucas arrived at Wolfe's, Sloan was examining the same NSX that Lucas had cruised in the morning.

"Heavy metal," he said, as he slouched over to Lucas. "Makes the Porsche look like a fuckin' Packard."

Sloan was a thin man, a man who looked at the world sideways, with a skeptical grin. He liked brown suits and had several of varied intensity: in the summer he leaned toward off-tans and not-quite-beiges, and striped neckties, and straw hats; in the winter, he went for darker tones and felt hats. He'd just shifted to winter wear, and was a dark spot in the parking lot.

"The NSX could bite you on the ass," Lucas said, looking at the car. He flipped the engagement ring in the air, caught it, and slipped it over the end of his thumb. The stone sparkled like high-rent fire.

"What're we doing?" Sloan asked.

"Good guy–bad guy with Nancy Wolfe, Manette's partner. You're the good guy."

"What has she got to do with it?"

"You know about the call from the asshole?" Lucas asked.

"Yeah, Lester played the tape for me."

"I've been running around asking questions," Lucas said. "Nobody—none of the papers, none of the stations—carried anything about the shirt. Nobody had anything about me working the case. The only people who knew, outside the department, were the family and a few people close to the family. Wolfe. A lawyer."

"Christ." Sloan scratched his head. "You think somebody's talking to him? The asshole?"

"Maybe. I can explain him knowing about me," Lucas said. "I can't explain the shirt, unless he made a pretty big intuitive leap."

"Huh." They passed the chewing-gum sculpture. Sloan looked up at it and asked, "How about Miranda?"

"Yep. We do the whole thing . . . And she asks for an attorney, we say *fine*. I'm going after her pretty hard. We want to shake her up. Same thing for the rest of the family, when we get to them."

"Lucas. Hey, Lucas." They'd started across the bridge, stopped for just a second to look at the koi, heard the woman's voice, turned and saw Jan Reed hurrying across the street. A TV van was making an illegal U-turn that would take it into the parking lot.

"*This* one makes my dick hard," Sloan muttered.

Reed had large dark eyes, auburn hair that fell to her shoulders, and long, tanned legs. She wore a plum suit and matching shoes, and carried a Gucci shoulder bag. She had a slight overbite; a tiny lisp added to her charm.

"Are you working this?" Lucas asked as Reed came up. "This is . . ."

"Detective Sloan, of course," Reed said. She took Sloan's hand, gave him a two-hundred-watt smile. Then to Lucas: "I'm trying for an interview with Nancy Wolfe. I understand her records were subpoenaed this morning by the local Nazis."

"That was me," Lucas said.

Reed's smile widened slightly: she'd known. "Really? Well, why'd you do that?"

Lucas glanced toward the truck and then said to Reed, "Jan, Jan, Jan. You've got a sleazy unethical microphone in the truck, don't you? I mean, my golly, that's very slimy, a really tacky, disgusting, snakelike invasion of my privacy. In fact, it's very close to criminal. It may even be criminal."

Reed sighed. "Lucas . . ."

Lucas leaned close to her ear and whispered, "Go fuck yourself."

She leaned close to his ear and said, "I like the basic concept, but I hate flying solo."

Lucas, backing away, felt the ring in his pocket and said, "C'mon, Sloan, let's see if we can get to Mrs. Wolfe before the media does . . ."

"Goddamnit, Lucas," Reed said, and she stamped her foot.

Inside, Sloan asked, "Do you really think they had a mike?"

"I'm sure they did," Lucas said.

"Do you think they heard what I said? About Reed making my dick hard?"

"No question about it," Lucas said, biting back a grin. "And they'll use it, too, the treacherous assholes."

"You're giving me shit, man. Don't give me shit, I need to know."

The receptionist looked like she wanted to hide when she saw Lucas and Sloan coming down the hall. Lucas asked to see Wolfe, and she said, "Dr. Wolfe is with a patient. She should be finished"—she looked at a desk clock—"in five minutes or so. I hate to interrupt . . ."

"When she's done," Lucas said. "We'll be in Dr. Manette's office."

Sherrill and Black were sitting on the floor, working through a pile of manila folders.

"Anything new?" Lucas asked.

"Hey, Sloan," said Sherrill.

"These people are nuts," Black said, patting a small stack of folders. "These are neurotic"—he pointed toward an-

other, larger stack—"and the big stack are just fucked up,"
he said, pointing at a third pile. "Some of the nuts are in jail
or in hospitals; some of them we don't know about. When
we get one, we call it downtown."

"What are we doing about the bank guy?" Sherrill asked.

"I unloaded it on the chief," Lucas said. "Did you find
any more of those?"

"Maybe. There are a couple where it seems like she's
getting cute . . . cryptic notes. References to other files,
which we haven't found. There are computer files somewhere, but we haven't found the disks. Anderson's gonna
come down and take a crack at her system." She nodded at
an IBM computer on a credenza behind Manette's desk.

Wolfe walked in then, her face grim, her anger barely
suppressed, and faced Lucas. Her arms were straight to her
sides, her fists clenched. "What do you want?"

"We need to ask you some questions," Lucas said.

"Should I get my attorney?"

Lucas shrugged. "It's up to you. I do have to warn you:
you have a right to an attorney."

Wolfe went pale as Lucas recited the Miranda warning.
"You're serious."

Lucas nodded. "Yes. We're very serious, Dr. Wolfe."

Sloan broke in, his voice cheerful, placating. "We really are
just asking basic stuff. I mean, you have to make the decision,
but we're not gonna sweat you, Miz Wolfe, I mean, we're not
gonna pull a light down over your head. We're just trying to
figure out a few angles. If this wasn't done by one of her
patients, why was it done? It was obviously planned, so it
wasn't just some maniac picking people at random. We need to
know who would benefit . . ."

"This man"—Wolfe, talking to Sloan, jabbed a finger at
Lucas—"suggested this morning that I would benefit from
Andi's death. I resent that. Andi's my dearest friend, a
life-long friend. She's been my best friend since college,
and if something should happen to her, it would be a
personal disaster, not a benefit. And I bitterly . . ."

Sloan glanced at Lucas, shook his head, looked back at

Wolfe and said, "Sometimes Lucas and I don't see eye-to-eye on these things . . ."

"Sloan," Lucas said, in a warning tone. But Sloan held up a hand.

"He's not a bad guy," Sloan said to Wolfe. "But he's a street guy. I'm sure he didn't mean to offend you, but sometimes he sort of . . . overstates things."

Lucas let the irritation show. "Hey, Sloan . . ."

But Sloan put up a warning hand. "We're really just looking for facts. Not trying to put pressure on you. We're trying to find out if anyone would benefit from Andi Manette's death or disappearance, and we don't mean you. At least, I don't."

Wolfe was shaking her head. "I don't see how anybody would benefit. I would get some key-person insurance if Andi died, but that wouldn't make up for the loss, financially or emotionally. I would imagine that George Dunn would get quite a bit—you know, she started out with all the money in her family. George would be a carpenter someplace if he hadn't married Andi."

"Can we do this down in your office? We should be someplace a little more private, huh?" Sloan asked winningly.

On the way to Wolfe's office, with Wolfe several steps ahead, Sloan leaned to Lucas and muttered: "You know that Sherrill? She makes my dick hard, too. I think something's going on with my dick."

"That's not what you'd call a *big* change," Lucas said. He flipped the ring in the air and caught it. Sherrill. Sherrill was nice; so was Jan Reed, and he most certainly would have bundled Reed off to his cabin if it hadn't been for Weather. Lucas liked women, liked them a lot. Maybe too much. And that was another item on the long list of mental questions he had about marriage.

He was always shocked when a married friend went after another woman. That never seemed right. If you hadn't made the commitment, all right—do anything you wanted. But now, with the possibility of marriage looming . . . would he miss the hunt? Would he miss it enough to betray Weather? Would he even be considering this question if he should ask her to marry him? On the other hand, he really didn't want Reed. He didn't want Sherrill. He only wanted Weather.

"What's wrong?" Sloan asked quietly.

"Huh?" Lucas started.

"You looked like you'd had a stroke or something," Sloan said. They were just outside Wolfe's office, and Sloan was staring at him curiously.

"Ah, nothing. Lot of stuff going on," Lucas said.

Sloan grinned. "Yeah."

Wolfe's office was a mirror of Manette's, with furniture of the same style, and the same files-and-coffee niche in one wall. Sloan was charming and got Wolfe talking.

She did not like George Dunn. Dunn was facing imminent divorce, Wolfe said. If Andi died, not only would he inherit and collect any life insurance, he would also save half of his own fortune. "That's what she'd get—when they got married, he had the shirt on his back, and that was all. He made all of his money since they were married, and you know Minnesota divorce law."

Tower Manette wouldn't get anything from his daughter's death, Wolfe said, except at the end of a long string of unlikely circumstances. Andi and both the children would have to die, and George Dunn would have to be convicted of the crime.

"All you would get is the key-man insurance?" Lucas asked.

"That's right."

"Who'd take Dr. Manette's patients?"

Wolfe looked exasperated. "I would, Mr. Davenport. And I would make a little money on them. And as quickly as I could, I would bring somebody else in to handle them. I have a full slate right now. I simply couldn't handle her patient load, not by myself."

"So there's the insurance and the patients . . ."

"Goddamnit," Wolfe said. "I hate these insinuations."

"They're not insinuations. We're talking serious money and you're not being very forthcoming," Lucas rasped.

"All right, all right," said Sloan. "Take it easy, Lucas."

They talked for half an hour, but got very little more. As they were leaving, Wolfe said to Lucas, "I'm sure you've heard about the lawsuit."

"No."

"We've gone to court to repossess our records," she said.

Lucas shrugged: "That's not my problem. The lawyers can sort it out."

"What you're doing is shameful," she said.

"Tell that to Andi Manette and her kids—if we get them back."

"I'm sure Andi would agree with our position," Wolfe said. "*We'd* review the records and pass on anything that might be significant."

"You aren't cops," Lucas snapped. "What's significant to cops might not be significant to shrinks."

"You aren't doing much good," Wolfe snapped back. "As far as I know, you haven't detected a thing."

Lucas took the composite drawing from his pocket: the accumulated memories of two eyewitnesses and Marcus Paloma, the game store owner. "Do you know this man?"

Wolfe took the picture, frowned, shook her head. "No, I don't think so. But he does look sort of . . . generic. Who is he?"

"The kidnapper," Lucas said. "That's what we've detected so far."

"There's a woman who doesn't think the sun shines out of your ass," Sloan said as they walked down the hall.

"Yeah, that's what?" Lucas didn't mind being disliked, but sometimes the taste was sour. "Six thousand that we know of?"

"I think it's eight thousand," Sloan said.

"Does *she* make your dick hard?" Lucas asked.

"No-no," Sloan said. He pushed through the door outside. "She's the one with the hard-on, and it ain't for me." After a moment, Sloan said, "Where now? Manette's?"

"Yeah. Jesus, I can feel the time passing." Lucas stopped to look at the koi, hovering in the pond, their gill flaps slowly opening and closing. Mellow, the koi: and he felt like somebody had stacked another brick on his chest. "Manette and the kids . . . Jesus."

Tower Manette again said that Dunn would get everything unless he was convicted of a part in the crime.

"Do you think he could do it?" Sloan asked.

"I don't know about the kids," Tower said. He took a turn around the carpet, nibbling at a thumbnail. "He always acted like he loved the kids, but basically, George Dunn could do anything. Suppose he hired some cretin who was supposed to . . . take Andi. And instead, the guy takes all of them because they're witnesses in this screwed-up kidnapping. George would hardly be in a position to tell you about it."

"I don't think so," said Helen Manette. Her face was lined with worry, her eyes confused. "I always liked George. More than Tower did, anyway. I think if he was in on this, he'd make sure that the kids weren't hurt."

Manette stopped, turned on a heel, poked a finger at Lucas. "I really think you're barking up the wrong tree— you should be out looking for crazy people, not trying to figure out who'd benefit."

"We're working every angle we can find," Lucas said. "We're working everything."

"Are you getting anything? Anything at all?"

"Some things: we've got a picture of the kidnapper," Lucas said.

"What? Can I see it?"

Lucas took the picture out of his pocket. The Manettes looked at it, and both shook their heads at the same time. "Don't know him," Tower said.

"And nobody benefits from her death, except George Dunn . . ."

"Well," Helen Manette said hesitantly. "I hate to . . ."

"What?" Sloan asked. "We'll take anything."

"Well . . . Nancy Wolfe. The key-man insurance isn't the only thing she'd get. They have a partnership and six associates. If Andi disappeared, she'd get the business, along with the insurance money."

"That's ridiculous," Tower Manette said. "Nancy's an old friend of the family. She's Andi's oldest friend . . ."

"Who dated George Dunn before Andi took him away," Helen said. "And their business—they've done very well."

"But Dr. Wolfe says that if Andi was gone, she'd just have to hire another associate," Sloan said.

"Sure, she would," Helen said. "But instead of a partnership, she'd be a sole owner and she'd get a piece of everybody's action." The word *action* tripped easily from Helen Manette's mouth, out-of-place for a woman in this house; too close to the street. "Nancy Wolfe would . . . make out."

"Another happy couple," Sloan said on the way to the car. "Helen is a tarantula disguised as Betty Crocker. And Tower looked like somebody was pulling a trotline out of his ass."

"Yeah—but that partnership business. Wolfe didn't exactly tell us everything, did she?"

George Dunn had two offices.

One was furnished in contemporary cherry furniture, with leather chairs, a deep wine carpet, and original duck-stamp art on the walls. The desk was clear of everything but an appointment pad and a large dark wooden box for cigars.

The other office, in the back of the building, had a commercial carpet on the floor, fluorescent lighting, a dozen desks and drafting tables with computer terminals, and two women and two men working in shirtsleeves. Dunn sat at a U-shaped desk littered with paper, a telephone to his ear. When he saw Lucas and Sloan, he said a few last words into the phone and dropped it on the hook.

"Okay, everybody, everybody knows what to do? Tom will run things, Clarice will handle traffic; I'll be back as soon as we find Andi and the kids."

He took Lucas and Sloan down to the green-leather office, where they could talk. "I've turned everything over to the guys until this is done with," he said. "Have you heard anything at all?"

"We've had a couple of odd incidents. We think we have a picture of the kidnapper, but we don't know his name."

Lucas showed the picture to Dunn, who studied it, scratched his forehead. "There was a guy, a carpenter. Goddamn, he looks something like this. He's got those lips."

"What's his name? Any reason to think . . . ?"

"Dick, Dick, Dick . . ." Dunn scratched his forehead again. "Saddle? Seddle. Dick Seddle. He thought he ought to be a foreman, and when he didn't get a job that opened up, he got pissed and quit. He was mad—but that was last winter. He went around saying he was gonna clean my clock, but nothing ever came of it."

"You know where we could find him?"

"Payroll would have an address. He's married, he lives over in South St. Paul somewhere. But I don't know. He's an older guy than what you were talking about. He's maybe thirty-five, forty."

"Where's payroll?" Sloan asked.

"Down the hall on your left . . ."

"I'll get it," Sloan said to Lucas.

As Sloan left, Dunn picked up his phone, poked a button, and said, "A cop is on his way down. Give him whatever he needs on Dick Seddle. He's a carpenter, worked on the Woodbury project until last winter, January, I think. Yeah. Yeah."

When he hung up, Lucas said, "We're talking to everybody, all over again. We're asking who'd win if Andi Manette's dead. Your name keeps coming up."

"Fuck those people," Dunn snarled. He banged a large fist in the middle of the leather appointment pad. "Fuck 'em."

Lucas said, "They say that Andi was going after a divorce . . ."

"That's bullshit. We'd have worked it out."

". . . and if you were divorced, you'd lose at least half of everything. They say you started this company with some of her money, and having to pay out half could be pretty troublesome."

"Yeah, it would," Dunn said, nodding. "But there's not a dime of her money in this place. Not a goddamn dime. That was part of the deal when I married her: I wasn't gonna owe her. And it would take a fucking lunatic to suggest I'd do anything to Andi and the kids. A fuckin' lunatic."

"Then we got a bunch of fuckin' lunatics, 'cause everybody we talked to suggested it," Lucas said.

"Yeah, well . . ."

"I know, fuck 'em," Lucas said. "So: who else would benefit?"

"Nobody else," Dunn said.

"Helen Manette suggested that Nancy Wolfe would pick up a pretty thriving business."

Dunn thought for a moment, then said, "I suppose she would, but she's never been that interested in business . . . or money. Andi's always been the leader and the businesswoman. Nancy was the intellectual. She publishes papers and that. She's still connected to the university and she's a bigwig in the psychiatric society. That's why they're good partners—Andi takes care of business, Nancy builds their reputation in the field."

"You don't think Wolfe's a candidate?"

"No, I don't."

"I understand you dated her."

"Jesus, they really did dump it on you, didn't they," Dunn said, his voice softening. "I took Nancy out twice. Neither one of us was much interested in a third try. So when we were saying good-bye that second time, the last time, she said, 'You know, I've got somebody who'd be perfect for you.' And she was right. I called up Andi and we got married a year later."

Lucas hesitated, then said, "Does your wife have any distinguishing marks on her body? Scars?"

Dunn froze: "You've got a body somewhere?"

"No, no. But if we should contact the people who have her, if there's a question . . ."

Dunn wasn't buying it. "What's going on?"

"We got a call from a guy," Lucas said.

"He said she's got a scar?"

"Yeah."

"What kind of scar?"

Lucas said, "He said it looked like a rocketship . . ."

"Oh, no," Dunn groaned. "Oh no . . ." .

Sloan came in, looked at the two men facing each other. "What's going on?"

Lucas told Dunn, "We'll get back."

Dunn swung a large workman's hand across the cherry desk, and the cigar safe flew across the room, the fat Cuban cigars spraying out like so much shrapnel. "Well, fuckin' find something," Dunn shouted. "You're supposed to be the fuckin' Sherlock Holmes. Quit hanging around my ass and get out and do something."

Outside the office, Sloan said, "What was all that?"

"I asked him about the rocketship."

"Oh-oh."

"Whoever it is, he's raping her," Lucas said.

As they stood talking in the parking lot, Greave called from the Minneapolis Public Library. "It's the Bible," he said. "The Nethinims are mentioned a bunch of times, but they don't seem to amount to much."

"Xerox the references and bring them back to the office. I'll be there in ten minutes," Lucas said. He punched Greave out and called Andi Manette's office, and got Black: "Can you bring a batch of the best files downtown?"

"Yeah. On the way. And we got another problem case. A guy who runs a chain of video-game arcades."

"So what're we doing?" Sloan asked.

"You want to work this?" Lucas asked.

Sloan shrugged. "I ain't got much else. I got that Turkey case, but we're having trouble getting anybody who can speak good Turk, so it's not going anywhere."

"I've never met any Turks who didn't speak pretty good English," Lucas said.

"Yeah, well, you oughta try investigating a Turk murder

sometime," Sloan said. "They're yellin' no-speaka-da-English when I'm walking down the street. The guy who was killed was outa Detroit, he was sharkin', he probably had thirty grand on the street and *nobody* was sorry to see him go."

"Talk with Lester," Lucas said. "We need somebody to keep digging around the Manettes, Wolfe, Dunn, and anybody else who might make something out of Andi Manette dying . . ." He flipped the engagement ring up in the air and caught it, rolled it between his palms.

Sloan said, "You're gonna lose that fuckin' stone. You're gonna drop it and the ring is gonna bounce right down a sewer."

Lucas looked in his hand and saw the ring: he hadn't been conscious of it. "I gotta do something about this, with Weather."

"There's pretty general agreement on that," Sloan said. "My old lady is peeing her pants, waiting for you to ask. She wants all the details. If I don't get her the details, I'm a dead man."

Greave was waiting with a sheaf of computer printer-paper and handed it to Lucas. "There's not much. The Nethinims were mostly just mentioned in passing—if there's anything, it's probably in Nehemiah. Here, 3:26."

Lucas looked at the passage. *Moreover the Nethinims dwelt in Ophel unto the place over against the water gate toward the east, and the tower that lieth out.*

"Huh." He passed the paper to Sloan and walked down the office to a wall map of the Metro area, traced the Mississippi with his finger. "One thing you can see from the river is all those green water towers," he said. "They're like mushrooms along the tops of all the tallest hills. The water gate could be any of the dams."

"Want me to check?"

Lucas grinned. "Take you two days. Just call all the towns along here." He snapped his finger at the map. "Hastings, Cottage Grove, St. Paul Park, Newport, Inver Grove, South St. Paul, like that. Tell them you're working Manette and ask them to swing a patrol car by the water towers; see if there's anything to see."

Black showed up ten minutes later, morose, handed Lucas a file and a tape. "Guy's messing with kids. Somebody ought to cut his fuckin' nuts off."

"Pretty explicit?"

"It's all there, and I don't give a shit what the shrinks say. This guy *likes* doing it. And he likes talking about it—he likes the attention he's getting from Manette. He'll never stop."

"Yeah, he will," Lucas said, flipping through the file. "For several years . . . I'll take it to the chief. We want to hold off until Manette's out of the way."

Black nodded. "We got some doozies in the files." He sat down opposite Lucas, spread five files on the desk like a poker hand, pushed one toward Lucas. "Look at this guy. I think he may have raped a half-dozen women, but he talks them out of doing anything about it. He brags about it: breaks down for them, weeps. Then he laughs about it. He says he's addicted to sex, and he's coming on to Manette . . . right here, see, she mentions it, and how she might have to redirect his therapy."

They were reading files an hour later when Greave hurried in. "They've got something in Cottage Grove."

Lucas stood up. "What is it?"

"They said it's like an oil drum under one of the water towers."

"How do they know?"

"It's got your name spray-painted on it," Greave said.

"*My* name?"

Greave shrugged. "That's what they said—and they are freaked out. They want your ass down there."

On the way down to Cottage Grove, the cellular buzzed and Lucas flipped it open. "Yeah?"

Mail cooed, "Hey, Davenport, got it figured out?"

Lucas knew the voice before the third word was out. "Listen, I . . ."

But he was gone.

9

Six blocks from the water tower, Lucas ran into a police blockade, two squad cars V-ed across the street. The civilian traffic was turning around, jamming up the street. He put the Porsche on the yellow line and accelerated past the frustrated drivers, until two cops ran toward him waving him off.

A red-faced patrolman, one hand on his pistol, leaned up to the window. "Hey, what the hell . . ."

Lucas held up his ID and said, "Davenport, Minneapolis PD. Get me through."

The cop ran back to one of the squads, yelled something through an open window, and the cop inside backed it up. Lucas accelerated through the gap and up toward the water tower. Along the way, he saw cops in the streets, two different sets of uniforms. They were evacuating houses along the way, and women with kids in station wagons hurried down the streets away from the tower.

A bomb? Chemicals? What?

The water tower looked like an aqua-green alien from *War of the Worlds*, its big egg-shaped body supported by fat, squat legs. Three fire trucks, a cluster of squad cars, a bomb squad truck, two ambulances, and a wrecker were parked a hundred yards away. Lucas pulled into the cluster.

"Davenport?" A stout, red-faced man in a too-tight cop's uniform waved him over. "Don Carpenter, Cottage Grove." He wiped his face on his sleeve. He was sweating heavily, though the day was cool. "We might have a big problem."

"Bomb?"

Carpenter looked toward the top of the hill. "We don't know. But it's an oil barrel, and it's full of something heavy. We haven't tried to move it, but it's substantial."

"Somebody said my name is on it."

"That's right: *Lucas Davenport, Minneapolis Police.* Standard bullshit graffiti-artist spray paint. We were gonna open it, but then someone said, 'Jesus, if this guy's fuckin' with Davenport, what's to keep him from putting a few pounds of dynamite or some shit in there? Or a gas bomb or something?' So we're standing back."

"Huh." Lucas looked up toward the tower. Two men were there, talking. "Who are those guys?"

"Bomb squad. We were all over the place before somebody thought it might be a bomb, so we don't think it's dangerous to get near. A time bomb doesn't make sense, because he didn't know when we'd find it."

"Let's take a look," Lucas said.

The bottom of the tower was enclosed by the hurricane fence, with a truck-sized gate on one end. "Cut the chain on the gate and drove right in," Carpenter said. They were at the crest of the hill, and below them a steady stream of cars was leaving the neighborhood.

"But nobody saw it."

"We don't know—we were talking about a door-to-door, but then the bomb idea came up, and we never got to it."

"Maybe later," Lucas said.

The two bomb squad cops walked over and Lucas recognized one of them. He said, "How are you? You were on that case out in Lake Elmo." The guy said, "Yeah, Bill Path, and this is Jesus Martinez." He threw a thumb at his partner, and Lucas said, "What've we got?"

"Maybe nothing," Path said, looking back at the tower. Lucas could see the black oil drum through the hurricane fence. It sat directly under the bulb of the four-legged water tower. "But we don't want to try to move it. We're gonna pull the lid from a distance and see what happens."

"We've drained the tower," Carpenter said. He wiped his sweating face on his sleeve again. "Just in case."

"Can I?" Lucas said, nodding at the oil barrel.

"Sure," said Path. "Just don't kick it."

The barrel sat in the shade of the tower, and Lucas walked over to look at it, and then around it: a standard oil barrel, with a little rust, and a lid that looked professionally tight.

"One of the first guys knocked on it, and nothing happened; so we knocked on it when we got here," Martinez said, grinning at Lucas. He stepped up to the barrel and knocked on it. "It's full of something."

"Could be water," said Path. "If it's full, and it's water, it'd weigh about four-fifty."

"How'd he move it?" Lucas asked. "He couldn't use a fork lift."

"I think he rolled it," Path said. "Look . . ."

He walked away from the barrel, peered around, then pointed. There was a deep edge-cut in the soft earth, then a series of interlocking rings along with a wavy line. "I think he rolled it to here, then tipped it up, then rim-rolled it to the middle."

Lucas nodded: he could see the pattern in the dirt.

- "Hey, look at this, Bill," Martinez said to Path. He pointed at a lower corner of the barrel. "Is that just condensation, or is there a pinhole?"

A drop of liquid seemed to be squeezing out of the barrel. Path got to his knees, peered at it, then grunted, "Looks like a pinhole." He picked up a dandelion leaf, caught the drop on the leaf, smelled it, and passed it to Martinez.

"What?" Lucas asked.

Martinez said, "Nothing—probably water."

"So let's jerk the lid."

Path fixed a block to an access ladder on the water tower, while Martinez fitted a harness around the lid. Then he tied a rock climber's rope to the harness, ran it up through the block and down to the tow truck. The truck let out all of its cable, and when they finished, they were a hundred and fifty yards from the barrel.

"You ready for a big noise?" Path asked Carpenter.

The chief said, "Don't talk like that. Do you mean that? Do you think?"

They all squatted behind cars, the wrecker rolled forward, and the lid flipped off like a beer cap. Nothing happened. Lucas could hear a plane droning down the river.

"Well, shit," Martinez said after a moment. He stood up. "Let's go look."

They walked slowly back to the barrel. From thirty feet away, Lucas could see that it was filled with water. When they got next to it, they looked carefully inside. A small body was at the bottom of the barrel, a pale oval face turned to look up at them. The water was cloudy with a sediment of some kind, and the body shimmered, out of focus, a white dress floating around it like gauze, black hair drifting around the head.

Martinez looked in the barrel and said, "No. I don't do this." And he walked away.

"Oh, shit. Who is it?" Carpenter asked, peering open-mouthed into the barrel.

The body was small. "Probably Genevieve Dunn," Lucas said. "Are we sure this is water?"

Path, looking in, put his face close to the surface and said, "Yeah. It's water. He could have a big chunk of white phosphorus in there, waiting for us to get rid of the water."

Lucas shook his head: "Nah. This is what he wanted me to see. A jack-in-the-box. The motherfucker is playing games . . . Is that the Medical Examiner down there?"

Carpenter nodded. "Yeah. I'll get him."

Lucas stepped away and looked down the hill, waiting. There should be something else—or Mail would call again, to gloat. Carpenter, standing beside him, said, "I'd pull the trigger on this guy. How can you kill a kid?"

Lucas said, "Yeah?" He remembered the line from a Vietnam vet, a street guy. How can you kill a kid? Just lead them a little less . . .

The Medical Examiner was a young man with a thin face,

thin spectacles, and a large Adam's apple. He walked up, glanced in the barrel, and said, "What's the shit in the water?"

Nobody knew.

"Well, give me something I can fish around with, huh?" He was unselfconsciously cheerful, even for a Medical Examiner. "Give me one of those fire axes. I don't want to put my hand in there if we don't know what it is."

"Take it easy with the ax," Carpenter said.

"Don't worry about it," the examiner said. He looked in the barrel again. "That's not a kid."

"What?" Lucas walked back.

"Not unless she had deformed hands and too big a head," he said confidently.

Lucas looked in the water again—it still looked like a child's body. "I think it's some kind of big plastic doll," the examiner said. A fireman came up with a long curved tool that looked like an oversized poker. "Here."

The Medical Examiner took it, grabbed the body, but it slipped away. "Anchored with something," he grunted. "Look, if this is just water, why don't we dump it?"

They did; the water spilled out on the grass, and the ME reached inside and pulled out a four-foot doll, plastic flesh, black hair, and paint-flaking baby blue eyes. Its feet were folded beneath it and tied to a brick to keep the doll from floating.

"Got the big sense of humor, huh?" said the examiner. A white plastic tag floated from the doll's neck. The examiner turned it. It said, in black grease pencil, "CLUE."

"I don't think he has a sense of humor," Lucas said. "I really don't think he does."

"Then what is this shit?"

"I don't know," Lucas said.

Lucas called in, then headed back toward Minneapolis. As he passed the refinery off Highway 61, Mail called again.

"Goddamn, you were fast, Lucas. Can I call you Lucas? How'd you like all those fire trucks? I drove by while you guys were up there. What were you doing? Somebody said they thought it was a bomb or something. Is that right? Did you have the bomb squad up there?"

"Listen, we think you might have some trouble, you know, making the world work right. And we think you might know it. We can get you help . . ."

"You mean I'm fuckin' nuts? Is that what you mean?"

"Listen, I personally had a bad episode of depression a few years back, and I know what it's like. The shit in your head is wrong, and it's not your fault . . ."

"Fuck that, Davenport, there's nothing wrong with my fuckin' head. There's something wrong with the fuckin' world. Turn on your TV sometime, asshole. There's nothing wrong with me."

And he was gone again.

The phone company was automatically tracing all calls to Lucas's cellular phone and alerting the Dispatch Department at the same time. Dispatch would start cars toward the phone. But when Lester called, two minutes after Mail hung up, he said, "He was too quick. He was on the strip near the airport. We had cars there in two minutes forty-five seconds after he rang you, but he was gone. We stopped seven vans, nothing going there."

"Damnit. He won't talk for more than ten seconds or so."

"He knows what he's doing."

"All right. I'm heading back."

"Sherrill came up with another problem case, a guy fooling around with children—he's been screwing ten-year-old girls at a playground. I don't know what's gonna happen, but if we get Manette back, she might wind up doing some time."

Lucas shook his head and looked at the phone, then said, "Frank, we're not secure here. This phone is a fuckin' radio."

Lester was waiting when Lucas got back.

"This Manette thing, the sex things," he said.

"Yeah?"

"An awful lot of people know. They know down in Sex,

and they're pissed that they can't move. It's gonna get out, and it won't be long."

"Are we running the names of all these guys?"

"All of them."

"How about people they've abused? Could somebody be trying to get revenge on Manette?"

Lester shrugged. "So we plug in all the victims. We got more goddamned names, and nothing coming up. What do you make of that thing out at the water tower?"

"I don't know," Lucas said. "He says it's a clue, but what kind of a clue? Why was it full of water? Watery grave? Was it the barrel?"

Anderson came through, handed each of them a fat plastic binder with perhaps three hundred pages inside. "Everything we've got, except what might come out of the lab on the doll. And we're not getting anything from the feebs."

"Big surprise." Lucas flipped through the text.

"Any ideas?" Lester asked.

"Watery grave," Lucas said. "That's about it."

Nothing moved. Nobody called.

Lucas finally phoned Anderson: "There's an interview in your book with one of Manette's neighbors."

"Yeah?"

"She said there was somebody hanging around in a boat, in a spot where there aren't any fish. Maybe we ought to run boat licenses against the other lists."

"Jesus, Lucas, we got hundreds of names already."

Later, Lucas called St. Anne's College and asked for the psychology department. "Sister Mary Joseph, please."

"Is this Lucas?" The voice on the other end was breathless.

"Yes."

"We were wondering if you'd call," the receptionist said. "I'll go get her."

Elle Kruger—Sister Mary Joseph—picked up the phone a moment later, her voice dry: "Well, they're all in a tizzy around here. Sister Marple goes off to solve another one. And this one's a gamer, I hear."

"Yeah. And it's ugly," Lucas said. "I think one of the kids is dead."

"Oh, no." The wry quality disappeared from her voice. "How sure?"

"The guy who took them left a clue: a doll in an oil barrel filled with water. I think the doll was supposed to represent one of the kids."

"I see. Do you want to come over and talk?"

"Weather should be home around six. If you'd like to walk over, I'll cook some steaks."

"Six-thirty," she said. "See you then."

On his way home, Lucas took University Avenue toward St. Paul and stopped just short of the St. Paul city line. Davenport Simulations occupied a suite of offices on the first floor of a faceless but well-kept office building. Most of the offices in the building were closed. Davenport Simulations was completely lit up: most of the programmers started work in the early afternoon, and ran until midnight, or later.

Lucas smiled at the receptionist as he went by; she smiled and waved and kept talking on her phone. Barry Hunt was in his office with one of the techies, poring over a printout. When Lucas knocked, he gave a friendly, "Hey, come on in," while his face struggled to find an appropriate expression.

Hunt had been finishing his MBA at St. Thomas when Lucas started looking for somebody to take over the company. For ten years, Lucas had run it out of his study, writing war and role-playing games, selling the games to three different companies. Almost against his will, he got involved in the shift to computer gaming. At the same time, he'd been forced out of the department; he wound up working full-time, writing emergency scenarios for what became a line of police-training software. The software sold, and everything began to move too quickly: he didn't know about payroll, taxes, social security, royalties, worker's comp, operator training.

Elle had met Hunt in one of her psych classes and

recommended him. Hunt took over the company operations and had done well, for both of them. But Hunt and Lucas were not especially compatible, and Lucas was no longer certain that Hunt was happy to see him drop by.

"Barry, I need to talk to the software guys for a minute," Lucas said. "I've got a problem. It's this Manette thing."

Hunt shrugged. "Sure. Go ahead. I think everybody's here."

"I swear, just a minute."

"Great . . ."

The back two-thirds of the office suite was a single bay, cut up into small cubicles by shoulder-high dividers, exactly the kind used in the Homicide office. Seven men and two women, all young, were at work: six at individual monitors, three clustered around a large screen, running a search-trainer simulation. Another man and a heavy-set young woman, both with Coke-bottle glasses, were drinking coffee by a window. When Lucas walked in with Hunt, the room went quiet.

"Hey, everybody," Lucas said.

"Lucas," somebody said. Faces turned toward him.

"You've all probably heard about the Manette kidnapping case. The guy who took her is a gamer. I've got a composite sketch, and I'd like you all to look at it, see if you recognize him. And I'd appreciate it if you'd fax it or ship it to everybody you can think of, here in the Cities. We really need the help."

He passed out copies of the composite: nobody knew the face.

"He's a big guy?" asked one of the programmers, a woman named Ice.

"Yeah. Tall, muscular, thin," Lucas said. "Crazy, apparently. Maybe medically crazy."

"Sounds like my last date," Ice said.

"Will you put it on the 'Net?" Lucas asked.

"No problem," Ice said. She was a throwback to the days of punk, with short-cropped hair, bright red lipstick that somewhat flowed out of the lines of her lips, and nose rings. Hunt said she wrote more code than anyone in the place. An idea began to tickle the back of Lucas's head, but he pushed it away for the moment.

"Good," he said. "Let's do it."

On the way out, Hunt said, "Lucas, we need to get together."

"Trouble?" Lucas feared the day that the IRS would knock on the door and ask for his records. *Records? We don't got no steenking records.*

"We need a loan," Hunt said. "I've talked to Norwest, and there won't be any problem getting it. You'd have to approve."

"A loan? I thought we were . . . "

"We need to buy Probleco," Hunt said. "They've got a half-dozen hardware products that would fit with ours like the last pieces in a puzzle. And they're for sale. Jim Duncan wants to go back to engineering."

"How much do you want to borrow? Maybe I could . . ."

"Eight mil," Hunt said.

Lucas was startled. "Jesus, Barry, eight million dollars?"

"Eight million would buy us dominance in the field, Lucas. Nobody else would be close. Nobody else could get close."

"But, my God, that's a lot of money," Lucas said, flustered. "What if we fall on our butts?"

"You hired me to keep us off our butts, and we are," Hunt said. "We'll stay that way. But that's why we've got to meet, so I can explain it all."

"All right; but we'll have to wait until after this Manette thing. And I'd like you maybe to come up with a couple of other options."

"I can think of one big one, right off the top of my head."

"What?"

"Take the company public. It's a little early for that, but if you wanted out, well . . . we could take the company public and probably get you, I don't know, something between eight and ten mil."

"Holy cats," Lucas said.

He'd never said that before, in public or private, but now it bleated out and Hunt jerked out a quick smile. "If we borrow the eight mil, and hang on for another five years, it'll be thirty mil. I promise."

"All right, all right, we'll talk," Lucas said, starting down the hall. "Give me a week. Thirty mil. Holy cats."

"Say hello to Weather," Hunt said. He seemed about to say something else but stopped. Lucas was halfway out the door before he realized what it was, and walked back. Hunt had just sat down in his office, and Lucas stuck his head in. "This Manette thing can't last for more than a couple of weeks, so set a meeting with the bank. And lay out the stock thing we talked about—the share plan."

Hunt nodded. "I've been meaning to bring it up."

Lucas said, "Now's the time. I told you if it worked, you'd get a piece of it. It seems to be working."

Weather.

Lucas toyed with the engagement ring: he should ask her. He could feel her waiting. But the advice was rolling in, unsolicited, from everywhere, and somehow, it slowed him down.

Women suggested a romantic proposal: a short preface, declaring that he loved her, with a more or less elaborate description of what their life together would be like, and then a suggestion that they marry; most of the men suggested a plain, straightforward question: Hey babe, how about it? A few thought he was crazy for tying up with a woman at all. A park cop suggested that golf would be a complete replacement for any woman, and cheaper.

"Fuck golf," Lucas said. "I like women."

"Well, that's the other half of the equation," the guy admitted. "Women are also a complete replacement for golf."

"Anything?" Weather asked as soon as he came in the door. He could feel the ring in his pocket, against his thigh. "With the Manettes?"

"Bizarre bullshit," he said, and he told her about the oil barrel. "Elle's coming over at six-thirty; I promised her steak."

"Excellent," Weather said. "I'll do the salad."

Lucas went to start the charcoal and touched the ring in his pocket. What if she said *no, not yet . . .* ? Would that change everything? Would she feel like she had to move out?

Weather was bustling around the kitchen, bumping into him as he got the barbecue sauce out of the refrigerator. She asked with elaborate, chatty unconcern, "Do you think you and Elle would have gotten married, if . . ."

"If she'd hadn't become a nun?" Lucas laughed. "No. We grew up together. We were too close, too young. Romancing her just wouldn't have seemed . . . right. Too much like incest."

"Does she think the same way?"

Lucas shrugged. "I don't know. I never know what women think."

"You wouldn't rule it out, though."

"Weather?"

"What?"

"Shut the fuck up."

Sister Mary Joseph—Elle Kruger—still wore the traditional black habit with a long rosary swaying by her side. Lucas had asked her about it, and she'd said, "I like it. The other dress . . . it looks dowdy. I don't feel dowdy."

"Do you feel like a penguin?"

"Not in the slightest."

Elle had been a beautiful child, and still ran through Lucas's dreams, an eleven-year-old blonde touched by grace and merriment: and later scarred by acne so foul that she'd retreated from life, to emerge ten years later as Sister Joseph. She'd told him that her choice was not brought by her face, that she had a vocation. He wasn't certain; he never quite bought it.

Elle arrived in a black Chevrolet as Lucas was putting the first of the steaks on the grill. Weather gave her a beer.

"What's the status?" Elle asked.

"One's dead, maybe; the others aren't yet," Lucas said.

"But the guy is cracking open and all the gunk is oozing out of his head. He's gonna kill them soon."

"I know her—Andi Manette. She's not the most powerful mind, but she's got an ability to . . . touch people," Elle said, sipping the beer. The smell of steak floated in from the porch. "She reaches out and you talk to her. I think it's something that aristocrats develop. It's a touch."

"Can she stay alive?"

Elle nodded. "For a while—for longer than another woman could. She'll try to manipulate him. If he's had therapy, it's hard to tell which way he'll jump. He'll recognize the manipulation, but some people become so habituated to therapy that they need it, like a drug. She could keep him going."

"Like Scheherazade," Weather said.

"Like that," Elle agreed.

"I need to keep him talking," Lucas said. "He calls me on the telephone, and we try to track him."

"Do you think he was in therapy with her? A patient?"

"We don't know. We're looking, but we haven't found much."

"If he is, then you should go to his problem. Not accuse him of being ill."

"I did that this afternoon," Lucas said ruefully. "He got pissed . . . sorry."

"Ask him how he's taking care of them," Elle suggested. "See if you can make him feel some responsibility, or that you think he's shirking a responsibility. Ask him if there's anything you can do that would allow them to go free. Something he would trade. Ask him not to answer right away, but to consider it. What would he like? You need questions on that order."

Later, over the steaks, Lucas said, "We've got another problem. We're going through Manette's records. She was treating people for child abuse—and she hadn't notified anybody."

Elle put down her fork. "Oh, no. You're not going to prosecute."

"That's up in the air," Lucas said.

Now Elle was angry. "That's the most primitive law this state has ever passed. We know that people are ill, but we insist on putting them into positions where they can't get help, and they'll just go on . . ."

". . . Unless we slap their asses in jail . . ."

"What about the ones you never find out about? The ones who'd like to get treatment but can't because the minute they open their mouths, the cops'll be on them like wolves?"

"I know you've got a point-of-view," Lucas said, trying to back out of the argument.

"What?" Weather asked. "What happens?"

Elle turned to her. "If a person abuses a child in this state, and realizes he's sick, and tries to get treatment, the therapist is required to report him. If she does that, her records get seized by the state and are used as evidence against the patient. So as soon as the state acts, the patient, of course, gets a lawyer, who tells him to get out of treatment and keep his mouth shut. And if the man's acquitted—they frequently are, since he's admitted that he's mentally ill and that casts doubt on the records, and the therapists are very reluctant witnesses—well, then he's turned loose and all he knows for sure is that he can't ever go back to treatment, because he might wind up in prison."

Weather stared at her for a moment, then said to Lucas, "That can't be right."

"Sort of a Catch-22," Lucas admitted.

"Sort of barbaric is what it is," Weather said sharply.

"Child abuse is barbaric," Lucas snapped back.

"But if a person is trying to get help, what do you want? Throw him in a hole somewhere?"

"Listen, I really don't want to argue about it," Lucas said. "You either believe or you don't."

"Lucas . . ."

"Listen, will you guys let me chicken out of this thing and eat my steak? For . . . gosh sakes."

"Makes me really unhappy," Elle growled. "Really unhappy."

• • •

Late that night, Weather rolled up on a shoulder and said, "Barbaric."

"I didn't want to argue about it with Elle right there," Lucas said. "But you know what I really think? Therapy doesn't work with child abusers. The shrinks are flattering themselves. What you do with child abusers is you put their asses in jail. Each and every one of them, wherever you find them."

"And you call yourself a liberal," Weather said in the dark.

"Libertine. Not liberal," Lucas said, easing toward her.

"Stay on your side of the bed," she said.

"How about if I put just one finger over?"

"No." And a moment later, "*That's* not a finger . . ."

10

John Mail watched the late news with a sense of well-being. He was alone except for the wide-screen television and his computers. He had a dial-up Internet link, and monitored twenty-four news groups dealing with sex or computers or both. He had two phone lines and three computers going at once. As he watched the news, he punched through *alt.sex.blondes* on the 'Net, and now and then pulled out a piece and shipped it to a second computer.

Mail was a little sleepy, a little burned out, with a pleasant ache in his lower belly and a burn on his knees. Andi Manette was a package, all right: he'd known that when he'd first laid eyes on her ten years earlier. She was everything he'd expected: nice body, and she fought him. He enjoyed the fight, and enjoyed smothering it. Every time he rode her, he finished with a sense of victory.

And now here he was, on television, dominating the news. Everybody was looking for him—and they might find him, he thought, given a few weeks, or months. He'd have to do something about that, eventually.

He pushed the thought away and went back to his favorite: Davenport. Davenport was in hiding. Nothing was said about him. Nothing.

Mail ran through the Internet news groups as he watched

TV, sorting the messages by subject. He was tempted to post something about Manette and what he was doing with her. He might do that, if he could get to a machine at the university. Some people on the *alt.sex* groups who would appreciate what he had to say . . .

Maybe just a quick note now, just a hint? No. There was always a path they could get back on, a way to trace him—his Internet link had his real phone number.

Though not his real name.

On the Internet, he was Tab Post and Pete Rate, names he got off his computer keyboard. Down at the store, and with the store van, he was Larry F. Roses. The real Larry F. Roses was down south somewhere, Florida, Louisiana. He'd sold the van and its papers for cash, to avoid having to split the money with his ex-wife. To the mortgage company, he was Martin LaDoux. He had Marty's papers—driver's license, with his own photo on it now, a Social Security card, even a passport. He paid Marty's income taxes.

He wasn't John Mail anywhere. John Mail was dead . . .

Mail sat up and pushed away the TV tray with the aluminum foil chicken-pot-pie tin. Chicken-pot-pie and a Coke; just about his favorite. And he thought about Grace. Got up, went to the kitchen, got another can of Coke, and thought about her some more.

Grace might be good. Fresh. Her body was just starting to turn, and she'd fight, all right. He dropped on the couch and closed his eyes. Still, when he looked at her, he didn't feel the hunger he felt for the mother. That still surprised him. The first time he'd taken Andi Manette to the mattress, he'd almost blacked out with the joy of it. Maybe, Grace. Sometime. As an experiment. Bet she'd freak out when she saw it coming . . .

He'd just finished the Coke when the phone rang on the corner table behind his head. He groped for it, found it. "Hello?"

"Yes, Mr. LaDoux." Mail sat up: *this* voice he paid attention to.

"They are looking for your boat. The police know you

were watching her from the lake." Click. Mail stared at the phone. Shit. He wished he knew who it was: a face-to-face talk would be interesting.

But the boat. He frowned. When he'd rented the boat, he'd had to show an ID, the LaDoux driver's license, his home name. The old guy at the rental place had stamped it on the back of a duplicate form. Where he put the form, Mail didn't know. Hadn't paid attention. Damnit. That's how Davenport would get him: when he didn't pay attention.

Mail stood up, got a jacket and a flashlight, and went outside. Chilly. But the clouds had vanished with the sun, and overhead, the Milky Way stretched across the sky like God's own Rolex. Drive up? Nah. Good night for a stroll. Maybe some pussy at the end of it, although his testicles were beginning to ache.

With the flashlight picking out the bumps and holes, Mail took the driveway down to the gravel frontage road, checked the rural mailbox out of habit. Nothing; the mailman always came before ten o'clock, and Mail had picked up the day's delivery when he'd got up. He shut the mailbox and went down the gravel road.

To the north, the lights of the Cities were visible as a thin orange glow above the roadside trees. But when he turned south, up the track to the shack where he kept the women, it was as dark as the inside of a bone; and it all smelled of corn leaves.

Mail lived on what once had been a small farm. A neighbor had bought it when the farm could no longer support itself, had shorn a hundred and fifty acres of crop land from the original plot, and had sold the remaining ten acres containing the original farmhouse and a few crumbling outbuildings. The new owner, an alcoholic slaughterhouse worker, had allowed the house to fall apart before he killed himself. The next owner built a small house closer to the road, and a two-horse stable out back. When his children had grown, he'd moved to Florida. The next owner converted the stable to a garage, got lonely in the country winter, and moved back to the city. The next owner was Mail.

By the time Mail took the place, the old house was a ruin, a shack. A caved-in chicken coop squatted behind the shack, with the remains of what might have been a machine shed, now reduced to a pile of rotting boards. A still-recognizable two-seater outhouse was out to one side, nearly buried in the corn. Further to the back was the foundation of a barn.

If the farmhouse was a ruin, the basement and root cellar were solid. Mail had run a new electrical cable out to the place from his own house, a job that had taken him two hours.

He had worried, for a while, about keeping the women in the house. A trespassing antique hunter might accidentally stumble over them. Antique hunters were everywhere, stripping old farmhouses of their antique brass doorknobs and doorstops and forced-air register fittings, old pickle crocks—those were getting hard to find—and even nails, if they were hand-forged and in good shape.

But antique scavengers were a nervous lot. Judges treated them like burglars, which is what they were, so Mail had put in two Radio Shack battery-operated motion alarms and felt fairly safe. Any antique hunter tripping an alarm would be out of the house in an instant; and if it was anybody else, the cops, for instance, the jig would be up anyway.

The only other danger was Hecht, the neighboring farmer. Hecht was a phlegmatic German, a member of some weird religious sect. He had no television, there was no newspaper box on his mailbox post. He had never shown much interest in anything beyond his tractor and his land. Mail had never seen him near the old house, except at planting and harvest time, when he was working in the adjacent fields. By then, the women would be long gone.

Mail walked in the thin oval of illumination from the flashlight, smelling the corn and the dust; and when he crossed the crest of the hill and turned the light toward it, the old farmhouse came up like a witch-house in a Gothic novel, glowing with a faint, ghostly luminescence often found in old clapboard houses that had once been painted white.

As Mail passed the porch, on the way around back, a nervous chill trickled down his spine: a finger of graveyard fear as he passed the cistern. Scratching sounds? No.

He clumped inside.

Grace heard him coming and pushed herself against the wall. She wasn't sure that her mother had heard: Andi had been lying on the mattress for hours, one arm crooked over her eyes, not asleep, but not conscious. She had drifted away again, after the last attack. Grace had tried to rouse her, but Andi wouldn't respond.

Grace had decided to go after Mail.

Mail had attacked her mother four times now, battering her each time, raping her after the beating. She could hear the crack of his hand through the steel door, and thinner, weaker sounds that must have been her mother's voice, pleading. He slapped, Andi had told her. Hit her with an open hand, but it was like being hit with a board. This last time, something had broken, and Andi was out of it, Grace thought.

She'd have to go after Mail, even if she had nothing but her fingernails. He was killing her mother, and when he'd done it, she'd go too.

"No." Andi pushed herself up. Blood ringed her nostrils, a dark reddish-black crust. Her eyes were like holes, her lips swollen. But she'd heard the footsteps, and roused herself, half-turning to croak the single warning word.

"I have to do something," Grace whispered. He was coming.

"No." Andi shook her head. "I don't think . . . I don't think he'll do anything when I'm like this."

"He's killing you. I thought you were dying already," Grace whispered. She was crouched on the back corner of the mattress, like a cowering dog at the pound, Andi thought. The girl's eyes were too bright, her lips pale, her skin stretched thin like tracing paper.

"He might be, but we can't fight him yet. He's too big.

We need . . . something." She pushed herself up, feeling the impact of Mail's footsteps on the stairs. "We need something we can kill him with."

"What?" Grace looked wildly around the cell. There was nothing.

"We have to think . . . but I can't think. I can't think." Andi put her hands to her head, at the temples, as though trying to hold her skull together.

He was close, on the stairs. "You have to lie down, just like you were," Grace said fiercely. "With your hands over your eyes. Don't say anything, no matter what."

She pushed her mother down, and they heard the slide-lock pulled back. Andi, too weak to argue, and without the time, nodded and put her arm up and closed her eyes. Grace pulled back in the corner, her feet pulled tight to her thighs, her arms around her legs, looking up at the door.

Mail peered through the crack, saw them, undid the chain, opened the door. "Get up," he said to Andi.

Grace, frightened, said, "You did something to her. She hasn't moved since you left."

That pushed him back.

Mail's forehead wrinkled and he said, harshly, "Get up," and he pushed Andi's foot with his own.

Andi rolled half over, then pulled herself away from him, toward the wall, like a cartoon woman dying of thirst in a desert. She inched away, pathetic.

"You really hurt her, this time," Grace said, and she began to bawl.

"Shut up," Mail snarled. "Shut up, goddamnit, little fuckin' . . . whiner . . ."

He took a step toward her, as though to hit her, and Grace choked off the sobs and tried to pull herself tighter to the wall. Mail hesitated, then pushed Andi again. "Get up."

Andi rolled some more, and began to inch away again. Mail caught her feet and twisted them, and she flipped onto her back. "Water," she whimpered.

"What?"

Her eyes closed and she lay limp as a rag. Grace began

bawling again, and Mail shouted, "Shut up, I said," and backed away, uncertain now.

"You hurt her," Grace said.

"She wasn't like this when I put her back in," Mail said. "She was walking."

"I think you did something to her . . . mind. She talks to Genevieve and Daddy. Where's Gen? What did you do with her? Is she with Daddy?"

"Ah, fuck," Mail said, exasperated. He probed Andi again, pushing her left foot with his own. "You'd best get better, 'cause I'm not done with you yet," he said. "We're not done, at-all."

He backed out of the room, and said to Grace, "Give her some water."

"I do," Grace sobbed. "But then she . . . wets on the floor."

"Ah, for Christ sakes," Mail said. The door slammed, but the bolt didn't slide shut. Grace held her breath. Had he forgotten? No. The door opened again, and Mail threw in a towel.

Grace had seen it, when he'd taken her mother out of the cell, lying on the floor beside the mattress he used when he raped her. "Clean her up," Mail said. "I'll be back in the morning."

The door closed again, and they heard his footsteps on the stairs. They waited, unmoving, but he didn't return.

"That was great," Andi whispered. She pushed herself up and felt the tears running down her face and she actually smiled through her cracked lips. "Grace, that was wonderful."

"That's once we beat him," Grace whispered back.

"We can do it again," Andi said. She propped herself up and tilted her head back. "But we've got to find something."

"Find what?"

"A weapon. Something we can kill him with."

"In here?" Grace looked around the barren cell, her eyes wide but not quite hopeless. "Where?"

"We'll find something," Andi said. "We have to."

• • •

Mail took the van—the van was blue now, and the sign on the side doors was clear: "Computer Roses"—and rode it down to Highway Three and I-494, filled the tank, and put a little more than four gallons in the red, five-gallon plastic gas can in the back. Inside the convenience store, he bought two quarts of motor oil and paid for it all with a twenty.

He took forty minutes riding out to Minnetonka, thinking it over. Mail thought a lot about crime, about the way things worked. If he were in a movie, he'd break into the boat works, use a flashlight, go through the files, and then play a breathless game of hide-and-seek with a security guard.

But this wasn't a movie, and his best protection was simply timing and invisibility.

Irv's Boat Works was tucked into a curve in the road just off the lake, along with a shabby gas station, a grocery store, and an ice cream parlor, all closed. He drove by once, looking for movement, looking for cops. He saw two moving cars, one in front and one behind, and no cops. Nobody walking. The only light in the buildings was in an ice cream freezer.

He drove a half-mile down the road to an intersection, did a U-turn, and went back the same way. Another car passed; a house a quarter mile past the station was fully lit, although he didn't see anybody around. He drove out to a Super-America store, parked, walked around to the back of the van, and let himself inside. He took just a minute to mix the motor oil with the gas, the fumes giving him a small mental charge: he hadn't done this since he got out of the hospital—he didn't need it anymore—but it still held something for him.

When he finished mixing, he went into the Tom Thumb and bought a cheap plastic cigarette lighter and a Coke. He already had a role of duct tape in the glove compartment. Back in the truck, he put the tape on the lighter so it'd be ready, opened the Coke and put it in the van's can-holder, and drove back toward Irv's.

The place was little more than a wooden shack, with a dock, gas pump, and launching ramp out back. Twenty aluminum fishing boats bobbed off the dock. Inside, he remembered a counter with a cash register, a half-dozen tanks for minnows and shiners, a few pieces of cheap fishing gear in wall racks, and a big, loose pile of green flotation cushions and orange round-the-neck life preservers. The whole place smelled of gas and oil, waterweed and rot.

Mail drove by once more, did his U-turn, looked for cars coming up behind, waited until one passed, and then followed it back to Irv's. Nothing out ahead. He swerved into the parking lot, stopped just outside the dusty picture-window where the fading red stick-up letters said, IRV'S BOAT WORK with a missing final "s."

He left the engine running, walked quickly around to the back of the van, took a jackknife out of his pocket, and cut a grapefruit-size hole in the top of the plastic gas can. The smell of gas was thick. He picked the can up, ready to ease it out the door, when headlights came up. He stopped, listening, but the car purred past.

He climbed out, got the lighter off the passenger seat, turned it up full, taped the sparking-lever down so he had a miniature torch, then picked up the five-gallon jug and heaved it through the window.

The window shattered with the sound of a load of dishes dropped in a diner: but nobody yelled, nobody came running. He tossed the lighter after the gas, and the building went up with a hollow *whoom*. By the time he was out of the parking lot, the fire was all over the inside of the building.

Damn. Wished he could stay.

He watched the building in the rearview mirror, until it disappeared behind a curve. When he was a kid, he'd torched a house in North St. Paul and had come back to sit on an elementary school embankment to watch the action. He liked the flames. Even more, he'd liked the excitement and companionship of the crowd, gathered to watch the fire. He felt like an entertainer, a movie star: he'd done this.

And listening, back then, he realized that everybody could find a little joy in watching one of their neighbors get burned out.

On the way back home, under the night sky, he thought about Andi Manette. Maybe this break was for the better. He'd been fucking her a lot, he could use the rest.

Tomorrow, though, he'd need her—need one of them, anyway.

He could feel that already.

11

Lucas got up a few minutes after Weather, struggling with the early hour, the morning light pale in the east windows. Weather put breakfast together while Lucas cleaned up. When he was dressed, Lucas got the ring from his sock drawer, fiddled with it, then dropped it in his pants pocket as he had almost every day for a month.

In the kitchen, Weather was standing at the sink, humming to herself as she sliced the orange heart out of a cantaloupe. Lucas still felt like he'd been hit in the forehead with a gavel.

"Anything good today?" he asked. His morning voice sounded like a rusty gate, but she was used to it.

"Not especially interesting," she said. "The first one is a woman with facial scarring from an electrical shock." She touched her cheek in front of her ear, to indicate where the scarring was. "I'm going to take out as much of the scar as I can—all of it, I hope."

"Sounds like she needs a plastic surgeon," Lucas said. He pushed two slices of bread into the toaster and started looking for the cinnamon.

"Sometimes I am a plastic surgeon," Weather said. "We do have that child coming up; that will be interesting. Six operations, probably. We're going to have to rotate her skull backwards . . ."

He liked watching her talk, her enthusiasm for the work, even when he had no idea of what she was talking about. He'd seen a half-dozen operations now, gowning up and learning where to stand, how to stay out of the way. The precision of it astonished him as did her easy way of command, and he found himself thinking that he could have done the work and been happy with it.

Although there was an odd, steely ego that went with surgeons, Weather had it—she ran the operating room like a sergeant major might—and so did George Howell, Weather's mentor. Howell was a fiftyish reconstructive surgeon who often stopped by when Weather was working, and Lucas usually felt a small, controllable urge to stuff the guy in a sewer somewhere, though Howell was a good enough guy.

"Are you listening?" Weather asked.

"Sure," Lucas said, peering down into the toaster. "It's just that I'm near death."

"There's something wrong with your metabolism," she said. "How can you be doing six things at three o'clock in the morning, but you can't add two and two at six o'clock in the morning? You should have a physical. How long has it been?"

Lucas rolled his eyes. "Having some guy shine his flashlight up my asshole isn't gonna improve my addition," he said. He looked glumly out the kitchen window. A robin hopped in the yard, peering this way and that for worms. "Christ, where's my .45 when I need it?"

Weather, up from the table, stopped to look outside, saw the robin and said, "I'd turn you in to Friends of Animals. You'd have bird lovers over here at five in the morning, making dove calls on the front porch."

"More fodder for the .45," he said. They ate together, talking about the daily routine, then Lucas kissed her good-bye, patted her on the ass, and went to lie facedown on the couch.

• • •

Sherrill and Black were finishing at Manette's office. Lucas stopped by at eight o'clock, still feeling that he was out of his time zone. Black was the same way, grumping at his partner, shaking his head at Lucas. "Six guys. No women. Anderson has the rundown on all of them. They'll all be in today's book. We're looking at all of them, and the FBI's going through its records. Now we're going back and looking at the second choices . . . the not-so-looney tunes."

"How about the six?"

"Severe goofs," Black said.

"Severe," Sherrill repeated. Like Weather, she was fairly chipper; in fact, seemed to soak up chipperness from Lucas and her partner. "I'd still like to know what we're doing about the sex cases."

"We'll get to them," Lucas promised. "We just don't want the media up in smoke. Not any more than they already are."

"I think Channel Three set new records in stupidity last night," Sherrill said. "The stuff they were saying was so stupid it made my teeth hurt."

"I don't understand what those guys are about," Black said. "I really don't."

"Making money," Lucas said. "That's all they're about."

As Lucas was leaving Manette's office, the receptionist, who'd been so flustered the first day, held up a hand, then looked both ways into the inner offices, a furtive look that Lucas recognized instantly. He continued out into the hall, looked back, caught her eye, and turned left. At the end of the hall was an alcove with Coke, coffee, and candy machines. A second later, she found him there, sipping a Diet Coke.

"I feel not so good, talking to you," the woman said. She wore a name tag that said "Marcella," and her voice was tentative, as though she hadn't made up her mind.

"Anything might help," Lucas said. "Anything. There are two kids out there."

She nodded. "It's just that with all the arguments and

lawyers, it makes me feel . . . disloyal. Nancy doesn't have to know?"

Lucas shook his head. "Nobody will know."

The woman glanced nervously back at her office again. "Well: Andi's files are complete, but only for here."

Lucas frowned, gestured with the cup of Coke. "Only for here? I was told that this is the only place that she worked."

"On her own. But when she was doing her post-doc work, at the U, she did lots of people in the Hennepin County jail. You know, court-ordered evaluations. Most of them were juveniles, but that was so long ago that lots of them would be adults by now."

"Did she ever mention anyone in particular?"

"No, she really couldn't, because, you know . . . confidentiality. But they scared her—she'd talk about that sometimes—about how a guy'd get her up against a door, or he'd hiss at her like a cat, and she could feel them getting ready to come at her. The sex ones scared her, especially. She said you could feel the hunger coming across the room. She said some of them would have attacked her right there, in the jail interview rooms, if they hadn't been restrained. I think the people she saw there . . . those are the worst ones."

"Well, Jesus, why didn't somebody say something?" Lucas asked.

The woman looked down at the floor. "You know why, Mr. Davenport. Everybody hates you getting these records. I'm not even sure you should. You might be undoing a lot of work. But then there's Andi, and I keep thinking about the girls."

"Okay. You've been a help, Marcella," Lucas said. "I'm serious. This is all between you and me, but if something comes out of it, and you approve, I'll let Miz Manette know you helped."

Lucas let her get back into the office while he finished the Diet Coke, then returned himself.

"What?" Sherrill asked, when she saw him coming back.

"I think we've been euchred—there's a whole other set of records. Criminal stuff. C'mon, we're way behind."

• • •

The university might have objected on grounds of patient privacy, but the chief called the governor, the governor called three of the Regents, and the Regents called down to the university president, who issued a statement that said, "Given the circumstances—that we may have a monster preying on innocent women and girls, and helping oppress all genders and races by making the streets unsafe—we have agreed to provide the City of Minneapolis limited access to limited numbers of psychological records."

"How limited?" Lucas asked the records section supervisor at the university. He'd gone with Black and Sherrill because his title added weight.

"Limited to what you ask for," the supervisor said wryly.

"These guys will do the asking," Lucas said, tipping his head at Black and Sherrill. "We really appreciate anything you can do."

Lucas learned about the fire at Irv's Boat Works while he ate a late breakfast at his desk. The fire was reported in a routine, four-inch filler in the *Star-Tribune*: FIRE STRIKES MINNETONKA BOAT RENTAL. The article quoted a fire marshal: "It was arson, but there was no attempt to hide it, and we don't have a motive as yet. We're asking the public . . ."

Lucas called the marshal, whom he'd known vaguely from the neighborhood.

"It was a bomb, essentially, a Molotov cocktail, gas and motor oil," the fire marshal said. "Not a pro job, but a pro couldn't have done it any better. Burned that thing right down to the foundation. Old Irv didn't have but six thousand dollars in insurance, so he didn't do it. Not unless I'm missing something."

At the university, Sherrill sat gloomily at a microfilm reader, operating the antiquated equipment by hand, eyes red from staring at the scratchy images of ten-year-old records. "Jesus Christ."

"What?" Black was on the next chair, three empty root

beer cans next to his foot. He was wearing tan socks with blue clocks.

"This guy went around fucking exhaust pipes," Sherrill said.

Black looked at her: "You mean on cars?"

"Honest to God." She missed the double entendre and giggled, her finger trailing down the screen, over the projected image. "You know how they caught him?"

"He got stuck," Black suggested.

"No."

Black thought for a second. "His lawnmower sued for sexual harassment?"

"He tried to fuck a hot one," Sherrill said. "He had to go to the hospital with third-degree burns."

"Aw, man," Black groaned. He reached into his crotch and rearranged himself, then scribbled a note on the pad next to his hand.

"Anything good?" Sherrill asked as he made the note.

"Kid who was into sex and fire," Black said. "I think he scared her bad." He rolled through to the next page. "She says he shows signs of 'substantial sexual maladjustment manifested in improper, aggressive sexual behavior and identification with fire.' "

"Guys are so fucked up," Sherrill said as Black pushed the printout button. "You never see women doing this stuff."

"Have you heard the 'best friend' joke's been going around?"

"Oh, no. Don't tell me." She shook her head unconvincingly.

"See, there was this guy goes to work, gets there late, and the boss jumps him . . ."

"C'mon, don't tell me," Sherrill said.

"All right. If you really don't want to hear it," he said. "Let me get this printout."

He came back a minute later with the printout and she said, "All right, let's hear it. The joke."

Black dropped the printout next to the microfilm reader and went on, ". . . so the boss says, 'Get the fuck out of here. You're fired. I don't want to see your ass again.' So the guy drags out the door, really upset, gets in his car, and halfway home he's t-boned at an intersection by a teenager. Trashes his car, and the kid's got no insurance. Jesus. This is turning into the worst day of his life. So his car is towed, and the guy has to take the bus home—and when he gets there, eleven o'clock in the morning, he hears sounds coming from the bedroom. Like sex. Moaning, groaning, sheets being scratched. And he sneaks back there, and there's his wife, having sex with his best friend."

"No shit," said Sherrill.

"And the guy freaks out," Black said. "He yells at his wife, 'Get out of here, you slut. Get your clothes, get dressed, and get out. Don't ever come back or I'll beat your ass into the floor.' And he turns to his best friend and says, 'As for you—Bad dog! Bad dog!'"

"That's really fuckin' funny," Sherrill said; she turned away to smile.

"So don't laugh," Black said, knowing she liked it. And on the top of the printout he wrote "John Mail."

Irv was a broad-shouldered old man with a crown of fine white hair, with a pink spot in the middle of it. His nose was pitted and red, as though he might like his whiskey too much. He wore a faded flannel shirt and canvas trousers, and sat on a park bench next to his dock. A cash box sat on the bench beside him. "What can I do you for?" he asked when Lucas rolled up.

"Are you Irv?" Off to the left, there was a scorched stone foundation with raw dirt inside, and nothing else.

"Yeah." Irv squinted up at him. "You a cop?"

"Yeah, Minneapolis," Lucas said. "What do you think? Will you get it back together?"

"I suppose." Irv rubbed his large nose with the back of one hand. "Don't have much else to do, and the insurance'll probably get me halfway there."

Lucas walked over to the foundation. There wasn't much evidence of fire, except for soot on the stones. "Got it cleaned up in a hurry."

The old man shrugged. "Wasn't anything in it but wood

and glass, and a few minnie tanks. It burned like a torch. What didn't burn, they took out with a front-end loader. The whole kit and caboodle was out of here in five minutes." He took off his glasses and cleaned the lenses on his flannel shirt. "Goddamnit."

Lucas turned away, inspected the foundation some more, and, when Irv got his glasses straight, walked back and handed him the flier. "Did you see this guy in here last week?"

Irv tipped his head back so he could look at the flier with his bifocals. Then he looked up and said, "Is this the sonofabitch that burned me out?"

"Was he in here?"

Irv nodded. "I believe he was. He doesn't look quite like this—the mouth is wrong—but he looks something like it, and I wondered what he was doing when he came in here. He wasn't any fisherman; he didn't know how to start the kicker. And it was cold that day."

"When was this?" Lucas asked.

"Two days ago—the day the rain came in. He came back in the rain."

"You remember his name?"

Irv scratched his chin. "No, no, I don't. I'd have his name off his driver's license, in my receipt box. If I had a receipt box anymore." He looked up at Lucas, the sun glittering off his glasses. "This is the one that took the Manette girl and her daughters, isn't it?"

"Could be," Lucas said. And he thought: *Yes, it is.*

John Mail called Lucas at one o'clock in the afternoon. "Here I am, figuring the cops are coming down on me at any minute. I mean, I'm buying my food a day at a time, so I don't waste any. Where are you guys?"

"We're coming," Lucas growled. The voice was beginning to get to him: he was looking at his watch as he talked, counting the seconds. "We're taking bets on how long you last. Nobody's out as far as a week. We can't give that bet away."

"That's interesting," Mail said cheerfully. "I mean, that's

very interesting. I best do as much fuckin' as I can, then, because I might not get any more for a while. Have to do with those hairy old assholes out at Stillwater."

"Be your asshole," Lucas snarled.

Mail's voice went cold: "Oh, I don't think so. I don't think so, Lucas."

"What?" Lucas asked. "You got a magic spell?"

"Nothing like that," Mail said. "But after people get to know me, they don't fuck with me; and that's the truth. But hey, gotta go."

"Wait a minute," Lucas said. "Are you taking care of those people? You've got them for now, and that puts some responsibility on you."

Mail hesitated, then said, "I don't have time to talk. But yeah, I'm taking care of them. Sometimes she makes me angry, but I don't know: subconsciously, she likes me. She always did, but she repressed it. She has a guilt complex about our doctor-patient relationship, but she used to sit there . . ."

He paused again, then said, "I've got to go."

Given a different context, he might have sounded almost human, Lucas thought, as the phone went *click*. As it was, he simply sounded insane.

"Fire," Lucas said to Black and Sherrill. "Sex. Probably he's been institutionalized—he talks about Stillwater like . . . I don't know. He doesn't really know about it, but he's heard a lot about it."

Lester came in. "He called from out in Woodbury somewhere."

"Woodbury. That's 494," Lucas said. "The guy's riding up and down the 494 strip, so he's someplace south."

"Yeah. We've whittled it down to one-point-two million people."

"The fire and sex thing," Sherrill said. "We got one just like that."

"Yeah." Black thumbed through a stack of paper. "This guy. John Mail. Let me see, he was fourteen when she saw him . . . Huh. He'd be about twenty-five right now."

Lucas looked at Lester. "That'd be pretty good. That'd be about prime time for a psycho."

Lester tapped the file. "Let's isolate that one and get on it."

Lucas looked at his watch: almost two o'clock. Nearly forty-eight hours since the kidnapping. He locked the door to his office, closed the blinds, pulled the curtains, put his feet back on his desk, and thought about it. And the more he thought about it, the more the telephone link seemed the best immediate possibility.

He closed his eyes and visualized a map of the metro area. All right: if they coordinated cops from all over the metro area—if they set everything up in advance—how far down could they push the reaction time? A minute? Forty-five seconds? Even less than that, if they got lucky. And if they caught him in a shopping center, someplace with restricted access, only a couple of exits—if they did that, they should be able to seal the place before he could get the car out. They could process every plate in the lot, check every ID . . .

Lucas was putting the idea together when another thought occurred: what had Dunn said? That he talked to Andi in her car? So Andi Manette had a cellular phone? What kind? A purse phone, or a dedicated car phone?

He sat up, turned on the desk light, rang Black's desk, got no answer, tried Sherrill, no answer. Got Anderson's daily book, flipped through it, found Dunn's phone number and dialed.

A cop answered. "He's probably on his car phone, chief."

Lucas got the number and called, and Dunn answered.

"Does your wife have a cellular?"

"Sure."

"A car phone, or a personal phone?"

"She carries it in her purse," Dunn said.

12

The FBI's agent-in-charge had a cleft chin and blond hair; his name was T. Conrad Haward, and he thought he looked like a Yale footballer, just now easing into his prime. But he had large, fuzzy ears and behind his back was called Dumbo.

Lucas, Lester, and an anonymous FBI tech sat in Haward's office underlooking the Minneapolis skyline. Haward interlaced his fingers in the middle of his leatherette desk pad and said, "It's all on the way, with the techs to operate it. The Chicago flight lands in an hour; the LA flight is still three hours out. The Dallas stuff, I don't know if we'll get that tonight. We'll go ahead in any case. Time is too much of a problem. In sixty-five percent of the cases, the victims have been terminated at this point on the time line."

"I just hope he's got that fucking phone," Lester said.

"He plays computer games—he won't throw out a piece of technology like a new flip phone," Lucas said.

The FBI tech, an older man with a silvery crewcut and striped clip-on tie, said, "The big question is, how do we hold him on the phone, if he answers it?"

"We're working on it," Lucas said, leaning forward in his chair. "We talked to one of the local rock-radio stations—

the general manager is a friend of mine, and the only people who'd know about this would be him, one DJ, and an engineer. We're gonna have the DJ call, with a contest they've been running. It's a real contest, real prizes, and it'll really go out over the air. The only difference being that we'll feed them the phone number. If he doesn't answer the first time, we'll try again in a few hours. If he answers— whenever he answers—we'll have the DJ ready to go. The typical air time, for one of these contest things, is only about a minute or a little more. We're working out credible ways to stretch it."

"Unless we're lucky, we'll need at least two or three minutes to get a really good fix," the tech said. "You gotta hold him on there."

"He's a gamer—we're gonna appeal to his vanity," Lucas said. "He'll stay on long enough to deal with the question. And when he answers, if he's right, the DJ's gonna say, 'Hang on while I do an intro to the next song.' Then he'll do it—take his time, maybe do a little ad—and then come back for a mailing address."

"We'll never get an address," Lester said. He grinned. "But wouldn't that be something?"

Lucas shook his head. "He'd just give us some bullshit. But if we can hold him on that long, we ought to get the fix."

"When you say, 'Really good fix,' what does that mean?" Lester asked the tech. Dumbo frowned. The conversation seemed to be flowing around him. "A half-mile, a block, six inches, what?"

"If we could risk riding the signal in, we could get it right down to the house," the tech said. "As it is, we'll be able to put you on the right block."

"Why not go closer?" Dumbo asked.

"Because if he's really nuts, he might slit their throats and run for it," the tech said, turning to his boss. "He'd hear the choppers coming when they were six blocks away."

Lucas said, "You get us to the block, we'll have him out of there in an hour, guaranteed."

"If you can get us the air time, we'll put you on the block," the tech said.

On the way out of the building, Lester said, "Do you believe them?"

Lucas nodded. "Yeah. This is what the feebs are good at—technology. If he answers the phone, and we can keep him on, they'll track him."

"Dumbo was right about one thing—it's getting long," Lester said. He glanced at his watch as if to check the date. "The asshole won't keep them much more than four or five days at the outside. The pressure'll get to him."

"How about the full-court-press idea?" Lucas asked.

"Anderson's trying to set it up, but it'll be tomorrow before we're ready. It's a goddamned administrative nightmare. Even then . . . I don't know. There are too many people involved. Somebody will fuck it up."

"It's a shot," Lucas said. "What about that guy Black and Sherrill were tracking? The kid who liked sex and fire?"

"John Mail," Lester said. "That's a definite washout. I don't know why, but Black left a note for me. They're looking into three other possibilities."

"Shit," Lucas said. "The guy sounded good."

With two sets of cellular tracking equipment, they would need six helicopters, one flying high and two flying low in each of two groups. The gear from Chicago arrived first, along with three techs, and they busied themselves fixing odd-looking globe antennas to the support struts on the choppers. The gear from Los Angeles arrived two hours later, and the other group was put together. When the choppers were ready, and the equipment checked, they assembled on a landing pad at the airport.

"All you have to do," one of the techs told the assembled pilots, "is generally face in the direction we tell you, and hold it there. The instruments will do the fine tuning. And keep track of what you're doing: I don't want to get hit by a goddamned jumbo jet because you get interested in what *we're* doing, and I don't want anybody running into anybody else."

"Glad he said that," Lucas muttered to Sloan, who was riding with the second group.

"You ready?" Sloan asked. Lucas feared airplanes in a way that amused other cops. Sloan no longer thought it was very funny.

"Yeah."

"They're pretty safe . . ."

"Helicopters don't bother me the way planes do," Lucas said. He grinned briefly and looked up at the chopper. "I don't know why, but I can ride a chopper."

At eight forty-five they were in the air, lifting out of the airport landing zone, Lucas's group of choppers fixing themselves over I-494 south of Minneapolis, while Sloan's group hovered south of St. Paul. Below them, the lights in the cars on I-494 went by like streams of luminescent salmon, and the street and house lights stretched into the distance in a psychedelic chessboard. At nine-twenty, the techs were happy: "Let's do it," said the tech in Lucas's chopper.

And at the radio station, the DJ picked up a phone, said, "OK," looked through the glass of the broadcast booth at the engineer and the general manager behind him, and nodded.

. . . wrapping up with "Bohemian Rhapsody" from Queen. Tell you what, sports fans, it's time to play a little squeeze. Here, I'll stick my hand in the fifty-five-gallon drum . . . (There was a deep thumping, a man trapped inside an oil drum) . . . and pull out one of these telephone numbers. We'll give it ten rings. If we don't get it in ten, then we push the prize up by ninety-three dollars and try again. So . . .

John Mail listened with half an ear: he was playing one of Davenport's fantasy games on a Gateway P5-90. He was in trouble: all of Davenport's games were full of traps and reversals. When you were killed, you could restart the game, carefully edge up to the point when you were killed—and get killed by something that passed you through the first time. A back-trail trap, a switchback ambush; must be some kind of circular counting mechanism in the program, Mail thought. He felt he was learning something about the opposition.

On the tuner, the DJ's voice followed a nice set of Queen. His phony bubble-gum rap was a subliminal annoyance, but not worth changing. Mail heard the *beep-beep-boop* of the phone dialing. And when the phone rang on the radio—at that very instant—the phone rang in Andi Manette's purse.

Mail sat up, pushed away from the game with a spasm of fear. *What was that? Something outside? The cops?*

When he'd finished with Andi Manette the first night, he'd gone to the store for groceries and beer. Andi's purse was on the front seat of the van, where he'd thrown it after the attack. He opened it as he drove and pawed through it. He found her billfold, took out almost six hundred dollars, a pleasant surprise. He found her appointment book, a calculator, miscellaneous makeup, and the two pounds of junk that women seem to accumulate. He'd pushed it all back in the purse.

Later, a little drunk, and preoccupied with the question of Genevieve—the presence of the too-young girl bothered him; a kind of psychological thorn, for no reason that he understood—he dropped the purse on the floor near the kitchen door, intending to get rid of it later.

Now he stood, tense, up on the balls of his feet. *Gun,* he thought. The .45 was on a bookcase, and in two steps, he had it. Lights? No, if he turned them off, they'd know he'd heard them.

The buzzing continued. Nothing furtive about it. The fear recoiled a notch, but he kept the gun. Somebody outside? Or the stove clock? A broken smoke alarm? He moved quickly toward the kitchen, looked around—and saw the purse. In the background, the phone was ringing on the radio, the DJ said, "That's four . . ." and Mail's ear picked up the synchronized ringing between the radio and the purse.

He dumped the purse on the table. No phone, but the purse still rang at him, and was too heavy in his hand. He pulled open the front pocket and found it, a portable phone.

As he looked at it, the DJ was saying, "That's six . . . and that's seven. George Dunn, if you're on the pot you better get off, 'cause . . . that's eight . . ."

Mail turned the phone in his hands, flipped it open, saw the phone switch. He looked out the window—nothing. If it was the cops calling, they didn't know where he was.

"He's not gonna answer," the tech said. "That's nine."

Mail answered on the tenth ring. "Hello?" And Lucas jabbed a finger at the tech: "That's him."

At the radio station, the DJ leaned into it. "George Dunn? Damn, boy, you almost missed the call of your life, of the week, anyway."

And Mail could hear it all on the radio.

"This is Milo Weet at K-LIK with a We-Squeeze-It, You-Suck-It-Up; one thousand, two hundred and nine dollars on the line. You know how we play—we squeeze out a classic rock song in five seconds, the whole song, and you have ten seconds to tell us what it is. Are you ready?"

Mail knew the game. They thought his name was George Dunn, that was Manette's husband, but Weet was asking again, "Uh, George, excuse me, this is where you're supposed to say, 'Go ahead, dude,' unless you been into the vegetable matter again, in which case, give me your address and I'll be right out."

"Uh, go ahead, dude," Mail said. He'd never been on the radio. He could hear himself with his other ear, a strange, electronic echo.

"Here it comes, then, Georgie." There was a second of dead air, and then a nearly incomprehensible packet of noise with a vague rhythm to it, almost recognizable. *What was it?* Da-duh-da-Duh-da-Duh . . . *Let's see.*

The tech was working what looked like a television set, shouting at the pilot, "Hold it there, hold it, hold it . . ." while yellow numbers scrambled across the screen, and then, "Go 160, go, go . . ." and they took off, southeast.

• • •

"George? You there, boy? You got it? Tell you what, buddy, this is getting old. I'll give you another five seconds, another song by the same group. Not the same song, the same group . . ."

The tech was saying, "We've got him on, goddamn, he's right between us." He clicked on his microphone. "Frank, you got him?"

From the radio: "We got him, we're heading out at 195, but we're getting some shake in the reception . . ."

The second squirt of sound ended, and Mail said to Weet, "'All Night Long, by AC/DC.'"

He added, on the air, "Davenport, you cocksucker."

And he was gone.

13

Mail punched the Off button and with the phone still in his hand, ran outside. Overhead, a jetliner passed in-bound for Minneapolis–St. Paul. *That's how they'd come,* he thought, looking into the sky for lights, red or white, blinking, swooping, focusing on him. Choppers. An envelopment.

He ran down to the drive and piled into the van, fumbled the keys out of his jeans pocket, roared backwards out of the driveway onto the gravel road. If they were coming, and if he could get just a little bit north, maybe he could lose himself in the suburban traffic . . .

Mail wasn't frightened as much as he was excited. And angry. They'd played him for a sucker. He'd bet a hundred-to-one that Davenport was behind the call. Hell, he'd go a thousand-to-one. It was all very slick. So slick that he found himself grinning in the night, then sliding into an angry sulk, then grinning again, despite himself. Slick.

But not quite slick enough, he thought.

From a mile away, atop a hill, Mail looked back at his house. He couldn't really see it, but he could see the lighted kitchen door, which he'd left open, a thin candlestick against the dark fields. There was nothing near him—

nothing coming. He shifted into park, and let the engine idle. Nothing at all.

After a moment, he turned off the engine and got out to listen: nothing but a thin breeze blowing through the goldenrod in his headlights . . .

Andi and Grace had nearly given up on the weapon idea. The only thing they could find, that might be anything at all, was a large nail that had bent over when it was being driven into the rafters above them. If they could pull it free, Andi thought, they might be able to hone it on the granite fieldstone in the walls.

"It'd be like a short ice pick, I guess," Andi said. They had nothing to work with, except the aluminum cans that the strawberry soda came in. While they were trying to figure out how to use the cans to pull the nail free, they began experimenting with the cans themselves. They could pull the tops and bottoms off without too much trouble—Andi wrapped her fingers in her shirt, and literally tore the aluminum free. They then had a thin, flexible sheet of aluminum. They tried folding it and flattening it, with the idea of sharpening the point and using it like a knife blade.

They could get a point, but not with enough stiffness to penetrate skin and muscle deeply enough to do damage. They might get an eye.

They tried twisting the stuff into spirals, but that wasn't as good as folding it. Grace suggested that since the edges of the aluminum were quite sharp when freshly torn, if they could somehow mount an edge between folded pieces, they might be able to use it like a razor. Again, it seemed that it might cut, but not enough to do mortal damage.

"If he was ̇. . . on you, and I tried to cut his throat . . ." Grace suggested, her face pale.

Andi shook her head and pressed a strip of aluminum ingot into the back of her arm. "It takes too much force," she said. "Look."

She pressed hard, and got a long red line with just a hint of blood at one end. "It's harder to cut really deeply than you'd think. I remember from med school: the bodies cut like clay." She looked at the ceiling, and the bent nail. "The nail would do it, though. If we could get it out . . ."

"We'll just have to work on it," Grace said.

And they did, Grace sitting on Andi's shoulders, digging at the wood with small pieces of the torn aluminum. The nail head was free, but stubbornly unmoving, when they heard him coming.

Grace took her arm, and Andi was struck at how old her daughter had become. "Don't fight him," Grace said. "Please, don't fight."

But she would.

She had to. If she didn't, he might start losing interest, and look at Grace, or . . . just get rid of them. Mail wanted her to fight. Wanted to conquer her, she'd figured that much.

Mail took her out of the cell, locked it, and then spun her toward the mattress. She let herself spin, stumbled, and went down hard. Better to go down than be knocked down.

And he liked the fear in her voice. He'd beat her to inspire it, if he had to, so she'd learned to beg: "Please, John," she said. "Please, you don't have to hurt me."

"Get out of the clothes," Mail said. Andi started pulling off her blouse. But now she looked around, carefully, the fearful look pasted on her face. Was there anything in the basement that might be used in a brawl?

"Come on, hurry up, goddamnit," Mail said. He was nude, erect, coming across the basement at her.

"John . . ."

He was standing over her. "We're gonna move on, try something new. If I get bit—I really don't wanna get bit—if I get bit, I'll beat the shit out of you, then I'll take Grace down to the house and put her hands in the garbage disposal, then bring her back here so you can look at her. You got that?"

She nodded dumbly, and he said, "Okay, then . . ."

Afterwards, lying on the mattress, he said, "You know what that fuckin' Davenport did?" And he told her about the radio. "I saw it, though," he bragged. "They took me for a minute, but I saw right through it and I said it right on the air, Davenport, you cocksucker,' I said." He was animated as he talked, and they might have been teenage lovers lying on a mattress in a cold-water flat, talking about dreams. "He thinks he's pretty fuckin' smart. But what he don't know is hurtin' him."

"I . . . what?" She was responding automatically, keeping the talk going as she inventoried the basement. Mail hadn't beaten her this time, and the sex had become inconsequential; there just wasn't much more that he could do to her, and she could handle it . . . she thought.

The inventory: a stack of old terra-cotta pots in the corner—they could be thrown, or used as a club. And over there, was that a beer bottle? God, if she could get that bottle, they could break off an end of it, maybe get some glass splinters. Those would be real weapons.

Mail said, "I've got a spy watching his every move."

Andi, doing her reconnaissance, had lost track of the conversation. A spy? "A spy?" she asked. A delusion?

"Somebody you know," Mail said to her, turning to watch her reaction. "A friend of yours; put me on you in the first place."

"Who?" His voice suggested this was more than a delusion—he was too matter-of-fact.

"Can't tell you," Mail said.

"Why?"

" 'Cause I want you thinking about it. Maybe it's your husband, trying to get rid of you and the daughters. Maybe it's your mother . . ."

"My mother's dead."

"Yeah? How'd she die?"

"She drowned."

"Huh." Mail seemed about to say something else, but then he rolled to his knees, looming over her again. "Well, then, maybe it's your partner. Maybe it's your father."

She took the risk. "John, I think you're making it up."

For a moment, she thought he might strike her—his eyes widened in instant, unreflective anger, and he seemed to pull within himself, as when he beat her. But then he smiled, slightly, and said, "Yeah, I'm bullshitting you. There really is a spy. But I don't know who it is."

She shook her head.

"Called me up out of the blue," he said. "Said, 'Remember Andi Manette who sent you away? She talks about you all the time . . .'"

"Somebody said that?" She believed him now—and she was appalled.

"Yeah. Said you thought I was some kind of devil. Pretty soon I couldn't get you out of my head. I never forgot you, but you were in the back of my mind someplace. I didn't have to deal with you. But the spy called . . ."

"Yes?" A psychiatrist's prompt, and she felt a little thrill of power.

"I can remember sitting in that detention room, and you always sat there in these . . . dresses . . . you had these tits, you wore this perfume, I could see up your legs sometimes, I used to think I could see your pussy in there; I'd lay up at night and think about it. Could I see it? Or maybe not . . ."

"I didn't realize . . ." Another prompt.

"You never knew what made me work, and I couldn't explain it," Mail said. "After a while I'd just sit there and look at your tits and burn."

"Somebody kept calling you?"

"I don't wanna talk any more," he said, the anger suddenly back. And his eyes turned inward, jelled over. "I want to fuck . . ." He swatted at her and hit her on a shoulder. She quailed away, and he said, "Get over here, or I'll really fuckin' beat your ass."

Later she said, "Can I call somebody? My husband, or somebody, to tell them that we're alive?"

He was irritated. "Fuck no."

"John, pretty soon they'll think we're dead. Pretty soon all this activity will die down, and it'll just be one long grinding hunt, and they'll get you and lock you up forever. If they know I'm alive, you might be able to . . . move better. There might be a deal somewhere, something you can work."

Again, talking almost like lovers: she concerned for his future. He shook it off. "There won't be any deal. Not with me."

"It gives you more power," she said. "If they convince themselves that I'm dead, they can do anything they want. If they know I'm alive, things'll be more awkward for them. As a gamer, I'm sure you can see that. And I just want people to know that I'm still out here. I don't want them to forget me."

Mail stood up, began to dress, kicked her clothes at her. "Put them on." And when she was dressed, he said, "I'll think about it. You can't call direct, but maybe we could tape something. I could call the tape in from somewhere else."

"John, that would be . . ." She almost laughed. "That would be great."

He reacted to that: he puffed up, she thought. He liked the flattery, especially from her. "I'll think about it."

Back inside the cell, after the door had closed and his feet had thumped away, she said to Grace, "We've got to think of a message to tape—he might tape a message for us. We have to figure out a code, or something."

She was excited, and Grace watched her, her young face solemn, withdrawn, and Andi finally said, "What? What?"

And Grace said, "You've got blood all over your face, Mom. It's all over."

Grace pointed to the right side of Andi's face and suddenly her hand began to shake with fear, and she began to cry, backing away from Andi, and Andi scrubbed at the side of her face and the blood from her nose that had dried there, after Mail, excited, had begun slapping her during the last sexual frenzy.

She hadn't noticed the blood, she thought, as Grace huddled in the corner. She was becoming used to it; a condition of her servitude.

But things had changed this time. Things had changed.

14

Rose Marie Roux, looking too tired to be a chief of police, her purse dangling from her hand, struggled up the stairs and through the open door.

Lucas followed the chief and T. Conrad Haward— Dumbo—into Manette's house, to a gathering in the ornate living room. Dunn was there, tense, unhappy, hair in disarray, eyes heavy; he had his back to a cold fireplace, a heavy crystal liquor glass in his hand. He looked past Roux and Dumbo to nod at Lucas.

Helen Manette perched on an antique chair, mouth too wide and too tight, and Lucas thought she might be drunk, although she wasn't drinking anything. Nancy Wolfe, in a soft, moss-colored suit, glared at him from across the room. When he looked steadily back, she bounced her hair and looked away. She was sipping from a small cognac glass, and posed in front of a nineteenth-century oil painting of a woman with cold, dark eyes, a coal-black dress, and a surprisingly sensual lower lip.

The gofer attorney was getting drinks; a Minneapolis Intelligence cop in a plaid sportcoat and t-shirt, with a bump on his hip that was probably a large automatic, leaned in a doorway and gobbled popcorn from a plastic sack. He was waiting for the phone call that had never come, and looked bored.

Manette stood in the center of the circle, wearing a gray suit with an Italian necktie, the knot tight at his throat. He was worn and older than he'd looked only the day before. But somehow, down in his soul, Lucas thought, watching him, Manette also enjoyed being at the center of a tragedy.

"No-go," the chief said to Manette, shaking her head. "I'm sorry."

"Shit." Dunn turned away from them, and Lucas thought he might chunk the bourbon glass into the fireplace. Instead, he leaned against the rock-facing, head down.

"Not a complete loss," Dumbo said. A fine patina of sweat covered his forehead. He hated dealing with the rich, people who knew U.S. Senators by their nicknames and toilet habits. "We had him on, but we couldn't hold him long enough. We had him for twenty seconds and he figured it out. We've got an idea where he is: south of the rivers, down in Eagan or Apple Valley."

"You've got projects down there," Manette said to Dunn.

Dunn turned around, his face sullen, a little heat lightning in his eyes. "Yeah, but I wasn't answering any telephones down there tonight," he growled.

"That's not what I meant," Manette said, squaring off to Dunn. "I meant, you know the area."

Nancy Wolfe caught Tower's jacket sleeve and pulled him back an inch, and Dunn said, "Yeah, and I know there're three hundred thousand people in the fuckin' area . . ."

"Watch your mouth," Manette snapped. "There are women here."

Lucas, now watching Wolfe, behind Manette, her hand on his sleeve, thought: *Huh.*

"He, uh, mentioned Davenport," Dumbo said, looking at Lucas. "He apparently, uh, feels Chief Davenport is"—he groped for a word, finally found one—"*responsible* for the"—he groped for another one—"radio procedure."

"Well, he is," Dunn said to Dumbo. "He's the only cop I've talked to so far doesn't have his head up his ass."

"George . . ." Manette said, his face still red under his shock of white hair. Dunn ignored him and stepped closer to Lucas. "I want to put up a reward. I don't care how much. A million."

"Not that much," Lucas said. "We'd have freaks coming out of the woodwork. Start at fifty thousand."

"Good. I'm gonna announce it right now," Dunn said. He looked at Manette, but Manette said nothing, just shook his head with a sour, skeptical smile and turned away from them all.

On the way out, the chief said, "Happy little family."

"Nancy Wolfe, Tower Manette, what do you think?"

Nothing surprised Rose Marie Roux: she'd been in politics too long. After a moment of silence, she said, in a voice that was almost pleased, "It's possible. When we briefed them last night, she touched the back of his hand."

"And tonight, she tried to stop him from fighting Dunn . . . or made a move that way. Protective."

"Huh," the chief said. Then, "You know, Lucas, you have a strong feminine side."

"What?"

"Never mind," she said.

"No, what'd you mean?" Lucas was amused.

The chief said, "You're more willing than most men to rely on intuition. I mean, you suspect that Nancy Wolfe and Tower Manette are having an affair."

"There's no question about it," he said. "Now that I think about it."

"Because she caught his sleeve." Now Roux was amused. "That's a pretty good leap."

"It was *how* she touched his sleeve," Lucas said. "If that's feminine, I accept the label."

"What'd you think I meant?" Roux asked.

"I don't know," he said vaguely. "Maybe, you know—I had nice tits."

Roux started to laugh: "Christ, I'm running a fuckin' zoo, the people I've got."

The middle of the night, all foul-mouthed, their shirts seeming to pull willfully out of their pants and rumple on their own, they stood around a six-by-five Metro wall map and looked at the red-crayoned box southeast of the airport.

"It's something," Lester insisted. "He was smarter than we gave him credit for. Christ, another minute. One more minute and we've got him."

Lucas threw a paper coffee cup at a waste basket, the old coffee like acid in his mouth. "We gotta go for the full-court press. He'll be calling back. I'm surprised he hasn't already."

"We can do it with the next shift," Anderson says. "Right now, we'd be eighty percent. By tomorrow morning, we'll be at full strength."

"We gotta be ready to do it now," Lucas said.

"We are—just not a hundred percent. It's a matter of getting people through the shifts," Anderson said.

"We should flood the 494 strip, and extra people down I-35 all the way through Apple Valley," Lucas said.

"Smart little fuck," Lester said, staring moodily at the map.

Weather was asleep and moaned softly when he slipped into bed. He needed to wake her up to talk, but she would be cutting on someone in the morning, and he didn't dare do it. Instead, he lay awake for an hour, plotting the twists and turns of the day, feeling the warmth from Weather seeping over him. He finally slept, one arm at her waist, the smell of Chanel around him.

Weather was gone, and Lucas was just out of the shower when the cellular phone rang. He stopped, listening, then hurried into the living room, trailing streams of water. He'd left the phone on the dining room table, and now he picked it up and clicked it on.

"Lucas, how they hanging?" Mail sounded unnaturally cheerful.

"Are they still alive?" The squad cars should be rolling. Thirty seconds.

"Are you trying to trace me?"

Lucas hesitated, then repeated his original question: "Are they alive, or not?" Lucas asked.

"Yeah, they're alive," Mail said grudgingly. "In fact, I've got a message for you from Andi Manette."

"Let me get a pencil," Lucas said.

"Oh, horseshit, this is all recorded," Mail said impatiently. "Not that it's gonna do you any good. I'm using the cellular, but this time I'm riding around, a long way from anywhere."

Shit. "Go ahead: I've got a pencil."

"Here it is. I don't know how clear it'll be . . ."

George, Daddy, Genevieve, Aunt Lisa, this is Andi. We're okay, Grace and me, and we hope Genevieve is back and everything is fine with her. The man with us won't let us say anything about him, but he was good enough to let us send this. I hope we can talk to you again, and this man with us, please give him whatever he wants so we can come back safely. That's all I can say . . .

Andi Manette's voice was plaintive, fearful, trembling with hope; cut off with a click of a recorder button.

"That's all for now, sports fans," Mail said cheerfully. "I have to say, though, I liked the disk-jockey thing. It really woke me up. Tell the guy I'm gonna stop by his house and visit his family some day while he's gone. I'm gonna bring a pair of wire cutters with me. We're gonna have a lot of fun."

When Mail hung up, Lucas turned the phone off, laid it on the table, and stared at it like an ebony cockroach; fifteen seconds later, Martha Gresham called from the communications center and said, "We got it all."

"Excellent. Is Lester there?"

"No, but Donna's talking to him now, so he knows."

Lucas hurried back to the bedroom and dressed, waiting for the phone to ring. It rang as he was knotting the tie: "Yeah, Frank. Was it her?"

"It's her. And she's trying to tell us something, but we don't know what," Lester said.

"How do you know?"

"Because she said hello to her aunt Lisa."

"Yeah?"

"I talked to Tower Manette one minute ago," Lester said. "Her aunt Lisa's been dead for ten years."

"Get somebody going: we need everything we can get on the aunt."

"We're going, but I want you looking at it," Lester said. "Goddamnit, Lucas, we need somebody to pull a rabbit out of a hat."

Lucas said, "You gotta cover Milo, over at the station. And his family. He's got two kids himself."

"We're on the way. But what about Genevieve?"

"Genevieve's dead," Lucas said. "We know that, but Andi Manette doesn't."

They did a group therapy with Manette and Dunn, in Roux's office: why Aunt Lisa?

"Lisa Farmer was my first wife's sister," Manette said. "She had this big place out in the country, with horses, and when Andi was a kid she'd go out and ride. Maybe she's telling us that the guy's a farmer—or that he's a horse guy, or something. It's gotta be something like that."

"Unless she's just lost it," Dunn said quietly.

"My daughter . . ." Manette started.

"Hey." Dunn pointed a finger at Manette, his voice cold. "I know you love your daughter, Tower, but I do too, and frankly, I know her better. She is fucked up. Her voice has changed, her manner's changed, she is desperate and she's hurt. I want to think that she's sending a message, but I don't want to cut off everything and just concentrate on that one thing. Because it's possible that she's lost it."

Manette looked away, sideways at nothing, down at the floor. Dunn, uncomfortable, patted him on the back, then looked across Manette at Lucas. "Genevieve's dead, isn't she?"

"You better be ready," Lucas said.

They would do a fast scan of farms and horses, running the Dakota County agricultural assessment rolls against sex crime records and other lists. Lucas got Anderson's running case log and carried it back to his office and read for a while. Nothing occurred to him. Restless, he wandered down to Homicide, and ran into Black and Sherrill.

"What's happening at the U?" he asked.

"We've got five more possibles, including one with fire and sex. We're looking for him now," Sherrill said. She held up a stack of files. "You want Xeroxes?"

"Yeah. Anderson said something about the one guy—Mail?—that he was a washout?"

"Yeah," Black said. "Really washed out. He washed out of the river. He's dead."

"Shit," Lucas said. "He sounded good."

Sherrill nodded. "They let him out of St. Peter and two months later he went off the Lake Street Bridge, middle of the night. They found him down by Fort Snelling. He'd been in the water for a week."

"How'd they ID him?" Lucas asked.

"They found a state ID card on the body," Sherrill said. "The ME went ahead and did a dental on him; it was him."

"All right," Lucas nodded. "Who's this other guy, the fire and sex guy?"

"Francis Xavier Peter, age—now—thirty-four. He set sixteen fires in ten days out in St. Louis Park, nobody hurt, several houses damaged. We talked to his parents, and they say he's out on the West Coast being an actor. They haven't heard from him lately, and he doesn't have a phone. Andi Manette treated him; he was a patient for two years. She didn't like him much. He came on to her during a couple of therapy sessions."

"An actor?"

"That's what they say," Sherrill said.

"This guy we're dealing with," Lucas said, "he could be an actor. He likes games . . ."

"One thing," Black said. "Francis Xavier Peter is a blond and wore his hair long."

"Jesus: could be the guy. Does he look anything like the composite?" Lucas asked.

"He has a round face, sort of German-country boy," Sherrill said.

"What you mean is, *No*," Lucas said. "He doesn't look like the composite."

"Not too much," she conceded.

"Well, push it," Lucas said.

15

The voice was tense: "They're getting close to you. You've got to move on."

Mail, standing in the litter of two decapitated mini-tower systems—he was switching out hard drives—sneered at the phone, and the distant personality at the end of it. "Say what you mean. You don't mean, *move on*. You mean, kill them and dump them."

"I mean, get yourself out," the voice said. "I didn't think anything like this was going to happen . . ."

"Bullshit," Mail said. "You thought you were manipulating me. You were pushing my buttons."

He could hear the breathing on the other end—exasperation, desperation, anticipation? Mail would have enjoyed knowing. Someday, he thought, he'd figure the voice out. Then . . . "Besides, they're nowhere near as close as you think. You just want me to get rid of them."

"Did you know that Andi Manette sent a message with that tape recording you let her make? Her aunt is dead—she's been dead a long time. Her name was Lisa Farmer, and she lived on a farm. And they're looking in Dakota County, at farmhouses, because that's where they put you with that little cellular phone trick. You don't have much time now."

Click.

Mail looked at the phone, then dropped it back on the hook and wandered around the living room, whistling, stepping over computer parts. The tune he whistled came from the bad old days at the hospital, when they piped Minnesota Public Radio into the cells. Simple Mozart: he'd probably heard it a hundred times. Mail had no time for Mozart. He wanted rhythm, not melody. He wanted sticks hammering out a blood-beat; he wanted drums, tambourines, maracas. He wanted timpani. He didn't want tinkly music.

But now he whistled it, a little Mozart two-finger melody, because he didn't want to think about Andi Manette tricking him, because he didn't want to kill her yet.

Had she done this? She had—he knew it in his heart. And it made him so *angry.* Because he'd trusted her. He'd given her an opportunity, and she'd betrayed him. This *always* happened. He should have known it was going to happen again. He put his hands to his temples, he could feel the blood beating through them, the pain that was going to come. Christ, this was the story of his life: when he tried to do something, somebody *always* spoiled it.

He took several laps around the living room and the kitchen, opened the refrigerator door, looked blindly inside, slammed it; the whistling began a humming noise deep in his throat, and the humming became a growl—still two-finger Mozart—and then he walked out the back door and cut across the lawn toward the pasture beyond, and the old house in the back.

He jumped the fallen-down fence, passed an antique iron disker half-buried in the bluestem and asters; halfway up the hill, he was running, his fists clenched, his eyes like frosted marbles.

They thought they were making progress, working on Mail: he hadn't become gentle, but Andi felt a relationship forming. If she didn't exactly have power, she had influence.

And they were still working on the nail. They couldn't

move it, but a full inch of it was exposed. A few more hours, she thought, and they might pull it free.

Then Mail came.

They heard him running across the floor above them, *pounding* down the stairs. She and Grace looked at each other. Something was happening, and Grace, who'd been squatting in front of the game monitor, rocked uneasily.

Then the door opened, and Mail's face was a boiled-egg mask with the turned-in, frosted-marble eyes, his hair bushed like a frightened cat's. He said, "Get the fuck out here."

Grace could hear the beating.

She could feel it, even through the steel door. She stretched herself up the door and pounded on it and cried, "Mom, mama, mother. Mom . . ."

And after a while, she stopped and went back to the mattress and put her hands on her ears so she couldn't hear. A few minutes later, weeping, she closed her eyes and put her hands on her mouth like the speak-no-evil monkey and felt herself a traitor. She wanted the beating to stop, but she wouldn't cry out. She didn't want Mail to come for *her*.

An hour after he'd taken Andi, Mail brought her back. Always, in the past, her mother had been clothed when Mail put her back in the room: this time, she was nude, as was Mail himself.

Grace huddled back against the wall as he stood in the doorway, facing her, the hostile frontality frightening as nothing else ever had been. Finally, she bowed her head between her knees and closed her eyes and began to sing to herself, to close out the world. Mail listened to her for a moment, then a tiny, bitter smile crossed his face, and he shut the door with a *clang*.

Andi didn't move.

When the door closed, Grace was afraid to look up—afraid that Mail might be inside the room with her. But after a few seconds, when nothing moved, she peeked. He was gone.

Grace whispered, "Mother? Mom?"

Andi moaned and turned to look at her daughter, and blood ran out of her mouth.

16

Lucas put down the file and picked up the phone. "Lucas Davenport."

"Yeah, um, I'm a game player?" The woman's voice was tentative, slightly unplugged. Her statements came as questions. "I was told I should talk to you?"

"Yes?"

He was impatient; he was waiting for the LA cops to get back with information on Francis Xavier Peter, the fire-starting actor.

"I think, um, I've seen the guy in the picture," the woman said. "I played D&D with him a couple of months ago, in this girl's house? In Dinkytown?"

Lucas sat up. "Do you know his name, or where he lives?"

"No, but he was with this girl, and we were at her house, so she knows him."

"How sure are you?"

"I wouldn't be sure except for his eyes? The eyes are the same. The mouth's different? But the eyes are right? And he was really a gamer, he was a good dungeon master, he knew everything. But he was scary? Really wired? And something this girl said made me think he'd been in treatment?"

Lucas looked at his watch. "Where are you? I'd like to come over and talk." He wrote it down.

"Sloan, c'mon," Lucas said.

The narrow man got his jacket, a new one, a new shade of brown. "Where're we going?"

Lucas explained as they walked out. "She had a sound about her," Lucas said. "I don't think it's bullshit."

The woman lived in a student apartment complex across I-494 from the university. Lucas put the gray city Plymouth in a fire zone and they went inside, following a blonde co-ed in a short skirt and bowling jacket. They all stopped at the elevator, Sloan and Lucas looking at the girl from the corners of their eyes; she was very pretty, with round blue eyes and a *retroussé* nose that might have been natural. The girl studied the numbers at the top of the elevator doors with rapt attention. Nobody said anything. The elevator came, they all got on, and all three watched the numbers at the top of the door.

The woman got off at three, turned, smiled, and walked away. The doors closed and Sloan said, "I think she smiled at me."

"I beg your pardon," Lucas said. "I believe it was me she smiled at."

"Bullshit. You stepped in front of it, that's all."

Cindy McPherson, the gamer, was a confused Wisconsin milkmaid. She was a large girl with a perfect complexion and a sweet country smile, who dressed in black from head to foot, and wore a seven-pointed star around her neck on a leather shoestring.

"The more I looked at the picture, the more I was sure it was him," she said. She sat on the edge of the Salvation Army couch, using her hands to talk: Lucas had the impression that under the black dress was a former high school basketball jock. "There's something about his face," she said. "It's like a coyote's—he's got those narrow eyes and the cheekbones. He could've been pretty sexy, but it was like there was something . . . missing. He just didn't connect. I think he connected with Gloria, though. She was pawing him."

"This Gloria—what's her last name?"

She shrugged. "I don't know. I've seen her around with people, we hang out over there, but she's not a good friend of mine. A couple of years ago, there were some raves over, like, in the industrial park up 280? That's where I met her. Then I'd see her over in Dinkytown, and a couple of months ago I saw her and she said they were starting a game. So I went up and he was the dungeon master."

"Can you show us the place?" Sloan asked.

"Sure. And Gloria's name is on the mailbox. She checked her mailbox when we were going up the stairs and I saw that it said Gloria something."

Dinkytown is an island of well-worn commerce off the campus at the University of Minnesota, two- and three-story buildings selling clothes and fast food and compact discs and pharmaceuticals and Xerox copies. They were backing into a parking space when McPherson pointed across the street and said, "There she is. That's Gloria. And that's her building."

Gloria was a thin, hunch-shouldered woman, dressed, like McPherson, in head-to-toe black; like McPherson, she wore an amulet. But while McPherson had that perfect, open face and peaches-and-cream complexion, Gloria was dark, saturnine, her face closed and wary like a fox's.

"Wait here, or go get a sandwich or something," Lucas said to McPherson. "We might have some more questions for you."

He and Sloan scrambled through the traffic and hurried through the apartment house door. Gloria was just locking her mailbox and held a green electric-bill envelope in her teeth.

"Gloria?" Lucas was out front.

She took the envelope out and looked at them. "Yes?"

"We're police officers, we'd . . .

"Like your help," Sloan finished.

• • •

Gloria Crosby might have been pretty, but she wasn't: she was unkempt, a little dirty, her face was formed in a frown. She reluctantly took them to her apartment on the top floor. "Been working on a thesis, haven't had much time to clean," she said. When she opened her door, the apartment smelled of tomato soup and feathers, with an overlay of tobacco and marijuana.

"Do a little grass from time to time?" Sloan asked cheerfully.

"I don't, no," she said. She seemed almost slow. "Marijuana makes you more stupid than you already are. Some people choose that, and I say, 'Okay.' But I don't choose it."

"Smells sort of grassy up here," Sloan said.

"A couple of people were visiting last night, and they smoked," she said offhandedly. "I didn't."

"You don't think that's wrong?" Lucas asked.

"No, do you?"

Lucas shrugged and Sloan laughed. Sloan said, "About two months ago, you played D&D up here with a group of five people. The dungeon master was this man. We need his name." He handed her a copy of the composite.

Crosby took the flier, looked at it for a long time. Then her forehead wrinkled and she said, "Well—this isn't the guy, but I know who you're talking about. He looks sort of like this, but the eyes are wrong. His name is . . . David." She dropped her hand to her side and went to a window and looked down at the street and pulled on her lower lip.

Lucas said, "What . . ."

She put up a hand to silence him, continued to look down at the street. After a moment, "David . . . Ellers. E-L-L-E-R-S. God, I almost forgot. Tells you about my relationships, huh?"

"Do you know . . ."

"How'd you know about the game?" she asked, turning to look at them. She was interested, but totally unflustered: so unflustered that Lucas wondered if she was on medication.

"I'm in the gaming net, besides being a cop," Lucas said.

She pointed a finger at him and said, with the first flicker of animation, "Davenport."

"Yeah."

"You did some wicked games, before you went to computers," she said. "Your computer games suck."

"Thanks," Lucas said, dryly. "Do you know where this guy lives?"

"He's the guy who took the Manette chick?"

"Well, we're looking into that . . ."

"I think you're barking up the wrong tree," she said. "David was from Connecticut and he was on his way to California."

"I got the impression that you knew him pretty well," Lucas said.

She sighed, dropped into a chair. "Well, he stayed here for a week and fucked me every day, but he was just here that one week."

"What kind of a car did he have?" Lucas asked.

She snorted and showed what might have been either a smile or a grimace. "A traveling gamer, on his way to California? What do you think?"

Lucas thought a minute, and then said, "A Harley."

"Absolutely," Gloria said. "A Harley-Davidson sportster. He tried to scam me: he said he'd love to take me with him, but he needed the money to trade up to a softtail. I told him to pick me up when he got it."

She had few details about David Ellers: she'd met him at a McDonald's, where he was arguing with some people about the MYST game. He didn't have a place to stay, and he looked nice, so she asked if he wanted to stay over. He did, for a week.

"I hated to see him go," she said. "He was *intense.*"

He was from Connecticut, she said. "I think his parents had money, like insurance or something. He was from Hartford, maybe."

"What do you think?" Lucas asked Sloan when they were back on the street. McPherson was walking back toward them, eating a cheeseburger, carrying a McDonald's bag.

"I don't know," Sloan said. "If she was lying, she was good at it. But it didn't sound like the truth, either. Goddamn dopers, it's hard to tell. They don't have that edge of fear."

They got to the car just as McPherson did; she offered some fries to Lucas and Sloan, and seemed slightly chagrined when Sloan took some. "What happened?" she asked.

"She said he was passing through," Lucas said, briefly. "She said his name is David Ellers, he's from Connecticut, and he was on his way to the West Coast."

McPherson had taken a large bite out of the cheeseburger, but she stopped chewing for a moment, then looked sideways out the car window, shook her head at Lucas, finished chewing, swallowed, licked her lips, and said, "God: when you said that, Connecticut, it popped into my head. I asked this guy if he knew my friend David, because they both came from the same town. Wayzata. But he said he went to a private school and didn't know him."

"Wayzata?" Sloan asked.

"I'm pretty sure," she said.

"Gloria said *his* name was David," Lucas said.

McPherson shook her head. "It wasn't. I would have remembered that—I mean, two Davids from the same town and the same age and all."

Sloan sighed and looked at Lucas. "God, it's a shame the way young people lie to us nowadays."

"And the old people," Lucas said. "And the middle-aged." To McPherson he said, "C'mon. Let's go see if she remembers you, and if that helps her remember the guy's name."

"Jeez, I kinda hate to be seen with cops," McPherson said.

"Is that what they taught you in Wisconsin?" Sloan asked as they got back out of the car.

"Nope. They taught me that if I get lost, ask a cop. So I got over here at the U, and I got lost, and I asked a cop. He wanted to take me home. With him, I mean."

"Must've been a St. Paul cop," Lucas said. "C'mon, let's go."

• • •

They climbed the stairs again, but when they knocked on Gloria's door, there was no answer. "Could be visiting another apartment," Sloan said. But it didn't feel that way. The building was silent, nothing moving.

Lucas walked down to the end of the hall and looked out a window: "Fire escape," he said. An old iron drop-ladder fire escape hung on the side of the building. He checked the window above it, and the window slid open easily. "The window's unlocked from inside. Goes down the back."

He leaned out: nothing moved.

Sloan said, "She's running."

Lucas said, "And she knows him—you go that way."

Sloan ran for the stairs, while Lucas went out the window and ran down the fire escape. At the top of the lowest flight, he had to wait for a counter-weight to drop the stairs to a narrow walkway between the apartment and the next building. The walkway was filled with debris, blown paper, a few boards, a bent and rusting real-estate sign, and wine bottles. Lucas looked one way toward the street, and the other toward an alley that ran along the back of the buildings. If she'd gone out to the street, they should have seen her. He ran the other way, toward the alley, high-stepping over dried dog shit and a knee-high pile of what looked like cat litter. Just down the alley was the rear door of a pizza shop, with a window. Behind the window, a kid was hosing down dishes in a stainless-steel sink. Lucas went to the door and pushed through: and a woman leaned against a counter, smoking a cigarette, and the kid looked up. "Hey," she said, straightening up. "You're not supposed to . . ."

"I'm a cop," Lucas said. "Did either of you guys see a woman come down the fire escape in back of the building across the alley? Five, six minutes ago?"

The woman and the dishwasher looked at each other and then the dishwasher said, "I guess. Skinny, dressed in black?"

"That's her," Lucas said. "Did you see where she went?"

"She walked up that way . . ." The dishwasher pointed.

"Was she in a hurry?"

"Yeah. She sort of skipped, and she was carrying like a laundry bag. She went around the corner. What'd she do?"

Lucas left without answering, ran down to the corner. There was a bus stop, with nobody waiting. He ran across a street, into a bakery, flashed his badge and asked to use a phone: a flour-dusted fat man led him into the back and pointed at a wall phone. Lucas called Dispatch: "She might be on a bus, or she might be walking someplace. But flood it: we're looking for a tall, pale woman in her middle twenties, dressed all in black, probably in a hurry, probably carrying a bag of some kind. Maybe a sack. Check for a car registration and get that out."

Back on the street, he looked both ways: he could see three or four women dressed in black. One might have been Crosby, but when she turned to cross a street, Lucas, running up from behind, saw it wasn't her. A cop flashed by: two guys looking out the windows. Lucas turned back: there were students everywhere.

Too many of them in black.

Lucas walked back to the apartment's front door. Sloan turned the corner and walked toward him from the other end of the street. Sloan shook his head, took off his hat, smoothed his hair, and said, "Didn't see a thing."

"Goddamnit, this is just like the fuckin' game store. We were this close," Lucas said, showing an inch between his thumb and forefinger. He looked up at the building. "Let's see if there's a manager."

A glassed-over building directory showed a manager in 3A; his wife sent them down the basement, where they found him building a box kite.

Lucas explained the problem, and asked, "Have you got a key?"

"Sure." The manager had a thick German accent. He gave the box kite a final tweak, tightened a balsa-wood joint with a c-clamp, and said, "Gum dis vay." He didn't mention a warrant.

• • •

McPherson was waiting in the hall outside Gloria's room. "Could you take a cab?" Lucas asked.

"Well . . ."

"Here's twenty bucks; that's to cover the cab and buy you dinner," he said, handing her the bill. "And thanks. If you think of anything . . ."

"I've got your number," she nodded.

The manager let them into Gloria's apartment. They did a quick walk-through: something was bothering Lucas—he'd seen something, but he didn't know what. Something his eye had picked up. But when? During the talk with Crosby? No. It was just now . . . he looked around, couldn't think of it. *Getting old,* he thought.

"Do you know any of her friends?" Lucas asked the manager, with little hope.

The German went through an elaborate, Frenchlike shrug, and said, "Not me."

They knocked on every door in the building, with the manager trailing behind them. Few people were in their apartments, and nobody had seen her. Two patrol cops showed up and Lucas said, "Go with the manager. He has legal access, so you don't need a search warrant. Check every single apartment. Don't mess with anything, just check for the girl." As they were walking away, he called, "Look under the beds," and one of the cops said, with an edge, "Right, chief."

Lucas, scowling, turned and said to Sloan, "Find the best picture you can, get it back to the office, and get it out. Tell Rose Marie to hand it out to the press."

"What're you doing?" Sloan asked.

Lucas looked around. "I'm gonna tear the place to pieces, see what I can see. Oh. Get somebody to check the phone company, see if she just made a call."

"All right. And maybe I ought to get a search warrant."

"Yeah, yeah, yeah."

Sloan started looking, while Lucas did another walk-through. The apartment had only three rooms—a living room with a kitchenette at one end, a tiny bath, and a small bedroom.

A battered bureau, probably from the Salvation Army store, was pushed against one wall of the bedroom. Several drawers stood open. He'd glanced in the bedroom during the original interview, and he didn't remember the drawers being open: so she'd taken some clothes. He lifted her mattress, looked under it. Nothing. He tossed the bureau drawers onto the mattress. Nothing. Rolled her shoes out of a closet, patted down her clothes. Nothing.

He walked back out to the kitchenette, looked in the refrigerator, pulled out the ice trays. He checked every scrap of paper within reach of the telephone. In ten minutes he had a dozen phone numbers, mostly scrawled on the backs of junk-mail envelopes, a few more on a phone book. He checked the exchanges: none was in Eagan, or Apple Valley, or down that way. He stacked the phone book on the counter with the envelopes, mentioned them to Sloan.

He went to the bathroom next and peered into the medicine cabinet. There were a dozen brown pill bottles on the top shelf, lined up like chessmen. "She's got some weird meds," Lucas called to Sloan. "Let's find out where she gets them and what they're for. Get somebody to check the local pharmacies and maybe the U clinic. This looks like serious shit, so she might need some more."

"Okay," Sloan called back. Lucas opened the door to a small linen closet—women hid things in linen closets, refrigerators, and bureau drawers. He found nothing useful.

Sloan stuck his head in. "She didn't like cameras," he said. He showed Lucas a handful of Polaroids and a couple of prints. She was always in black, almost always alone, standing against something. The few other people in the prints were women.

"So get them all out," Lucas said briefly. He slammed a drawer shut, and they heard glass breaking inside.

"All right," Sloan said. Then: "Chill out, man. We'll get her, sooner or later. You're freaking out."

"She knows him, goddamnit," Lucas said. He turned and kicked the bathroom wall, the toe of his shoe breaking through the drywall. They both stood and looked at the hole for a second. Then Lucas said, "She knows who the motherfucker is, and where the motherfucker is, and we let her go."

17

Anderson tracked Gloria Crosby through the state records, starting with a driver's license to get her exact age, then into the national crime computers—she'd been twice convicted of shoplifting from Walgreen's drug stores—and through the court records into the mental health system. Crosby had been in and out of treatment programs and hospitals since she was a young teenager; her home address was listed as North Oaks, a suburban bedroom north of St. Paul.

"We oughta get some people up there," Anderson said, leaning in the office door.

"I'm not doing anything except reading the book," Lucas said, taking his feet out of his desk drawer. "Is Sloan still wandering around?"

"He was drinking coffee down in Homicide."

They took Lucas's Porsche, Sloan driving it hard. Lucas said, "I hope Gloria doesn't set our guy off. If he gets the feeling that people *know* . . ."

Sloan, grunting as he shifted up and hammered the Porsche through the North Oaks entry, said, "If I was Gloria, I'd be very fucking careful. Very careful." The address came up, a small redwood rambler that looked out of place among the larger homes. The house was set into a low rise, with a split-rail fence defining the yard. Sloan asked, "Put it right in the driveway?"

"Yeah. I'll take the back."

"Sure."

Sloan squealed into the driveway, hit the brakes, and they were out, Lucas heading around the side of the house. The grass on the open parts of the yard had been thoroughly burned off, though the summer hadn't been especially hot or dry. In the shadier spots, it was long and ragged, untended.

Sloan walked up to the front door, passed a picture window with drawn curtains, stopped, peered through a crack in the curtains, saw nobody, and rang the doorbell.

Marilyn Crosby was a slight, gray-haired woman, stooped, suspicious, her face lined with worry. She stood in the doorway, one hand clutching her housecoat at the throat. "I haven't seen her or heard from her since last spring, some time. She wanted money. I gave her seventy-five dollars; but we're not close any more."

"We need to talk," Sloan said, low-keyed, relaxing. "She may be involved with the man who did the Manette kidnapping. We need to know as much about her as we can—who her friends are."

"Well . . ." She was reluctant, but finally pushed the door open and stepped back. Sloan followed her in.

"She's not here, is she?" Sloan asked.

"No. Of course not." Crosby frowned. "I wouldn't lie to the police."

Sloan looked at her, nodded. "All right. Where's your back door?"

"Through there, through the kitchen . . . What?"

Sloan walked through the kitchen with its odor of old coffee grounds and rancid potatoes and pushed open the back door.

"Lucas . . . yeah, c'mon."

"You had me surrounded?" Crosby seemed offended.

"We really need to find your daughter," Sloan said. Lucas came inside, and Sloan said, "So let's talk. Is your husband home?"

"He's dead," Crosby said. She turned and walked back into the house, Sloan and Lucas trailing behind. She led them to a darkened living room, with a shag carpet and drawn curtains. The television was tuned to *Wheel of Fortune*. A green wine bottle sat next to a lamp on a corner table. Crosby dropped into an overstuffed chair and pulled up her feet.

"He was out cutting a limb off an apple tree, got dizzy, and went like that." She snapped her fingers. "He had seventy thousand in insurance. That was it. I can't get at his pension until I'm fifty-seven."

"That's a tragedy," Sloan said.

"Three years ago last month, it was," she said, looking up at Sloan with rheumy eyes. "You know what his last words to me were? He said, 'Boy, I feel like shit.' How's that for last words?"

"Honest," Lucas muttered.

"What?" She looked at him, the suspicion right at the surface. Sloan turned so Crosby couldn't see his face, and rolled his eyes. Lucas was stepping on his act.

"Have you seen this man? He might have been younger when he came around," Sloan said, turning back to Marilyn Crosby. He handed her the composite drawing. She studied it for a moment and then said, "Maybe. Oh, last winter, maybe, he might have come around once. But his hair was different."

"Were they with anyone else?"

"No, just the two of them," she said, passing the composite back. "They were only here for a minute. He was a big guy, though. Sort of mean-looking, like he could fight. Not the kind Gloria usually came back with."

"What type was that?"

"Bums, mostly," Crosby said flatly. "No-goods who never did anything." Then, confidentially, to Sloan: "You know, Gloria's crazy. She got it from her father's side of the family. Several crazy people there—though, of course, I didn't know it until it was too late."

"We need the names of all her friends," Lucas said.

"Friends or relatives that she might turn to. Anybody. Doctors."

"I don't know anything like that. Well, I know a doctor."

"There's a reward for information leading to an arrest," Lucas said. "Fifty thousand."

"Oh, really?" Marilyn Crosby brightened. "Well, I could go get the things she left here. Or maybe you'd like to come up and look in her room. You'd know better than I do what you're looking for."

"That'd be good," Sloan said.

Gloria Crosby's bedroom was an eleven-foot-square cubicle with a window in one wall, a bed, and a small pine desk and matching dresser. The dresser was empty, but the desk was stuffed with school papers, music tapes, rubber bands, broken pencils, crayons, rock 'n' roll concert badges, drawings, calendars, pushpins.

"Usual stuff," Sloan said. He went through it all. Lucas helped for a few minutes, then found Marilyn Crosby in the kitchen, drinking from the wine bottle, and got the name of Gloria's last doctor. He looked the name up in the phone book, noted the address, and called Sherrill, who was doing phone work on the patients they'd uncovered at the university. "Anything you can get," Lucas said.

When he got back to the bedroom, he lay down on Gloria Crosby's bed, a narrow, sagging single-width that was too short by six inches. A Mr. Happy Tooth poster hung on the wall opposite the bed. "Hi! I'm Gloria!" was written in careful block letters on the cartoon molar. The molar was doing a root dance on a red line that might have been an infected gum.

"Three names so far," Sloan said, nodding at the pile of junk on the desk. He was halfway through it. "From high school."

"We've got a better shot at the pharmacy. She'll have to go in there sooner or later," Lucas said. He sat up. "We should check the places she was hospitalized and get the names of patients who overlapped with her, and run them against Manette's patient list."

"Anderson's already doing that," Sloan said.

"Yeah?" Lucas dropped back on the bed and closed his eyes.

After a minute, Sloan asked, "Taking a nap?"

"Thinking," Lucas said.

"What do you think?"

"I think we're wasting our time, Sloan."

"What else is there to do?"

"I don't know."

As they were leaving, Marilyn Crosby leaned in the kitchen doorway. She held a twelve-ounce tumbler of what looked like water, but she sipped like wine. "Find anything?"

"No."

"If, uh, my daughter got in touch—you know, if she wanted more money or something—and if I put you in touch with her, who'd get the reward?"

"If you put us in touch and we got the information from her, you'd get it," Lucas said. "We know she knows who it is. All we have to do is ask her."

"Leave a number where I can get you quick," Marilyn Crosby said. She took a sip from the glass. "If she calls, I'll get in touch. For her own good."

"Right," Lucas said.

Sloan took the wheel again, and Lucas slumped in the passenger seat and stared out the window as they dropped past the wooded lawns and headed toward the gate.

"Listen," he said finally, "have you met the new PR chick? I only talked to her a couple of times."

"Yeah. I met her," Sloan said.

"Is she decent?"

Sloan shrugged. "She's okay. Why?"

"I'd like to get a story written about my company, but I don't want to go around and ask somebody to do it. I'd like to get the PR chick to talk the idea around, and have the TV people come to me."

Sloan said doubtfully, "I don't know, it's a private business and all. What're you thinking?"

"This guy, whoever he is, is fairly intelligent, right?"

"Right."

"And he plays computer games. I'd be willing to bet that he's a computer freak. Ninety percent of male gamers are," Lucas said. He was staring sightlessly out the window, thinking of Ice, the programmer. "His girlfriend knows my computer games, 'cause she said they suck. So I'm wondering, if there were stories on TV and in the papers about how my computer guys were counter-gaming this asshole, I wonder if he'd take a look? You know, cruise the building. How about if we had a really . . . progressive-looking woman talking to him?"

"Sounds a little thin," Sloan said. "He'll be suspicious after that radio gag. But he might."

"I'll talk to the PR chick," Lucas said. "See if we can get something going."

"Don't call her a chick, huh? You make me nervous when you talk that way. She carries a can opener in her purse," Sloan said.

"Okay."

Sloan was driving too fast through traffic, and when Lucas tilted his head back, he punched the radio up, a country station, and they listened to Hank Williams, Jr., until Lucas said, "I feel like my head's stuffed with cotton."

"What?"

"Nothing's going through it at all." He was fumbling with his hand and looked down and saw the ring on his thumb at the same moment that Sloan saw it.

"You gonna ask her, or what?"

"Every time I go home, she's asleep," Lucas said. "When I get up, she's gone."

"You're a cop; that's the way it goes. She's smart enough to know that," Sloan said. "At least you're not doing shift work."

"Yeah, it's just this fuckin' case," Lucas said, holding the ring up to the windshield, peering through the rock. "After this case, we can get back on some kind of schedule."

• • • •

Lucas cleared the idea with the chief, then talked to Anita Segundo, the press liaison.

"I don't know whether we should tell them it's bullshit, and that they're helping catch the kidnapper, or just feed them the story," Lucas said.

"It wouldn't be honest to just feed them the story—but that's the way I'd do it," Segundo said. She was dark-haired, with a smooth, olive complexion and large black eyes. She spoke with a slight West Texas accent, biting off her words like a TV cowgirl.

"How fast could we get it done?" Lucas asked.

"I could tip the TV stations to what might make a good story—and they'd jump all over it. Anything to do with Manette is hot stuff. Of course, the papers'll bite if TV does."

"Give me an hour," Lucas said. "Then put it through."

Lucas found Barry Hunt in a huddle with salesmen, pulled him out, and outlined the story idea. Hunt thought about it for fifteen seconds, then nodded. "I don't see a downside, as long as we have enough cops around for protection."

"You'll have the cops. But the downside is, it might not work," Lucas said.

"That's not what I meant," Hunt said. "I meant, there's no downside for *us*. Whether or not we catch the guy, we can use the stories—video and print—in our PR. You know, tracking a vicious nut kidnapper blah blah blah."

"Oh." Lucas scratched his head. He'd hired the guy to think like this. "Yeah. Listen, then, I'd like Ice to make the presentation to the TV people."

Hunt studied him for a moment and then said, "You're going a little deeper than I expected. But you're right—if we have the protection."

The programmers thought the idea was great: Ice almost hopped up and down when Hunt said she'd lead the presentation of the story. The idea fit with her sense of humor.

"Listen, you guys," Lucas said anxiously, "if you pull their weenies too hard, they're gonna *know*. Then they're gonna screw us, because the press don't like to get their weenies pulled. Worse than that, this guy, this asshole, *he* might know. He's no dummy. We gotta play this straight: or mostly straight. We gotta look good. So let's, like, you know, try not to . . ." He trailed off.

"What?" somebody asked.

"Geek out," Lucas said.

"One thing we could do," said Ice, "is we could take that composite you've been passing around, and make up a hundred different variations of what he looks like. We could do that in an hour with one of the landscape programs. Then we could call them up for the TV people. It'd be very visual . . ."

"Do that," Lucas said, jabbing a finger at her. "Now, I was thinking—when we tried to grab him by tracing the phone call . . ." He explained the FBI's cellular phone direction-finding gear. "That's really high tech. I thought there might be something in it."

"All right, how about this," said another programmer, a short redhead with a yellow pencil behind each ear. "We scan in a map of Dakota County, do some lift-up 3-D shit, then program where the helicopters were and do some graphic overlays on the signal strengths, like we're trying to refine where on the map the signals came from . . ."

"Can you do that?" Lucas asked. "I mean, really?"

The programmer shrugged: "Beats the shit outa me. Maybe, if we had the data. But I was thinking more like, you know, making a cartoon for the TV people."

"Jesus, I can see it. We'd do the whole screen in blood red," Ice said. She looked at Lucas. "It'd look great: they'd eat the whole thing."

"That's what we want," Lucas said. "It's only gotta hold water for a couple of days."

The receptionist stepped into the doorway of the work room, looked around for Hunt, saw him perched on the end of a work bench. "Barry? We've got Channel Three on the phone. They want to do a story."

Hunt hopped off the bench. "How long do you guys need?"

Ice looked around the room, said, "We'll need a few hours to set up, get everything together."

"Could you do it tomorrow morning?"

"No problem," Ice said.

"Excellent," said Lucas.

18

Gloria was walking up to Mail's front porch when the sheriff's car pulled into the driveway. She turned, smiling, and waited. The cop wrote something on a clipboard on the passenger seat, then got out of the car, smiled, nodded politely.

"Ma'am? Are you the owner?"

"Yes? Is there a problem?"

"Well, we're just checking ownership records of houses down here," the police officer said. "You're . . ." He looked at his clipboard and waited.

"Gloria LaDoux," Gloria said. "My husband is Martin, but he's not home yet."

"He works up in the Cities?"

"Yup." She thought quickly, picking out the most boring job she could think of. "He's at the Mall of America? At Brothers Shoes?"

The cop nodded, made a mark on the board. "Have you seen anything that would be, like, unusual along the road here? We're looking for a man in a van . . ."

Mail was a half-mile from the house, the passenger seat full of groceries, when he saw the car in the driveway.

He stopped on the side of the road and closed his eyes for

a moment. He knew the car, a rusty brown Chevy Cavalier. It belonged to a guy named Bob Something, who had a ponytail and a nose ring and bit his fingernails down to the quick. Bob didn't know where he lived, but Gloria did—and Gloria drove Bob's car when she needed one.

Gloria.

She'd been a good contact at the hospital. She worked in the clinic. She could steal cigarettes, small change, candy, and sometimes a few painkillers. Outside, she'd been trouble. She'd helped him with the Marty LaDoux thing, she'd switched the dental records, she'd collected John Mail's life insurance when the body was found in the river. Then she started going on about their *relationship*. And though she'd never made any direct threats, she'd hinted that her knowledge of Martin LaDoux made her special.

He'd worried about that. He hadn't done anything, because she was as implicated as he was, and she was smart enough to know it. On the other hand, she had *liked* it inside. She'd told him that when she was inside, she felt secure.

And she loved to talk.

If she'd figured out the Manette kidnapping, she wouldn't leave it alone. Eventually she'd tell someone. Gloria was always in therapy. She'd never get enough of talking about her problems, of hearing someone else analyze them.

Shit. *Gloria . . .*

Mail pulled the van off the shoulder and went down the road to the house.

Gloria Crosby felt *expansive*. For weeks, she'd felt as though she were living in a box. One day was much like the next as she waited for something to happen, for a direction to emerge. Now it was happening. John had Andi Manette and the kids, she was sure of that: and he must have a plan to get at the Manette money. When they had it, they'd have to leave. Go south, maybe. He was smart, he had ideas, but he wasn't good at details. She could do the detail work, just like she had with Martin LaDoux.

Martin LaDoux had been a robo-geek, the worst of the worst, frightened by everybody, allergic to everything, crowded by Others who'd keep him up all night, talking to him. Her mental picture of Martin was of a tall, thin, pimply teenager with a handkerchief, rubbing his Rudolph-red nose while his eyes watered, trying to smile . . .

He was useless until the state swept them all out of the hospital and gave them, in a ludicrous gesture at their presumed normalcy, both medical and life insurance, along with their places in a halfway house. The life insurance had doomed Martin LaDoux.

Gloria was sitting on Mail's front porch, waiting, not at all impatient. The house was locked, but John was around—through the front window, she could see the pieces of a microwave meal sitting on a TV tray in the living room.

The question was, where was he keeping Manette and the kids? The house felt empty. There was nothing living inside. A feather of unease touched Gloria's heart. Could he have gotten rid of them already?

No. She knew about John and Manette. He'd keep her for a while, she was sure of that.

Gloria was sitting on the front steps, chewing on a grass stem. When Mail pulled the van into the yard, she stood up—dressed all in black, she looked like the wicked witch's apprentice—and sauntered down to meet him.

"John," she said. Her face was pallid, soft, an indoor face, an institutional face. "How are you?"

"Okay," he said, shortly. "What's going on?"

"I came out to see how you're doing? Got a beer?"

He looked at her for a moment, and her face shone with knowledge and expectation. *She knew.* He nodded to the question. "Yeah, sure. Come on in."

She followed him inside, looked around. "Same old place," she said. She plunked down on his computer chair and looked at the blind eyes of the computer monitors. "Got some new ones," she said. "Any new games?"

"I've been off games," he said.

He got two beers from the refrigerator and handed one to the woman, and she twisted the top off, watching him.

"You've got a Davenport game," she said, picking up a

software box. There was a pamphlet inside, and three loose discs.

"Yeah." He took a hit of the beer. "How's your head?" he asked.

"Been okay." She thumbed through the game pamphlet.

"Still on your meds?"

"Ehh, sometimes." She frowned. "But I left them back at my apartment."

"Yeah?"

"Yeah. I don't think I can go back there." She said it as a teaser. She wanted him to ask why not. She tossed the pamphlet back in the software box and looked up at him.

"Why not?"

"The cops were there," she said. She took a drink from the bottle, eyes fixed on him. "Looking for you."

"For me?"

"Yup. They had a picture. I don't know who told them that I know you, but they knew. I managed to put them off and slid out of there."

"Jesus, are you sure? That they didn't follow . . ." He looked at the front window, half-expecting squad cars.

"Yeah. They were stupid; it was easy. Hey, you know who one of them was?"

"Davenport."

She nodded. "Yeah."

"Goddamnit, Gloria."

"I jumped a bus, rode it eight blocks, hopped off, walked through Janis's apartment building, and took the walkway to Bob's, borrowed the car key from Bob . . ."

"Did you tell him you were coming to see me?"

"Nope." She was proud of herself. "I told him I had to bring some school stuff home. Anyway, I got the key, went down into the parking garage, and got his car. There was nobody around when I left."

He watched her as she talked, and when she finished, he nodded. "All right. I've been having some trouble with the cops."

"I know," she said. And she popped it out, a surprise: "They were here, too."

"Here?" Now he *was* worried.

"A cop pulled in just after I got here—they're checking all the farmhouses. I don't think he was too interested after I told him I was your wife, and we lived here together."

Mail looked at her for a moment, and then said, "You did."

"I did," she said. "And he left."

"All right," he said, his voice flat.

She caught the hems of her dress and did a mock curtsey, oddly crowlike in its bobbing dip. "You took the Manette lady and her kids."

He was dumbstruck by the baldness of it. He tried to recover: "What?"

"Come on, John," she said. "This is Gloria. You can't lie to me. Where've you got them?"

"Gloria . . ."

But she was shaking her head. "We took down fifteen thousand, remember?"

"Yeah."

"That was sweet," she said. "I'd like to help you collect on Manette . . . if you'll let me."

"Jesus." He looked at her and scratched his head.

"Can I see them? I mean, you know, put a stocking over my head or something? I assume they haven't seen your face or anything."

"Gloria, this isn't about money," Mail said. "This is about what she did to me in the old days."

That stopped her. She said, "Oh." Then: "What're you doing to her?"

Mail thought about it for ten seconds, then said, "Whatever I want."

"God," Gloria said. "That's so"—she wiggled in the chair—"neat."

Mail smiled now and said, "C'mon. I'll show you."

On the way out the back, Gloria said, "You told me you'd stopped thinking about her."

"I started again," Mail said.

"How come?"

Mail thought about not answering, but Gloria had been inside with him. As dreary and unlikable as she was, she was one of the few people who really might know how his mind worked, how he *felt*.

"A woman started calling me," he said. "Somebody who doesn't like Andi Manette. I don't know who—just that it's a woman. She said Manette still talks about me, about what I was like. She said Manette said I was interested in her sexually, and that she could feel the sex coming out of me. She must have called fifteen times."

"God, that's a little weird," Gloria said.

"Yeah." Mail scratched his chin, thinking about it. "The really strange thing is, she called me here. She knows who I am, but she won't tell me who she is. I can't figure that out. But she doesn't like Andi, that's for sure. She kept pushing, and I kept thinking, and pretty soon . . . you know how it gets. It's like you can't get a song out of your head."

"Yeah. Like when I was counting to a thousand." Gloria had once spent a year counting to one thousand, over and over. Then, one day, the counting stopped. She didn't feel like she'd had much to do with it, either starting or stopping it, but she was grateful for the silence in her brain.

Mail grinned: "Drives you nuts . . ."

On the way down the stairs, into the musty basement, Gloria realized who the woman was—who was calling John Mail. She opened her mouth to tell him, but then decided, *Later*. That would be something to tease him with, not something simply to blurt out. John had to be controlled, to some extent; you had to fight to maintain your equality.

"I built a room," Mail said, gesturing at a steel door in the basement wall. "Used to be a root cellar. Damn near killed me, working in that hole. I'd have to stop every ten minutes and run outside."

Gloria nodded: she knew about his claustrophobia. "Open it," she said.

Andi and Grace had used the snap tab from Grace's bra to work on the nail in the overhead joist but could work only a half-hour or so before the skin on their fingers grew too painful to continue. They were making progress—a half-inch of the nail was in the clear—but Andi thought it might take another week to extract it.

She didn't think they had a week: Mail was becoming more animated, and darker, at the same time. She could feel the devils driving him, she could see them in his eyes. He was losing control.

"Never get it out," Grace said. She was standing on the Porta-Potti. "Mom, we're never gonna get it." She dropped the snap tab and sat down on the Potti cover and put her face in her hands. She didn't cry: both of them had gone dry-eyed, as though they'd run out of tears.

Andi squatted next to her, took her daughter's hand, and rolled it: the skin where she'd been holding the too-small tab was pinched and scarlet, overlying a deeper, dark-blue bruise. "You'll have to stop. Don't do any more until the red goes away." She looked up at the joist, rubbing her thumb against the shredded skin of her own forefinger. "I'll try to do a little more."

"No good anyway," Grace said. "He's too big for us. He's a monster."

"We've got to try," Andi said. "If we can only get a weapon, we can . . ."

They heard the thumps of feet overhead. "He's coming," Grace said. She shrank back to the mattress, to the corner.

Andi closed her eyes for a moment, opened them, said, "Remember: no eye contact."

She spit into her hand, dabbed a finger into a dusty corner, reached up and rubbed the combination of dirt and saliva on the raw wood where Grace had been digging around the nail. The moisture darkened the wood and made the rawness less noticeable. When she was satisfied—when the footsteps were on the stairs, and she could wait no longer—she stepped down, pushed the Porta-Potti against a wall, and sat on it.

"Don't talk unless he talks to you, and keep your head down. I'll start talking as soon as he comes in. Okay? Grace, okay?"

"Okay." Grace rolled onto the mattress, facing the wall, pulled her tattered dress around her legs.

Mail was at the door.

"John," Andi said, her voice dull, her face slack. She was desperately trying to project an image of weariness, of lifelessness. She wanted to do nothing that would provoke him.

"Come on, up, we've got a visitor." Andi's head snapped up despite herself, and from the corner of her eye, she saw Grace roll over. Mail stepped down into the cell, and as Andi got to her feet, he took her arm, and she shuffled to the door.

"Can I come?" Grace squeaked. Andi's heart sank.

"No," Mail said. He never looked at the girl, and Andi said, quickly, so he wouldn't have a chance to think of her, "Who is it, John?"

"An old nuthouse friend of mine," Mail said. He thrust her through the door, stepped out behind her, and closed the door and bolted it. A woman, all dressed in black, was standing at the bottom of the dusty basement stairs. She had a long, thin stick in her hand; a tree branch. In her other hand, she held a bottle of beer by the neck.

Witch, Andi thought. And then, *Executioner*.

"God, John," the woman breathed. She came closer and walked around Andi, looking her up and down, as though she were a mannequin. "Do you hit her a lot?"

"Not a lot; I mostly fuck her."

"Does she let you, or do you make her?" The woman was only inches away, and Andi could smell her breath, the sourness of the beer.

"Mostly, I just go ahead and do it," Mail said. "When she gives me any trouble, I pound her a little." Andi stood dumbly, not knowing what to do. And Mail said, "I try not to break anything. Mostly I just use my open hand. Like this."

He swatted Andi's face, hard, and she went down, but her head was clear. Mail hit her almost every time he took her out of the room, and she had learned to anticipate the motion. By moving with it, just a bit, the blow was softened.

By falling, she assuaged whatever it was that made him hit her.

Sometimes he helped her pick herself up. Not this time. This time he stood over her, with the woman in black.

"Brought some rope," he said to Andi. He showed her several four-foot lengths of yellow plastic water-ski rope. "Put your hands up—no, don't stand up. Just put your hands up."

Andi did what he told her, and he tied her hands at the wrist. The rope was stiff and cut into her skin.

"John, don't hurt me," she said as calmly as she could.

"I'm not going to," Mail said.

He tied a second length of the rope to the bindings at her wrist, led it over a joist-mounted rack in the ceiling, and pulled on the end until Andi's hands and arms were above her head, then tied it off.

"There you go," Mail said to Gloria. "Just the way you wanted her."

"God," Gloria said. She walked around Andi, and Andi turned with her, watching. "Don't turn, or you'll really get it," Gloria snapped.

Andi stopped, closed her eyes. A second later, she heard a thin, quick whistle and then the tree branch hit her in the back. Most of the impact was soaked up by her dress, but it hurt, and she screeched, "Ahhhh," and arced away from the other woman.

Gloria's voice was hot, excited. "God. Can we get her dress off? I want to hit her on the tits."

"Go ahead," Mail said. "She can't do anything to you."

Gloria walked straight up to Andi, and, as she reached for her blouse, said, "You should have taken her clothes away from her, anyway. We oughta cut them off with a knife. Same with the kid, we oughta . . ."

Mail had come up directly behind her, a third length of the rope held between his hands. He flipped it over Gloria's neck and twisted: the rope cut into the woman's throat, and she tried to turn, tried to grab the rope. Her face, eyes bulging, was inches from Andi's. Andi tried to swing away, to turn, but Mail shouted, "No, watch this. Watch."

She turned back. The woman's tongue was out now, and she did a little dance, her feet tapping on the floor, her arms windmilling for a moment, then her fingers would pluck at the rope, then she'd windmill again.

The muscles stood out in Mail's arms and face as he twisted the rope and controlled the woman at the same time; eventually, he held her slack body like a puppet, held her, held her, until her bladder relaxed and the smell of urine floated through the room. He held her for another ten seconds, but now he was watching Andi's face.

Andi was watching, but without much feeling: her capacity for horror had dried out as thoroughly as her tears. She'd imagined John Mail killing herself, or Grace, much in this way. And she'd dreamed of Genevieve, not at home, but in a grave somewhere, in her first-day-of-school dress. The murder of Gloria seemed almost insignificant.

Mail let go of the rope, and Gloria fell face-first to the floor, wide-eyed, and never flinched when it came up to meet her. Mail put a knee in her back, tightened the rope again, held it for another minute, threw a quick sailor's knot into it, then stood up and made a hand-dusting gesture.

"She was a pain in the ass," he said, looking down at the body. Then he smiled at Andi. "You see? I take care of you. She would've beat the shit out of you."

Andi's hands were still over her head, and she said, "This is hurting my shoulders . . ."

"Really? Tough shit." He walked behind her, put his hands around her waist, pressed his teeth against the back of her shoulder, and looked down at the body. "This is kind of"—he looked for a word and remembered Gloria's—"kind of *neat*," he said.

19

Lucas's cellular phone buzzed, and he looked down at his pocket. "I told all my friends to stay off, unless it was an emergency," he said. Lester picked up another phone and dialed, and Lucas let the phone ring once more before he snapped it open and said, "Yeah?"

"Ah, Lucas." Mail's voice. Traffic was busy in the background. "Is your ass getting tired of chasing me? I'm thinking of going on vacation, tell you the truth."

"Are you driving around?" Lucas asked. He flapped his hand at Lester, nodding, and Lester whispered urgently into his phone, then dropped it and sprinted out of the room. "Feel pretty safe?"

"Yeah, I'm driving," Mail said. "Are you trying to track me?"

"I don't know. Probably," Lucas said. "I need to talk to you and I need to finish what I've got to say, with no bullshit."

"Well, spit it out, man. But don't take too long. I've got a clue for you. And this is a good one."

"Why don't you give me that, first?" Lucas said. "Just in case I piss you off."

Mail laughed, and then said, "You're a funny guy. But

listen, this is a real clue. Not sort of remote, like the first one."

"Tell me about the first one?"

"Fuck no." Mail was amused. "But I'll tell you—if you figure this one out, you'll get me fair and square. You ever watch Monty Python? It'd be like"— he lapsed into a bad British accent—"a fair cop."

"So what is it?"

"Just a minute, I got it written down. I've got to read it to you, to get it right. Okay, here it is . . ." He paused, then said, in a reading voice: "A little blank verse, one-twelve-ten, four-four, one-forty-seven-nine, and a long line; twenty-three-two, thirty-two-nine, sixty-nine-twenty-two."

"That's it?" Lucas asked.

"That's it. This is a very simple code, but I don't think you'll crack it. If you do, I'm done. Mrs. Manette bet me that you'd break it. And I'll tell you, I have to be honest about this, you sure don't want her to lose the bet, Lucas. Hey, did you say it was all right for me to call you Lucas?"

Lucas said, "Mrs. Manette's still okay? Can I talk to her?"

"After the stunt she pulled last time? Bullshit. We had a hard little talk about that. What do you cops call it? Tough love?"

"She's still alive?"

"Yeah. But I'm gonna have to go. I feel like a whole cloud of cops are closing in on me."

"No, no—listen to me," Lucas said urgently. "You don't feel it, but you're ill. I mean, you're gonna die from it. If you come in, I swear to God nothing will happen to you, except we'll try to fix things . . ."

Mail's voice turned to a growl. "Hey, I've been fixed. Best and the brightest tried to fix me, Davenport. They used to strap me to a table and fix the shit out of me. Sometimes I remember whole months that I'd forgotten because they fixed me so good. So don't give me any of that fixed shit. I been fixed. I'm what you get, when they fix somebody." His voice changed again, went Hollywood. "But, hey, dude, I gotta run. Got a little pussy lined up after dinner, know what I mean? Catch you later."

And he was gone.

Lucas ran down the hall and through the security doors on the 911 center. Lester was already there, with a man Lucas recognized as an FBI agent. They were looking over the shoulder of one of the operators, who was speaking into a microphone: "Dark Econoline van or like that, probably no further west than Rice Street . . ."

Lester said to Lucas, "Probably 694, east to west. We're flooding it right now. We're taking every van off the road."

They hung around Dispatch for fifteen minutes, listening as vans were pulled off the highway wholesale. After a while, they walked back to the Homicide Office together and found Sloan with his feet on his desk, looking at a printout.

"Da clue," he said, waving the printout at them.

"Already?" Lucas said. "What do you think?"

"Could be Bible verses," Sloan said. "They got that kind of numbers and he used the Bible last time."

"Unless he's cooked up something clever and he's fucking with us," Lester said. "Maybe it's got something to do with the numbers."

"Maybe it's his address," Sloan said. "And his driver's license number."

"And maybe it's the Bible," Lucas said. "I've got somebody who can look into that possibility."

"Elle," Sloan said, looking up from the list of clues. "Does a nunnery got a fax machine?"

"Yeah," Lucas said, vaguely. He read through a transcript of the tape. "Shit."

"What?"

"Don't go away," Lucas said. "Let me fax this to Elle."

When he came back, five minutes later, he glanced around the Homicide Office. A half-dozen detectives were sitting at desks, talking, looking at maps, eating. Two of them had found a Bible and were paging through it with some perplexity.

Lucas stepped close to Sloan's desk and crooked a finger at Lester. Lester stepped over and Lucas said, in a low voice,

"There were two things he said. He was fixed—so our guy has been in a state hospital. We've gotta be sure that every state hospital employee and every long-term resident has seen the composite."

Lester nodded. "Why are we whispering?"

"'Cause of the other thing," Lucas said. "Remember how he knew that we'd spotted his gamer's shirt? Now he knows that Andi Manette tried to send a message to us. He *knows*. He's gotta be getting information. He's gotta."

"From here?" Lester breathed, looking around.

"Probably not, but I don't know. I'd bet it comes out of the family briefings. Somebody out there has a motive to get rid of Manette. Whoever it is, is talking to this guy."

Lester scratched his nose, nervous, his Adam's apple bobbing up and down. "The chief is gonna be delighted," he said.

"Maybe we shouldn't tell her," Lucas said. "I mean, for her own good."

"What're you thinking about?" Lester said.

"I'm thinking that we ought to come up with a bunch of little nuggets, different nuggets, bullshit, that we feed through all the different family members—and then we wait to see if anything comes out the other side. Stuff that our guy would react to. If we can find who's feeding him, we can crack him. Or her."

"Christ." Lester scratched his nose, then his head. Then, "We gotta tell Roux. That's what she's paid for."

Roux said, "I wish you hadn't told me."

"That's what you're paid for," Lucas said, straight-faced.

Roux sighed and said, "Right. So. Anything critical, we keep to ourselves, though I don't see how we could keep Manette's message to ourselves. We wouldn't have known what it meant."

Lester explained Lucas's idea about feeding false information through the family: Roux grudgingly approved but rolled her eyes to the ceiling and said, "Please, God, don't let it be Tower."

"One other thing," Lucas said. "We've got recorders on

everybody's listed numbers, because we were only looking for incoming calls from a stranger. We should start looking at the private phones, too, the unlisted numbers, the outgoing calls. And we need to be quiet about it."

Roux looked at Lester, who nodded and said, "I agree," and then closed her eyes and said, "They'll be pissed when they find out."

"When they find out, we can explain it," Lucas said. "But we need to get on this right now. I mean, *right now*. We're running out of time."

"But I really don't think whoever it is would call from his own phone."

"They might, if they think they know what's being monitored," Lucas said. "And when the asshole needs to get in touch with them, *he's* got to call. We need to know about anything anomalous—odd rings, cryptic phone calls, funny-sounding wrong numbers, anything."

Roux sighed, spread her hands on her desk, looked at them. "I knew there'd be days like this," she said.

"You gotta do it," Lucas said.

"All right," Roux said. "I'll call Larry Baxter—he'd sign a warrant on the Little Old Lady Who Lived in a Shoe."

"Tonight," Lucas said. "Get Anderson to call the phone company and get a list of all their numbers, on every single one of the family members. Then get a guy over to the phone company and have him sit there and listen."

"We're running out of guys," Lester said.

"Pull some uniforms," Lucas said. "We don't need Einstein over there."

One hundred and forty-four vans were stopped along I-694 after Mail's call to Lucas. Two men were held briefly while checks were run on them, and then they were released.

"You know what he was doing?" Lucas said, looking up at a wall map in the Homicide Office. He pointed at the top of the map, at the belt highway. "I bet he's on a secondary road driving parallel to the highway. I bet he was on County Road C, knowing that if we're tracking him, we'd be looking on 694."

"So . . . that's gonna be tough," Lester said, looking at the map. "We'll have to try to flood a whole area, instead of just a road, or a street."

"We won't get him that way," Lucas said. "He'll keep changing up on us."

Lucas was just ready to leave again when Elle called back. "I'm pushing the button on my fax. You should have a fax coming in."

A second later, Lucas heard the fax phone ring once, and then the fax machine started buzzing at the other end of the office: "It's coming now."

"Okay," she said. "Now. If it's the Bible, it's Psalms, of course."

"How do you know that?"

"Psalms is the only book that has chapter numbers as high as the ones he cited," she said. "If they're not from Psalms, then it's just a bunch of gibberish. It could be anything."

"But what if they're all from Psalms?" Lucas asked.

"This is what he said," Elle intoned. "He said, 'A little blank verse' and then the numbers. And here are the first three verses. These are from the King James Version, by the way—I think he'd probably be using one, since I doubt that he's religious, and if he's not, he's probably got a James."

"All right. But the pope'll be pissed." There was silence on the other end and Lucas said, "Sorry."

She said, "Why don't you go get that fax?"

"Just a minute." He put the phone down, got the fax, and walked back. "Ready."

"Psalm 112:10," she said. Lucas followed along on the fax as she read, *"The wicked shall see it, and be grieved; he shall gnash with his teeth, and melt away: the desire of the wicked shall perish.*

"Psalm 4:4: *Stand in awe and sin not: commune with your own heart upon your bed, and be still. Selah.*

"Psalm 147:9: *He giveth to the beast his food, and to the young ravens which cry."*

There was a rustling of paper and Elle said, "Got that?"

"Yeah. But what is it?" He studied the Psalms but found no pattern at all.

"I couldn't see *anything* at first. I kept thinking that the verses must relate to his condition, or the condition of the women. I thought he must've made a psychotic connection between them. These are powerful images—gnashing teeth, ravens and beasts, the wicked and the grieved. The problem is, I couldn't relate them to anything. There was no thread."

"Elle? What are you leading up to?" Lucas asked.

"A silly question," the nun said. "It's so silly that I don't want to explain it unless the answer is yes."

"So ask."

"Is there anybody named Crosby involved with this whole thing?"

After a moment of silence, Lucas said, "Elle, we're getting ready to plaster the papers and the TV newscasts with pictures of a woman named Gloria Crosby. She knows our man. How did you know?"

Elle laughed softly and said, "I thought it was so stupid."

"What?"

"The sequence of single words in the first three verses, with that 'blank verse' coming first."

"Elle, damnit . . ."

"Each verse has one of these words, in order: Blank, Gnash, still, young."

Lucas closed his eyes and then grinned. "God, I like this kid. It's the group: Crosby, Nash, Stills and Young. I think the order is wrong, but . . ."

"I think that's it."

Lucas's smile faded. "Then he's got her. Crosby."

"That would be my interpretation. After that verse, he says, 'long line.' That breaks the meaning of the top three verses from the next three. For the first two of those three, I have no clue. Well, I have some clue, but it's pretty general."

Lucas read the two verses, under the long line she'd drawn across the paper. The first was Psalm 23:2: *He maketh me to lie down in green pastures; he leadeth me beside the still waters.*

"She's dead," Lucas said. "That's the verse you read at a funeral."

"Unless he's hinting that he's taken her to Stillwater."

"Yeah." He scanned the fifth verse, Psalm 32:9: *Be ye not as the horse, or as the mule, which have no understanding: whose mouth must be held in with bit and bridle, lest they come near unto thee.*

After a long moment of silence, Lucas said, "Doesn't mean anything to me."

"Me either. But I'll think about it."

"How about the last one?"

"That's the one that worries me: 69:22: *Let their table become a snare before them: and that which should have been for their welfare, let it become a trap.*"

"Huh," Lucas said.

"Be careful," Elle said. "He's warning you."

"I will. And Elle: thanks."

"I'm praying for Dr. Manette and the children," Elle said. "But you've got to hurry, Lucas."

Before Lucas left, he called Anderson and said, "Check and see if there are any horse farms—or mule farms, for that matter—out near Stillwater."

"There are," Anderson said. "Lots of them. It's sorta St. Paul's horsey country."

"Better start running the owners," Lucas said. "Make a list."

20

Weather was sleeping soundly when Lucas finally got home. He slipped out of his clothes to the light from the hall, coming through a crack in the door, and dropped his jacket, pants, and shirt over a chair. After tiptoeing to the bathroom, and then back out, he took off his watch, put it on the bed table, and slipped in beside her.

She was warm, comfortable, but Lucas was unable to sleep. After a few minutes, he got up and tiptoed out to the study, sat in the old leather chair, and tried to think.

There were too many things going on at once. Too much to think about. And he was messing around with facts, rather than looking for patterns, or for revealing holes. He put his feet up, steepled his fingers, closed his eyes, and let his mind roam.

And in ten minutes concluded that the case would break when they identified the probable killer through hospital records, or when they cracked the kidnapper's source of information. Two solid angles, but not enough pressure on them.

So: Dunn, Tower and Helen Manette, Wolfe.

Of course, there was a small chance that the leak was not from the family. It could be an investigation insider—a cop. But Lucas thought not. The kidnapper was clearly crazy. A cop would be unlikely to stick his neck out for a nut, even a family nut. They were simply too unreliable.

No. Somebody had to benefit.

Wolfe. Wolfe was sleeping with Manette. Manette didn't have much left, in the way of money. Dog food . . .

Lucas frowned, glanced at his watch. Dunn was up late every night. Lucas got Anderson's daily log, looked up Dunn's home phone, and dialed. Dunn picked it up, a little breathless, on the second ring: "Hello?"

"Mr. Dunn, Lucas Davenport."

"Davenport—you scared me. I thought it might be the guy, this time of night." In an aside to somebody, he said, *Lucas Davenport*. Then: "What can I do for you?"

Lucas said, "When I talked to you the night of the kidnapping, you told me that Tower and Andi Manette shared money from a trust."

"That's right."

"If your wife was gone, and the kids were gone, what would happen to the trust?"

After a long moment of silence, Dunn said, "I don't know. That would be up to the terms of the trust, and the trustees. The only beneficiaries are Tower and his descendants. If he didn't have any descendants . . . I suppose it'd go to Tower."

"If Tower croaked . . . excuse me . . ."

"Yeah, yeah, if Tower croaked, what?"

"Would his wife get it?"

"No. I mean, not if Andi and the kids were still around. Jesus, listen to the way I'm talking, for christ sakes." And the phone went dead. Lucas looked at the receiver, unsure about what had happened. He redialed.

A cop picked up on the first ring, and without preamble said, "Chief Davenport?"

"Yeah, I was talking to Dunn."

"Well, Jesus, sir, I don't know what you said, but he cracked up. He's back in his bedroom."

"Ah."

"Do you want me to get him?"

"No, no, let him go. Tell him I'm sorry, okay?"

"Sure, I will . . ."

"And after he's got back together, ask him if I could get a copy of the Manette Trust document. They must have one around."

Lucas, still wide awake, crawled back into bed and lay looking at the ceiling for a moment, then rolled over and gripped Weather's shoulder and whispered in her ear, "Can you wake up?"

"Hmmm?" she asked sleepily.

"Are you operating in the morning?"

"At ten," she said.

"Oh . . ."

"What?" She rolled more on her back and reached up and touched his face.

"I need to talk to you about the case. I need an opinion from a woman. But if you're working . . ."

"I'm fine," she said, more awake now. "Tell me."

He told her, and finished with, "Tower could die anytime. If Andi and the kids are gone, his wife is gonna get a load. Whatever he's got, plus—maybe—whatever's in the trust. Probably four million, plus a million-dollar house. So the question is, could Nancy Wolfe do that? How about Helen?"

Weather had been listening intently. "I can't say—it could be either one. Normally, I'd say no to Wolfe. Even if she's having an affair with Tower, she can't be so sure that he'll marry her, that she'd already be maneuvering for the money. Not to the extent of killing three people. Helen, well, Helen doesn't have anything invested in Andi and the children. She was having an affair with Tower before Andi's mother was gone—so she and Andi probably dislike each other. And if Helen knows about the affair with Nancy Wolfe, maybe . . ."

"Yeah. If Andi and the kids are gone, she gets more from a divorce, if there is one. If Andi and the kids are gone, and Manette croaked from the stress, or from the stress before a divorce, or both . . . well, all the better. So Helen looks good."

"Except."

"Except," Lucas repeated.

"Except that we don't know much about Wolfe's relationship with Andi Manette. They are partners and old friends, we're told—but that's exactly where you'll find some really deep, rich, suppressed hatreds. Things that go back decades. My best friend in high school got married when she was nineteen, had a bunch of kids, and wound up flipping burgers in a motel. The last time I saw her, I realized . . . I think she hates me. Andi was always rich, Wolfe didn't have money; Andi married a man who Wolfe met first, and who went on to become a multimillionaire. Andi has good-looking kids, Wolfe is at the time of life when she's got to face the possibility that she won't get married and have children at all. And maybe Andi would interfere with this affair. I wonder if she knows about it. Anyway—that's all pretty emotional stuff and pretty tangled up."

"Yeah. And there's something else," Lucas said. "If somebody sicced a fruitcake killer on Andi Manette, who'd know more about picking a fruitcake killer than Wolfe?"

"Maybe you're looking at the wrong files," Weather said. "Maybe you should be looking at Nancy Wolfe's." After a moment, "And there's always George Dunn."

"He doesn't feel right to me, anymore," Lucas said. "He'd have to be a great liar, a great actor."

"In other words, a sociopath," Weather said.

"Glad you said that," Lucas said.

"A lot of very successful businessmen are—at least, that's what I've heard anecdotally. Like surgeons . . ."

"Nancy Wolfe once called him a sociopath," Lucas said.

". . . and if he were facing a divorce that would cut his business in half . . . How much did you say he was worth?" Weather asked.

"If he wasn't lying, could be anything up to thirty million."

"So Andi Manette's death could be worth fifteen million dollars to him," Weather said. "I'll tell you something. Rich people get very attached to their money. It's like one of their organs, or more than that. If you asked most people who have two million dollars whether they'd rather lose one million, or lose a foot, I think most of them would rather lose the foot."

"But that only holds if Andi Manette really wants a divorce," Lucas said. "Dunn says he was trying to put it back together."

"What else *would* he say? That he hates her and he's glad they were kidnapped?"

"Yeah." The problem wasn't a lack of motive. The problem was picking one.

"Don't forget the last possibility," Weather said. "Tower. Her father."

"You've got a sick mind, Karkinnen."

"It wouldn't be the first time that a father went after his daughter. If he's desperate . . ."

Lucas lay flat on his back, his fingers laced across his stomach, and he said, "When I had my little bout of depression, whenever that was, one of the worst things was lying awake at night with everything running through my head, in circles, and not being able to stop it. This isn't quite the same, but it's related. Jesus. I keep going around and around: Dunn, Wolfe, the Manettes; Dunn, Wolfe, the Manettes. The answer is there."

Weather patted his leg. "You'll figure it out."

"Something else is bothering me. I saw something in Gloria Crosby's apartment, but I can't remember what it was. But it's important."

She pushed herself up: "You *forgot?*"

"Not exactly forgot. It was there, but it's like I never really recognized it. It's like when you see a face in the street, and an hour later you realize it was an old classmate. Like that. I saw something . . ."

"Sleep on it," she said. "Maybe your subconscious will kick it out."

After a while in the dark, after Weather had rolled back to her own pillow, he said, "You know, those two Bible verses have me whipped, too. Must be Stillwater. That would be too much of a coincidence—or a trick, or something—not to be right. But what's he talking about?"

And Weather said something that sounded like "ZZZzzt-tug."

When he woke, before he opened his eyes, he thought of the Bible verses. Maybe the *not* was the key. *Be ye* not *as the horse, or as the mule, which have no understanding; whose mouth must be held in with bit and bridle, lest they come near unto thee.* But even if the *not* was the key word, he thought wryly, ye had no understanding. And who was coming near unto whom?

He thought about it through shaving, through the shower, and came up with nothing brilliant, and began dressing. The day was gorgeous: sunlight slanted in through the wooden blinds in the living room, and the whole feel was that of a perfect fall day. As he put on a shirt and tie, he watched the *Openers* morning show. The weatherman said that the low pressure system responsible for all the rain had rambled off to the east and was presently peeing on Ohio; additional micturatory activity could be expected in New York by evening, if you were going there. The weatherman said neither *peeing* nor *micturatory,* but should have, Lucas thought. He found himself whistling, stopped to wonder why, and decided a nice day was a nice day. The kidnapping wasn't the day's fault, but he stopped whistling.

"So we're stuck?" Roux asked. She lit a cigarette, forgetting the one already burning in an ashtray behind her. Her office stank of nicotine, and would need new curtains every year. "All we can do is grind along?"

"I had those Bible verses sent out to Stillwater," Lucas said. "Maybe the local cops will figure something out."

"And maybe the fairy godmother will kiss me on the sweet patootie," Lester said.

"Nasty thought," Roux said. "Nasty."

"I think we ought to start pushing the big four: the Manettes, Dunn, Wolfe. Start taking them apart. Somebody is talking."

Roux shook her head. "I haven't entirely bought that.

We've got the wiretaps going, but I don't think I'm ready for a full-scale assault."

"Who's listening to the wires?" Lucas asked.

Lester made a sound like he was clearing his throat.

"What?"

"Larry Carter, from uniform, then tonight, uh, Bob. Greave."

"Ah, shit," Lucas groaned.

"He can do that," Lester said defensively. "He's not stupid, he's just . . ." He groped for a phrase.

"Investigatively challenged," Roux suggested.

"That's it," Lester said.

Lucas stood up. "I've gotten everything I can out of the raw paper on Dunn, Wolfe, and the Manettes, and I want to look at all the stuff from the hospitals and the possible candidates from Andi Manette's files," he said. "That's where it'll break—unless we get a piece of luck."

"Good luck; there's a lot of it," Lester said. "And you better pick up a new copy of Anderson's book. There's more new stuff in there. We got lists coming out the wazoo."

Lucas spent the day like a medieval monk, bent over the paper. Anything useful, he xeroxed and stuck in a smaller file. By the end of the day, he had fifty pieces of paper for additional review, plus a foot-tall stack of files to take home. He left at six, enjoying the lingering daylight, regretting the great day missed, and gone forever. This would have been a day to go up north with Weather, to learn a little more about sailing from her. They were talking about buying an S2 and racing it. Maybe next year . . .

They spent a quiet evening: a quick mile run, a small, easy dinner with a lot of carrots. Afterwards, Lucas dipped into the homework files, while Weather read a Larry Rivers autobiography called *What Did I Do?* Occasionally she'd read him a paragraph, and they'd laugh or groan together. As she sat in the red chair, with the yellow light illuminating half of her face, he thought she looked like a painting he'd seen in New York. Vermeer, that was it. Or Van Gogh—but

Van Gogh was the crazy guy, so it must have been Vermeer. Anyway, he remembered the light in the painting.

And she looked like that, he thought, in the light.

"Gotta go to bed," she said, regretfully, a little after nine o'clock. "Gotta be up at five-thirty. We oughta do this more often."

"What?"

"Nothing, together."

When she'd gone, Lucas started through the stack of files again; came to the one marked JOHN MAIL; after the name, somebody had scrawled [*deceased*].

This one had looked good, Lucas thought. He opened it and started reading.

The phone rang and he picked it up.

"Yeah?"

Greave: "Lucas, I'm peeing my pants. The asshole is talking to Dunn."

21

Greave met Lucas at the elevator doors. He was in shirtsleeves, his tie hanging around his shoulders, his hair sticking up in clumps. "Christ, lit me up like a fuckin' Christmas tree," he said. "I couldn't believe what I was hearing."

He led Lucas down a bare but brightly lit hallway toward an open office door, their heels echoing on the tile floor.

"You call the feebs?" Lucas asked.

"No. Should I?"

"Not yet." The office was furnished with a cafeteria-style folding table, three office chairs, and a television. A group of beige push-button telephones and a tape recorder sat on the table with a plate of donut crumbs; the TV was on but the sound was off, Jane Fonda hustling a treadmill. A pile of magazines sat on the floor beside the table.

"Got it cued up," Greave said. He pushed a button on the recorder, and the tape began to roll with the sound of a phone ringing, then being picked up.

"*George Dunn.*"

"*George?*" Mail's voice was cheerful, insouciant. "*I'm calling for your wife, Andi.*"

"*What? What'd you say?*" Dunn seemed stunned.

"*I'm calling for your wife. Is this call being monitored? And you better tell the truth, for Andi's sake.*"

"No, for christ sakes. I'm in the car. Who is this?"

"*An old friend of Andi's . . . Now listen: I want a hundred thousand for the package. For the three of them.*"

"*How do I know this isn't a con?*" Dunn asked.

"*I'm gonna play a recording.*" There was some apparent fumbling, then Andi Manette's voice, tinny, recorded: "*George, this is Andi. Do what this man tells you. Um, he said to tell you what we talked about the last time we talked . . . You called me from the club and you wanted to come over, but I said that the kids were already in bed and I wasn't ready to . . .*"

The recording ended in mid-sentence and Mail said, "*She gets a little sloppy after that, George. You wouldn't want to hear it. Anyway, you got any more questions about whether this is real?*"

Dunn's voice sounded like a rock. "*No.*"

"*So. I don't want you to go to the bank and get a bunch of money with the numbers recorded and dusted with UV powder and all that FBI shit. If you do it, I'll know, and I'll kill them all.*"

"*I gotta get the money.*"

"*George, you've got almost sixty thousand in case money, mostly kruggerrands, that nobody knows about, in a safety deposit box in Prescott, Wisconsin. Okay? You've got a Rolex worth $8,000 that you never wear anyway. Andi has $25,000 in diamond jewelry and a ruby from her mother, all in your joint safety deposit box at First Bank. And you've got several thousand dollars in cash hidden in the two houses . . . get that.*"

"*You sonofabitch.*"

"*Hey. Let's try to keep this businesslike, okay?*" Mail's voice was wry, but not quite taunting.

"*How do I get it to you? I've got cops staying with me, waiting for you to call.*"

"*Take I-94 east all the way to the St. Croix, get off on Highway 95, get back on going west, and pull off at the Minnesota Welcome station. You know where that is?*"

"Yeah."

"There's a phone by the Coke machine. Get on it just before seven o'clock, but keep your finger on the hook. I'll call right at seven o'clock. If it's busy, I'll try again at five after seven. If it's still busy, I'll try at ten after, but that's it: after that, I'm gone. Don't even think about telling the cops. I'll be driving around, and they can't track me when I'm moving. They've been trying. When I get you on the phone, I'll give you some instructions."

"Okay."

"If I see any cops, I'm gone."

The phone went dead.

"That's it," Greave said.

"Jesus." Lucas walked in a quick circle, stopped to look out the window at the lights of the city, then said, "We talk to Lester and the chief. Nobody else. Nobody. We've got to get a team going."

Roux brought the FBI in. Lucas argued against it, but she insisted: "For christ sakes, Lucas, this is the thing they do. This is their big specialty. We can't leave them out—if we do, and if we blow it, it'll be all our asses. And it should be."

"We can handle it."

"I'm sure we can, if it's real. But if it's anything else, we'd be in deep shit, my friend. No, they've got to come in."

Lucas looked at Lester, who nodded, agreeing with Roux.

"So. I'll call them, and you two can brief them. We'll want representatives on the team that tracks Dunn. You, Lucas, somebody else."

"Sloan or Capslock."

"Whichever, or both," Roux said. She turned away from them, flicked her lighter, and touched off another cigarette. "Christ, I hope this is the end of it."

Lucas, up all night, arguing with Roux or briefing the feebs, stopped home at five-thirty and ate breakfast with Weather.

"Do you think it's real?" she asked. She was running a

seminar for post-docs that morning, and was dressed in a pale linen suit with a silk scarf.

"It sure sounded good," Lucas said. "Dunn was absolutely spontaneous. We didn't have that phone monitored until yesterday, and we didn't tell him about it . . . so, yeah, I believe the call. I don't think this asshole is gonna hand over his wife and kids, though."

"Then the call was good for one thing," Weather said.

Lucas nodded. "If it's real, it eliminates Dunn from the list."

"Unless . . ." Weather said.

"What?"

"Unless he's talking to somebody in his office, and that person is passing the word along."

Lucas waved her off. "That's too complicated to think about. Possible, but we'd never get to them."

They heard the *Pioneer-Press* paper-delivery car slow outside the house, and the paper hit the walk. Lucas ran out to get it, and as he did, the *Star-Tribune* car came by, and he got that, too. Both papers had photos of Crosby above the fold.

"For all the good it does us," Lucas said, scanning the stories. "He's got her."

"Aren't you planning to talk to the papers today?"

Lucas slapped his forehead. "Yes. Damnit. Noon."

"Get some sleep," she said.

"Yeah." He glanced at his watch. Almost six. "A few hours, anyway."

Weather took her coffee cup and the plate on which she'd had her toast, carried them to the sink, then laughed as she walked back to the table and ruffled his hair.

"What?" he asked.

"You look like you're fifteen and going on your first date. You always do when you get something going. And the more awful it is, and the more tired you get, the happier you look. This whole thing is terrible: and you're getting high on it."

"It's interesting," Lucas admitted. "This kid we're talking to, he's an interesting kid." He looked out the window, where the neighbor from across the street was walking his elderly cocker spaniel, and the day was beginning as quietly as a mouse. "I mean, you know, for a nightmare."

Reporters from five television stations and both major papers showed up at the company headquarters at noon. Lucas talked for five minutes about police tactical simulation software and gaming programs, then passed the reporters to Ice.

Ice said, with the camera rolling, "We're gonna show you how we're gonna catch this sucker and nail his butt to the wall."

Lucas saw the quick smiles from the cameramen and the reporters: he had a hit on his hands. Barry Hunt caught his eye and they nodded at each other.

"The first thing is, we know what he looks like."

Ice ran the art program that manipulated the facial characteristics of the composite drawing of the suspect, adding and deleting hair, mustaches, beards, glasses, and collar styles. The other techies set up a camera to take pictures of the on-air reporters and manipulate their faces through the various styles. Then they put up a show that involved rotating three-dimensional maps of the Twin Cities, supposedly showing general locations of the kidnapper's hideout.

"It's going fuckin' great, as long as nobody asks what it means and how it'll help catch the guy," Ice muttered to Lucas just before he left.

Lucas looked back at the crowd of laughing reporters standing around the computer displays: "Don't worry about it," he said. "This is great video. Nobody'll be stupid enough to ask anything that'd spoil it."

At three o'clock the Dunn task force met at the federal building, with Roux, Lucas, and Sloan representing the city. Roux and Sloan were just walking in when Lucas arrived, and Roux said, "Dunn's picking up the money. The feds are all over him."

"Excellent," Lucas said.

Dumbo and twenty FBI agents were packed in a conference room, with space left for the three city reps. Lucas sat down next to a girl whom he thought must be an intern of some sort, though she hardly seemed old enough. Fifteen, he thought, or sixteen. She looked at him, a level, speculating glance that struck him as too old for her body and face. He felt uncomfortable with her sitting behind him as he faced Dumbo.

Dumbo laid out the procedure: fourteen agents on the ground in seven cars, plus a chopper with a spotter in the air. "We've already marked his car with an infra-red flasher wired into the taillight. I understand that Minneapolis uses the same technique," Dumbo said, his ears flapping.

"Something like it," Sloan said. "I like the taillight deal. That's a nice touch. We oughta talk."

Dumbo looked pleased: "So. You guys want to ride in the chopper or go on the ground?"

"I'm ground," Lucas said.

"I'll go with Lucas," Sloan said. "We've got to coordinate on the radio codes."

"Sure." Dumbo pointed at one of the FBI technical people.

"Who's going into the rest stop?" Lucas asked. "It's gotta look good."

"Marie," Dumbo said, and nodded at the woman behind Lucas. Lucas glanced back at her and she grinned. "We'll put her in a high school letter jacket and a pleated skirt, give her some bubble gum. She'll go in right behind Dunn and head for the phones. There are four of them in a pod. We're monitoring all four. If Dunn has to wait, so will she. If they don't, she'll get on one and start talking to her boyfriend. She'll be looking for anything and anybody."

Roux, peering at the woman from across the table, said, "You're either precocious or older than you look."

"I'm thirty-two," the woman said, in a sweet young soprano.

"And Danny McGreff"—Dumbo nodded at a man with a large square face and two-day beard—"will get there a half-hour before Dunn is scheduled to, will get Dunn's phone and stay on it until he sees Dunn come in the door. Then he'll say good-bye, and drop it on the hook and leave. We don't think anyone should be waiting—there's never been a time when all four of them have been tied up, in the time we've been monitoring them."

"So you'll have one agent in the place and at least one outside . . ."

"We'll have three in the place," Dumbo said. "There's a storage room, lockable, and we'll put two men in there a couple of hours ahead of time. They simply won't come out, and there won't be any way to check inside without a key."

As the meeting was breaking up, Dumbo said, "Let's try to keep the radio communications clean, huh? Washington has asked us to allow a cameraman to ride with us tonight, for a documentary being made, uh, anyway for a documentary. I've agreed."

. On the way out the door, an FBI technician muttered at Lucas, "Keep your box on Fox."

Sloan said, "We could be in a world of hurt."

"How?" Roux asked. They pushed through the brass revolving doors onto the street.

"They've got everything figured out," Sloan said. He started peeling a Dentine pack. "Everything's on a schedule. But this can't be as easy as it looks—there's a joker in the deck somewhere."

Lucas looked up and down the street, and saw a one-time pimp named Robert Lika, whom the local wits called Leica because of his fondness for flashing preteen girls. Lika was peeing into a doorway, one hand braced on the door jamb as though the doorway were an ordinary urinal. "Will you look at this?"

"Rather not," said Roux, and her face colored.

"You're a little pink," Lucas said.

"You know, you didn't see much of that until the last two or three years," Roux said, looking down at Lika. "Now you see it all the time. It's such a weird . . . turn."

• • •

The federal operation was already moving, but Lucas and Sloan wouldn't be involved until Dunn started toward the rest stop. The feds were monitoring him: after making a morning round of the banks, he'd gone to his office and was still there.

Sloan's wife had had a bunion removed, and her foot was still tender, and Sloan snuck off to do some grocery shopping on city time. Lucas, restless, caught lunch at a cop bar, put twenty dollars on the Vikes over Chicago, eating the eight-point spread—the Bears sucked—walked the sky-ways for a while, looking at women and clothes, and played with the ring in his pocket.

He was gonna do it, he decided. Something simple—no juvenile tricks, no sophomoric misdirection or declarations. He'd just ask. What could she say, other than no? But she wouldn't say no. She had to know what he was thinking— she could read his mind, she'd proved that. Hell, she was probably getting impatient; maybe she saw all this delay as some kind of insult. But the main thing was, she wouldn't say no. Well, technically, you know, she *could* say no. What if she started out to be really nice about it . . . Fuckin' women.

Wonder what Dunn's doing?

At four-thirty, he went back to the office, got the files out, and started reading through again. The file on the dead kid, where was he? Let's see, subject reported to have jumped from the Lake Street Bridge, reporting officers called boat . . .

The PR woman stuck her head in the door. "Lucas, they're talking about you on TV, on the promos, so you'll be up in the next couple of minutes if you want to watch."

"Yeah, I want . . ." Lucas had just turned the page on the report and looked up at the PR lady, but an after-image stuck in his eye and the after-image was *Gloria*. He looked back down at the page, trying to find it.

"Lucas?"

"Yeah, I'll be along . . ." Where was it? He found it at the bottom of the page:

". . . witness Gloria Crosby said he'd been depressed since getting out of the state hospital and had stopped taking his prescription medication. Crosby said he may have been taking street drugs and had been acting irrational and that on 8/9 she had him admitted to Hennepin General for apparent drug overdose. Crosby said subject called her and asked to meet him at the Stanley Grill on Lake Street and that when she got there he was already walking toward the bridge. She walked after him, but when she got to the bridge the subject was standing on the railing and stepped off before she could approach him. Crosby said she ran back to Stanley Grill to call for assistance . . ."

Damnit. Gloria Crosby. Crouched over the desk, he thumbed through the rest of the papers, trying to figure out what had happened. The phone rang and he snatched it off the desk:

"What?"

"Lucas, you're on . . ."

"Yeah, yeah." He banged down the receiver, went back to the papers, and then picked up the phone again, punched in Anderson's number.

"This is Lucas . . ."

"Lucas, you're on . . ."

"Yeah, yeah, fuck that, listen, you gotta get everything you can find on a guy named John Mail, DOB 7/7/68. Did time in the state hospital. We need the most recent photo we can find. Check the DMV and find his parents . . . wait, wait, I've got this . . ." Lucas shuffled through the papers. "His folks lived at 28 Sharf Lane in Wayzata. Goddamnit, that's where McPherson said he was from."

"Who?"

"Just get that shit, man. This is something."

Off the phone again, he went through the file on Mail and found the reference to the dental records. Damnit. He got his book, looked up the Medical Examiner's number.

"Sharon, this is Lucas Davenport . . . yeah, fine, it's all healed up, yeah, listen, I need you to pull something for me.

You should have some records on a guy named John Mail went off the Lake Street Bridge a few years back, I can get you the date if you need it. John Mail. Yeah, I'll wait."

Ten seconds later, she was back. Mail was on the computer. "Just hold it there," Lucas said. "I'm gonna run over right now."

Lucas was out the door and down the street, a fast five-minute walk to the Medical Examiner's. An ME's investigator named Brunswick was peering at a computer.

"Something hot?" he asked.

"You say a guy is dead," Lucas said. "I think he might still be alive."

"Well, the guy we saw was dead," Brunswick said. "I've been looking at the pictures." He passed a group of eight-by-ten color photographs to Lucas. The remains of the body. Still partly wrapped in the remains of a pair of Levi blue jeans, was spread on a stainless steel table. Most of it was bone, although the torso looked like a gray ball of string or grass. The face was gone, but the dark hair was still there. Both hands were missing, as was one leg.

"Bad shape. Were the hands—is that natural? Is there any possibility they were taken off?"

Brunswick shook his head. "No way to tell. The body was falling apart. The one unusual thing is that there was evidence of a ligature around the torso—wire, or something. God knows, in that part of the Mississippi, it could have been anything."

"Could somebody have anchored the body somewhere? Until it was ready to be found?"

"You've got a nasty turn of mind, Davenport."

"But you already thought of that," Lucas said.

"Yeah. And it's possible. Whatever it was tied him down, had him for a while. Nearly cut the body through, in the end. There was no sign of any ligature when the body was found, though."

"What about the dental records?"

"It's the right guy, by the records. Here are the X rays on the body, and you can see the dental X rays."

Lucas bent over them and looked: they were patently

identical. In the corner of the dental records was a response phone number at the state hospital. Lucas picked up Brunswick's phone and punched the number in.

"Can't be right," Lucas said.

A woman answered. Lucas identified himself and said, "I need to talk to Dr. L. D. Rehder, does he still work there? I'm sorry, she? Yeah, it really is important. Yeah."

To Brunswick, he said, "I'm on hold."

Brunswick said, "Is this the Manette case?"

"Part of it," Lucas said.

"My wife went on a march last night to protest violence against women," Brunswick said.

"Hope it works," Lucas said.

On the phone, a woman said, "This is Dr. Rehder."

"Yeah, Dr. Rehder, some time ago one of your patients apparently committed suicide. The body ID was confirmed by dental records from your office," Lucas said. "A kid named John Mail."

"I remember John." Her voice was pleasantly clipped. "He was with us for quite a while."

"Is there any way he could've gotten to the records to switch them with somebody else's? I mean, before he got out of the hospital?"

"Oh, I don't think so. He was confined in a completely different area. He would have had to escape over there, break in here without being detected, then get out of here and break back in over there. It would have been very difficult."

"Damnit," Lucas said.

"Is there some question about whether it was John who jumped off the bridge?" Rehder asked.

"Yes. Have you by any chance seen the police composite pictures of the man who kidnapped Mrs. Manette and her daughters?"

Rehder said, "Yes, I have. John had dark hair."

"He may have changed the hair color . . ."

"Just a minute, let me get my paper."

"Getting her paper," Lucas said to Brunswick. He shuffled through the pictures of the body while they waited. Then

Rehder came back on and said, "If the hair was changed, if the hair was black, I've just colored it in with my felt-tip pen. It could be John. There's something not quite right about the chin line."

Lucas nodded. He knew he was right. "Okay. Does the name Gloria Crosby mean anything to you?"

"Gloria?" Rehder said. "Gloria was an aide—Gloria worked for us."

Lucas closed his eyes. *Gotcha.*

22

Anderson, harried, his hands full of paper, his sharecropper's face pickled in a permanent squint, said, "Sloan said to tell you he's bringing the car. Dunn's moving: you gotta get out of here."

"Stay on the Mail thing," Lucas said, pulling on his jacket.

Anderson ticked it off on his fingers. "We're tracking his friends, to see if anybody's run into him since the bridge, if anybody has a name. We're trying to figure out who the body really was, but that will be a problem. It has to be somebody at the hospital who had dental care, who was close to Mail's size and age, and who was out at the same time, but there are hundreds of people who fit, all of them are mentally ill, and a lot of them are impossible to find. We're trying to find Mail's parents—his mother and stepfather. We think they might have split up. We know they moved to the Seattle area, but one of the stepfather's friends heard they split out there, and the mother might have remarried."

"What about decent photos of the guy?"

"We've got photos coming from the hospital and the DMV, but they're all years old," Anderson said.

"Yeah, but with something real to work from, we can age

him. Get them over to the company, if you need to. They were doing some good stuff this morning."

"Okay. But you need to talk with the chief about whether to release them to the press. If he's as close to the edge as you say he is . . ."

"Yeah. I'll be back. Don't do anything until we talk about it. And if anything breaks—*anything*—call me. I'll be on the phone."

When Lucas ran out, Sloan was walking up to the building, carrying a baseball cap.

"Where is he? Dunn?"

"He's coming through town right now," Sloan said over his shoulder as he turned and headed back into the street. He had a gray, four-year-old Chevy Caprice sitting in traffic with its engine running. "We've got to motivate."

The radios they'd gotten from the feds were standard: Lucas called in, checking the identification protocols, and was told that *zebra is underway; the subject has been acquired.*

"That means they can see the car from the chopper," Lucas said.

"Fuckin' wonderful," Sloan said.

"It's better than the ten-four bullshit," Lucas said. "I never did understand that."

"Did you bring the maps?"

"Yeah, and I got one for the Hudson area, just in case." Lucas took the maps out of his pocket. The radio burped: *Approaching White Bear Avenue Interchange.*

"This is really fucked, you know?" Lucas said. "I'm sitting here thinking that it's a little too strange."

As they paced Dunn's car through the city and into the 'burbs, Lucas told Sloan about the identification of John Mail. "Haven't pinned him yet," Lucas said.

"If he's the guy, we will," Sloan said confidently. "Once we get a face . . ."

"I hope," Lucas said.

They were in the countryside now, and white puffy clouds cast long shadows on new-cut hay, the last cut of the year.

The beans and corn, as far as Lucas could tell, were about as good as they ever got in Minnesota, the corn showing stripes of gold along the edge of the leaves, the beans already brown and drying. A few miles out of St. Paul, an ultra-light aircraft circled over the highway, the pilot plainly visible in his leathers and black helmet. Further on, toward the St. Croix River, a half-dozen brightly colored hot-air balloons drifted east toward Wisconsin.

And the radio said, *He's off at 95 . . . he's back on, heading east.*

This is five; we got him coming in.

Dumbo: *Everybody in position, now.*

"Get off at Highway 15," Lucas said, pointing at an exit sign. "Go north, find a place to turn around and start back. We don't want to sit anywhere. If Mail is out roaming around, and sees us, he'd recognize me."

Sloan took the off-ramp, paused at the top, and started north on the blacktopped road. "Van coming up from behind," Sloan said.

Lucas slid down in his seat and Sloan took the first left. The van stayed on the main road. Sloan, looking in the rearview mirror, said, "Blonde. Woman." He did a U-turn and started back.

He's inside. We've got him covered.

"They're doing okay," Lucas said nervously.

"Give them time," Sloan said. "The feebs could fuck up a wet dream."

Lucas and Sloan both looked at their watches simultaneously. Sloan said, "Five minutes," and Lucas grunted.

They were headed back toward the interstate, no other cars in sight. The landscape was littered with new suburban houses with plastic siding in pastel tints ranging from sunset to sage; here and there a farm field came up to the edge of the road. A flock of sheep grazed over a pasture.

Lucas said, "Green pastures."

"Say what?" Sloan looked at him.

Lucas said, "These are the green pastures, from Psalms. Elle was right. I'll bet my ass that he's about to lead us into Stillwater. How far are we from Stillwater? Ten miles?"

"About that."

"Let's head that way," Lucas said urgently. "We're pretty useless anyway."

"If he's leading us, then this might not be what it looks like . . ."

"Yeah, yeah," Lucas said. "Exactly right."

And the radio said, *We've got a confirmed hit, confirmed hit. He's off, he's gone, Jimmy get me . . . what? We've got cellular confirmed but no cell designation, it was too quick. Can we run that, Jimmy? Jimmy? Subject is out of the rest stop on his way to the car, can we get the intercept up . . .*

"What the fuck did he say?" Lucas asked. "What'd Mail say?"

And the radio said, *Subject was told to go to a picnic table and pull a note off the bottom side and follow instructions . . . subject is at the picnic table, subject is walking back to the car, he's reading a paper, he has the instructions . . .*

"Come on, goddamnit, we gotta move," Lucas said. "It's Stillwater."

Subject is in car proceeding west on I-94.

"Wrong way," Sloan grunted.

"He's got no choice from there," Lucas said. He slapped his own forehead. "And think about it, think about it: the guy makes the initial contact on Dunn's cellular phone, and routes him to a public phone? Why'd he do that? Why didn't he call him on the cellular again? Then he wouldn't have to fuck around with the possibility that somebody else was using the pay phone. Why'd he do that, Sloan?"

"I don't know." Sloan frowned as he thought about it. "Maybe . . . no. If he doesn't trust the cellular now, why'd he trust it yesterday?"

"He didn't. Maybe he figured we'd be monitoring it," Lucas said. "Maybe he did it so we'd be close by, but he'd know where we were at. I'll bet that sonofabitch is in Stillwater right now. Goddamnit, what's he doing?"

Three minutes later the radio burped, *Subject exiting*

at Highway 15 . . . crossing Interstate, reentering Inter-state . . .

"What's he doing?" Sloan asked. "Why didn't he go this way?"

"He's going down to 95 and he'll take 95 north to Stillwater," Lucas said. "It's simpler, if you don't have a map. How fast can we get there?"

"We'll be there in six or seven minutes. He'll be ten minutes behind us. If you're right."

"I'm right."

"Yeah, I know." Sloan had the Chevy up to ninety, sloughed past the Lake Elmo airport with its pole-barn hangars, and onto Highway 5 east toward Stillwater.

"Goddamnit, I wish we were set up with the Stillwater cops. Just a few guys to sit and watch. We could've shipped a picture of Mail out here."

They listened to the parade moving east on the interstate, then Lucas got on the radio to Dumbo. "We're headed to Stillwater, we think he's playing out the Bible verses he sent us. You probably ought to have your lead cars get off at Highway 95 and start north. And take it easy: we've got two more verses to go, but the last one talks about a trap."

"Got it covered, Minneapolis," Dumbo said. "Keep your heads down. We don't want a crowd."

"Thanks for the technical advice," Sloan muttered.

As Dunn and the federal parade turned off the interstate, Sloan blew past a Dodge pickup on the Highway 36 entrance ramp. The truck swerved onto the shoulder as they passed, and the driver, a young, long-haired man, leaned on his horn and then came after them as they weaved through the traffic, down a long passage of convenience stores and fast-food joints.

"Asshole," Sloan said, grinning into his rearview mirror.

"Better hope he doesn't kill any kids," Lucas said.

"Yeah. The fuckin' paperwork alone. We gotta light coming up, you wanna hop out and chat with him?"

"Unless you want to run the light."

"All right."

The truck loomed behind them as they slowed for the light, closed to eight inches from their bumper, and the kid was back on the horn.

Lucas turned to look over the backseat. The trucker had one hand on the wheel and the other on the horn; a young woman, next to him in the passenger seat, seemed to be yelling—he could see the points of her canine teeth—but Lucas couldn't tell whether she was yelling at the driver or at him. Then she gave him the finger and Lucas decided that he was definitely the target. The trucker dropped the transmission into park, popped his door, and started to climb out, and Sloan went through the red light.

"Goddamn, he's coming through the red," Sloan said, peering in the mirror.

The radio: *Two miles out of Bayport, slow and steady.*

"We gotta do something about this guy," Sloan said as they took the long sweeping curve toward the St. Croix River. They'd cut the corner off Dunn's route and were approaching Highway 95 ahead of him. "Dunn's not five miles away. Going through Bayport'll slow him down, but this asshole . . ." He looked in the mirror, and the truck was coming after them.

"All right," Lucas said. "There's a marina up ahead. Pull in there. He'll come in behind us and I'll take him in the parking lot." Lucas pulled his .45 out of the shoulder rig, popped the magazine, jacked the shell out of the chamber, slapped the magazine back in the butt, and dropped the extra shell in his coat pocket. "What a pain in the ass."

"Ready?" Sloan asked.

"Yeah. You got cuffs? If we need them?"

"Glove compartment."

Sloan kept the speed up until he was on top of the marina entrance, then stood on the brakes and took them off the highway. The trucker almost rammed them, swerved out at the last minute, then cranked the truck down the road behind them. Sloan kept moving until they hit the parking lot, then pulled around in a circle. The trucker cut inside them, and they stopped, nearly nose-to-nose.

Lucas popped the door and climbed out, the pistol back in

its holster. The trucker was already on the ground, running around the back of his truck, reaching into the open truck bed for something. Lucas ran toward him and the trucker pulled out a length of two-by-four and Lucas screamed, "Police," showed his badge in his left hand, and pulled the pistol in his right. "On the ground. On the ground, asshole."

The trucker looked at the two-by-four, his eyes puzzled, as though it had gotten into his hand by mistake, then chunked it back into the truck. "You cut me off," he said.

"Get on the fuckin' ground," Lucas shouted.

The woman started out of the passenger side, but when she saw the gun, she got back in and punched down the door locks. Sloan got out and held up a badge where she could see it.

The trucker was flat on the blacktop, looking up, and Lucas said, "We're on an emergency run, we're in a big goddamn hurry or I'd kick your ass into fuckin' strawberry jam. As it is, I'm gonna take your truck license number. I want you to sit here, out of the way, for a half-hour. You can sit in the truck, but you sit for a half-hour, and then you can leave. If you leave before then, I'll be all over your ass. I'll put your ass in jail on fifteen fuckin' traffic counts and a couple of felonies, like interfering with officers. You understand that?"

"I understand, sir." The trucker had grown calm.

"All right. Get in the truck and sit. Half an hour."

Lucas hurried back to the car and Sloan pulled it around in a circle and they were halfway out of the parking lot before they started laughing.

"Funny, but Christ, I wished that hadn't happened just then," Lucas said as he reloaded the .45. "They say anything more on the radio?"

"Yeah, they said . . ." Before Sloan could get it out, the radio said, *He's into Bayport, still proceeding north. We got him.*

"We've got five minutes," Sloan said.

"Main Street's only about ten blocks long. Let's run down it and see what we can see," Lucas said.

• • •

Stillwater was an old lumber mill town, with most of the turn-of-the-century mercantile buildings still in place, crowding Main Street. The buildings had been renovated with tourists in mind, and were now filled with bricks-and-copper-pot restaurants, fern bars, and butter-churn antique stores; the long row of brick store fronts was inflected by the white plastic of a Fina station.

Lucas slumped in his seat, Sloan's baseball cap on his head, only his eyes above the window sill. He hoped he looked like a child but wouldn't have bet on it. "Two million vans," he said. "Everywhere you look, there's a van, if the sonofabitch is dumb enough to still be driving that van around."

The chopper: *Subject proceeding through Bayport.*

Sloan idled the length of the town, and they saw nothing of interest: storefronts full of tourists, teenagers idling along the walks, one kid who might've been Mail but wasn't. In the light of a pizza place, his face was five years too young.

At the north end of town, Lucas said, "We've got three or four minutes to set up. Let's go back to the other end and find a spot where we can watch the street. If he turns off right away, we should be able to see him. If he goes on past, we can fall in behind."

"Piss off the feds," Sloan said.

"Fuck 'em. Something's happening."

Sloan made a U-turn in the parking lot of a run-down building with a line of dancing cowboy boots painted on the bare, corrugated metal in flaking house paint. They waited for a break in traffic and then drove back to the south end of town, pulled into a parking lot, and found an empty handicapped parking space facing the street. A line of pine trees separated the lot from the street. "Probably get a ticket," Sloan said as he pulled into the handicapped space.

"I don't know," Lucas said. "I've always thought of you as handicapped."

Radio: *The subject has exited Bayport and is proceeding north.*

"Why's he talking like that?" Sloan asked.

"He's got that camera with him. He'll say *perpetrator* in a minute."

From their vantage in the parking lot, they could look through the line of trees and see the cars coming into town on Highway 95. Dunn drove a silver Mercedes 500 S, and as the chopper radio said *Subject is entering Stillwater,* Lucas picked it out in the traffic stream.

"See him?"

"I've got him."

"Let him get past."

Sloan backed the car out of the handicapped slot. "I wonder where the feds are?"

"Probably not real close."

They waited behind the trees until the Mercedes went past, and then Sloan pulled out of the lot and back onto Main Street. There were two cars between them and Dunn. Lucas, slumped in his seat, couldn't see him.

"What's he doing?" he asked, when they all stopped for a red light.

Sloan had edged a bit to the left, and said, "Nothing. Looking straight ahead."

"What do you think? Is Dunn legit?"

Sloan looked at him. "If he's not, they had to set it up ahead of time."

"Well, he's a smart guy."

"I don't know," Sloan said. The traffic started moving again. "That'd be awful tricky."

"Yeah."

After a moment, Sloan said, "It looks like he's going all the way through town. Unless he's going to that old train station. Or one of the antique places."

"Shit: I hope he doesn't take a boat somewhere. Did the feds think of a boat? Boy, if the sonofabitch goes out on the water . . ."

"We could grab a boat from somebody," Sloan said.

"I'd give ten bucks to see that note he got from the picnic table."

"With your money, you could do better," Sloan said.

"Hey. He's slowing down. Goddamn, he's turning around right where we did."

"Go on past," Lucas said. He sat up a bit and saw the silver Benz turning in the gravel parking lot outside the building painted with the cowboy boots. Sloan pulled into the next parking lot, a marina, and found a space with two cars between them and Dunn.

"Goddamnit," Lucas said. He put his hand to his forehead.

Subject has stopped. Subject has stopped. Five, are you on him?

We see him, we're proceeding into parking lot down the street.

"The whole fuckin' lot's gonna be full of cops," Sloan said. "That must be them." A dark Ford bumped into the lot, and Lucas could see that it was full of adult-sized heads.

"Can you see the name of that place?" Lucas asked. "Where he's at?"

"No light," Sloan said. Across the street, Dunn was getting out of his car. He looked up at the boot store and started toward it, ponderously. He carried a briefcase and slumped with it, as though it weighed a hundred pounds.

Lucas picked up the federal radio. "This is Davenport. We're in the same parking lot with your guys. If he tries to go into that building, I'm going to stop him. We need you to spread your people out on the street, set up a net and look at faces, see if you can spot Mail. He's around here."

Dumbo was sputtering. "Davenport, you stay the heck out of here. You stay out of here, we've got it under control."

Sloan was looking at him curiously, and said, "Lucas, I don't think . . ."

"Fuck me, fuck me," Lucas said. He pushed open the door.

"Lucas!" Sloan was whispering, though Dunn was a long way away.

A concrete loading dock ran along the front of the cowboy building, and Dunn was climbing heavily up the steps at one end. The building was dark, with no sign of movement. Dunn went to the door, and Lucas climbed out of the car, radio in his hand.

Sloan said, "Lucas . . ."

And Lucas put the radio to his mouth and said, "I gotta stop him. Get your men out." He tossed the radio back into the car and started running, yelling at Dunn: "Dunn, Dunn! Wait. George Dunn . . ."

Dunn stopped, his hand on the door of the store. Lucas waved, and, glancing back, saw Sloan coming after him. "Take the back of the building," Lucas shouted. Sloan yelled something and broke off, and Lucas ran toward Dunn, who simply stood.

"Get down off of there," Lucas shouted as he came up.

"You sonofabitch," Dunn shouted back. "You've killed my kids . . ."

"Get out of there," Lucas yelled. He ran up the steps— saw in the dark window the barely discernible words, "Bit & Bridle"—and reached for his gun.

"What the fuck are you doing here?" Dunn asked. His face was stretched with tension and anger.

"There's something wrong," Lucas said. "This whole thing is a set-up."

"Set-up," Dunn shouted. "Set-up? You just fuckin' . . ." And before Lucas could stop him, Dunn turned the door knob and shoved the door open. Lucas flinched. Nothing happened. ". . . fuckin' killed my kids . . ."

Lucas pulled his .45 and stepped past Dunn into the building, groped for a light switch, found it, flicked the switch up. To his surprise, the lights came on. The store was empty, and apparently had been for some time. He was facing a long bare counter top, with vacant shelves behind it. All of it was covered with a patina of dust.

A fed ran up the steps. "What the hell are you doing?" he shouted at Lucas. Lucas waved him away, then said, "You oughta get out on the street and watch for Mail. He's watching this from somewhere."

"Watching what?"

"Whatever he's got going here," Lucas said. "This used to be a place called the Bit and Bridle. One of those Bible verses said something about a bit and bridle. It was all too fuckin' easy."

The fed looked around the empty room, then reached back under his jacket and pulled out a Smith & Wesson automatic. "You want to try that door? Or you think we should wait for the bomb squad?"

"Let's take a look," Lucas suggested. To Dunn, he said, "You wait outside."

"Yeah, bullshit."

"Wait the fuck outside," Lucas said.

Dunn dropped the briefcase and said, "You wanna find out right now if you can take me?"

"Ah, Jesus," Lucas said. He turned away from Dunn and went to a doorway that led into the back of the building. The doorway was open just an inch, and Lucas, standing well off to the back side of it, pushed it open another inch. Nothing happened. The fed moved in from the opening side, reached around the corner, groped for a minute, found the light switch, and turned it on.

The place was deadly silent until Dunn said, "There's nothing here. He's gone."

Lucas looked through the two-inch opening, saw nothing, then pushed the door open a foot, then all the way. The door opened into what looked like a storage room. A stack of shelves, covered with dust, sat against one wall. A handful of blank receipt forms was scattered over the wooden floor. A 1991 Snap-On Tool calendar still hung on a wall.

"Somebody's been here," the fed said. He pointed his Smith at the floor, at a tangled line of footprints in the dust. The prints came through another door further back. The door was open several inches. Lucas stood next to it and called out, "Mail? John Mail?"

"Who's that?" Dunn asked. "Is that the guy?"

"Yeah."

"There's a light switch," the fed said. "I'm gonna get it, watch it."

He hit the switch, and three light bulbs, scattered around the central shaft of the building, popped on. The building had been remodelled since it had last been used to store grain, and the grain storage shaft had been partitioned into storage rooms and a receiving dock. The rooms had no ceilings, but looked straight to the top of the shaft. The light inside the shaft was weak—the volume was too big for the three operable bulbs.

But in the gloom above them, something moved. They all saw it at once, and Lucas and the fed pressed back against the walls, their guns up.

"What is it?"

"Aw, Jesus," Dunn shouted, turning in his own footprints, head craned up. "It's Andi, Jesus . . ."

Then Lucas could see it, the body in black, the feet below it, twisting from a yellow rope at the top of the shaft. The door they had not yet tried went into the receiving dock and the main part of the shaft itself. Dunn broke toward it, hands out to stiff-arm the door . . .

"Wait, wait," Lucas screamed. He launched himself cross the room in a body block, caught Dunn just behind the knees, and cut him down. The fed stood frozen as they thrashed on the floor for a moment, and Lucas, gun still in one hand, trying to control it, sputtered at the fed, "Hold him, for christ sakes."

"That's Andi," Dunn groaned as the fed put away his pistol and grabbed Dunn's coat. "Let me up."

"That's not your wife," Lucas said. "That's a woman named Crosby."

"Crosby? Who's Crosby?"

"A friend of Mail's," Lucas said shortly. "We've been trying to track her, but he got to her first."

Lucas, back on his feet, holstered his pistol and went to the partially open door to the shaft. There was a slight draft through the doorway, but nothing else. Lucas reached through, found another light switch, hesitated, then flipped it on. Again, the lights worked. He looked through the crack in the door, saw nothing. No wires, nothing that might be a bomb. He gave the door a push and was ready to step through.

But the door seemed to resist for a split second, just a

hair-trigger hold, and then a break, almost imperceptible, but enough that Lucas jumped back.

"What?" The FBI man was grinning at him.

"I thought I felt . . ." Lucas started. He put his hand out toward the door and took a step.

And was nearly knocked off his feet as the door seemed to explode a foot from his face.

Can see, he thought, his hands up in front of his face. *Nothing hurts . . .*

"What?" the fed was shouting, his gun out again, pointing at the shattered wooden door. "What? What? What was that?"

Dust filtered down on them and rolled out of the back room like smoke. Lucas could taste dirt in his mouth, feel the grit in his eyes. Dunn had reflexively turned away, but now turned back, his hair and shoulders covered with grime.

"What was that?"

Lucas stepped back to the door, pushed it, pushed it again, pushed hard. It opened a foot and he looked through. On the other side, the floor was littered with river rocks, granite cobblestones the size of pumpkins, fifteen or twenty of them.

"Trap," Lucas said. He pushed the door again and a rock rolled away from it. Lucas stepped through and saw the rope from the top of the door leading up into the darkness. "They fell a long way. If one of them hit you, it'd be like getting hit by a cannonball."

"But that's not Andi?" Dunn said, following him through, looking up at the body. In the stronger light, they could now see the soles of the woman's feet, like dancing footprints above their heads.

"No. That's just bait," Lucas said. "That was to get us to run through the door without thinking about it."

"Asshole," said the fed. He was dusting himself off. "Somebody could have got hurt."

23

Mail's trap had snapped, but it had come up empty. Still, it had excited him: figuring it out, setting it up. He hadn't planned to put Gloria's body in the loft section, but it had worked so well in his mind—the cheese to pull them, unthinking, into the trap.

And it must've been close, because they'd tripped it. He could tell by the way they were acting.

"We knew there'd be a booby trap, that there'd be *something*," Davenport said. He seemed to find the situation almost funny, in a grim way. He stood with his back to the Bit & Bridle, his hard face made even harder by the television lights; his suit seemed unwrinkled, his tie went with his cool blue eyes. "We were hoping that by flooding the area with unmarked cars, we'd spot him. We're still processing license numbers."

"You're lying, asshole," Mail shouted at the television screen. Then he laughed, pointed at the screen with a beer bottle. "You got lucky, motherfucker."

Davenport looked out at him, unblinking. Behind Davenport, cops swarmed over the Bit & Bridle storefront. He missed some of what Davenport had said, and picked up on, ". . . we'll have to wait for the Medical Examiner's report on Gloria Crosby. She may have been up there for quite a while. We don't think he'd risk confronting us."

"You're fuckin' lying," Mail shouted. He jumped out of the chair and punched the TV off, sat down, bounced twice, picked up the remote, and punched it back on.

This was not right: he'd pulled them into Stillwater with the phony verses—he'd known that they'd look at Stillwater, but they wouldn't have gone into the city when Dunn was just outside it. They would've stayed with Dunn. Mail had been in Stillwater in the early morning hours, just after his first call to Dunn, and there'd been no cops anywhere. Unmarked cars, bullshit. He would have noticed.

But he worried about his plates: *were* they on a list somewhere?

The talking head had moved on: Davenport was gone, and the news program had gone to a room full of computer cubicles, and a group of young people gathered around a monitor. There was an air of urgency among them, like a war room.

The reporter was saying, ". . . is also the owner of a company that makes police and security-oriented computer training software. He has placed those resources at the command of the department, for the duration of the hunt for Andi Manette and her children. A working group of gaming and software experts anticipated the kidnapper's moves, including the possibility of a booby trap . . ."

What?

". . . believe they are closing in on the kidnapper or kidnappers . . ."

"That's bullshit," Mail said. But as he watched the video of the group crouched over their screens, he envied them. Good equipment, good group. They were all dressed informally, and two of the men were holding oversized coffee mugs. They probably all went out at night for pizza and beer and laughed.

The reporter was saying, ". . . but everybody just calls her by her last name, Ice." A startlingly attractive young woman with a punk haircut and a nose ring grinned out at Mail and said, "We've almost had him twice. Almost. And it's really a rush. I never worked with the cops before—I mean, except for Lucas—and it's pretty interesting. Totally better'n programming some pinball game or something. Totally."

"Do you think you'll get him?" the reporter asked.

Ice nodded. "Oh, yeah, if the cops don't get him first 'cause of some routine f—— mistake." She'd been about to say fuck-up, Mail thought. And he liked her. "Right now, over there"—she pointed at two women huddled over keyboards—"we're keying in everything we know about the guy, and we know quite a bit. We include a list of all the possible suspects, you know, like profiles of previous offenders from the police department, Andi Manette's patients, and so on. Not too long from now, we'll push a button and some names'll come out, cross-referenced by the other things we know. I'd bet my [beep] that our guy's name's like totally on the list."

When the story ended, Mail went into the kitchen and pulled out a phone book, looked up Davenport's company. He found it on University Avenue, in Minneapolis, down in the old warehouse and rail yard district west of Highway 280. Huh. Probably cops all over the place.

Back in the front room, a different talking head was going on about a troop movement in the Middle East, and Mail picked up the remote and surfed.

Ice came up again—Channel Three. "The guy has shown a certain crude intelligence, so we think it's possible that he wore a wig or colored his hair during the actual attack. One of the witnesses mentioned that his hair didn't look quite right. If he's really dark-haired, he'd look more like this . . ."

The TV went to a composite. Mail was riveted: the computer composite didn't look exactly like him, but it was close enough. And they knew about the van, and about the gaming.

He nibbled nervously on a thumbnail. Maybe these people really did amount to something.

This Ice chick: she was as good as Andi Manette. He'd like to try her sometime.

But Davenport and this computer operation . . . something should be done.

Andi and Grace had lost their grip on passing time: Andi tried to keep them alert but found that more and more they were sleeping between Mail's visits, huddled on the mattress, curled like discarded fetuses.

Andi had lost count of the assaults. Mail was becoming increasingly violent and increasingly angry. After the episode with the witch-woman, Mail had beaten her with her arms overhead, and she'd been unable to protect herself; that night, she'd found blood in her urine.

She was disappointing him, now, but she didn't know what he had expected and so couldn't do anything about it. He had begun talking to Grace—a word or two, a sentence—when he took Andi out and put her back in. Andi could feel his interest shifting.

So could Grace, who hid from it, in sleep. And sometimes, in nightmares, she'd groan or whimper. Andi first held her, then tried to cover her own ears, then got angry at the girl for her fear, then was washed at guilt because of her anger, and held the girl, and then she got angry again . . .

When they talked, Andi had little to suggest. "If he takes you, wet yourself. Just . . . pee. That's supposed to turn off a lot of people like this."

"God, mom . . ." Grace's eyes pleaded with her to do something: a nightmare of Andi's own, but she couldn't wake from it.

The nail in the overhead beam was perhaps half-exposed, and was as unmovable as before. They'd given up working on it, but when Andi rolled onto her back, she could see the nail head glowing faintly in the dark wood. A reproach . . .

She and Grace hadn't spoken for two hours when Grace, exhausted but unable to sleep, rolled from her left side to her right, and a spring-tensioner broke in the mattress. The spring pushed up into the pad that covered it, and thrust a small, uncomfortable bump into Grace's cheek.

"God," was all Grace said.

Andi: "What?" She rolled onto her back and looked up at the light bulb. Sooner or later, it'd burn out, she thought, and they'd be in the dark. Would that be better? She tried to think.

"Something broke in the mattress," Grace said. She pushed herself up with one hand and punched the bump with the other hand. "It makes a bump."

Andi turned her head to look: the bump looked like somebody were gently trying to push a thumb through the pad. "Just move over . . ." Then, suddenly, she sat up. "Grace—there's a spring in there."

Grace said, "So?"

"So a spring is as good as a nail."

Grace looked at her, then at the mattress, and some of the dullness seemed to lift from her face. "Can we get one out?"

"I'm sure."

They crawled off the mattress, flipped it over, and tried to scratch through the fabric. The fabric was as tough as leather; Andi broke a nail without even damaging it.

"We're trying to go too fast," Grace said. "We've got to go slow, like with the nail. Let me chew on it."

Grace chewed on it forever—for five minutes—then Andi chewed on it for another two, and finally cut through. The hole was small, but with a little worrying, they opened it enough that Grace could get a finger through. Tugging on the hole, she started to split the fabric, and then Andi could get fingers from both hands through at once, and she ripped a two-foot hole in the bottom of the mattress.

The springs were coiled steel, both tied and sewn in. They took another twenty minutes working one free, using their teeth.

"Got it," Andi said, lifting it out of the hole. Grace took it, turned it in her hands. The spring had a sharp, nipped-off tip. She used it to pick at the stitching around another spring, and in a minute had the second one free.

"I bet we could get the nail out with these," Grace said, looking up at the overhead. Her face was grimy, with dirt grimed into wrinkles around her eyes.

"We could try—but let's see what happens when we

stretch these things out. Maybe we won't need it." Andi rubbed the end of the spring on an exposed granite rock in the wall, the concrete floor: after a moment she looked at it, and then at Grace. "It works," she said. "We can sharpen them."

A moment later, they heard the feet on the floor above. "Back in the mattress," Andi snapped. They put the springs back in the hole, flipped the mattress over, shoved it against the wall, curled up on it.

Grace's back was to Andi, so she whispered to the wall, "Be nice to him. Maybe he won't hurt you."

"I . . . can't be," Andi whispered. "When he takes me out there, something turns off."

"Try," Grace pleaded. "If he keeps beating you, you'll die."

"I'll try," Andi said. As the steps got closer, she whispered, "Head down. No eye contact."

24

Roux had her feet up in the half-dark of her office. She was looking pensively out at the night street, the glow of her cigarette like a firefly.

"I made nice with Stillwater," she said without turning her head.

"Thanks." Lucas popped the top on a Diet Coke and sat down. "What about Dunn? Are the feds gonna charge him with anything?"

"They're making noises, but they won't. Dunn's already talking with Washington," she said. She blew a smoke ring toward her curtains.

"We should have known that it was too easy—that Mail was jerking us around," Lucas said. "By the way, I don't know if Lester told you, but Crosby was killed before she ever got to the loft. We didn't kill her."

"He told me. You looked great on the tube, by the way. You almost might've been telling the truth, about figuring out the trap business," Roux said.

"The feds are going along," Lucas said.

"Not much choice. If they don't, they look like fools." Roux turned to tamp the cigarette out in an ashtray, fumbled another one out of the pack, and lit it with a plastic lighter. "Are you sure we're looking for this Mail guy?"

"Yeah. Pretty sure," Lucas said.

"But you don't want to go out with it."

"I'm afraid it might trigger him. If we put his actual face on the air, he'd have to run for it. He wouldn't leave anybody behind."

"Huh." Roux tapped ashes off the cigarette. "I could use something that would look like progress."

"I don't have anything like that."

"Mail's name is gonna get out," she said.

"Yeah, but maybe not for a day or two. I don't see it going much longer than that."

"I wonder if she's still alive? Manette."

"I think so," Lucas said. "When he kills her, we won't hear from him any more. There wouldn't be any point. As long as he's fucking with us, as long as he's calling me, she's alive. And I think one of the girls."

"Christ, I'm tired," she said.

"Tell me," Lucas said. He yawned. "I'm sleeping at the company tonight. On a cot."

"Who's with you?"

"Intelligence guys. And Sloan is over there tonight."

"You still think he'll come in?"

"If he's watching TV, he might. He'll be curious. And in the meantime, we're trying to nail down his friends."

A few clouds had come through in the late evening and dropped just enough rain to clear the air. Now they'd gone, and the brighter stars were visible through the ground lights. Lucas got the car and cut across town to University Avenue. He noticed a van in his rearview mirror and thought about it: there were tens of thousands of vans in the Twin Cities. If Mail showed up at the company during the day, and they flooded the area with squads, as they were planning, how many vans would be in the net? A hundred? A hundred might be manageable. But what if it were five hundred, or a thousand?

Maybe the techies at the office had some kind of statistics software that would tell him how many vans he could expect in, say, a ten-minute period in a square mile of the city. Would the density of vans be higher in an industrial area than in a suburb?

He was still mulling it over when he pulled into a Subway shop off University. He could see two young sandwich makers through the front window, both red-haired, maybe twins. Nobody else was in the shop. He yawned, went inside. The place smelled of pickles and relish; the clean, watery odor of lettuce mingled with the yeast smell of bread.

"Give me a foot-long BMT on white, everything but the jalapeños," he said.

One of the redheads had disappeared into the back. The other started working on the sandwich. Lucas leaned on the counter and yawned again and turned his head. A van was parked across the street. As Lucas turned his head, the taillight flickered. Somebody inside the dark vehicle had stepped on the brake pedal. The van looked like the one he'd seen in his rearview mirror.

"Hey, kid," Lucas said, turning back to the sandwich man. "I'm a cop and I've got to make a cop call. I don't want you to look up while I'm talking. Just keep working on the sandwich, huh?"

The kid didn't look up. "What's going on?"

"There's a van across the street, and it might be trouble. I'm gonna call in a squad car to check. Hand me one of those large root beer cups and keep working on the sandwich."

"I'm almost done," the kid said, glancing up at Lucas.

"Make another one. Same thing. Don't look out the window."

Lucas carried the root beer cup to the soda machine, where he was out of sight, took the cellular phone out of his pocket, and called in. "This is Davenport. I've got a van tailing me out to a Subway on University Avenue, I need a couple of cars here quick." He gave the dispatcher the address and asked that the cars come in at the corners on either side of the van. "Get one guy out of each car to walk to the corner on foot. Let me know when they're in position, and I'll come out."

"Hang on." The dispatcher was back fifteen seconds later. "Two cars on the way, Lucas. They'll be there in a minute or a little more. Stay on, and we'll let you know."

"Do they know what they're supposed to do?"

"Yes. They'll wait until they see you moving out of the Subway."

The kid was finishing the second sandwich when Lucas moved back to the counter with the cup full of cellular telephone.

"We gonna get robbed?" the kid asked, keeping his head down.

"I don't think so," Lucas said. "I think this is something else."

"Been robbed twice, this place has," the kid said. "I wasn't here. My brother was."

"Just give them the money," Lucas said, handing the kid a ten-dollar bill.

"That's what everybody says." The kid handed him some change, and the cellular scratched from the cup. Lucas put it to his face and said, "Say that again?"

"We're all set."

"I'm on my way out."

A hell of a way to end it, Lucas thought as he walked toward the entrance. He was tight: something was wrong at the van. Something was about to happen. Anyone who had been on the streets would have seen it, would have felt it coming.

At the door, the sandwich bag in one hand and the cup and cellular phone in the other, he paused, put his hand in his pocket as though fumbling for car keys, and checked the van. It was older, with rusted-out holes on the fenders, side panels, and around the taillights. The cup said something to him, and he put it to his mouth. "What?"

"Two men just got out of the other side of the vehicle where you can't see them. They may be armed."

"Okay." Two men?

Lucas pushed through the door and started toward the Porsche. He was halfway to the car when the two men came around the back of the car and started toward him. One was tall and thin, with a thin goatee; the other short and muscular, with long, heavy arms. The tall one wore a thin cotton jacket; the short one wore a high school letter jacket without a letter. They were pointing toward him, and he thought: *A mugging? Maybe nothing to do with Mail?*

They were twenty yards away and walking fast, hands in their pockets, looking at him, cutting him off from the car. Lucas stopped suddenly, and they changed direction toward him, and he stooped and put the sandwiches on the blacktop and drew his pistol in the same motion, pointed it at them.

"Police. Stop right there. Get your hands in the air, get your hands up."

And two uniformed cops came running in from behind, guns drawn, and one shouted, "Police."

The van tried to leave—the driver, unseen behind the dark glass, cranked the engine, gunned it forward, and a squad popped out of the street halfway down the block, and paused. The van driver stopped, then pulled to the side of the street. The two men in the street were looking around, uncertainly, and one pulled his hands from his pockets slowly and said, "What? What do you want?" The other slowly lifted his hands.

"On the ground," Lucas shouted. "C'mon, you know the routine: on the ground."

And they knew. They dropped to their knees, then lay on the ground with their hands behind their heads.

Lucas moved in close and asked, "Is that Mail in the van?"

"Don't got no mail," the taller of the two men said. "What're you doing to us?"

"You know what the fuck I'm talking about," Lucas said harshly. "You've got Andi Manette and her daughters, and if we don't find out real fuckin' quick where they're at, we're gonna turn you over to the feds. The federal penalty for kidnapping is the electric chair, my fine friends."

The shorter man now turned his eyes up. He was scared and puzzled. "What? What're you talking about?"

The two cops on foot had arrived, while the two squads boxed the van. "Cuff 'em," Lucas said.

He walked down to the van, where the driver was slowly climbing out, keeping his hands in sight. He was black. Lucas said, "Shit," and walked back to the two men on the ground. The uniforms had frisked them and had come up with a Davis .32 and a can of pepper gas.

"So what are we doing?" asked one of the uniforms, a sergeant named Harper Coos.

"Aw, they were gonna mug me," Lucas said. "Probably picked up on the car. I thought it might be the other thing."

The cops at the van called, "We got a gun."

"Run 'em, and if you can do a gun charge, do it," Lucas said. "Otherwise, you're gonna have to cut them loose. I never gave them a chance to actually start mugging me."

"Too bad," Coos said.

"Yeah," Lucas said. "Fuckheads had me excited."

There were a half-dozen cars in the parking lot outside the company, and almost every light in the building was turned on.

"Bring me a sandwich?" The voice floated down out of the sky.

"Who's that?" Lucas looked up, but with the brightly lit windows couldn't see anything in the dark along the roof line.

"Haywood."

"I got an extra sub."

"I'd pay a hundred bucks for a sub."

"I'll run it right up."

"How about, uh, three bucks? Which is what I got."

"You can owe the ninety-seven," Lucas said.

Sloan and three young programmers were staring at a single screen, when one of the programmers saw Lucas come in. He prodded the guy working the keyboard, who turned and said, "Ah. Hi." The screen in front of him went blank.

"Hey. I'm gonna run this sub up on the roof. What you got going?"

"Um, just messing around."

"Show him," said Sloan. "He'll probably make another million with it."

"Yeah, show me," said Lucas, walking over to the group.

The programmers were all grinning at the guy in the chair, who shrugged and started tapping on keys. "You know those screen-savers? The flying toasters, and the tropical fish that swim around the screen, and all that?"

"Yeah."

"And you know how some of the magazines put out, uh, pinups as screensavers?"

"Yeah."

"Well . . ." A pinup appeared on the screen, one leg lifted coyly, but her almost impossibly perky breasts in full view.

"Yeah?" Lucas waited. The woman was pretty but nothing special.

Until her breasts took off and began flying around the screen on their own, like the flying toasters.

"Flying hooters—Davenport Simulations' answer to the Flying Toasters," the kid said.

"If Davenport Simulations' name appears anywhere on this product, I'll be forced to take out my gun and kill you all," Lucas said.

"Some people might feel it's in poor taste," the kid in the chair conceded.

"Does this mean you wouldn't be interested in the swimming pussys?" asked Sloan.

"I'll pass," Lucas said.

He started away and then turned. "What does Ice think about these things?"

The programmer in the chair shuddered: "She doesn't know. If she knew, she'd hunt us down and kill us like vermin."

"Which reminds me," said one of the others. "She called and asked if you were around. She said she'd try you at the police department."

"When was this?"

The other man shrugged. "Ten, fifteen minutes ago. She's

at home—I got her number." He handed Lucas a slip of paper.

"Okay." Lucas stuck the paper in his pocket and walked through the back to the stairs, took them to the second floor, then on up a shorter flight to the roof.

Haywood was pacing the perimeter of the building when Lucas came through the roof door.

"Anything?"

"A bunch of juvie skaters coming and going, that's about it," the cop said. He was wearing a black, long-sleeved shirt and blue jeans, with a black-and-green Treebark camo face mask. He'd be invisible from the street. "There's a little coke getting served outside the Bottle Cap, down on the next block."

"Nothing new there," Lucas said.

The night was pleasant, cool, with the stars brighter away from the heavy lights of the loop. Lucas handed him a sandwich and they sat on the wall along the edge of the roof and unwrapped them. Haywood alternately chewed and scanned the streets with a pair of Night Mariner glasses, not saying much.

Lucas finished his sub, then took the cellular phone and the note from Ice out of his pocket and punched the number in. She answered on the second ring.

"Ms. Ice, this is Lucas Davenport."

"Mr. Davenport, Lucas." She sounded a little out of breath. "I think somebody is here. Looking at me. At my house."

25

Ice lived in a brick two-story in St. Paul's Desnoyer Park, a few blocks from the Mississippi. Only the upper floor was lit: when Del touched the doorbell, he said, without looking back, "Nothing."

Lucas was in the back of Del's van, invisible behind the tinted glass, a radio in one hand, a phone in the other. His .45 was on the floor; he could see almost nothing in the dark. Behind them was a hurricane fence, and on the other side, the Town and Country Club golf course. "The guy on the porch can't see anything," he said into the phone.

"Should I go down?" Ice asked.

"No, no, just wait. He'll be up, if the door's open."

"It should be . . ."

"Hang on," Lucas said to Ice. And to Del, on the radio, "Go on in. Straight ahead to the white door, through it, then a hard right up the stairs."

"Jesus, I love this shit," Del said. He was wearing a Derby hat, a white shirt pulled out at the waist, pants that were too large and too short, and a cotton jacket. A guitar case was slung over his shoulder. In the dark, from a distance, he might pass for a musician in his twenties. "I'm going in."

Del pushed through the front door, his right hand crooked

awkwardly in front of his belly. He was holding a Ruger .357, trying to keep it out of sight from the street.

When he disappeared into the house, Lucas crawled to the other side of the van and looked out, then quickly checked the street through the front and rear windows. There were only a few lights on. Nothing moved on the street. Lights went on, then off, in Ice's house. Then Del's voice burped from the radio. "I'm at the stairs. Not a sound. I'm on my way up."

Lucas said into the phone, "He's coming up," and to himself, *He's gone* . . .

Mail hadn't decided what to do about Ice. Actually, he thought, he'd like to date her. They'd go well together. But that didn't seem possible, not anymore. He was beginning to feel the pressure, to feel the sides of the bubble collapsing upon him. He was beginning to think beyond Andi Manette and her body.

When he became aware of it—became aware of the barely conscious planning for "afterwards"—a kind of depression settled on him. He and Andi were working something out: a relationship.

If he moved on, something would have to be done about her and the kid. He'd started working through it in his mind. The best way to do it, he thought, would be to take Andi out, and upstairs, and out in the yard, and shoot her. There'd be no evidence in the house, and he could throw the body in the cistern. Then the kid: just go down, open the door, and do it. And after a while, he could dump some junk into the cistern—there was an old disker he could drag over, and other metal junk that nobody would want to take out. Then, when somebody else rented the place, even if they looked in the cistern, there'd be no attempt to clean it out. Just fill it up with dirt and rebuild.

Getting close to the time, he thought.

But it depressed him. The last few days had been the most fulfilling he'd known. But then, he was young: he could fall in love again.

With somebody like Ice.

Mail was parked a block from Ice's house, in the driveway of a house with a For Sale sign in the front yard. He'd been driving by when a saleswoman pulled the drapes on the picture window so she could show the view to a young couple from Cedar Rapids. Mail looked in: there was no furniture in the place. Nobody living there. When the saleswoman left, he pulled into the driveway, all the way to the garage, and simply sat and watched the lights in Ice's house. He knew the layout of the neighborhood from fifteen minutes circling the golf course. If he wanted, he could probably get down the alley and come up from the back of the house, and maybe force the back door.

But he wasn't sure he wanted that. He just wasn't sure what he was doing—but Ice's image was in his mind.

He was still waiting when the guitar player arrived in a blue minivan. And he was waiting when the guitar player left with Ice. An odd time to leave, he thought.

He followed them, staying well back.

Ice and Del came down the sidewalk together, Ice wearing a Korean War–era Army field jacket and tights, smoking a cigarette. She flicked the cigarette into the street, blew smoke, and climbed in the passenger side of the van.

As they headed across the interstate back toward the company offices, she half-turned to talk to Lucas. And he thought how young she was: her unmarked face, the way she bounced in the front seat, out of excitement, engagement.

She was emphatic. "Three people saw him, two of them out front, one of them around by the alley; he was going through in a van, and Mr. Turner, who's the guy behind me, saw his face up close. When I showed him the composites we made, he picked out the one where we aged Mail's face. He was sure. He said Mail was the guy in the alley."

"He saw you on television," Lucas said. "I thought he'd go after the company. I didn't think he'd come after you in person."

"Why me?"

"'Cause of the way you look," Del said bluntly, after a

couple seconds of silence. "We've got an idea of the kind of kid he is. We thought he might go for you."

"That's why the TV people were all over you," Lucas said. "You sorta stand out in a crowd of techies."

She looked Lucas full in the face. "Is that why you were so happy to have me involved?"

Lucas started to say no, but then nodded and said, "Yeah."

"All right," she said, turning back to the front. He saw her eyes in the rearview mirror. "Is this a good time to ask for a raise?"

Lucas grinned and said, "We can talk about it."

"How come you didn't come in with Del?" Ice asked.

"He knows who I am, that I write games," Lucas said. "And he probably knows me by sight. I think I actually ran into the sonofabitch the day after the kidnapping."

"At least he's sniffing around," Del said.

"Yeah," Lucas nodded, looking out the back windows. Another van was back there—and yet another was waiting at a cross street. "He's out there."

"Good thing I had a gun," Ice said.

Lucas turned back to her and said, "What?"

Ice dug into her waistband and came up with a blued .380 automatic, turned it in the dome light, worked the safety.

"Gimme that," Lucas said, irritated, putting his hand out.

"Fuck you, pal," she said. She pushed it back in her waistband. "I'm keeping it."

"You're asking for trouble," Lucas said. "Tell her, Del."

Del shrugged: "I just bought one for my old lady. Not a piece of shit like that, though." He looked at Ice. "If you're gonna have one, get something bigger."

Ice shook her head: "I like this one. It's cute."

"You gotta shell in the chamber?"

"Nope."

"Good. You don't have to worry about blowing your nuts off, carrying it in your pants like that."

Mail stayed a full two blocks back, following them up St. Anthony to Cretin, across the interstate to University. When they turned left, he let them go.

Davenport's, he thought. *She's going back to work.*

He wondered who the musician was—a full-time relationship, or just a ride?

He'd like to take a look at Davenport's, but it simply smelled wrong. Of course, maybe he was simply being paranoid. Mail laughed at himself. He *was* paranoid; everybody said so. Still, if he had to look at Davenport's, it might be a good idea to make a test run. To send in a dummy.

He thought, *I wonder where Ricky Brennan is* . . .

26

Haywood called from the roof. "We got somebody coming in.

Lucas had been on the cot for an hour, half-wrapped in an unzipped sleeping bag, his mind moving too restlessly for sleep. He kicked the bag off, groped for the radio. "Coming in? What do you mean?"

"I mean there's this asshole down there along the tracks, coming straight in, kind of dodging in and out like he's in fuckin' Vietnam. But he's coming here. I can see his face, he's looking at the building."

"Stay on him," Lucas said. He stood up and flipped on the storeroom lights. The radio burped again. Sloan asked, "We moving?"

"Maybe." Lucas called Dispatch. "You're up on the flood plan?"

"Yes." A little tension popped into the dispatcher's voice.

"I might call it," Lucas said. "On my address. Put out a preliminary call right now, get people to their staging points, but don't bring anybody in yet."

"Got it."

They'd been sleeping in a conference room, Sloan on an air mattress under the conference table, Lucas next to the door. Sloan fumbled into his pants and shirt, in the dark. "What's going on?"

Lucas had slept in his clothes, except for his jacket. He pulled on his pistol rig and said, "Got somebody coming in. Hay's watching him."

Haywood called. "He's coming up to the back of the building, boys. He's like sneaking up on the place. I think he's heading for that old loading dock . . . that's padlocked, right?"

"Yeah. He'll probably come around the dark side, going for the windows," Lucas said. "Stay on him, call him for us. We're going to plug in."

"Hate these fuckin' things," Sloan grumbled, pushing the flesh-colored radio plug into his ear. Lucas had trouble with his, finally got it in as they started down the stairs. Lucas said, "You go around the building to the left, I'll go around to the right."

"Take it easy," Sloan said. He had his piece out, pointing down his leg.

"Yeah." Lucas jacked a round into the chamber of the .45, a harsh, ratcheting noise in the tiled hallway.

"He's headed for the windows," Haywood said. His voice seemed to come from the middle of Lucas's skull. "This guy is something else. He's like tiptoeing. He looks like Sylvester the Cat sneaking up on Tweety Bird."

Lucas shook his head: his mental picture of Mail was neither funny nor stupid. "We're out," he muttered into his microphone. "We'll take him."

Sloan ran around to the left, while Lucas moved slowly to the right, the pistol up and ready. At the corner, he waited, listening. Too many cars, and a voice floating down from the doper bar: *You see that? Did you see what she did? Do that again . . .*

"He's trying the windows. I'm right over his head." Haywood spoke softly into Lucas's ear. Sloan should be ready.

Lucas stepped around the corner of the building. A man was just breaking out a corner of a window, just swinging a piece of rerod, when Lucas stepped around and shouted, "Freeze."

Sloan, coming from the other side, shouted "Police," a second later, and they both moved out from the building a step, two steps, the guy pinned between them at the point of a widening triangle. The trapped man had blond, shoulder-length hair, and Lucas thought of the first descriptions of the kidnapper. He was muscular, too—but short. His head snapped first at Lucas, and then at Sloan, then back to Lucas.

And then without a word he rushed at Sloan, lifting the rerod.

"Stop, stop . . ." Sloan and Lucas were both screaming, but the man rushed in. Lucas brought up his weapon, but the man was closing on Sloan too quickly.

Sloan shot him.

There was a quick, flat muzzle flash and the man screamed, staggered, and went down, and Sloan said, "Ah, shit, ah, shit."

Lucas said to Haywood, "Get Dispatch. Tell them we got a guy down. Tell them to get an ambulance over here."

"Calling," Haywood said.

"Got it, Lucas. Ambulance on the way."

The man on the ground was rolling, holding his leg, and Lucas put his pistol away and walked over, knelt on the man's back, cuffed him, patted him, found a cheap chrome .38 and handed it to Sloan, who put it in his pocket. Then Lucas rolled the wounded man: he groaned, swore. He had a fat, round face and pale blue eyes. This was not John Mail. "Can you talk?"

"Fuckin' leg, man." The wounded man's eyes glittered with tears. "My leg's broken. I can feel the fuckin' bone."

"Ah, Jesus," Sloan said. "What a fuckin' day."

Lucas checked in the bad light and saw the spreading wet patch on the man's right thigh. "Where're the Manettes?" he asked.

"Who?" The man was frightened and seemed genuinely confused.

"Who are you? What's your name?" Lucas asked.

"Ricky Brennan."

"Why'd you come here, Ricky? Why'd you pick this place?"

"Well, man . . ." Ricky's eyes slid away from Lucas, and Lucas thought he might lose him.

"Come on, asshole," Lucas said.

"Well, this dude said I could pick up a little toot from the computer freaks. Said they had a bag of toot in the back room, like a couple ounces to keep them going all night. My fuckin' leg, man, my fuckin' leg is killing me."

"Shit," Sloan said, and he looked like he was going into shock.

Lucas got on the radio: "Janet? Flood it. I'm calling the flood."

"You got it."

Sloan sat down beside the wounded man. "Got an ambulance coming," he said.

"I'm really hurting, man."

Haywood ran up and Lucas said, "You got a flash?"

"Yeah."

Lucas pulled a folded pad of paper from his pocket, unfolded it, sorted through the composites, and found the one of Mail with dark hair.

"Is this the dude?" Lucas turned the flashlight on the paper.

Ricky was slipping away again, but the light brought him back and he focused on the paper. "Yeah. That's the dude."

"Where is he?"

"He was gonna wait in the parking ramp." He flopped an arm out. The ramp was out of sight, on the far side of the building. Lucas got back on the radio. "Janet, goddamnit, this is the real thing, he's here, somewhere. Keep them coming."

"They oughta be there, Lucas. They're already out on the perimeter with the dogs."

And then Lucas heard the sirens: fifteen or twenty of them, coming from every direction. More would be arriving later. The patrol people had decided to use the sirens in an effort to pin Mail down, to frighten him. "Tell them to look in the information packets they got tonight, and look at composite *C* as in Cat. That's our guy."

"*C* as in Cat."

Lucas bent over Ricky again. "The guy's name is John Mail, right?"

"Oh, man, my fuckin' leg."

"John Mail?"

"Yeah, man. John. I see him around. You know. I see him around and I say, 'Hey, John.' And he says 'Hey, Ricky.' And that's all. Said there was some toot over here. He seen it. My fuckin' leg, man, you got something? You got any, like, Percodan?"

"You know where he lives?"

"Oh, man, I don't even know the dude, you know, I used to see him when we were inside, he'd just be, 'Hi, Ricky.' That's all." Ricky groaned. "How about the Percodan, man?"

"Sent in a decoy, to see what we'd do," Lucas said to Sloan. Then: "You stay here. They're gonna want a statement and your gun."

To Haywood: "C'mon. You got those glasses?"

"Yeah."

And to Sloan, "You okay?"

Sloan swallowed and nodded. "First time," he said. "I don't think I like it."

"Just get him in the ambulance and don't worry about it." Lucas grinned at him and slapped him on the back. "I can't believe you shot low, you dumb shit," he said. "If you'd missed him, he'd of sunk that rerod about six inches into your skull."

"Yeah, yeah." Sloan swallowed. "Actually, I was aiming at the middle of his chest."

Lucas grinned and said, "I know how that goes. C'mon, Hay."

Lucas and Haywood ran around to the front of the building, Lucas glancing back once. Sloan was standing over Ricky, and Lucas thought he might be apologizing. He'd have to watch his friend: Sloan seemed unbalanced by the shooting. And that was in character, Lucas thought.

Sloan liked the relationships that came out with cop work, the tussle. He even enjoyed an occasional fight. But he never really wanted to hurt anybody.

Then Lucas turned back toward the parking ramp and he and Haywood ran up the sidewalk together, weapons out. Far up University, they could see the roadblocks going in, and everywhere, in every direction, the red flashing lights.

"Looks like a fuckin' light-rack convention," Haywood panted.

Lucas heard him but had no time to answer: they'd rounded the office building on University and were coming up on the ramp. Lucas said, "Let's go up. Ready?"

"Outa fuckin' shape," Haywood said. "Let's go."

Lucas took the first set of steps: there were a half-dozen cars parked in the first floor, and they checked them quickly. Then up the next set of steps, and Lucas, looking over the low, concrete deck wall, saw taillights flicker to the north, headed toward the railroad tracks.

"Did you see that?"

"What?"

The lights flickered again. "There."

"Yeah. Somebody crawling along in the dark, no headlights," Haywood said.

"Sonofabitch, that's him." Lucas put the radio to his face: "I need a car at the . . . what the fuck is the name of this building? I need a car by the Hansen dairy place, first road west of the Hansen dairy trucks. We've got the suspect in sight, going down toward the elevators."

Haywood was already running across the slab and down the stairs, Lucas a few steps behind. The blacked-out vehicle was almost two blocks away, and once they were on the ground, they could no longer see it. They were running awkwardly over the uneven ground toward the grain elevator when one set of headlights caught them in the back, then another. They turned and saw two squads coming down toward them; Lucas waved them on and kept running.

When the cars caught up, Lucas pointed up ahead. "He was going under the elevator."

The driver in the lead car was a sergeant. "No way out of there," he grunted. "That's all dead end back there."

"Could he just bump it across the tracks?"

The cop shrugged. "Maybe. But we'd see him. He might be able to snake his way out alongside of them." He picked up his radio and said, "We need a car on the 280 overpass across the tracks. Put some light down onto the tracks. Where's the chopper?"

"Chopper's just leaving the airport, he'll be five minutes. We're confirming the car on the tracks."

"Get some K9 down here," Lucas said.

The sergeant said, "We called them; they're on the way." And the car pulled ahead of them, the second car close behind him. The sergeant spoke into the radio: "We need some guys north of the tracks."

"Gonna be dark in there," Haywood grunted as they jogged up toward the elevators.

"But once we got him, even if we only get his van, we get the VIN even if he's pulled the plates . . . then we get a name and an address."

"You're counting your chickens," Haywood said.

"First goddamn chicken we've had to count, and I'm counting the sonofabitch," Lucas said.

27

The cop slipped down the side of the building, his right hand cocked away from his body.

Carrying a gun, Mail thought. The night air was thick, cool, and moist, and the night seemed particularly dark; he couldn't see that well, but the cop was too small to be Davenport.

Still, it *had* been a trap, a rudimentary one. Mail smiled and turned to go, then slowed, turned back, lingered. Davenport's building was a block away and he felt remote from it, as though he were watching a movie. The movie was just getting good.

He'd found Ricky on a Hennepin Avenue street corner, half-drunk, his face sullen, his hair stuck together like cotton candy. He'd whispered *cocaine*, and *just a bunch of computer pussies in there*, and Ricky'd started slavering. He couldn't wait to get started.

Ricky needed drugs to function: without cocaine, speed, acid, grass, peyote, alcohol, even two or three of them at a time, the world was not right. He'd spent years on the inside and barely remembered a time where he didn't have a drug flowing through his veins—and what he remembered about that drugless state, he didn't like. He needed more dentists, he thought, people who'd say, "Here—I'll numb that up for you."

Even inside, with very strange people around—people who spoke to God, and got personal letters back—Ricky had been considered mad as a hatter.

But he could function in society, the shrinks said, so they had let him out and seemed proud of themselves when they did it. Now Ricky ate from trashcans and shit in doorways and carried a piece-of-crap revolver in his waistband. He gobbled up any pill he could beg, buy, or steal.

Now Ricky was out of sight, trying the windows on the far side of the building. The cop was running along the back of the building, to the side where Ricky was; he looked like an inmate in a prison movie, caught in a spotlight as he ran along a wall. The cop stopped at the corner, did a quick peek, pulled his head back, peeked again, ran out from the building, pointing his gun, and the shouting began, the words indistinguishable in the distance.

Again, Mail turned to go. Then he heard the gunshot, and turned back: "Sonofabitch."

He smiled again, amused; he almost laughed. What a joke. They'd shot Ricky, or Ricky had shot one of them. The cop he could see had dropped his pistol to his side and moved forward. So it had been Ricky.

Time to move.

He ran across the parking ramp, down a short flight of stairs, to the street. The van was already pointed into University Avenue. He'd be a mile away in a minute and a half. He unlocked the door, hopped in—he'd leave the lights blacked out for a few hundred feet—pulled up to the corner, looked right, looked left. And heard the sirens, saw the lights.

A cop car, far down the street to the left, coming in a hurry: but that was the way he wanted to go. If he turned right, he'd have to drive past Davenport's building. He didn't want to do that.

He hesitated. The cop was probably on the way to the shooting. He could wait until he passed.

Mail shifted into reverse and started to back up—but then the cop car, still six or eight blocks away, unexpectedly slewed sideways across the street. And then he saw more lights far down to his right, and then another car joining the squad blocking the street to his left.

"Motherfuckers."

He felt as though a hand had grabbed his heart and squeezed it. He'd underestimated Davenport. The building wasn't the trap. The whole goddamn area was the trap.

Headlights still off, he did a quick U-turn and rolled down the street toward a grain elevator at the end. He hadn't been down there, didn't know what to expect, but once out of the immediate neighborhood, he could work his way through back streets until he was completely clear.

A cold sweat broke on his face, and his hands held the steering wheel so tightly that they hurt. He had to break out of this.

But he couldn't see much without the lights. Strange, odd shapes, wheelless tractor trailers, loomed off to the left. Here and there, a machine with claws, like mutated, earth-moving equipment. He drove between two elevator buildings, slowed. The van dropped into a pothole seven inches deep and half as long as the van itself, then climbed out the other side. Two trailers were parked against a loading dock. Another van was tucked in between them, facing out.

Mail leaned toward the windshield, trying to see better, then rolled down the side window, trying to hear. The area smelled of milled grain, corn, maybe. He bumped along through the dark, then into a lighter patch, the light thrown from a naked bulb over an office door.

No lights on in the office, though . . .

The road ended at a gate, a gate closed and locked, with dark buildings behind it. A dead end? There'd been no dead-end sign. He backed up, found a gravel track that went east along the side of the grain elevator. Ahead, he could see the lights of a busy street, a little higher than he was, maybe up a hill? If he could work his way over there . . . But what was that?

A cop car, lights flashing, stopped on the hill, and Mail realized it was not a hill at all but an overpass. No way up, no way to the street. The track he was on went from gravel to dirt. To the left, there was nothing but darkness, like an unlit farm field. To the right, there was a line of the boxes that looked like the wheelless tractor trailers he'd seen back in the lot.

He slowed, thought about going back, looked over his shoulders, and saw the cop lights at the elevator. Had they seen him? He had to go forward.

Suddenly, a huge dark shape slid past to his left, almost soundlessly, and he jerked the van to the right.

"What?" he shouted. Frightened now, gripping the wheel, peering out into the dark. The shape made no noise, but he could feel the rumble of it: the thing had materialized from the dark, like some creature from a Japanese horror flick, like Rodan . . . and he realized it was a string of freight cars, ghosting by in the night. There was no engine attached to them. They simply glided by.

And he realized that off to his left, in the darkness that looked like a farm field, were multiple lines of railroad tracks. He could see some of them now, in the dim, ambient light, thin, steely reflections against the field of black. He couldn't see how many there were, but there were several.

The cop car on the overpass suddenly lit up, and a searchlight swung across the tracks, left to right. If it had come the other way, right to left, it might have caught him, though he was still a half-mile away. As it was, he had time to drive into a hole in a wall of the boxes that lined the track.

In between the boxes, he couldn't see at all—he had to risk the parking lights. The cop searchlight swept the field behind him, and he edged forward again, and found another row of boxes parallel to the boxes he was crossing through. Another dirt track ran between the rows of boxes, and he turned onto it. His parking lights caught a sign that said "Burlington Northern Container Yard—Trespassers Will Be Prosecuted."

Containers. Huh. The track ended when the containers did: nothing ahead but dirt and grass and the certainty of being seen. A second cop car had joined the first on the overpass, and a second searchlight popped out and probed the tracks. He could see the cops, like tiny action figures, standing along the overpass railing.

"Goddamn. Goddamn." He was caught, stuck. He reached under the seat, got his .45. The gun was not comforting: it was a big, cold lump in his hand. If he had to use it, he was dead.

He put the gun between his thighs, backed the van up until he was out of sight of the overpass, turned it off, started to get out—but the overhead light flickered and he quickly pulled the door closed. Shit. How to do this? He finally reached back, scratched the dome off the overhead light, and twisted out the bulb. Then he got out, put the gun in his pocket, and slipped down to the end of the line of boxes.

There were sirens everywhere, like nothing he'd ever heard before, not even when he was starting fires, all those years ago. The sirens didn't seem especially close, but they came from every possible direction.

"Fucked," he said, half out loud. "I'm fucked." And he kicked one of the containers. "Fucked."

He ran his hands through his hair. Had to get out. He ran back to the van, stopped for a second, then ran further down the line of containers. The container boxes were stacked two by two, end to end, in two long rows, with the track between them. In places, a container had been pulled. In a few, both containers had been pulled—like the hole he'd driven through.

In those spots, he could see out, either across the tracks, or into the neighborhood on the other side of the elevators. He found one of the double breaks and walked carefully down it, trailing his hand along the edge of the container, feeling the clumped weeds underfoot. The neighborhood on the other side of the elevator was coming awake. Lights were on all up and down the street, and he heard a man shouting. The reflections of red flashing lights bounced off the side windows of the houses. Cops all over the place.

Damnit, damnit.

They had him, or they would have him. The van, anyway. He walked back toward it, and it occurred to him that if he backed it into one of the spaces left where a single container had been pulled, then nobody could see it unless they walked down the center track and looked into each space. If a cop simply looked down the track, the track would appear to be empty.

That might give him some time.

Mail hurried down to the truck, backed it up fifty feet, then maneuvered it into a single container space. He doubted that he'd see it again. He'd have to abandon the Roses name along with the van, and probably all his computers.

What about fingerprints? If they found the Roses name, that would be fine—but if they found his fingerprints, he'd never have any peace.

He stripped off his jacket, shirt, and t-shirt, put the shirt and jacket back on, and used the t-shirt to wipe everything he might have touched in the van. His mind was working furiously: *get the door handles, the wheel, of course, the ash tray, the seats, the glove compartment, the dashboard . . . get rid of all the paper crap on the floor.*

But then he thought: *the computers. Damn. Everything at the self-storage would have his prints. If they found the van, they'd find the storage place, and get his prints there.*

He continued wiping, working the problem in his mind. He finished inside, got out, pushed the door shut with his elbow, and started wiping outside. *The goddamn computers.*

He did the outside handles, plates, took a swipe at the wipers. He never messed with the engine, had never lifted the hood in his life, so that wasn't a problem.

And he thought: *Fire.*

If he could get back to the store, there could be a fire. A fire would do it. Ten gallons of gas, a little oil, and the computers would burn like kindling.

Even so, he couldn't take any chances. He might not get everything—they might find a print, or two. So he'd have to get lost for a while, and that meant he'd have to settle Andi Manette and the girl. He could dump them in the cistern; that'd only take a second. He felt a small, dark tug at the thought—but he'd known it was coming.

Okay. Done. He took a last swipe at the door handles, stuffed the t-shirt in his jacket pocket, and walked through the dark shadows of the containers to an opening that looked across the tracks.

With the dark jacket and the jeans, he was almost invisible in the rail yard. He started walking through the dark, one hand in front of him for balance, his feet picking the way over the rough ground. Behind him, back toward the elevator, a dog barked; then another.

A patrol captain arrived as Lucas was punching the driver's side window out of the van. He used a piece of paving stone to break out the glass, then reached through the broken window and popped the lock. Haywood was beside him, trying to peer through the dirty windows.

"Paper," Lucas grunted when they got the door open. A clipboard lay on the floor of the passenger side, and he picked it up. A pad of pink paper was clipped into it, with a letterhead that said "Carmody Foods."

"Got him?" the captain asked, coming up.

Lucas frowned, shook his head. "I think this belongs here . . . we oughta check it out, but we better look for another van. It's here, we saw it coming back here."

The captain walked around to the front of the van, fished around for a moment, then said, "Engine's cold."

"Then this ain't it," Lucas said. He tossed the clipboard back in the truck. "C'mon, Hay, let's go down the tracks."

"How do you want to work this, chief?" the captain asked. "It's your call."

"You run it," Lucas said. "You know how to do this shit better than I do. Just tell your people that Haywood and I'll be out there, wandering around."

Captain nodded. "You got it." He jogged away, yelling for somebody, and they heard a K9 car arrive, and a moment later, the helicopter buzzed overhead on its first pass. The elevator yard had been dark, forbidding, when Lucas and Haywood first ran down into it. Now there were headlights everywhere, and the chopper lit up a searchlight. There were still dark areas, but there was less and less room to hide.

"That was an elevator down in Stillwater, wasn't it? Where you found the hanged girl?" Haywood asked, craning his neck to look at the elevator above them. "I wonder if there's a connection?"

"That doesn't seem . . . reasonable. That's got to be a coincidence," Lucas said.

"You don't believe in coincidences," Haywood said.

"Except when they happen," Lucas said. They were walking behind a canine officer with a leashed German shepherd. When the cop and his dog went to examine the back of the elevator, Haywood said, "What do you think?"

Lucas looked around: there were a number of buildings, ranging from small switch shacks to the huge elevators, on the near side of the tracks, and more on the far side. Another set of elevators loomed back to the west. "I doubt that he's hiding. Given the chance, he'd run. And there's no van, and all these little side tracks tend to go east. He probably picked one out and rode it as long as he could."

"There were squads up on 280 before he could've gotten through there."

"Yeah. So he's between here and there." They heard the beat and then the lights of the chopper coming in, and then a searchlight lit up the tracks beyond them and the chopper roared overhead. "Let's go down that way . . . follow the lights."

Mail decided to cross the tracks: there was less activity on the other side, and in the growing illumination provided by the cop cars, he could see the rows of dark houses and small yards on the other side. Once in there, he could sneak away.

He started across, nearly got caught by a searchlight: they came more quickly than he'd expected, and he had to drop to his face, his hands beneath himself, to hide the flesh.

The light didn't pause but swept on, and he got to a crouch and started running again, and the light swept back and he went down again. He didn't bother to stand up the next time but simply scuttled on his hands and knees, over the rails, down the other side of the roadbed, then up the next, and across the rails. The rocks bit into his hands, but he felt more scuffed up than injured.

He was halfway across the yard when the helicopter showed up: the light tracking beneath it was fifty feet across. He watched it coming and realized that if he were caught in the chopper's light, he'd be done.

Mail got to his feet and ran, fell down, got up and ran, head down. The cop searchlight from the bridge flicked over and past him and he kept going, the helicopter light tracking more or less toward him, but sliding back and forth across the tracks as it came. A small shack loomed dead ahead, and he dove into the grass beside it and rolled hard against it as the searchlight burned overhead.

Even with his face turned down, the powerful light cut through the grass, dazzling him. And the light passed on.

He looked up, saw the zigzagging chopper chattering slowly toward the overpass. He got to his feet and began running again.

A cop car, lights flickering, ran through the neighborhood on the other side of the tracks, but a street or two west of him. He was running toward some kind of commercial building with trees around it. He swerved toward it; he could hide in the brush. The cops on the bridge swept him with the searchlight and he went down. A second later, the light came back, swept overhead, picking away at him. When it drifted back toward the tracks, he made it the last few feet to the trees.

And found his way blocked by water.

"No-no," he said, out loud. He couldn't catch a break.

He was in a small neighborhood park, with a pond in the middle of it. The light came back, and he dropped to his hands and knees and crawled toward the water. His hands slipped on the grass and a stench reached up to him. What? Whatever he was crawling through was slick; then a small thing moved to his right, and he realized it was a duck. He was crawling through duck shit. The light came back and he dropped into the stuff, then slithered down the bank into the chill water. And heard the shouting behind him.

• • •

The night glasses were useless. They were fine in steady, low light, but the sweeping searchlights were screwing up the sensors, and Haywood put them away.

"That way," Lucas said. "Up in those containers."

They ran along the track and were quickly pinned and dazzled by the searchlights from the overpass. Lucas got on the radio, waved the lights off.

"Can't see a fuckin' thing," Haywood said. "I never been on the other end of those lights."

Lucas stepped into a hole in the line of containers, found a second row of containers with a track between them, all dark as pitch.

"If he's down there and he's got a gun, it'd be suicide to go in," Haywood said.

"Yeah." Lucas got on the radio, got the chopper. "Can you come back toward the elevator? There's a double line of containers; we want the light right down the middle."

The pilot took a minute to get lined up, then hung above them, the downwash from the rotors battering down at them as they walked up the line. A hundred feet from the end, Lucas caught an edge of chrome in a hole in the wall. He shouted "Whoa" into the radio and caught Haywood's arm, shouted, "There's the van, there's the van."

Haywood went right while Lucas went left, and the chopper moved up, found the hole, and dropped the light on it.

The cops were walking through the neighborhood, and lights were coming on. Mail could hear their voices, far away, but distinct enough: a woman yelling to a neighbor, "Is it the gas? Is it the gas?"

And the answer, "They're looking for a crazy guy."

Mail dog-paddled across the pond to a muddy point, where a weeping willow tree hung over the water. A half-dozen ducks woke and started inquisitively quacking. "Get the fuck . . ." he hissed and started out of the water. The ducks took off in a rush of wings, quacking.

Christ, if anybody heard that . . .

He crawled up on the bank, shivering—very cold now—and had started through the trees when he heard the cops coming, marked by a line of bobbing flashlights. He looked around, then back at the water, and reluctantly slipped in, his head below the cutbank under the willow.

The chill water was only about three feet deep but wanted to float him. Groping along the bank, his hand caught a willow root, and he used it to push himself down and stabilize. He turned his face to the bank and pulled the dark jacket over his head.

"Probably breathing through a straw," a cop said, the voice young and far away.

"Yeah, like you're talking through your ass," said another, equally young. "Jesus, there's goose shit all over the place."

"Duck shit," the first voice said. Farm boy. "Goose shit's bigger; looks like stogies."

A third voice: "Hey, we got a shit expert."

"Somebody ought to kick through those bushes . . ."

"I'll get it . . . ?"

Mail bowed his head as the footsteps got closer. Then the cop began kicking through the brush overhead. The cop came all the way down to the willow tree: Mail could have reached out of the water and grabbed his leg. But the cop just shined his light out over the water and then headed back for the others, calling, "Nothing here."

Mail was on the same side of the pond as the cops. When they'd moved on, he dog-paddled across the pond and crawled out, picking up more duck shit. Now he began shivering uncontrollably. Cold; he'd never been this cold. He crawled straight ahead, toward the corner of the commercial building, the rubble on the ground cutting into his hands. He pushed into a clump of brush, where he stopped, and pulled his legs beneath him, trying to control the shivering. His hair hung across his forehead, and he pushed it back with one hand; he smelled like duck shit.

Across the tracks, the helicopter was hovering in one spot, and three cop cars were bumping along the line of containers.

"Found it," he said out loud. They'd already found the goddamn van. The barking started again: were they tracking him with dogs? Jesus.

More dogs were barking through the neighborhood, aroused by all the cops walking through. He had to move. Had to get out of here. He crawled back through the bushes, finally stood up and looked around. The cops seemed to have set up a perimeter, with more cops sweeping the area inside of it. He'd have to cross it, sooner or later.

He thought: Sewer.

And dismissed it. He didn't know anything about sewers. If he crawled down a sewer, he'd probably die down there. And the idea of the sewer walls closing in . . .

He'd always been claustrophobic, one reason he'd never go back to the hospital. The hospital didn't fuck around with beatings; they knew how to really punish you. His claustrophobia had come out early in his stay, and they'd introduced him to the Quiet Room . . .

Half-crouching, Mail crossed a driveway and climbed a short fence into the first yard. He crossed the yard, ran behind a house with several lights on, and down a line of bridal-wreath bushes, where he crawled over a wire fence, crossed the next yard, and climbed the fence again. He crossed the next yard, came to another fence, and heard the dog. Large dog, woofing along in the night at the other end of the yard. Take a chance? The dog smelled him at the same time he heard it, turned, and rushed the fence where he was hiding, snarling, slavering for him. Big black-and-tan body, white teeth like a tiger's. No way.

Mail went back, crawled over a fence, and turned left, looking for another way.

A cop car flashed past, light rack spinning; dogs were barking everywhere, now, a mad chorus of mutts.

This could take a while . . .

Lucas called in the plate number on the van, and the VIN.

Thirty seconds later, on the radio: "Lucas: we've got an address down in Eagan."

28

The bedsprings were too flexible to make decent weapons. They'd hoped for something like an icepick, but the springs would not fully uncurl. When pressed against anything resistant, they flexed.

But if they couldn't get icepicks from the springs, they got two fat, three-inch-long needles, honed on the granite rocks in the fieldstone walls.

Grace stood on the Porta-Potti and began picking at the nail: "Lots better," she told Andi. "This works great."

She picked for ten minutes and Andi picked for ten minutes more, then Grace started again. Grace was working on it when it finally came free. She thought it moved under the spring-needle, and grabbed it between a thumb and forefinger. It turned in her fingers, and she held tighter and put weight on it, felt it twist again.

Grace said, breathlessly, "Mom, it's coming. It's coming out." And she pulled it free, like a tooth.

Andi put a finger to her lips. "Listen."

Grace froze, and they listened. But there were no thumps, no footsteps, and Andi said, "I thought I heard something."

"I wonder where he is?" Grace looked nervously at the door. Mail had been gone a long time.

"I don't know. We just need a little more time." Andi took

the nail, sat on the mattress, and began to hone it on a granite pebble. The nail left behind what looked like tiny scratches in the rock, but were actually whisper-thin metal scrapings. "Next time he comes, we have to do it," she said. "He'll kill me, soon, if we don't. And when he kills me, he'll kill you."

"Yes." Grace nodded. She'd thought about it.

Andi stopped honing the nail to look at her daughter. Grace had lost ten pounds. Her hair was stuck together in strings and ropes; the skin of her face was waxy, almost transparent, and her arms trembled when she stood up. Her dress was tattered, soiling, torn. She looked, Andi thought, like an old photograph of a Nazi prison-camp inmate.

"So: we do it." She went back to scraping the nail, then turned it in her hand. The rust was gone from the tip, and the wedge-shaped nail point was fining down to a needletip.

"What we have to do is figure out a . . . scenario for attacking him," she said. Grace was sitting at the end of the mattress, her knees pulled up under her chin. She had a bruise on her forearm. Where'd she gotten that? Mail hadn't touched her, yet, though the last two times he'd assaulted Andi, he hadn't bothered to dress before he pushed her back in the cell. He was displaying for Grace. Sooner or later, he'd take her . . .

She put a finger to her lips. "Listen."

There was nothing. Grace whispered, "What?"

"I thought I heard him."

Grace said, "I don't hear anything."

They listened for a long time, tense, the fear holding them silent; but nobody came. Finally, Andi went back to honing the nail, the ragged *zzzt zzzt zzzt* the only sound in the hole.

She had Mail in her mind as she honed it. They'd been in the hole for almost five days. He had attacked her . . . she didn't know how many times, but probably twenty. Twenty? Could it be that many?

She thought so.

She honed the nail, thinking, with each stroke, *For John Mail. For John Mail . . .*

29

Lucas and Haywood went past Lucas's building at seventy—Sloan still standing in the lot, now in the center of a circle of plainclothes cops; an ambulance had hauled Ricky away—slipped onto Highway 280 and then I-94, east to I-35E, south through St. Paul, Haywood hanging on the safety belt, three cars trailing, all with lights.

A dispatcher came back. "Eagan's in. They're pulling a search warrant right now and they ought to have it by the time you're there."

"Patch me through—get them to pull us in there."

The directions from Eagan burped out over the radio and they crossed the Mississippi like a flock of big-assed birds, jumped off on Yankee Doodle Road, killed the flashers, and headed east.

"That's them," Haywood said. He was holding on to the safety belt with one hand and had the other braced on the dashboard. Below them, in a shallow valley, two squad cars and a gray sedan were lined up at the curb. Lucas pulled over next to the sedan and hopped out. A man in a suit hustled around the nose of the car.

"Chief Davenport?"

"Danny Carlton. I'm the chief out here." Carlton was

young, with curly red hair and a pink face. "We got your search warrant, but I don't think you're gonna be happy."

"Yeah?"

Carlton pointed down the road, where it rose along the opposite wall of the valley. "The place you're looking for is right up there. But it's one of them self-storage places. You know, like two hundred rental garages."

"Damnit." Lucas shook his head: this sounded unlikely. "We have to check it, we can't fuck around."

The self-storage warehouse was a complex of long, one-story, concrete-block buildings, the long sides of the buildings each faced with twenty white garage doors. The whole place was surrounded by an eight-foot chain-link fence topped with barbed wire. A small blue gatehouse stood next to the only gate through the fence. An elderly man, pale, worried, met them at the gate. He carried a .38 that looked older than he was.

"No problem," he said when they gave him the warrant. "Roses, that'd be fifty-seven."

"Have you seen him?" Lucas asked.

"Hasn't come through here, not tonight."

Lucas showed him a copy of the computer-aged Mail photo. "Is that him?"

The guard held it under a light, tipping his head back the better to use his bifocals, stuck out a lip, raised his eyebrows, then handed it back. "That's him. Got him to a T," he said.

The garage door was padlocked, but one of the Eagan cops had a pair of cutters and chopped the hasp. Lucas knocked it away, and with another cop, raised the door.

"Computers," Haywood said.

He found the light and flipped it on. The room was lined with tables, and the computers were stacked on them, dozens of beige cases and sullen, gray-screen monitors. Under the tables were plastic clothes baskets full of parts—disk drives, modems, sound and color cards, a mouse with its cord wrapped around it, miscellaneous electronic junk.

Nothing human.

A desk and an old cash register sat off to the left. Lucas walked over to the desk, pulled open a drawer. Scrap paper, a single ball-point. He pulled open another, and found stick-on labels, an indelible pen missing its cap, a dusty yellow legal pad. The middle drawer had another pencil and three X-Men comics in plastic sleeves.

"Tear it apart," Lucas said to the Minneapolis cops crowding up behind them. "Any piece of paper—anything that might point at the guy. Checks, receipts, credit card numbers, bills, anything."

The Eagan chief lit a cigarette, looked around, and said, "This is him, huh?"

"Yeah. This is him."

"I wonder where *they* are?"

"So do I," Lucas said.

He stepped outside and tipped his head back, and the Eagan chief thought for a moment that he was sniffing the wind. "I bet they're close—I bet this is the closest self-storage to his house. Goddamnit. Goddamnit, we're close."

The guard had come along out of curiosity, but when not much happened, started tottering back to the gatehouse. Lucas walked after him. "Hey, wait a minute."

The guard turned. "Huh?"

"You see this guy come and go? You ever see him spend any time here?"

The guard looked slowly left and right, as if checking for eavesdroppers. "He runs a store here on weekends. All kinds of long-haired kids running around."

"A store?"

The Eagan chief had come up behind him. "It's illegal, but you see it quite a bit, now," he said. "Part-time shops, nobody talks to the IRS, no sales tax. They call them flea markets, or garage sales, but you know—they're not."

"Does he have any employees? Any regulars?"

The guard touched his lips with his middle and index fingers, thinking, scratched his ass with the other hand, and finally shook his head. "Not that one. The guy in the next, uh, spot, sells lawnmowers 'n' hedgetrimmers and stuff. He might know."

"Where's he?"

"I got a list."

Lucas followed him back to the gate shack, where the guard fumbled under a counter top and finally produced a list of names and telephone numbers.

"What's under Roses' name? What number?"

The old man ran a shaky index finger down the list, came to ROSE, and followed it across to a blank space. "Ain't got one. Supposed to."

"Gimme the other guy's name, the lawnmower guy."

The cop wasn't going to leave.

Mail lay behind a bush thirty feet away and watched him. The cop checked his shotgun, then checked it again— playing with it, flipping a shell out, catching it in mid-air, shoving it back in—hummed to himself, spoke into a radio a couple of times, paced back and forth, and once, looking quickly around first, moved up close to a maple tree and took a leak.

But he wasn't going anywhere. He idled back and forth, watching the cars come and go at the end of the block, turned the shotgun like a baton. Whistled a snatch of a Paul Simon song . . .

The cop was at the thinnest spot along the line, a place where the street made an odd little curve before straightening again, as though it had been built around a stump. The curve had the effect of changing the angles, pushing out toward the next set of lawns.

If he could just get across. He thought about using the .45, but if the cop tried to fight him for it, or went for his gun, and he had to shoot—that'd be the end. If he was going to take the cop out, he had to be quick and silent and sure.

Mail pushed himself back, a foot at a time, until he reached the back edge of the house, where he got to his hands and knees. He couldn't see much, but he could see the dark shape of some kind of yard shed. He scurried over to it, looked around quickly, pulled open the door, and slid inside.

And felt instantly safe with the roof over his head. Nobody could see in, no light would catch him. The shed was full of yard tools and smelled of dead autumn leaves and old premix-gasoline. Groping in the dark, he found a couple of rakes, a hoe, a shovel. He could try the shovel, but it was awkward, and he groped along the floor for something else. He found a short piece of two-by-four, thought about it, decided he liked the shovel better. Moved on, found two snow shovels, a pair of hedge clippers; he touched a gas can, smelled the gas on his fingers; and then, in the corner, a spade handle.

The handle had broken off just above where the blade had been. He hefted it, made a short chopping motion. Okay. This would work.

He didn't want to go back outside, but he had to. He slipped outside, scrambled back to the corner, and eased down the side of the house to the bush where he'd watched the cop. The cop was still there, hat off, rubbing his head. Then he put the cap back on, said something to his radio, got something back, and whistled the snatch of Paul Simon again.

Like he had the song on his mind, Mail thought.

The cop turned, looking away from Mail, drifted toward the maple tree where he'd taken the leak. Mail tensed, and when the cop's head was behind the tree, stood up and padded toward the tree, slowly at first, but more quickly as the cop came out from behind it, his back still turned.

The cop heard him coming, though.

When Mail was ten feet away, he flinched and turned his head, his mouth open. But even a slow man can cross ten feet in a small fraction of a second, and Mail hit him with the spade handle, the steel grip burying itself in the cop's forehead with a wet crunch.

The cop dropped, his shotgun flying out to the side and clattering down the sidewalk. Mail dropped the spade handle, caught the cop under the armpits, and dragged him back between the houses. In a few seconds, he'd pulled off the cop's jacket, hat, and gunbelt. His own dark jeans would do well enough for uniform pants. The gunbelt was heavy and awkward, and he struggled to get it on.

The cop said a word, and Mail looked down at him, prodded him with a foot. The cop's head rolled to the other side, limp, loose.

"Die, motherfucker," Mail said. And he walked away, out to the sidewalk, pulling on the hat. It was too small, and perched on top of his head. But it would do. He picked up the shotgun, crossed the street, walked between a dark house and a lit one, and started running again.

A man in the dark house, standing in the kitchen drinking coffee, saw him pass. Watched him go across the fence; couldn't see the police uniform, only the movement of the running man. He walked quickly back through his house, to tell the cop out front. But the cop out front was missing.

Huh. The man, cold in his undershirt, went out on his stoop, picked up the newspaper. In the very thin predawn light, he could see what looked like a shotgun lying on the sidewalk . . . and something else, further down the walk. Where was the cop?

The man looked around, then hurried across the street. What he thought was a shotgun turned out to be a spade handle. He turned, shaking his head, to go back to his house. Then he noticed the other object again. He stepped toward it, picked it up. A police radio.

And the cop on the grass groaned, and the man in the t-shirt said, "What? Who is that?"

They'd found a thick wad of computer printout, and Lucas and Haywood were taking it apart a page at a time, looking for anything. They heard the running footsteps before they saw anyone coming and looked up. The Eagan chief spun in the door, grabbing the edge of the doorframe to stop himself.

"Lucas, you better call in. They got a big problem up there."

Lucas said, "Keep reading," to Haywood and started back toward the car. "What happened?"

"I think your guy killed a cop. And he might have gotten through your perimeter."

"Sonofabitch."

As they hurried back to the car, Lucas said, "Have your guys talked to MacElroy yet?" MacElroy ran the lawn-mower shop.

"Talking to him now."

Lucas got the radio, called in. The dispatcher said the cop was still alive. "It's Larry White, Bob White's kid. He's really messed up, the guy hit him with a pipe or something. They're taking him to Ramsey."

"Jesus. What about Mail? Is he gone?"

"Maybe not. A guy who lives down there called us on 911 within a couple of minutes of White getting hit. They backed the perimeter off, making the house the middle of it. He should still be inside."

"All right. I'm coming back up there. Call Roux and Lester, tell them we need to talk."

"They're headed over to Ramsey. Both of them, along with Clemmons." Clemmons ran the Uniform Division.

"Are they on the air?"

"Yeah."

"Tell them to wait for me."

Mail made it through the new perimeter, but not by much. Once outside the original lines, he stayed out of sight for two blocks, then simply ran down a long dark alley, stumbling now and then as he raced over the uneven ground. He'd been running for a minute or perhaps a minute and a half, when he heard the sirens screaming behind him. Christ, they'd found the cop. He ran faster.

Another minute, and a cop car flashed down a cross street in front of him but continued past the alley. Mail slowed just a bit. He was breathing hard now, still carrying the shotgun, the hat perched on his head.

At the end of the alley, he edged cautiously out toward the street. The cop car was a block away, dropping off two foot patrolmen. They were crouched over the car window, intent on what the man inside was saying, or the radio. Mail took a breath, took two quick steps across that put him behind a car, then another behind a maple tree. The cops were still talking. Mail took another breath and walked quickly across the street to a maple on the other side.

And waited—but the cops had missed him.

Watching them, trying to keep the tree between himself and the mouth of the alley, he walked backwards until he was into the alley, then turned and broke into a run. A dog barked at him, and Mail ran faster, and the dog barked a few more times. But there were still dogs barking everywhere. Nobody came after him.

Mail stayed in the alley until it ended, then walked down a block to another alley, and ran down that. The sirens were getting fainter, and he could no longer see lights. But he *could* see houses against the sky. Dawn was getting close— and the traffic would be picking up.

He would be more visible, now, and there'd be more people around.

He needed wheels.

30

A surgeon in a scrub suit was wandering aimlessly outside the emergency room exit, a mask hanging down on his chest, paper operating hat askew. He was smoking a cigarette, head down, shoulders humped against the cool air.

"Did you do the White kid?" Lucas asked as he hustled up the drive to the door.

The surgeon shook his head. "They're still working on him."

Inside the door, Lester was talking to two Minneapolis cops, while Roux was facing Bob White, the cop's father, and his mother, whose name Lucas couldn't remember. But he remembered that she liked hats, although this morning she was bareheaded, and holding on to a white handkerchief like it was a lifeline. Lucas walked up, nodded, said, "Bob, Mrs. White . . . how is he?"

"His head is real bad," White said. "But he's a fighter."

Lucas didn't know the son, but had the impression that he was somewhat dull; not a bad kid, though. "Yeah, he is. And this is the best trauma place in the country. He's gonna do good."

Mrs. White pushed the handkerchief into her face and started to shake and her husband turned toward her. Lucas looked at Roux and tilted his head toward the door. She gave him an almost imperceptible nod and lifted a hand at a priest who was talking with a St. Paul cop. The priest broke away and Roux stepped toward him and whispered, "I think Mrs. White could use a hand . . ."

Lester joined them, and Roux lit up as soon as they were outside. The surgeon was starting a new cigarette and stamped his feet and said, "Cold."

Roux and Lester and Lucas walked to the end of the driveway as Roux puffed on the cigarette and Lucas filled them in on Mail's computer shop. When he finished, he said, "We couldn't put his picture out before, because it might touch him off. Now he knows we're close, and that'll do it—he's gonna kill them. We've got to get that picture on the air, everywhere."

"How do you know he'll kill them?" Roux asked.

"I know. He's had them a long time. The pressure must be terrific. With this chase, he'll have cracked like a big fuckin' egg. And he's smart. He'll know we've got the van, and he'll know that we'll get the computer store, that we'll get his prints, that we'll identify him as John Mail. He'll figure all that out—or he already has." Lucas nodded toward the hospital. "A cop has a shotgun, and Mail took him on with a club. He's freaking out."

Roux nodded. "All right. We can have the photo out in twenty minutes. He'll make all the morning news shows."

"Ask the TV guys to show the pictures at the beginning of the broadcasts, and to tell everybody to get their friends and come and watch, and show them again a couple of minutes later. As many times as they can. Flatter 'em: tell 'em if TV can't find the guy, Andi Manette's gonna die, and the kids, too. That'll keep them pushing the picture out there."

"How long have we got?"

"No time," Lucas said. "No time at all. If we don't find Manette in the next couple of hours, they're gone."

"Unless he's still in the perimeter," Lester said. "They think he might be, the guys up there."

"Yeah. We've gotta keep the perimeter tight. I'm gonna go over there, see if I can figure the odds that he's inside."

"Is there anything else?" Roux asked. "Any goddamn thing?"

Lucas hesitated, then said, "Two things. The first one is, I'd be willing to bet that wherever he's got them, it's within a few miles of that computer shop. That's where the phone calls were coming from, when we were trying to pinpoint the cellular phone. I think we oughta get everybody with a gun—highway patrol, local cops, everybody—and send them down there. We oughta filter every goddamn road. We don't have to stop everybody, but we ought to slow everything down, look in every backseat, see if we can spot somebody trying to elude the blockade."

"We can do that," Roux said.

Lucas looked at Lester, grinned slightly, and said, "Frank, could you call in? Could you get the picture thing going?"

Lester looked from Lucas to Roux and back, and then said, "What? I don't want to hear this?"

Lucas said, "You really don't."

Lester nodded. "All right," he said. "Back in a minute," and he went inside.

"What?" Roux asked when Lester was gone.

"I might call you later in the morning and suggest that you . . . I don't know, what?" He looked around, and then said, ". . . that you come over here and visit White. Spontaneously, without telling anybody exactly where you're going. You won't have to be out of touch long. Maybe half an hour."

She narrowed her eyes. "What're you going to do?"

"Are you willing to perjure yourself and say you didn't know?" Lucas asked. "Because you might want to say that."

Roux's vision seemed to turn inward, although she was gazing at Lucas's face. Then she said, "If it's that way . . ."

"It's that way, if you want to get them back—and keep your job."

"I'd do any fucking thing to get them back," she said. "But I hope you don't call."

"So do I," Lucas said. "If I do call, it'll mean that everything's gone in the toilet."

• • •

Mail picked out a house with lights on in the back. From the alley, he could see an older woman working in what must be the kitchen. He crossed a chain-link fence into the yard, wary of dogs, saw nothing. As he passed the garage, he stopped to look in the window. There was a car inside, a Chevy, he thought, not new, but not too old, either. That would work.

He went on to the house, to the back door, leaned the shotgun against the stoop, took out the pistol, looked around for other eyes, other windows, and knocked on the door.

The woman, curious, came to look. She was sixty or so, he thought, her gray hair pulled back in a bun, her thin face just touched with makeup. She was wearing a jacket over a silky shirt. A saleswoman, maybe, or a secretary. She saw the police hat and the uniform jacket and opened the inner door, pushed out the storm door, and said, "Yes?"

Mail grabbed the handle on the storm door, jerked it open, and before she could make another sound, shoved her as hard as he could, his open hand hitting her in the middle of the chest. She went down, and he was inside, and she said, "What?" She tried to crawl away, slowly, and he straddled her and gripped the back of her neck and asked, "Where are your car keys?"

"Don't hurt me," she whimpered. Mail could hear a television working in the other room and turned his head to look at it. Was somebody else out there?

"Where're the fuckin' car keys?" he asked, keeping his voice down.

"My purse, my purse." She tried to crawl out from under him, her thin hands working on the vinyl floor, and he tightened his grip on her neck.

"Where's your purse?"

"There. On the kitchen table."

He turned his head, saw the purse. "Good."

He stood up to get a better swing, and hammered her on the side of the head with the butt of the shotgun. She went down, hard, groaned, kicked a couple of times, and was still. Mail looked at her for a moment, then made a quick check of the small house. A weatherman with what looked like false teeth was pointing at a satellite loop of the Twin Cities area: ". . . a lake advisory with these winds, which could kick up into the thirty-mile-per-hour category by this afternoon . . ."

The bedroom had only one bed, a double, already made up.

A black-and-white photograph of a man in a Korean War Army uniform sat on the nightstand, under a crucifix. Nobody else to worry about.

He started back to the kitchen, and was stopped by his own image peering out of the television.

A woman was saying, ". . . John Mail, a former inmate at the state hospital. If you know this man, if you have seen him, contact the Minneapolis police at the number on your screen."

Mail was stunned. They knew him. Everything was gone. Everything. But they didn't know where he was. And they didn't say anything about the LaDoux name, they didn't say anything about finding Andi and the kid. And the TV would have that. So he was okay, for a while, anyway. But he had to get out, and get out now.

That fuckin' Davenport. Davenport was the one who'd done this. And it made him angry. That fuckin' Davenport, he wasn't fair. He had too much help.

The woman hadn't moved, and he dumped her purse on the kitchen table: car keys and a billfold. He opened the billfold, found twelve dollars.

"Shit."

He went back to the door, pausing to kick the woman in the side: twelve fuckin' dollars. You can't do anything with twelve fuckin' dollars. Her body moved sideways under the blow, leaving a trail of blood on the vinyl; she was bleeding from her ear.

Mail went on, through the door, picked up the shotgun at the stoop, and walked back to the garage. The side door was locked, and none of the keys fit it. He walked around to the alley side, tried the overhead door. That wouldn't budge, either. He walked back to the side door, used an elbow to put pressure on a window pane in the door, and pushed it in. Then he reached through, unlocked the door, and went inside.

A doorbell button was fixed to a block of wood beside the door. Mail pushed it, and the overhead door started up. He climbed in the car, started it, checked the gas. Damnit. Empty, or close enough. He'd have to risk a stop, or find another car. But there was enough to get him out of the neighborhood, anyway.

After Mail had gone, a neighbor woman looked out the back of her house and said, "That's odd."

"What?" Her husband was eating toast while he read the *Wizard of Id* in the comics.

"Mary left her garage door up."

"Getting old," her husband said. "I'll get it on the way to work."

"Don't forget," the woman said.

"How can I?" he asked, irritated. "I'm right across the alley."

"*You* could forget," his wife said. "That's why you've been shaving with soap for what, four days now?"

"Yeah, yeah, well, I'm not supposed to do the shopping for this family."

They argued. They always argued. In the heat of the argument, the woman's odd feeling evaporated—when her husband left, she went to get dressed herself, without waiting to see if he closed Mary's garage door.

The man who found White's body showed Lucas the window. "I saw the guy running, and I went right out front."

"So let's walk through it," Lucas said. He looked at his watch. "You're back here, you walk to the door."

They walked through it, out the front, down to the walk, all the way to the point where the man found White's body.

"Did you hear the cop cars moving out before or after the ambulance got here?" Lucas asked.

"Uh, about the same time. There was sirens everywhere. I remember hearing all the sirens, and then the ambulance got here. There was already four cops here, and they sent everybody running around after the guy."

Sloan walked up as Lucas looked at his watch again. "So it was probably five minutes."

The man said, "It didn't seem like it was that long. The cops, they was here in a couple seconds, it seemed like."

"Listen, thanks a lot," Lucas said. He slapped the man on the shoulder.

"That's fine, I hope I helped."

As they walked away from him, Sloan said, "I go on administrative duty starting with the next shift, until the shooting's okayed."

"Yeah."

"Makes me nervous," Sloan said.

"Don't worry about it," Lucas said. "You got witnesses up to your eyeballs."

"Yeah." Sloan was still unhappy. "What's happening here?"

"I'm not sure," Lucas said. "They probably didn't have the new perimeter up for six or seven minutes. The new perimeter is a half-mile out there. He *could* have run through it—we haven't found any sign of him. If it was *me*, I would have run through it."

"Sonofabitch could be in somebody's home," Sloan said, looking at the rows of neat, anonymous little houses. "Laying up."

"Yeah. Or he could be out."

Mail found a cut-rate gas station with no customers and no visible television. He pulled in—the shotgun, the hat and cop jacket in the backseat—and pumped ten dollars' worth of gas into the car. A bored kid sat behind the counter eating a packet of beer nuts, and Mail passed him the old woman's ten-dollar bill. Another customer pulled in as he paid for the gas. Mail walked back out, head averted, got in the car, and left. The other customer filled his tank, walked inside, and said, "That guy who just left—he looked like the guy they've got on TV."

"Don't got no TV. Asshole owner won't let me," the kid

said dully. He did the credit card, and the other man said, "Sure looked like him, though," and went off to work, where he talked about it most of the morning.

Mail went on down the block, stopped for a red light, turned on the radio. They were talking about him. ". . . apparently a long-time mental patient who faked his own death. Police have not yet identified the body found in the river."

Good. A break.

But they could be lying. Davenport could be mousetrapping him.

Another voice said, *No big difference. There's no way out anyway.* Anger cut through him, and he thought: *no way out.*

Another voice: *sure you can . . .*

He was smart. He could get down to the house, pick up what cash he had, take care of Manette and the kid, make it out to the countryside, knock off some rich farmer, somebody whose death wouldn't be noticed right away. If he could get a car for forty-eight hours, he could drive to the West Coast. And from the West Coast . . . he could go anywhere.

Anywhere. He smiled, visualized himself driving across the west, red buttes on the horizon, cowboys. Hollywood.

As the light changed to green, Mail saw the free-standing phone booth at the side of an Amoco station. He hesitated, but he wanted to talk. And shit, they *knew* who he was—they just didn't have the LaDoux name. He pulled into the station, dropped a quarter, and dialed Davenport.

The phone rang and Sloan looked at Lucas, and said, "If it's him, give me the high-sign, and I'll tell the Cap."

Lucas took the phone out, flipped it open. "Davenport."

Mail's voice was dark but controlled. "This was not fair. You had a lot more resources on your side."

"John, we're all done," Lucas said, jabbing a finger at Sloan. Sloan ran off to where the uniform captain was talking by radio with the cars on the perimeter. "Come on in. Give us Manette and the kids, huh?"

"Well, I just can't do that. That'd just be losing all the way around, you know? I mean, if they go away, then you've lost, too. You know? You've really lost, completely, in fact, because that's all you really want."

"John, I'm not worried about winning or losing . . ."

"I gotta go," Mail said, interrupting. "You've got those assholes tracing this."

"Are you trying to protect your friend? The one who's feeding you information on us?"

There was a moment of silence, then Mail laughed. "My friend? Fuck my friend. Fuck her."

And he hung up.

Lucas ran to the uniform captain's car, and the captain was saying, "Are you sure that's it? All right, I'm on the way."

To Lucas, he said, "It's an Amoco station not five miles from here. We didn't have anybody close. He's out."

Lucas said, "Shit," walked in a circle.

The uniform cop screeched out, leaving them, and Sloan said, "What'd he say?"

"He's gonna kill them."

"Aw, shit."

"But it's gonna take him a while to get there," Lucas said. "Patch through to Dispatch. Call Del, get him in. Get Loring from Intelligence and that rape guy, Franklin. Get him. Get them out of bed, anything you have to do, but tell them to meet me downtown in fifteen minutes. Tell them don't shave, don't clean up, just get there. Fifteen minutes."

"What're you gonna do?"

"You know somebody's feeding information to Mail?"

"I know you think that," Sloan said.

"I'm gonna arrest her," Lucas said.

Sloan's eyebrows went up. "Her? Who is it?"

"I don't know," Lucas said. "Get going."

Sloan, puzzled, hurried away. Lucas went back to the telephone, dialed. When the phone at the other end was picked up, he said, "Time to make your humanitarian visit to White."

"Lucas . . ." Roux was worried.

"Leave there in fifteen minutes."

"Lucas . . ."

"I just got a call from Mail. He's out, and he's going home to kill them. So go see White and keep your head down. Better keep it down for an hour."

"You gonna get him?"

"Yeah. I'm gonna get him."

31

"We have to be very fast," Andi said. "If we don't kill him, if we don't blind him, I'll try to hold his legs while you run. Run out and hide in the cornfield. He won't find you there. Just run out by the road and hide until you see cars. Wait until you see more than one, in case he's in one, then run out."

Andi rambled along, hoping that she was making sense. Sometimes, now, she wasn't sure. She'd see Grace looking at her oddly, and she'd say, "What?" and Grace would say, "You're calling me Gen," or "You were talking to Dad just now."

For a very long time, the sound of Andi scraping the nail had been the only noise in the cell, and then Grace sighed and said, "I think I could get the sole off my shoe. You know, with a piece of the bedspring."

Andi stopped scraping. "What for?"

"We could put the nail through it. We could use it like a push-handle."

When they were trying to work with the mattress springs, they'd found that the small pieces of metal were impossible to grip. Mail had given Andi some Band-Aids to patch a cut on her forehead, and Andi tried wrapping the wire with a bit of rag and the sticky-tape parts of the Band-Aids, but without much success.

Andi said, "Grace, that's a great idea. Let's see . . ."

Grace slipped her shoe off and handed it to her mother. The heel was capped by a thin slice of hard plastic. "We could break the plastic in half and make a hole in one half and put the nail through, and then put the other half over the nail head and tape it all together," Grace said. "When you stick him, you could have the nail coming out between your fingers with the heel in your hand."

Andi stared at her daughter: Grace had been thinking about this, how to kill him. Had visualized it, right down to the fatal punch. And it should work.

"Do it," she said. "I've got to keep scraping."

Another two hours, and they were done. The broken heel-cap and tape made a knob at the end of the nail, and held in her closed fist, with the nail protruding between her ring and middle finger, Andi could strike—and strike hard. The nail was five inches long. Nearly four were exposed beyond her fingers, and the last inch glittered with raw steel, like the tip of a new hypodermic needle.

"Now," Andi said, hefting the nail. "Let's go over it. When he comes, you're in the corner, playing with the computer. I'm lying on the mattress. I start to cry, but I don't get up. He comes to get me, just like he did the last couple of times. When he pulls me up, I put my left arm around his neck and pull up close, and my right hand hits him right below the breastbone, pointing up toward his heart. I do it a whole bunch of times, and try to turn him toward the wall . . ."

"And I come up from behind him and hit him in the eye with the spring," Grace said. She held up one of the thin needles she'd used to free the nail.

"So we should have room."

They danced it out, in the small cubicle: Grace was Mail, and bent over her mother, pulling her up. Andy struck at her midsection, pulled back, did it again.

Then Andi was Mail, her back turned, standing on the Porta-Potti, and Grace came from behind, striking a roundhouse blow at the left eye with the wire. The wire wasn't stiff enough to penetrate muscle, but it would blind him.

When they'd gone through it a half-dozen times, they sat down, and Grace said, "He's been gone a long time. What if something happened? What if he doesn't come?"

"He'll come," Andi said. She looked around the hole and touched her temples. "I can feel him out there, thinking about us."

32

Del looked like he'd been stuffed in a gunny sack and beaten with a pool cue. A patch of his blue jacket was discolored and stiff with something—ketchup? beer? His face was cut with stress lines, his hair was spiked from a pillow.

Franklin was not much better. He was a large black man, who wore a partial plate where his front teeth had been knocked out in a fight. He had the habit of dislodging the plate and rolling it with his tongue when he was thinking. Worse, a wandering eye gave him the appearance of a medieval insanity. He'd put on a suit, but he wore white gym shoes and a discolored t-shirt that said "Logan Septic Service: Satisfaction Guaranteed or Double Your Shit Back."

Loring was the prize. He was very large—fat—with a head the size and shape of a pumpkin, and eyes set so deep they were almost invisible. He hadn't shaved, and his beard was as thick and dangerous as a blackberry bramble. Sitting on top of the fat of his face, the beard shook like a bowl of cactus jelly. With his pale lavender suit and piss-yellow shirt, he looked crazier than Franklin.

Sloan simply looked worn out.

And all four were worried.

"You're talking about our ass," Franklin said. They were

all standing, jammed into Lucas's office, the desk dwarfed by the bulk of the five large bodies.

"I can cover it," Lucas insisted. "You're just taking orders and there's no time to argue about it. You argue about it, those two are gonna be dead."

Del nodded. "I'll do it."

Franklin growled, "Yeah, you're Lucas's pal. But shit . . ." He looked at Loring. "What do you think?"

Loring shrugged, then sighed. "Fuck, what can they do to us?"

"Fire us, take our pensions away, put us in jail, and these chicks could sue us for every dime we got."

After a moment of silence, Loring said, "What else?"

Franklin and Del started laughing, and Lucas knew he had them.

Lester stuck his head in the office. "I just saw a gang of your buddies running across the street. What's going on?"

Shit. "What're you doing here, Frank?" Lucas asked.

Lester straightened, frowned. "What do you mean?"

"Frank, you don't want to be here. Not for an hour or so."

"Why not?"

"You just don't."

Lester stepped inside, pushed the door shut with his foot. "Cut the bullshit, Lucas. Tell me what's happening."

"On your head," Lucas said.

"I'm willing to lie about it," Lester said. "I was never here."

Lucas said, "Somebody is feeding information to Mail. I'm sure of it."

"Who?"

"I don't know—but I'm fairly sure it's either Nancy Wolfe or Helen Manette. None of the other people were around for both the sessions that Mail got information from."

"But which?"

"I don't know," Lucas said. "There just isn't any way to tell. They've both got motives—money, emotional problems, or both. In fact, it could have been Tower Manette or

Dunn, but they didn't feel right, and when I talked to Mail, he said it was a she. So now I think it's got to be either Manette or Wolfe."

"So what're you going to do?"

"I'm arresting both of them," Lucas said. "I'm gonna have them dragged down here, searched, I'm gonna give them jail smocks and have them stuck in separate rooms, and I'm gonna have Franklin and Loring and Del and Sloan yell at them, until one of them cracks."

"Jesus Christ." Lester stared at him. "What about the innocent one?"

"I'm gonna apologize," Lucas said.

"You're fuckin' crazy," Lester said.

"Mail's on his way to kill those people. You heard the tapes. But he was a long way out, up north, and we've got cars tangling up traffic all over the south side of the Metro area. It'll take him a while to get there—but he *will* get there, and when he does, he's gonna kill them. That's how much time we've got."

"Does Roux know about this?" Lester asked.

"She's outa touch . . ."

"So am I," Lester said. He pulled open the door. "I never talked to you."

And he was gone. Lucas felt peculiarly alone, standing in his empty office. Nothing to do now except wait for the women to arrive. Then he heard footsteps outside, and Lester was back.

"How are you gonna cover it?" Lester demanded. "You got anything?"

Lucas shook his head. "Moral appeals. We were doing the only thing we could to save Manette's life, and the kid, if she's still alive."

Lester turned in a circle and said, "Christ, twenty-four years on the force." He ran a hand through his hair and said, "I gotta go do some paperwork."

Lucas said, "Frank: could you get us a helicopter in here? Across the street on the government center plaza?"

Lester thought for a second, then gave a quick nod. "Yeah, I can do that." And he was gone again.

• • •

Nancy Wolfe came in screaming. Helen Manette came in weeping.

Helen Manette arrived first, wrapped in a nightgown, with Tower Manette six feet behind her. They were moving fast, a tight clutch of cops, the fat Franklin and the frightening Loring and the middle-aged suspect, Tower Manette trotting a few feet behind, his white hair standing up in peaks. He spotted Lucas and ran at him, his thin face white with anger, his thin-man's wattles shaking with rage.

"What in the hell is going on?" He turned to point at the cops with his wife. "I'm told you're behind this . . . this fucking travesty of justice."

"Your wife has been arrested in the course of our investigation," Lucas said coldly. "I'd suggest you shut up."

"We've got a lawyer coming," Manette shouted. The cops were almost out of sight and Manette turned to run after them, shaking his finger at Lucas. "It's all over for you, you . . ."

"He sounded pleased," Lester said, stepping into the hall-way.

Lucas couldn't suppress a cop-smile, an unhappy rictus that appeared when the world had turned to shit and there was no way out. "Yeah . . . how about the helicopter?"

"It's coming; it'll be across the street on the plaza."

"Excellent."

Nancy Wolfe, dressed in pajamas, a housecoat, and slippers, was frightened and angry, a towering rage that expressed itself in tears and nearly incoherent screaming: "I will sue, goddamn you, goddamn you all."

She saw Lucas and wrenched away from Del. "You will never again," she said, but couldn't finish. Del had cuffed her and when he tried to lead her past Lucas, she jerked her arm away and Lucas thought she was going to come after him with her teeth. "You are, you are . . ." she said. Again, she failed to find the word, but a thin line of saliva dribbled out the left side of her mouth.

"Take her down," Lucas said to Del. "Send the pajamas to the lab."

"My pajamas," she said. "My pajamas . . ."

Lucas waited until they were down the stairs, and out of sight, then hurried after them. Del, Sloan, Franklin, and Loring were gathered outside the processing room. Helen Manette had already been searched, photographed, and isolated, and her clothes had been packaged for a lab inspection. She'd been given a jail smock to replace them.

Wolfe was being photographed, and would be searched and her clothes taken away.

And Franklin said, "Ah, man, this scares the shit outa me. This scares the shit outa me, man. Christ, I think we oughta let up."

"Too late," Lucas said. "We're already in it. If we break one of them, we're out the other side. Now, when you get in there with them, I want them scared. We need all the pressure you can put on them: nobody gets hit, but you get your face right down in theirs, you . . ."

Loring said, "Behind you . . ."

Lucas turned around. Tower Manette was coming through the glass doors, an attorney in tow.

"I want to see my wife."

"When we're finished with the processing," Lucas said.

"We want to see her right fucking now," Manette shouted, jostling past Sloan toward Lucas.

"Touch another fuckin' cop and we'll put *your* ass in jail," Lucas snapped.

The attorney pulled Manette's sleeve, said, "Tower, cool off." And to Lucas: "We want to see Mrs. Manette, and we want to see her immediately. We have reason to believe that her civil rights have been grossly violated."

"Get a court order," Lucas said.

"We will," the attorney said. "We'll have one here in fifteen minutes." To Manette, he said, "C'mon, Tower: this is the way to do it."

"You motherfucker," Manette said to Lucas. "I met you in my house, I treated you like . . . like . . . quality, and you do this, you fuckin' . . ."

"What?" Lucas asked, genuinely curious. "Fuckin' what?"

"Trash," Manette said. And he was gone.

Franklin, who had been turning the partial plate in his mouth so his large front teeth rotated through his lips, clicked the plate back in place with his tongue, chuckled, and said, "You WASPs, he didn't know what to call you. Wanted to call you a nigger or a spic, but you're as white as he is."

"He's gonna be black and blue if something don't happen," Loring said, looking back at the processing rooms. "You think they'll get that court order?"

"Yes, I do," Lucas said. "That's why you get to be like Tower Manette. So you can wake up a judge and get a pal out of jail. Now: when you get in those rooms . . ."

Wolfe sat in the bare interview room, small with the bodies around her, her hair wild, her eyes large and frightened. The three men pressed in around her, Loring smoking, the smoke gathering around her head; she tried to stand up, once, but Del pushed her back into the chair. Lucas had never seen anything quite like it, an interrogation from a bad movie.

"How did you talk to him?" Loring asked. "That's all we want to know. How did you get in touch with him? Was he a patient? Were you treating him?"

"I don't know him, I don't . . ."

"Bullshit, bullshit, bullshit, we know he was a patient. Were you fucking him? Was that it? Is that why you're protecting him?"

"I'm not protecting anybody," she wailed.

"Aw, c'mon, for christ sakes, he's gonna go out there and kill your partner, and I'll tell you what, honey, you're gonna go into the women's prison and the dykes out there are gonna make a meal outa you. You don't wanna spend the rest of your life snuffin' up strange pussy, you better start talking right now."

Del, standing behind her, put his hands over his eyes: Loring was over the edge. Del waved him off, and, playing the soft guy, said, "Listen, darling, I know what it's like to be attached to somebody. I mean, you get involved with a guy like Mail . . ."

"I wasn't involved," she shrieked, her head twisting. "I didn't do anything, Christ, I want a lawyer, I want a lawyer now, you can't do this."

"You'll get a lawyer when we fuckin' well say you can," Loring said, his voice a slap in the face. "Now, what I want to know is how we can reach him. All we want is a phone number, or somebody who can tell us where we can get a phone number."

Del's voice, softer: "We can get you a deal. You'll do five years. Now, we know one of the girls is dead, and that's thirty years inside. No parole. You'd be an old . . . what's the word?"

"Crone," Lucas said.

". . . crone when you get out," Del said, his voice still soft, still reasonable.

"I want my husband, I want him in here," Helen Manette wailed. She spent much of the time weeping uncontrollably, and questions were difficult to press.

Franklin finally got down on his knees, thrust his face to within an inch of hers, and said, "Listen, bitch, if you don't shut up, I'm gonna slap the shit out of you. You got that? You shut the fuck up, or I'm gonna stomp a mudhole in your white ass, and I'll fuckin' enjoy doing it. Your pal is gonna slice Miz Manette and her daughter into fuckin' dog food, and I want to know how to stop him, and you're gonna tell me."

"I want my husband . . ."

"Your husband doesn't give a shit about you," Franklin shouted. "He wants his daughter. He wants his granddaughters. But he's not gonna get his granddaughters, he's not gonna get both of them anyway, 'cause you and your pal killed one of them, didn't you?"

"Hey, c'mon, take it easy, take it easy," Sloan said, gently shoving Franklin out of the way. "You're gonna have a heart attack, man. Let me talk to her."

Sloan was sweating, though the room was cool. "Now

listen, Miz Manette, we know there are all kinds of stresses in a person's life, and sometimes we do things we regret. Now we know that your husband is sleeping with Nancy Wolfe, and we know that you know. And we know that if Tower Manette left you, there just wouldn't be that much to share, would there? Now . . ."

Franklin looked at Lucas and shook his head, and Lucas made a *keep rolling* sign with his hands.

Franklin nodded and pushed and said to Sloan, "Hey, cut the psychological bullshit, Sloan; you know the bitch did it. Give me two minutes alone with her, and I'll get it out." He squatted, his face close to Helen Manette's, and he turned the partial plate with his tongue. "Two minutes would do it," he said.

He chuckled, a long gravelly roll, and Lucas winced.

Wolfe looked at Lucas and pleaded: "Get me out of here, just get me out of here. Please, get me out."

"I could help you, but you've got to help us," Lucas said. "We could use anything. A phone number would be great. An address. How did you get to know him? A little history . . ."

"I don't know him," she said hoarsely.

"Let me explain," Loring said, circling her. Del stood behind her, very close, so she could feel his pants leg near the back of her head. "We know that you're fucking Tower Manette. We know that Tower Manette's money is going to his daughter. Now, if you shoot Tower's old lady out of the saddle, and you were getting close, and if there was no daughter around, you'd get a bundle, right?"

"That's crazy," she blurted.

"And even if you don't get Tower, you'd get the key-man insurance from the shrink business, right? That's a bundle all by itself. You could buy a fleet of Porsches with that money alone."

"That . . ." she started, but Loring stuck a warning finger in her face.

"Shut the fuck up. I'm not done," he said. "Now we know that you were going out with George Dunn before Andi

Manette took him away, and we've been having this argument: could that have triggered this off? Is it all because of George Dunn? Are you fucking Andi Manette's father to get back at Andi Manette because you can't fuck her husband? There's a pretty big kettle of psychological stew right there, huh? What'd old Desmond Freud have to say about that, huh?"

She went cool: "I want a lawyer. I promise you, if you don't get me a lawyer, none of you will ever again work as police officers. I'm willing to overlook . . ."

The door opened behind them, and Sloan stuck his head in: "Lucas. You better come in here." And to Loring and Del, he said, "Go easy."

Helen Manette was slumped in the plastic chair; she'd stopped weeping and was chewing on a fingernail. She had snapped: she had a foxy look on her face, a dealer's look.

Lucas said, "What?" and Sloan said, "Miz Manette, tell Chief Davenport what you just told us."

"I don't know anybody like this Mail person," Helen Manette said. "But I know a boy, a renter in one of my apartments."

"Oh, shit," Lucas said. He turned away, put a hand to his face.

Sloan said, "Lucas? What?"

"The goddamn building directory card in Crosby's building. We both looked at it, and it had that blue bird on it, just like in Andi Manette's office building." He looked at Manette. "That's your management company, isn't it?"

"That's our logo, a royal blue bird, yes," she nodded brightly.

"Remember that? We saw it the first day. I didn't put it together, but I knew there was something . . ."

He squatted, looked into Helen Manette's watery eyes. "So you knew Mail from the apartment building."

"I didn't know who he was. He seemed like a nice boy."

"Then why did you call him?" Sloan asked.

"I didn't—he called me," she said. "He said he heard

what was going on, and he wanted to say he was sorry and we . . . talked."

Lucas knew she was lying, but right now didn't care. "You have his phone number?"

Still bright: "Why, yes, I believe I do. Somewhere. If it's the same boy. He looks the same."

"Can you get it for us?"

"I believe I could, if I could go back home . . ."

Lucas said, "We'll get you back." He looked at Franklin. "Take Loring, put her in a squad, get her down there, full lights and sirens. I want it in six fuckin' minutes."

"You got it," Franklin said.

Lucas took his arm, pulled him to the side: "And you and Loring stay on top of her. Anything it takes."

On the way down to the room where Wolfe was being questioned, Lucas said to Sloan, "You're not supposed to be out with a gun. Stay here with Wolfe. Help her out. Be nice to her. Apologize. Explain what we were doing, and why. Get her home. If she wants a lawyer, help her out. But suggest that she talk with me before she does anything."

"What're you gonna tell her?"

"I'm gonna beg her to let it go," Lucas said, grinning.

"I don't think it's gonna work, man," Sloan said.

He stuck his head in the interview room, where Del and Loring were leaning against a wall, Loring smoking again. Wolfe was sitting straight in her chair, dry-eyed, expectant. Lucas said, "You two guys—let's go." And to Wolfe: "You're okay. You're free to go. Detective Sloan will help you."

Sherrill was coming in the door as Del and Lucas ran up the stairs to the front of the building: "I heard on the radio," she said. She was wearing jeans, boots, a plaid shirt, and her ball cap.

"Gotta go," Lucas called back as they passed her.

"I'm coming," she said, and she followed them out the door.

"I don't think . . ." Lucas said.

Sherrill interrupted: "Bullshit. I'm going." Then: "Where're we going?"

They ran together across the street to the plaza in front of the Hennepin County Government Center. A helicopter sat in the middle of the plaza, blades turning, and a TV crew was shooting film of it. When the cameraman saw the three running cops, he turned, and the camera followed them to the chopper.

"Let's go," Lucas said to the pilot.

"Where?"

"Down toward Eagan. Fast as you can."

33

The chopper took off head-down, Lucas's stomach clutching as the black-visored pilot poured on the power and threw the machine out of the loop. They crossed I-94, rising over the tumult of the early rush hour, then projected out over the Mississippi and down the valley, past a tow with a barge, past a solitary powerboat running full-out on twin outboards, and past Lucas's house on Mississippi River Drive. Del tapped him on the shoulder and pointed down, past the pilot, and Lucas pushed up against the safety belt and saw his house, in strobelike flashes between the brilliant autumn maples, and Weather's car slowly backing out of the driveway. He felt the cut in the palm of his hand, looked down, and found the ring. Weather: Jesus. He strained to see her, but the car was out of sight, lost in the trees.

"I'll take us right down to the I-35 intersection with Highway 55. We'll orbit there until we get better directions," the pilot said. "I got maps."

She handed Lucas a spiral-bound book of Metro area maps, and Lucas held it between his legs. Del, in back, said, "What if this is some kind of dead-drop, like the computer shop?"

Lucas shook his head. "Then they're gone, Manette and the kids." He looked at his watch. "We may be too late now.

We're an hour and fifteen minutes from when he called me. He could make it down there in forty-five minutes, except for the traffic tangles. We gotta hope that he takes her on one last time."

The pilot looked at him. "You gotta hope he takes her on . . . you mean, rapes her?"

"Yeah, that's what he's been doing," Lucas said. "It's better than death."

"Ah, my God," the pilot said. She turned away from him, and sent the chopper in a sickening swoop toward a twisted intersection below. "That's it, there. Look at that mess. Jeez, what happened?"

Below them, traffic was tied up in all directions, and blue lights winked through the worst jam Lucas had ever seen. "They're doing it, they're tying it up," he said, and he had to laugh, once, a short bark. "They'll be two hours getting that loose again. Maybe we got a chance. Maybe we got a chance."

Lucas found the map for the intersection as they orbited, once, twice, then again, like a bee in a bottle; and Del explained the interrogation scene to Sherrill.

"So where in the heck is Franklin?" Sherrill asked.

"Five minutes to the Manettes' house," Lucas said. "He oughta be calling."

"What's gonna happen to this guy?" the pilot asked.

"Gonna chain him in the basement of the state hospital," Lucas said. "Throw him a cheeseburger once a week."

"Better to shoot him," she said.

Lucas said, "Shhh," and they went around again.

Sherrill, huddled in the back, was greener than Lucas. "If Franklin doesn't call quick, I'm gonna blow a corn dog all over our pilot."

"Don't do that," the pilot said. Then: "I'll try to smooth things out."

Sherrill said, "C'mon, Franklin, you asshole, call."

And Franklin came then, patched through from Dispatch: "Lucas, we got it. His name is LaDoux. He's just north of Farmington, about a mile off Pilot Knob Road on Native American Trail. I got the address here."

Lucas found the map as Franklin read out the address, and the pilot poured it on, heading south.

And Franklin asked, "What about Miz Manette? I mean, this one?"

"Take her back downtown, get her a lawyer," Lucas said.

Del, from the backseat, shouted, "And read her rights to her."

Sherrill, marginally more cheerful, also shouting: "Yeah, we want it to be on the up-and-up."

Lucas, ignoring them, was talking to Dispatch. "Can you get us closer? These street numbers don't mean anything up here."

"Yeah, we're looking for the mailman on that route, and we've alerted Dakota County, but they don't have a lot of assets down there."

"I know, I can see them all from here," Lucas said. Down below, roof racks were lighting up the major intersections for miles, and he could see cops on the streets, peering into southbound cars. "But get some going south, if you can."

"Strangest thing I ever saw," Del said from the back as Lucas signed off the radio. Del, who liked high places, had his face pressed against his window. "A man-made traffic jam. God, look at those guys. I'd hate to be down there, though."

"Is that Pilot Knob there?" the pilot asked, pointing at a street with a gloved hand. "Or is that Cedar?"

"I don't know," Lucas said, turning the map. He hated flying, didn't like the exposed front on the helicopter: he would have preferred something solid, like sheet steel. "Where's due south?" The pilot pointed and he turned the map. "Okay, there should be a golf course."

"There's a golf course," the pilot said, pointing to her right. "But . . . there's another one."

"There should be a lake, a crescent-shaped lake," Lucas said.

"Okay, there's a lake."

"Okay, yeah, that's it—there's the little lake by the big one. So that's gotta be Pilot Knob right there."

They churned south, following the road, past another golf

course, out into the countryside, corn going brown, a green-and-yellow John Deere rolling through a half-cut field of alfalfa.

Dispatch called back. "Lucas, we got the mailman, here he is . . ." There was a pause, and then a man's distant voice. "Hello?"

Lucas identified himself. "Did the dispatcher tell you what we need?"

The mailman said, "Yes. You want the fifth house from the corner, on the south side of the road. It's about three-quarters of a mile from the corner, sits up on a slope with a gravel driveway. White house—needs paint, though—and it's got a porch and a screen door and a couple old tumble-down buildings out back. There's a shutter off on the front; one window's only got one shutter. The mailbox is silver and there's an orange *Pioneer Press* delivery box on the same post under the mailbox."

"Got that," Lucas said. A swamp flicked past, a thousand feet down. "Thanks."

"Listen, you still there?"

"Yeah."

"One of the guys here has a TV going, and I just saw the picture. You got the right guy. That's him, all right. He's not around there much, but I saw him a couple times."

"Got that," Lucas said.

In the backseat, Del said, "Hot dog," and slipped his pistol out from under his jacket and punched out the clip.

Sherrill said, "Don't say that."

"What?"

"The dog thing," Sherrill said, and she swallowed, and started fumbling for her gun.

"Hold on, I'll have you on the ground in two minutes," the pilot said. She'd been looking at the map, where Lucas's fingers pinched the road. "So we're looking for a loop, like a suburb or something, and then it's three miles on."

"There's the loop coming up," Lucas said, pointing at a cluster of houses, with tiny trees sprouting in the expansive front yards. They all looked the same, variations of beige with simple, peaked roofs, like properties on a Monopoly board.

"Okay. Then that must be the road, right there," the pilot said. Up ahead, Native American Trail was a beige thread in a blanket of green. "There's somebody heading down there . . ."

A red car was throwing up a cloud of gravel dust as they closed on the road. "One-two-three-four-five, Jesus, I think he's heading in there, he's slowing down, he's turning," Lucas said.

"Wrong drive, wrong drive. The fifth house is over there, down further," the pilot said, pointing.

"I don't know," Lucas said. "Look, he's in a hurry, he's moving."

The pilot groped at her feet and handed Lucas a pair of battered 8 × 50 marine binoculars. "You call it: whatever you want to do."

They were coming in fast, but they were still a half-mile out; Lucas put the heavy binoculars on the house, picked out the mailbox and the brilliant orange paperbox on the post below it. To the right, the red car had topped a hill, and as Lucas watched, a man got out of the car, turned his pale face toward them: black hair, tall; the white face, at the distance, a featureless wedge. But a wedge that felt right.

The man darted into the ramshackle house in the cornfield; he carried something—a shotgun? He was too far away to be certain. "That's him," Lucas said, half-shouting. "Put us on him, put us on him."

"What are we doing?" Sherrill shouted from the back. She had a revolver out, and a speed loader in her other hand. Below them to the front and right, three Dakota County sheriff's cars were pounding up Pilot Knob Road from the south. Lucas waved Sherrill off and got on the radio: "Tell the sheriff's guys it's the first road west of the house. Not the house, it's a track, goes across a ditch just west of the house . . . tell them to look for the chopper, where we're going in. We've got him in the house, we see him in the house."

"What're we doing?" Sherrill yelled again. "Are we going in? Are we going in?"

"Gotta try," Lucas said over his shoulder. "He's goofier than shit, and he might have some kind of long gun with him. Didn't he take a shotgun off White?"

"Shotgun," Del said.

"Yeah, so take it easy. But Christ, if he kills them now, we're thirty seconds late; and he's goofier'n shit, man, goofier'n shit."

The pilot said, "Hold on," and then, smiling beneath the black visor, dropped them out of the sky.

34

Mail drove north, cut I-694, the outer beltline around the Cities, took it east and then south, across I-94, where the highway changed numbers and became I-494. He was driving the old woman's car on remote control, his head thumping with the call to Davenport, the treachery of the cops, the humiliation of the duck shit, the nose-ring blonde at Davenport's computer company.

Had Davenport used the blonde to suck him in? Had he figured him that well? He relived the attack on the cop, the satisfying whack of the spade; the hit on the old lady, last seen crumpled on her kitchen floor, one leg under a chair, a broken plate on the floor by her head, a piece of buttered toast in the middle of her back; Gloria floated through his mind, her neck crooked with the nylon rope around her, her feet swinging like a pendulum overhead as he laid the river rocks into the booby trap.

And the parts of Andi Manette: tits, legs, face, ass, back. The way she talked, the way she curled away from him, fearing him.

He almost ran into the truck ahead. He cut left and saw the traffic jam. Cars, trucks, backed up a half-mile away from the river bridge. Blue cop-lights flashing along the road.

He sat in the traffic jam for five minutes, steaming, the bright movies in his brain now reduced to shadows. Up ahead, a Jeep cut onto the shoulder of the road. Mail edged over to watch: the Jeep rolled slowly along the shoulder, then cut across to an exit heading north on Highway 61. Mail followed. He didn't want to go back north, but he could make a U-turn, head back south. Must be a hell of an accident; there were cops all over the place.

He slid off the exit, running north; made an illegal U, and started south again. Everything around the bridge was blocked, but there was another bridge, little used, down in Newport.

More cops. He turned out east of the oil refinery, continued on Highway 61. The radio . . .

WCCO was full-time on the story, the announcer wearing his Tornado Alert Voice: ". . . the entire south end of the Metro area is tangled up as the police search for John Mail, identified as the kidnapper of Mrs. Andi Manette and her daughters Grace and Genevieve. There are checks at many of the major intersections in Dakota County, and all bridges across the Mississippi. All we can do is ask for patience as police check cars as quickly as possible, but delays are now running up to an hour on outbound lanes of I-35E and I-35W, all outbound bridges in downtown St. Paul. That would include the High Bridge, the Wabasha and Robert Street Bridges, and Highway 3, plus the Mendota Bridge, both I-694 bridges."

Christ, he couldn't get back home.

He was heading down to Hastings, straight into a checkpoint. The announcer hadn't said anything about Prescott, the St. Croix Bridge into Wisconsin.

If they were stopping cars on all those bridges, they hadn't found the house, hadn't found the women, still didn't have the LaDoux name.

He left Highway 61 just north of Hastings, crossed the St. Croix into Wisconsin, struck out in a wide southern swing through Wisconsin, and crossed the Mississippi back into Minnesota on the unguarded bridge at Red Wing. From Red

Wing, he took Highway 61 north, and finally turned cross-country to Farmington.

There were no cops on the highway, none in town. None. It was almost eerie. Even the highway north seemed thinly traveled. At Native Americans Trail, he turned east, taking it slow, looking for lights, for cars, for movement. For anything.

There was nothing.

He shoved the gas pedal to the floor, moving now, breathing again, heart pounding, everything coming to a close. He flashed on Andi Manette, all those parts—and turned left off the road.

He stopped. He felt a beat, but couldn't identify it, listened for a second, then reached in the backseat, got the shotgun, and climbed out of the car.

The chopper was just coming in. He looked up, to the north, and saw the machine dropping out of the sky, screaming in on him.

He ran to Andi . . .

They heard him running across the floor, pounding down the stairs. He'd never run before. Andi sat up, looked at her daughter. "Something's happening."

"Should we . . . ?" Grace was terrified.

"We've got to," Andi said.

Grace nodded, dropped to her knees, lifted the edge of the mattress. She took the needle and handed the nail to her mother.

Andi fitted it to her hand, kissed her daughter on the forehead. "Don't feel anything. Don't think, just do it," she said. "Just like we practiced; you get back there . . ."

The first day Mail had put them in the cell, she remembered the smell of old potatoes. She hadn't noticed the odor since—it had simply become part of the background—but she smelled it now. Potatoes, dust, urine, body sweat . . . The hole.

"Kill him," Grace rasped at her. Grace's eyes were too large, sunken. Her skin was like paper, her lips dry. "Kill him. Kill him."

Mail was rattling at the door, fumbling at it. When he opened it, he was carrying a shotgun, and for just an instant, Andi thought he was going to kill them without a word, open fire before they had a chance.

"Out," he screamed. "Both of you, out." His young-old face was dead white; he had a white bead of spittle at the corner of his mouth. He gestured with the gun, not pointing it at them, a sweep of his arm. "Get out here, both of you."

Andi had the nail by her side, and went first; she felt Grace reach out and grab the top of her tattered skirt, and pulled along behind.

"What?" Andi started.

"Get," Mail snarled, looking up the stairs. He grabbed her by the skin of her throat and pulled her, stepping back, still looking over his shoulder, expecting someone to burst in, the shotgun barrel straight up.

And she stepped straight into him and struck.

She rammed the nail into the space below his breastbone, trying to angle it into his heart, looking at his eyes as she struck.

And she screamed, "Grace, Grace . . ."

The shack's outside door was half-open; Lucas kicked it the rest of the way, Del flattened against the outer wall, sweeping the fallen-down mudroom just inside.

Sherrill was on the other side of the house, watching the back. Lucas went through first, through the mudroom, following the sights of the .45, his thumb-knuckle white in the lower rim of his circle of vision.

The shack smelled of wood rot, and dim light shifted in through dirty windows. A broken-legged table crouched in the kitchen beyond the mudroom, and tracks were etched in the dirt of the floor, heading into the interior. There was an open door to the left, hung with cobwebs; another on the other side, showing a down-slanting wall: and from there, a light, and a man's voice shouting.

Del, just behind, slapping him on the shoulder: "Go."

Lucas went straight ahead, scrabbling along in a half-crouch, while Del covered the doorway. Lucas did a peek at the door, looking down the stairs, and a woman screamed, "Grace, Grace . . ."

When Andi Manette struck with the nail, Mail's eyes widened and his mouth opened in surprise and pain, and he jerked forward, turning away. Grace struck at his right eye and missed as he turned his head, the point of the needle skidding across the bridge of his nose, burying itself an inch deep in his left eye.

He screamed, pulled back, and Andi shouted, "Grace, run."

Grace ran, and Mail flailed at her and the girl was batted off her feet, lurching into the pile of tumble-down shelving on the back wall of the tiny cellar. She scrambled to her feet and tried for the stairs, and Andi saw the shotgun coming around and she pulled the nail out and struck again, felt it skid along his ribs. The shotgun stopped in its track and Mail hit her in the face with an elbow and she fell, and saw her daughter's legs flying up the stairs. Mail fired the shotgun, a flash and a blast like thunder, straight up, into the ceiling, either by accident or simply to startle, to slow down whoever was up the stairs. He turned, and Andi saw his good eye fix on her—the other eye was a blotch of blood and she felt a thrill of satisfaction—and the barrel of the gun came around and opened at her face. They stood just for a second that way, Mail's face contorting. She could see his hand working on the trigger, but nothing was happening, and she rolled out of the line of fire.

Lucas started down the stairs in a crouch, heard the man scream and a girl, a scarecrow, hair on end, blood on her face, ran to the stairs and started up, stopped when she saw Lucas. A shotgun went off, the blast like a physical blow; plaster sprayed around them, and Lucas fell sideways, tried to catch himself.

There wasn't much pain when Andi Manette stuck him, but Mail knew he'd been hurt. He pulled back, tried to get some space, but Manette clung to him and then the girl was there.

He saw the hand coming up, the thin, steel glitter between her fingers, and turned his head. The needle slashed at him, hurt more than Manette's knife, or whatever it was. There was a black flash—was that possible?—in his left eye, and he wrenched away, spasmodically pulling at the trigger. The shotgun went off, the barrel not more than a foot from his ear, deafening him.

As dust and plaster rained on them from the ceiling, Manette struck again; she was screaming and he saw the girl running for the stairs. He swung at her; he felt no impact, but saw the girl go down. Everything was moving at a berserker's speed, like a movie cut too often, clips of this and that too fast for his brain to process . . . but he looked for Manette, his betrayer, found her at his feet.

Her mouth was open, she was screaming, and he pointed the barrel at her mouth and pulled the trigger. The trigger pulled back slackly, without tension. Nothing happened. He pulled it again, and again, saw the girl screaming on the stairs, Davenport falling, a gun in his hand.

Mail ran.

He ran behind the furnace, into the old rat's nest coal bin, up the coal chute to the rotten wooden door at the top. He knocked the door open with the stock of the gun and a shaft of light hit him full in the face.

Del was at the top of the stairs, frozen by the blast, his gun pointing down past Lucas. Lucas twisted, falling, struck the scarecrow girl, knocking her sideways, and staggering, caught himself on the post at the bottom of the stairs, his gun sweeping the room, looking for the face, the target.

"Grace," Andi screamed, and screaming again, "Run, Grace . . ."

Then a man was there with a gun, a large man in a suit, shouting at her, then another man, a man who looked like a tramp, with another gun, maneuvering toward the cell. She shrank away, but heard, through the pain and fear, the single word, "Where?"

She pointed toward the furnace; and as she pointed, a

shaft of sunlight broke into the room, from behind the furnace. Del was at another door, looking down, then back at him, and Lucas took three leaping steps across the room, past the furnace into a small wooden-sided room. Light poured through a hatchlike door in the foundation.

Andi heard the gunshots, the quick bite of a pistol, the deeper boom of the twelve-gauge. . . .

On the grass, outside, on his knees, Mail looked left and brought the gun up. This time, he pumped the slide, saw an empty shell flip out to the right. That's why it hadn't fired. In the chaos in the basement, he'd forgotten to pump it.

But there were more cops here: he heard a man's voice, screaming, and more shouting in the basement. A chopper roar picked up, and the chopper slipped from behind the house, six feet off the ground, hovering.

Sherrill ran around the side of the house.

They saw each other at the same instant. Sherrill's pistol was up and a single shot plucked at Mail's coat. Mail returned the shot, firing once, and Sherrill went down, her legs knocked from beneath her. The helicopter came in like a giant locust, and he pointed the shotgun at the black-visored pilot behind the glass, pulled the trigger; again, nothing happened. Cursing, he pumped the gun, and as the chopper pilot roared two feet overhead, he ran beneath the machine, past Sherrill, to the corner of the house.

Cops coming up the track. Three cars at least.

He turned and sprinted thirty yards across the yard toward the cornfield, vaulted the fence, and submerged in the deep green leaves.

Sherrill was on the ground, screaming, the chopper thirty yards away, the pilot gesturing frantically, when Lucas crawled up the coal chute. Lucas turned and saw Mail vault a barbed-wire fence into the cornfield; he vanished in an instant.

A sheriff's car slewed sideways in the yard as Lucas ran to Sherrill, put his hand on her back: "Hit?"

"My legs, man, my legs, it hurts so fuckin' bad, it just fuckin' burns . . ."

Del was out now, and Lucas waved at the pilot, pulling her down, then ran to the uniformed deputy, who stood by the fender of his car, a shotgun on his hip.

"He's in the cornfield—he's right in there," Lucas shouted over the blast of the chopper blades. Grass and bits of weed whipped past them as the chopper settled. "Get a couple guys on the road, and get in those hayfields. Cut him off, cut him off . . ."

The deputy nodded and ran back to the other cars. Lucas went back to Sherrill. Del was kneeling over her, had ripped open her pants leg. Sherrill had taken a solid hit on the inside of her left leg between her knee and her hip; bright red arterial blood was pulsing into the wound.

"Bleeding bad," Del said; his voice was cool, distant. He pulled off his jacket, ripped off a sleeve, and pressed it into the wound.

"Hold it there," Lucas said to Del. "I'll carry her."

"How bad? How bad is it?" Sherrill asked, her face a waxy white. "I hurt . . ."

"Just your leg, you'll be okay," Del said, and he grinned at Sherrill with his green teeth.

Lucas picked her up, cradling her, and carried her groaning with pain to the chopper, where the pilot had shoved open the passenger-side door. "Bleeding bad, hit an artery," Lucas shouted over the prop blast. "Got to get her to Ramsey."

The pilot nodded, gave him a thumbs-up. Lucas shouted at Del, "You go—keep the hole packed up."

"You're gonna need help . . ."

"Gonna have a lot of help in one minute," Lucas shouted back. "This is just gonna be a dog hunt now."

Del nodded, and they fitted Sherrill into the passenger seat with Del straddling her; and the chopper lifted off.

Lucas turned and saw Andi Manette at the door of the old farmhouse. She had her daughter under one arm, and with her hand, tried to hold together the pieces of what once had been a suit.

"You're Davenport," she said. She looked bad: she looked like she was dying.

"Yes," Lucas nodded. "Please sit down, both of you. You're okay ‹. . .›"

"He's afraid of you," Andi said. "John's afraid of you."

Lucas looked from Andi Manette and Grace toward the cornfield. "He should be," he said.

The Dakota deputies had pursued people into cornfields before; they knew how to isolate a runner. The field itself covered a half-section, a mile long by a half-mile wide. The road ran along one edge, and recently cut alfalfa fields along two more. A bean field, still standing, stretched along the fourth side. Cop cars were stationed at three of the corners of the field, and cops climbed on top, with binoculars, so they had clear views down the road and the surrounding alfalfa and soybean fields.

Mail might try to crawl out through the beans, but that was on the far side of the corn, a long run; and within a couple of minutes, a cop car bumped down into the beans and quickly ripped a three-car-wide path along the edge of the corn, then retired to the highest point along the path. A deputy with a semiautomatic rifle set up behind the car.

For now, that would hold; in five minutes, there would be twenty cops around the field. In ten minutes, there would be fifty.

Lucas stood with Andi Manette, on the handset. "I've got Mrs. Manette and Grace. We need to lift them out of here, we need a medevac now."

"Lucas, the chief is here."

Roux came on. "They say you got them."

"Yeah, but we need to get them out, we need to get a chopper down here."

"Are they hurt bad?"

"Not critical," Lucas said, looking at the two women. "But they're pretty beat up. And Sherrill's hurt bad."

"I was listening to Capslock on the radio. They'll be at Ramsey in three or four minutes. We've got another chopper on the way. Dunn's being notified."

Andi Manette, now with both arms wrapped around her sobbing daughter, said, "Genevieve. Do you have Genevieve?"

Lucas shook his head, and her face contorted and she choked out, "Do you know . . . ?"

"We hoped she was with you," Lucas said.

"He said he would drop her off in a mall. I gave her a quarter to call with."

"I'm sorry . . ."

A caravan of police cars, now including city cars, barrelled up the track: two more jammed into the driveway at Mail's house, and all around them, cops with rifles and shotguns were posting around the cornfield. The ranking sheriff's deputy hurried toward them.

"Davenport?"

"Yeah. Who're you?"

"Dale Peterson. Are you sure he's in the corn?"

"Ninety-five percent. We saw him go in and there wasn't anyplace to get out."

"He's hurt bad," Andi Manette said. Peterson reached a hand out to her, but she edged away and Lucas backed him off with a quick shake of the head. "I stabbed him," she said. "Just before he ran."

She lifted her hand; she still held the spike, and her fingers were smeared with blood. Grace turned her head in her mother's arms and said, "I did, too. I stabbed him in the eye." And she showed them the bedspring needle.

"He was going to kill us," Andi said numbly.

Lucas said, "You did right." And he laughed, and said, "Goddamn, I'm proud of you." And he lifted his hand to pat her shoulder, and remembered, and turned instead toward Peterson. "You gonna handle this?"

The deputy nodded: "We can."

"Do it, then," Lucas said. "I'd like to help out. He just shot a friend of mine."

Peterson nodded. "We heard. But, you know . . . take care." He meant, *Don't murder him.*

"I'm fine," Lucas said, and Peterson nodded. To Andi:

"Miz Manette, if you guys would like to ride down to the road, a helicopter will be picking you up."

"Got media coming," a deputy called from the last car down.

"Keep them out," Lucas said.

"Block them out at the corner," Peterson called. "And get Hank to call the FAA, keep the TV choppers out of here."

"Thank you," Andi Manette said to Peterson. And to her daughter, "Come on, Grace."

Grace said, "Genevieve?"

"We'll look for her," Andi promised.

Lucas walked with them toward the last of the sheriff's cars. "I'm sorry it took so long," he said. "He isn't stupid."

"No, he isn't," Andi said. A deputy opened the back door of his car. Andi helped Grace into the backseat, then turned to say something else to Lucas. Her eyes reached up toward his face, then stopped, looking past his shoulder. Lucas turned to see what she was looking at, his hand dropped toward his pistol. Had she seen Mail? Then she brushed past him, took three quick steps, and suddenly was running toward the house.

Lucas looked at the deputy, said, "Watch the kid," and started after her, walking quickly, and then, when he saw where she was going, broke into a run, shouting, "Mrs. Manette, wait, please wait, wait . . ."

Peterson was on the radio, but he dropped the microphone when he saw Andi Manette running toward the house, and he hurried after her.

She was running toward a six-foot square of weathered wood set on a six-inch-high concrete platform. Lucas, forty feet behind her, shouted, one last time, "Don't, wait," but she was already there. She stooped, caught the edges of the old cistern cover, and heaved.

Lucas had to stop her, because he'd realized what Andi Manette knew by instinct: this was where Genevieve was. The doll in the oil barrel was the girl in the cistern; a watery grave.

When Lucas had still been in uniform, he'd worked a kidnapping case where the child had been shot and thrown in a creek. The body had washed up on the bank, and he'd been with the group of searchers that had found it. He'd seen so much death in his years on the force that it no longer affected him, much. But that child, early in his career, with the white, pudding flesh, the absent eyes . . . he still saw them sometimes, in nightmares.

The cover on the cistern was too heavy for Andi Manette. There was no way that she could lift it. But she got it up a foot, staggered, and as Lucas reached her, slipped it sideways and heaved, opening the hole.

Lucas grabbed her, wrenched her away as she screamed, "No," and Lucas, turning, looked down and saw . . . What?

Nothing, at first, just a bundle of junk on the side of the hole, above the black water at the bottom.

Then the bundle moved, and he saw a flash of white.

Peterson had wrapped his arms around Andi Manette, pulling her away, when Lucas, eyes wild, waved at him, shouted, "Jesus Christ, she's alive."

The cistern was perhaps fifteen feet deep, and the bundle hung just above the water. It moved again, and a face turned up.

"Get something," Lucas screamed back at the cars. "Get a goddamn rope."

A uniformed cop was pulling Andi Manette away; Andi was fighting him, crazy. Another cop popped the trunk on a patrol car, and a second later was running toward them with a tow rope. Lucas peeled off his shoes and jacket.

"Just belay the end, get a couple of guys," Lucas yelled. There were cops running at them from all over the yard.

Andi Manette was pleading with the cop who held her; Peterson shouted into the swarm of men now around the cistern, "Let her come up, but hold her, hold her."

Lucas took the end of the rope and went over the side, feet against the rough fieldstone-and-concrete wall. The cistern smelled like new, wet earth, like early spring, like moss. He went down, passed the bundle on the wall, lowered himself into the water.

The water was three feet deep, coming up just to his hip joint; and it was cold.

"Genevieve," he breathed.

"Help me," she croaked. He could barely make out her voice.

Some kind of mechanism—a secondary pulley, perhaps—had once been mounted about three feet above what was now the water line. Whatever it was, was gone: but there were two metal support fixtures on either side of the cistern, and Genevieve had managed to crawl high enough up the rocks to spear the bottom of her raincoat over one of the fixtures.

With the coat buttoned, she had created a sturdy cloth sack hanging on the side of the cistern, above the water, like a cocoon. She'd crawled inside and hung there, legs in the sleeves, for nearly a hundred hours.

"Got you, honey," Lucas said, taking her weight.

"He threw me in . . . he threw me in," she said.

Peterson shouted down, "What do you want us to do? You need somebody else down there?"

"No. I'm gonna leave her in the coat, I'm gonna hook the rope through this hole. Take her up easy."

He hooked it up, and Genevieve groaned, and Lucas shouted, "Easy."

And Genevieve went up into the light.

35

Half-blind, his ears ringing with the blast of the shotgun, Mail crawled down the rows of corn, the field as dense as a rain forest. He couldn't see very well; he didn't really understand why, he just knew that one eye didn't seem to work. And every time his weight came down on his hand, pain shot through his abdomen.

But part of his mind still worked: fifty feet into the field, he went hard to his right, got to his feet, and running in a crablike crouch, one hand carrying the shotgun, the other pressed flat against his stomach, he headed downhill toward the road. Any other direction would lead to an open field, but if he could somehow get across the road, there was another mile-long cornfield, coming up to a farmhouse. The farmhouse would have a car.

And a culvert crossed under the road.

It wasn't large—maybe not even big enough to take his shoulders—but he remembered seeing the rust-stained end of it sticking out into a small cattail swamp in the ditch. If he could make it that far.

He was breathing hard, and the pain was growing, beating at him with every step. He fell, caught at the cornstalks with his free hand, went down. He lay there for a moment, then turned, rocked up on his butt, looked down at his stomach, and saw the blood. Lifting his shirt, he found a hole two inches below his breastbone, and a cut; blood was bubbling out of the hole.

The whole sequence, from the time he'd opened the door of the cell, through the shooting in the yard, was a shattered pane of memories, flashes of this and that. But now he remembered Andi Manette coming into him, and the bite of pain as she stabbed him with something.

Jesus. She'd stabbed him.

Mail's face contorted, and his shoulders lifted and he shuddered, and he began to sob. The cops would kill him if they found him; Manette had stabbed him. He had nowhere to go.

He sat, weeping, for fifteen seconds, then forced it all back. If he could get out of the field, if he could get through the culvert, if he could get a car and just get *away* from these people, just for a while; if he could *rest*, if he could just close his eyes—he could come back for Manette.

He *would* come back for her: she owed him a life.

Mail put his head down and began to crawl. Somewhere, he lost the shotgun, but he couldn't go back for it; and the pistol still rode in his belt. He looked back, once; there was nobody behind him, but he could see a thin trail of blood, winding down through the corn to where he lay.

Lucas lay on his back on the long grass next to the cistern, catching his breath. The cops who'd pulled him out were walking away, coiling the tow rope. Peterson hurried up. "Another chopper's coming. Be here in a minute."

Lucas sat up. He was soaked to the waist, and cold. "How's the kid?"

Peterson shook his head. "I don't know. She's not good, but I've seen worse that made it. Are you all right?"

"I'm tired," Lucas said. A chopper was coming in, and cops were down at the road, waving it in. He could see two other cops, walking along the road, and more were forming around the edges of the field.

Lucas pulled on his shoes and jacket, and said to Peterson, "Tell your people I'm going into the field. I'm only going in a few feet."

"He's got a shotgun," Peterson objected.

"Tell them," Lucas said.

"Look, there's no point . . ."

"He's not waiting for us to do something," Lucas said, looking out over the field. "I know how his head works, and he's running. He won't set up an ambush and go down shooting. He'll always try to get out."

"We'll have a couple more choppers here in a few minutes, knock down that field . . ."

"I just want a peek," Lucas said, walking away from the house, toward the fence where Mail had gone over. "Tell your guys."

Lucas crossed the fence line, his city shoes filling with plant debris. Sand burr hung from his damp socks, cutting at his ankles. Just inside the field, the sweet smell of maturing corn caught him; the fat ears hung off the stalks, dried silk like brown stains at the top of the ears. He worked slowly along the weedy margin until he saw the fresh foot-cuts in the soft gray dirt.

He slipped his pistol out, stooped, turned, and duck-walked into the field. And here was a flash of blood, more scuffs in the dirt, more blood. Mail was hurt. Lucas stopped, listened, heard a few leaves rustling in the light wind, the sound of car engines, distant sirens, the beat of a chopper. A ladybug crawled up a corn leaf, and he duckwalked a little further into the field, following the sights of his .45.

At knee-level, the cornfield was incredibly dense, and Lucas could see almost nothing, except straight up. Mail's track went straight into the field; Lucas followed it for two minutes, and then the trail turned sharply to the right and disappeared down a corn row. Lucas couldn't see anything at all up ahead. Mail was apparently shifting between rows; following him would be suicidal.

Lucas stood up and looked in the new direction the trail had taken. From where he was, he could see the phone poles along the road. Moving slowly, carefully, he worked his way back to the edge of the field, and recrossed the fence.

Peterson was waiting. When he saw Lucas coming back, he put a handset to his face, said something, and then, to Lucas: "See anything?"

"Not much," Lucas said. "He might be tending down toward the road."

"We'll have ten guys there in five minutes, but there's no way he could get across," Peterson said. "I'm more worried about that damn bean field. We don't have enough people down there—if he could get into one of those rows, he could crawl a good way."

"He's hurt," Lucas said. "There's quite a bit of blood. Manette and the kid both stabbed him, and it could be bad."

"We can always hope the sonofabitch dies," Peterson said. "That'd be some kind of justice, anyway."

Mail reached the end of the field. The nearest cops were standing on top of a squad car three hundred yards away, but he could hear sirens, all the sirens in the world. In a few minutes, they'd be elbow-to-elbow.

The pain in his stomach was growing, but tolerable. He crawled sideways through the corn, careful not to disturb the stalks, then low-crawled to the fence. The cattails were now between him and the deputy, and he could see the open end of the culvert. A thin, keening excitement gripped him: it wasn't big, but he thought it would do. This just might be possible. Just barely. He'd slip these cocksuckers after all, Davenport and his thugs.

He lay on his back and edged under the lowest strand of barbed wire, then slid down the side of the ditch into the swampy patch. The cop turned his head, looking the other way, and Mail gained three feet, into the cattails, and stopped. If anybody walked down the shoulder of the road now, they'd look right down at him. But looking from down the road—from where the deputy stood, scanning the field with binoculars—he was covered. He found himself holding his breath, watching the deputy through a half-inch opening between blades of the cattails, and when the deputy turned his head again, he made another two feet, the water now almost covering him, like an alligator in wait.

The culvert was only ten feet away.

"Choppers coming in—the medevac one and a federal one. They say they've got some plate in the floor, they can get right down on the deck with it," Peterson said.

Lucas nodded. "I'm gonna walk out along the road."

"Okay," Peterson nodded. "We'll flush him."

Lucas watched as Andi Manette, Grace, and Genevieve were loaded into the medical helicopter, Genevieve as an unrecognizable bundle of blankets. Andi Manette stared blank-faced at him as the chopper lifted off. In a few seconds, it was a speck in the northern sky. At the same time, another machine, larger, powered in from the north. The feds, Lucas thought.

He walked down the road, slowly, a step or two at a time. There were only three deputies along the whole length of the road: the visibility was so good that Peterson was routing newcomers to the other edges. But Mail had come this way.

The corn waved in the light breeze, ripples running through it like wind fronts on a lake. Nothing jerky, nothing too quick. Lucas came up to the first deputy, a chunky blond with mirrored sunglasses and a shotgun on his hip.

"Was that the kid there in the well?" he asked as Lucas came up.

"In the cistern, yeah," Lucas said. "She's gonna make it. See anything at all?"

"Nothing. There's just enough wind that the corn's moving, and you can't see much." He pointed his nose into the wind and sniffed, like a hunting dog, and Lucas continued down the road, studying the field.

Two-thirds of the way to the next deputy, he saw the culvert poking through under the road. It wasn't more than eighteen inches in diameter, he thought, maybe too small.

But this was where Mail was headed.

In fact . . .

A thin vein of water led from the fence to the shallow puddle near the end of the culvert pipe. Could he already be inside?

Lucas stepped carefully down the embankment.

And saw the grooves in the mud heading to the culvert. Thighs and shoe tips. And there . . . a speck of blood, almost black on the green grass. The culvert was small, and he risked a quick peek inside. He could see only a tiny crescent of green on the other side. As he watched, the crescent vanished. Mail was pulling himself through. The space was tight, but he was moving.

Lucas climbed the bank, walked to the other side, and looked over the edge. The pipe emptied into another cattail swamp on the opposite side, with a little mud delta leading away from the pipe itself. The delta was undisturbed and Lucas again let himself down the bank. He could hear Mail, possibly halfway through, scraping along, struggling.

And what did Mail's file say? That he was a frantic claustrophobic?

Mail had gone headfirst into the pipe, his shoulders tight against the corrugated sides. There was mud in the bottom of the pipe, and halfway through, the pipe itself was more than half-blocked by a rotten wooden board and a clump of dead weeds. But on the other side of the blockage, he could see a disk of light. If he could get that far . . .

He pulled the board and the weeds away with his hands, passing them down the length of his body, then kicking them back with his feet. He had barely enough room to maneuver his arms, and his breath came harder. He kicked, found one foot held tight; he kicked again, and still was stuck.

Now the claustrophobia seized him, and he began tearing frantically at the mud, whimpering, spitting, grunting, his breath coming harder and harder . . . and he broke free. Twenty feet from the end, fifteen feet. Pain burned through his stomach, and he had to stop. Goddamn; he touched his shirt, pulled his hand away; he couldn't see it, but he could smell it. He was bleeding worse. When he tried to move, he found he was stuck again, and he kicked frantically at whatever held him; splashed water, where part of the pipe had corroded away. Heard a noise. A rat?

Was there a rat in here with him?

Close to panic, he bucked down the pipe, the pain tearing at him. But could see green at the end of the pipe.

Okay. Okay. He pushed the panic back: he'd have to be careful now. He'd have to make himself move slowly, even with the impulse to dash into the cornfield. If he could get in undetected, he could do this. He'd never really thought there was a chance, but now . . .

A heavy clump of something—dirt, sod—dropped into the circle of light at the end of the pipe, half-blocking it. Then another clump.

Mail, shocked, froze.

And a familiar voice said, "Is it wet down there, John?"

The embankment had been seeded with some kind of heavy, thick-bladed grass. The recent rain had softened it, and by grabbing clumps of the grass by the base, Lucas found he could pull up a foot-square clump of sod. He pulled out a half-dozen clumps, then sat down on the embankment above the pipe. When Mail was close enough, he dropped the first of the clumps into the mouth of the culvert.

"Is it wet down there, John?"

There was no answer for a moment, then Mail's voice, low, desperate. "Let me out of here."

"Nah," Lucas said. "We found the little girl in the cistern. She was alive, but not by much. How in the fuck could you do that, John? Throw the kid in the hole?" He dropped another clump of grass into the entrance of the culvert.

"Let me out of here, I'm hurt," Mail screamed.

"Not for long," Lucas said. "The water's draining through from the other end. I'll block this up, the pipe'll fill up . . . it won't take long. Nobody will know. They'll think you got away. It'll almost be like you won—except you'll be dead. And I'll have a good laugh."

Mail screamed, "Help . . . help me," and Lucas could hear his hands and feet beating on the inside of the pipe. He was apparently trying to move backwards.

Mail pushed himself away from the sound of the voice, aware now that the water under him was moving with him. Must be downhill. Maybe the pipe would fill up . . . must get out. Must get out . . .

He backed away, frantically, until his feet hit the muck he'd passed behind himself coming in: and he remembered. He kicked at it, couldn't see it, couldn't move. He was stuck. Ahead, there was only a small square of light at the mouth of the culvert. He crawled forward again, stopped, twisted around enough that he could free the pistol, and pushed it out ahead of him.

"Let me out," he screamed. He fired the pistol. The muzzle blast and flash stunned and deafened him. He inched forward like a mole, in the water, fired again.

He couldn't see much at all, just a thin rim of light. Davenport said something, but Mail couldn't make it out. He simply lay in the deepening water, in the dark, with the pain in his stomach, the strange blindness in his eye, the world closing in on him. Davenport would bury him alive, he could feel the water rising. He thrashed and couldn't move, couldn't move; he had the gun, and without thinking, pushed it under his chin.

Lucas heard the muffled shot, and waited.

"John?"

He listened, heard nothing. The frantic beating had stopped. He looked back up the road, where the cops were still standing on the tops of their cars, looking the wrong way, into the cornfield. The shots from inside the culvert had been almost inaudible on the outside. Lucas started pulling the clumps of muck out of the pipe.

A little flow of water came out.

And then some blood.

And a clump of bloody, pulped flesh, floating like a child's leaf-ship, on the thin stream of muddy water.

Lucas stood up, and with the toe of one ruined shoe, pushed the clumps of grass out of the mouth of the culvert, and climbed to the road.

"Hey." He yelled at the cop on the closest car. When the cop turned, he pointed into the ditch and people began to run toward him.

36

Sloan drove down to the farm, gunless, suspended, afraid he was missing the action. He found a dozen cops on their hands and knees next to a culvert, and Lucas sitting on the steps of the tumble-down farmhouse.

"Need a ride, sweetheart?"

"I need a cigarette," Lucas said. "I don't know why I ever quit."

Sloan told him about it as they headed back to town:

"Wolfe wouldn't have anything to do with me, so I went with Franklin and Helen Manette. I sort of bullshitted her, being nice, and Helen opened her mouth and everything came out."

"Won't do much good," Lucas said. "A court won't take anything after the first time she asked for a lawyer, and we didn't get one."

"I wasn't thinking about that," Sloan said. "I just wanted to know why she did it."

"Money," Lucas said. "Some way or another."

Sloan nodded. "She knew all about Tower and Wolfe. Tower is in a lot worse financial shape than anybody knows. Almost everything is gone. His salary at the foundation has been cut, and they took a big equity loan on the house five years ago, and they've had a hard time making payments.

The only thing they had going for them was the money from the trust—and there's a provision in the deed of trust that if the trustees decided that there was no possibility of the last benefactor having children, then the trust would be dissolved and the last benefactor would get the whole thing. A lump sum. Right now, thirteen million dollars."

"Jesus," Lucas said. "That much?"

"Yep. The trust was in bonds. The trust company had to put aside enough income every year to cover inflation, and the rest of the income was divided up among the eligible people—Tower, Andi, and her two daughters. They were all getting about a hundred grand a year. If Andi and the two daughters were dead, and Tower pushed for it, the trust would be dissolved and he'd get the lump. And that's what Helen Manette was looking for. She figured Tower was about to dump her. She figured she'd get half."

"And she met Mail at the apartment?"

"Yeah. He asked about her name, said he'd had a doctor named Manette. He said some things that made her realize that he was the guy Andi had talked about a few times—the guy so crazy that he scared the life out of her. He gave her a name, Martin LaDoux. She found his phone number and started calling him."

"We could have seen it," Lucas said.

"We would have," Sloan said. "But man, it's only been five days. Not a whole five days, yet."

"Seems like a century," Lucas said.

A moment later, Sloan said, "You know what she asked me?"

"What?"

"If her helping us would qualify for Dunn's reward money . . ."

Halfway back, they got a call from the chief's secretary, saying Roux was on the way to the hospital. She wanted Lucas and Sloan to stop by. When they arrived, the hospital's turnout was clogged with cars.

Sloan looked him over. "Maybe I oughta drop you at emergency," he said. "You look like shit."

"I'm all right," Lucas said, getting out of the car. His

shoes were ruined, his suit pants, still wet, clung to his legs. His underwear and shirt, both soaked, felt like they were full of sand. His tie was a wet, twisted wreck; he hadn't shaved.

Sloan looked him over. "Your suit coat looks nice," he said.

Roux saw him first, hurried down the tile hallway, and caught him in her arms with a powerful hug. "Jesus, you got them back. I never would have believed it."

Dunn was there, pounding him on the back. "Jesus Christ, all of them." His face was luminous.

"Easy," Lucas said. "How's Genevieve?"

"Exposure," Dunn said, his face going dark. "She wouldn't have lasted the rest of the day. And she may have nerve damage in her legs. Maybe not too serious, it's too soon to tell. But the way she was caught up in the coat, the nerves were all pinched up . . ."

"Andi and Grace?"

Dunn looked at the floor, and then away. "Physically, they'll be okay; psychologically, they're in terrible shape. Andi is just . . . just rambling. God, I don't know . . ." And he turned and walked away without another word, back toward a cluster of doctors.

"You heard about Helen Manette?" Lucas asked Roux.

"From Franklin," she said. She shook her head. "I don't know what's gonna happen. We gotta talk with everybody from the state's attorney's office. We're gonna arrest her, but if we ever get her in court, I just don't know. But she's not our biggest problem."

Lucas nodded. "Wolfe?"

"Yeah. We're meeting with her and her lawyer." Roux looked at her watch. "In about forty-five minutes. You better be around, in case I need you."

"I'd hoped she'd go away, on her own," Lucas said.

"She hasn't," Roux said grimly.

There was a buzz of noise at the hospital, and Lucas looked down the hall. The mayor pushed through, and Roux said, "I gotta go. Stick close to your office."

"Sure," Lucas said.

• • •

Roux called an hour later, as Lucas sat in his office, talking with Sloan and Del. "You better come down."

The chief's secretary waved him through, saying, "They're waiting," and "God, that was great this morning. You're my hero."

"Yeah, but for how long?" Lucas asked.

"Rest of the week," she promised.

Nancy Wolfe, a loose-fleshed man with freckles and shiny red hair, Lester, and Rose Marie Roux faced each other in a tense rectangle around Roux's desk. The red-haired man's hands were steepled, and he wore a careful gray suit with a gold lapel pin. A lawyer, Lucas thought.

Roux pointed at an empty chair next to Lester. "Sit down. We're trying to work out what happened this morning."

"You know what happened," Wolfe snapped. She looked across the desk at Lucas, her eyes on fire. "The question is, what are you going to do about it?"

"What do you want?" Lucas asked.

"I want you out," she said. "I'll reserve the right to go to court no matter what happens, but I want you out now."

"We saved your partner's life," Lucas said.

"You should have found another way to do it . . ."

"There was no time."

". . . without . . . *violating me*."

Lucas shook his head. "No time."

"You should have made some," Wolfe said.

Rose Marie cleared her throat. "Lucas will be staying. I won't fire him. In fact, I'm putting him in for a commendation. I'm sorry that you were inconvenienced."

"Inconvenienced?" Wolfe shrilled. "I was strip-searched and given these prison clothes and they made me sit there while they shouted at me"—her lip trembled—"and they wouldn't let me call anybody, a lawyer, or anybody."

"Rose Marie, we're talking about a lot of money," the lawyer said, dryly. "Guys have done a lot less than Davenport, to people who deserved it a lot more, and they've been hammered. People are tired of this department, the way it handles people. You lose a million, two million, five million—and that's possible, in this case—and you'll be out of here. If you fire Davenport, at least it'll be a sign that you disapprove."

Rose Marie was shaking her head, and said, "Won't do it."

The lawyer nodded at Wolfe and said, "Well, that's it, then."

Wolfe gathered up her purse. "We're definitely going ahead."

Lester said, out of nowhere, "You can go to court, but I don't think we'll lose. We had some good reasons to interview Dr. Wolfe."

Lucas glanced at Lester, uncertainly, then looked at Roux, who raised her eyebrows. She didn't know what Lester was talking about, either.

The lawyer, who had dropped his hands to his lap when he was talking about the five million, resteepled his fingers, then peeked at Lester from behind them. "I know what you're thinking. And if the jury was deciding right this minute, you might get away with it. Ms. Manette and her daughters are in the hospital, the TV people are going crazy, there'd be a lot of sympathy for what Chief Davenport did. But when we get to court, six months from now, or a year from now? You'll lose. And Ms. Wolfe has expressed a determination to follow up on this."

Lester tried to break in during the speech, and finally got in with, "That's not what I'm thinking. I'm not talking about the Manette case at all."

The lawyer stopped and asked, "Then what are you talking about?"

"I'm talking about William Charles Aakers and Carlos Neroda Sonches," Lester said. "Two of Dr. Wolfe's patients . . . and Andi Manette's. We were planning to ask Dr. Wolfe about these cases when Chief Davenport found out where the suspect Mail was hiding, and he had to leave. But we *will* come back to Dr. Wolfe on these . . ."

He had two manila folders in his hands. They were empty, but a cursive feminine handwriting on the tabs said, *Aakers* and *Sonches*. He passed the folders to the lawyer.

"What are these?" the redhead asked, looking at Wolfe.

"Two patients," she hissed. "This man is trying to blackmail me."

"I'm not trying to do anything of the sort," Lester said. "The contents of these two files have been temporarily misplaced, due to some bureaucratic confusion with the other files in the case, but we'll find them and continue our evaluation. We feel that there might well be cause for prosecution."

"What?" the attorney asked. He was looking at Lucas.

Lucas shrugged, and Lester said, "Your client has been treating child molesters without informing the required law enforcement officials. It's all in the records. And we'll find these records. I'm gonna tear the department to pieces if I have to."

Roux leaned back in her chair; Lester looked intent, and Lucas looked away.

After a moment, Wolfe said, "You fuckers."

"Blackmail," Weather said that night. She was eating the back end of a lobster.

"I suppose," Lucas said. "She reserved the right to do whatever she wanted, but she won't do anything. She'll let it go."

"I don't think I approve," Weather said.

"I could burn the papers, I suppose—if I could find them," Lucas said. "Then we could call her up, tell her we're sorry, and let her sue."

"You were pretty rough with her."

"Shit happens." Lucas yawned, stretched, and smiled. "Just like the bumper sticker says."

"Are you okay?" she asked. They'd gone into the living room and parked on the couch, Weather leaning back with her head on his shoulder.

"I'm tired," he said. "I'm so tired."

"I heard a cop was shot, that there had been a shooting, a surgical tech told me . . ." The words were tumbling out in an uncontrolled spate, and her body tensed against him. "I couldn't believe it, I called Phil Orris over at Ramsey. you remember him, the orthopod . . ."

"Yeah."

"He said, 'No, no, it's not Lucas, it's a woman.' I was like, thank you, Jesus, thank you. I was so glad this poor woman was shot, that it wasn't you."

"She's kind of messed up, Sherrill is," Lucas said. "The bone's broken."

"Better than you getting shot," she said. "You've been shot enough."

They sat quietly for a second, then Lucas said, "I think we ought to get married."

She went absolutely still against him, and a second later, said, "So do I."

"I've got a ring for you," he said.

"I know, it's been driving everybody crazy," she said.

He grinned, but she couldn't see it. She was still facing away, the top of her head just under his nose.

"Why don't you go sit in the tub?" she suggested. "Then get in bed. You could use about fifteen hours of sleep."

"All right. Here, move away." He pushed her off a bit, and dug in his pocket, found the ring. "I could never think of what to tell you when I gave it to you," he said. "Except, I love you."

She put it on her finger, and it fit. "You could go on for a while," she said. "But that's certainly an excellent start."

Lucas sat in the tub for fifteen minutes, but he was never any good at relaxing in hot water. He got out, toweled off, put on a robe, and wandered through the house, looking for Weather, to say good night. He found her on the telephone, and heard her say, "Guess what?"

She was telling friends about the proposal, about the ring. He watched her for a moment, and her face was luminous, like Dunn's had been at the hospital, glowing with a light of its own.

He felt a sudden pang of fear: the moment was too perfect to last. He shook it off, walked into the kitchen, touched her hair, her cheek, kissed her chin.

"Taking a nap," he said.

She dropped the phone to her lap. "Del is pissed," she said. "He had until noon today, in the proposal pool. Some guy named Wood won six hundred and twenty dollars."

Lucas grinned. "Pretty romantic, huh?"

"Go to bed," she said. He walked back toward the bedroom, stopped, and listened.

He heard her punch new numbers into the phone, and heard her say again, "Guess what?"

POCKET
BOOKS

Hidden Prey
John Sandford

On the shore of Lake Superior a man named Rodion Oleshev is found dead – three holes in his head and heart. When it turns out the victim is a Russian with very high government connections, that's when it really hits the fan.

A female Russian cop flies in from Moscow, Lucas Davenport flies in from Minneapolis; law enforcement and press types swarm the scene – and in the middle of it all there's another murder. Could the two be connected? What is the Russian cop hiding from Davenport? Is she really a cop at all? Why was the victim shot with fifty-year old bullets?

Before he can find the answers, Davenport must follow a trail back to another place, another time, and battle the shadows he discovers there. Shadows that turn out to be both very real and very deadly . . .

PRICE £6.99
ISBN 0 7434 8416 9

POCKET
BOOKS

Naked Prey
John Sandford

Lucas Davenport has a new role – as a special trouble-shooter assigned to cases that are too complicated or politically touchy for others to handle. Like the two corpses found hanging from a tree, in the woods of northern Minnesota. What makes the case particularly sensitive is that the bodies are those of a black man and a white woman – and they're naked. 'Lynching' is the word that everybody's trying not to say – but, as Lucas begins to discover, the murders are not what they appear to be. Nor are they the end of it. There is worse to come – much, much worse . . .

'The sheer quality of the writing makes him unmissable'
Literary Review

PRICE £6.99
ISBN 0 7434 6869 4

POCKET
BOOKS

Chosen Prey
John Sandford

The deadliest of crimes . . .
The coolest of killers

In the mist and rain of a Minnesota spring,
a shallow grave is found. It contains the body of a young
woman, apparently strangled. When the murder is connected
with a brilliantly-executed erotic drawing, where the victim's
face has been grafted onto a pornographic internet image,
Lucas Davenport becomes involved. More of the drawings
come to light and Davenport makes a grisly discovery –
the drawings may represent more murder victims.

The case begins to come together in Lucas' mind,
but the mixture of ferocious intelligence and madness which
he faces means that the deaths must continue,
that the chosen prey must be stalked . . .

'A brilliant writer' GUARDIAN

'Few do it better than Sandford' DAILY TELEGRAPH

PRICE £6.99
ISBN 0 7434 1555 8

POCKET
BOOKS

Mortal Prey
John Sandford

Clara Rinker is a pleasant, soft-spoken, low-key Southerner.
She's also the best hitwoman in the business. Lucas Davenport
should know – she almost killed him.

That was then and this is now. Clara is retired and living in
Mexico with her boyfriend, the son of a local drug lord, and for
the first time in her life, she's happy. But when her boyfriend is
killed by a bullet that was meant for her, Clara is understandably
angry. And when Clara Rinker gets mad, people get hurt.

It's up to Lucas Davenport to stop the bloodbath but between
Clara, her old bosses in the St. Louis mob, the Mexican
druglord, and the combined, sometimes warring, arms of the
U.S. law enforcement, this is one case that will get more
dangerous as it goes along. And when the shooting starts,
anyone standing in the middle won't stand a chance . . .

PRICE £6.99
ISBN 0 7434 1556 6

POCKET
BOOKS

Sudden Prey
John Sandford

Lucas Davenport knows why people kill. Some do it for thrills.
Some do it for profit. Some do it because they must. But when
his team guns down two bank robbers in the middle of a heist,
Davenport falls prey to the purest, simplest criminal motivation
of all: revenge.

The husband of one of the victims wants Davenport to suffer as
he has. So he's not going after Davenport himself. He's going
after his family . . .

'In a crowded market, Sandford shines at the quality end'
Daily Telegraph

'Sandford knows all there is to know about detonating the gut-
level shocks of a good thriller' *New York Times*

PRICE £6.99
ISBN 0 7434 8421 5

POCKET
BOOKS

Secret Prey
John Sandford

The company chairman lay dead in the woods, his orange hunting jacket punctured by a bullet at close range. Around him stood four executives with whom he had been hunting, each with a reason not to be sorry about the man's death. A classic murder mystery, it would seem: the kind where the detective gathers everyone together at the end and solves the case.

But Lucas Davenport knows it's not going to be that easy. There are currents running through this group: hints and whispers of something much greater than the murder of a single man. Some time soon, unless he can stop it, there will be other deaths – and Davenport can't help but wonder if maybe the final death might be his own . . .

PRICE £6.99
ISBN 0 7434 8420 7